AMAZON NIGHTS
Classic Adventure Tales from the Pulps

When one thinks of the classic adventure-story authors of the pulp fiction era, H. Rider Haggard, Talbot Mundy, and Rafael Sabatini may come first to mind. But Arthur O. Friel's stellar contributions – particularly his stories featuring Lourenço and Pedro, two workers on a rubber-tree plantation in the Amazon, and the adventures they have exploring the rain forest's mysterious back-country during the flood season – certainly deserve honorable mention.

Here are tales of peril and last-minute rescue, brutal savages and men of honor, snake-worshipping armies and half-ape Lost Races —and many more! For in the shadows of the rain-forest, many evils lurk . . . human and otherwise!

Features a new introduction by Darrell Schweitzer, 8 short stories, and *The Jararaca*, a complete novel.

WILDSIDE PULP CLASSICS

AMAZON NIGHTS
Classic Adventure Tales from the Pulps

ARTHUR O. FRIEL

WILDSIDE PRESS

AMAZON DAYS:
CLASSIC ADVENTURE TALES FROM THE PULPS

CONTENTS

INTRODUCTION

ARTHUR O. FRIEL is one of those writers is whose identity has diminished to a byline on old books and magazines — but not entirely. A vague outline remains. Somewhere beyond that is the man, who probably would have been an interesting person to know. He led an adventurous life. He had a good mind.

What we do know is that Arthur Olney Friel was born in Detroit in 1885, and died in Concord, New Hampshire in 1959. He graduated from Yale, in a time when less than 5% of American men attended any college at all. His occupation might be described as "novelist, explorerer, and adventurer." No known military service. Some newspaper work. Began writing free-lance in 1919.

As is revealed in his 1924 book, *The River of the Seven Stars,* Friel, a fellow of the American Geographical Society, participated in a number of exploratory expeditions up the Orinoco River and into the Venezuelan jungle in the early 1920s. This experience colored much of his later writing. He seems to have traveled in much of the same area as the once-famous Colonel Fawcett, who vanished in those parts in the mid-1920s.

We remember Friel as one of the most popular contributors to the prestigious pulp magazine *Adventure,* where he published thirteen serials and fifty-five shorter pieces. He was extremely popular there and came to the attention of the most famous of all *Adventure* readers, Robert E. Howard, who never quite managed to become an *Adventure* writer, but doubtless would have if he'd stuck around longer. Howard wrote to fellow pulpster Carl Jacobi in 1934, "I was much interested to note that you are acquainted with Arthur O. Friel. He has been one of my favorite authors for years."

This doesn't so much suggest that Jacobi knew Friel, but that he, too, read him in *Adventure.*

An influence on Robert E. Howard? Just possibly. Other

Adventure writers, including Harold Lamb and Talbot Mundy, represented an ideal to which many pulp writers — not just Howard — aspired. There was a mystique about them, something which comes across strongly in the "Camp Fire" department of that magazine. *Adventure* writers, the best of them anyway, wrote what they knew. They had *been there*, wherever *there* was, and wrote from first-hand knowledge. Friel was the genuine article. He really *was* one of those pith-helmeted explorers in a canoe paddling into the unknown, just as depicted on the dustjacket to his 1922 novel, *The Pathless Trail*. He also wrote vividly and well. He was the perfect *Adventure* author.

Friel left behind a series of books, some of which have been reprinted in modern times. *The River of Seven* Stars is something of a classic of exploration literature. Among his novels, *The Pathless Trail* (1922) and *Tiger River* (1923), both first serialized in *Adventure*, were reprinted in the Timelost series from Centaur Press about twenty-five years ago. These novels, and a few of his others, use their extremely authentic detail to edge over the borderline into the fantastic convincingly. Some of them have Lost Race elements. *Mountains of Mystery* (1925) is about a quest for a legendary white race dwelling in the depths of the South American jungle.

Other Friel titles include *The King of No Man's Land, Cat O'Mountain, King of Kearsarge, Hardwood, Renegade,* and *Forgotten Island.* Not all his books are set in South America. *King of Kearsarge* is about the North Woods. Later in life, he had at least one story, "Long Hand," in *Mystery Stories* in 1942.

Much more research needs to be done if we are to flesh out these fleeting impressions of who Friel was and what happened in his life, but even from such scraps (you might say we know about as much about Friel as we do about Shakespeare) it is clear that he is a subject worth more research. It is obvious, too, that his fiction is worth reprinting and reading.

— Darrell Schweitzer
Philadelphia PA
January 30, 2005

THE SPIDER

I WOULD not attack that spider again, *senhor*, if I were you. You have seen for yourself that you can not hit him. No matter how quickly you strike, he is inches away when the blow falls.

Those huge, bird-killing spiders all are incredibly swift. I have heard that not even a bullet is fast enough to kill one — that at the flash of the gun he jumps so quickly that the whole seven inches of him is out of danger when the shot strikes. Whether that be true or not, I know you will never hit him with your fist; you will only tire yourself out. Besides, he may grow angry and attack you in return. His fangs are half an inch long, *senhor*, and he is full of poison. It is not wise to risk his springing at you.

This is an odd place to find such a monster — here in the middle of the broad Amazon, on a steamer outward bound toward the Atlantic. Yet strange creatures sometimes come aboard these river boats while they are tied up at the bank. Some of them are harmless, and some are deadly. And not all of the deadly things are found on the outgoing steamers, nor are they all bred here in the jungle.

Sometimes they come up the river from the outside and are the more deadly because they are human. The memory of one of them came into my mind just now while I watched that great spider leaping aside from your blows. He, too, was called the "Spider," that man, though his name was Schwartz.

What is that? You say that *schwarz* means "black"? That is very droll, *senhor*, for the Spider was black. Black of hair, black of beard, black of eye he was — yes, and black of heart, too, though at first we did not know that. We called him Spider because he looked like one. His little eyes were set close together with a sort of spidery look in them. His body was small and bunchy, while his arms were long and thin and covered with black hair. His legs were short and crooked. Yet he could run amazingly fast on those little legs; that made him seem all the more like a spider. And later he made himself a spider's lair — and came to a spider's end.

An upriver boat brought him to us one day, and with him a small brown bag and a rifle. He had no letters to Coronel Nunes, owner of the great rubber estate where I worked, nor anything else to show who he was or whence he had come. The *coronel*, however, received him with the courtesy he shows to all who come to him; and when this man told him he had had another bag, containing letters of introduction and other things of value, but that it had been stolen from him on the boat, the *coronel* believed him — or at any rate seemed to, for theft is a thing that may happen to any man in almost any place.

Schwartz boldly made himself at home there at the head-quarters and talked vaguely about looking over the country for the people he said he represented. He went out in the jungle with us men and saw all he could see. Always he carried two weapons — the rifle, and a pistol.

It may be a foolish fancy, *senhores*, but I have sometimes thought that a man may be judged by his weapons, and not only the man himself, but the country whence he comes — for a man usually carries the weapons made in his own land. Now you two Americans, I have noticed, carry with you that flat pistol made by the Senhor Colt, which you say was used by your army in the war in Europe. There is about it a square, solid look which fits well with the things I have observed about you and with what I have heard about your great country. Also, the shape of that pistol is such that it seems to say —

"I do not seek trouble with any man, but if any man wants it — I am ready."

Your Winchesters, too, have something of that same air of solid readiness.

The guns of the Spider had a much different appearance. The pistol looked venomous; it leaned forward from the ugly butt to the thin muzzle, as if always eager to kill. It reminded me of a striking snake. The name of it, he once told me, was a Loo — let me see — ah yes, that is it, *senhor* — a Luger. The rifle, too, looked wicked, but I can not remember its name; it does not matter. But that pistol and the look of the spidery man who carried it were such that, when he was following behind me in the bush, I got a cold feeling between my shoulder blades, as if death were about to strike me in the back.

My mates, too, said that they had the same feeling when he was behind them; yet he gave us no real cause for it. He did not bluster nor threaten us by word or act. Indeed, he was very quiet. He had the spider's way of remaining still in one place for a long time, watching everything and making no move. It might be our work that he watched, or it might be something in the jungle that aroused his interest; but whatever it was, you felt that when he stopped looking at it he had seen everything about it and remembered it all.

One thing that amused us was his habit of watching other spiders — real spiders of the bush, which we often met. No matter what sort of spider it might be, he would study it and learn its ways and how it lived and got its prey. When he did this we would wink at one another and laugh behind our hands, and one of my mates named Pedro — a, tall, handsome young fellow who was very droll — would pretend to pounce on something, and then say under his breath:

"Take care, little spider, the big Spider will eat you!"

It seemed very funny to us at the time. But later on things came about which made it not funny at all.

After he had been among us for some time, another boat came. It brought us welcome guests: the *coronel*'s daughter, who had journeyed all the way from Rio to visit him, and her cousin, a gentleman of Rio, Senhor Affonso da Fonseca. Every year the Senhorita Flora made this long trip from the great city where she was receiving the finest education the *coronel*'s wealth could give her, to see her lonely old father. And though he would never allow her to remain very long, lest she become ill from the climate or meet some mischance from snakes or other things, we all knew that he looked forward to these short visits of hers as the brightest days of all the year.

We knew, too, that he planned eventually to make his own home again in Rio, where he had lived until his wife died. And we knew also that Senhor Affonso, who was somewhat older than the *senhorita*, had a deeper feeling for her than that of a cousin, and that, though he accompanied her partly because he was interested in our rubber country and partly because he felt it his duty to protect her on the long journey, he came more for the pleasure of being with her. We were glad of this, for she was a handsome, gracious girl — the true daughter of her father — while the senhor was every inch a man and would make her a fine husband. The *coronel* himself approved the match.

Now it happened just at this time that I met with a rather bad accident in the bush — my right leg was cut by a machete — and so I had to go back to headquarters to let the injury heal. My old *coronel* had a very friendly feeling for me because in past days I had done some dangerous things for him which many men would not have done. So, while I was recovering from my hurt, he often had me come to the house and sit and talk to him, and, being there, I saw a number of things.

For one thing, I noticed that the Spider stopped going into the jungle so much. He stayed around the headquarters, sitting quiet for hours in that spidery way of his and watching the *senhorita* or Senhor Affonso. Sometimes he talked, in his throaty foreign way, and the others answered him with all politeness, but I could see that none of them liked him.

The *coronel* was displeased at the way the Spider's eyes followed his daughter, and the girl herself avoided him. Senhor Affonso, though, was much interested sometimes by the black-bearded man's talk of things he had studied in the jungle, and now and then he went out with him to see those things for himself. At such times I always felt uneasy, and Senhorita Flora, too, kept watching anxiously until they returned.

Mind you, *senhores*, the Spider never had done anything to make us distrust him. But dark crimes can easily be committed when two men are alone in the bush, and we knew that Senhor Affonso was wealthy and that, no doubt, he had a tempting sum of *milreis* with him; and, as I have said, there was that about the Spider which made one feel that it would not be well to trust him too far. So I always felt relieved when the Rio gentleman came back unharmed, and I knew the *senhorita* did also, though she never spoke of what was in her mind.

Then one day a man of ours reported seeing a splendid black jaguar in the forest, and Senhor Affonso and the Spider went to hunt it. They made the longest trip they had yet taken, for they were gone two days. This time we were more at ease about them, however, for by the *coronel's* order two of our men went with them — the man who had seen the jaguar and another who was a good hunter.

Not long after they departed, another boat came. It was the one which had brought the Spider to us. My leg was better now, though still stiff, and I limped down to watch the unloading of the supplies. As I started, the *coronel* asked me to request the captain to come up for a moment. I did so and thought no more of it. After the boat went, though, I noticed that the *coronel* seemed disturbed. At times his eyes would snap angrily and then he would walk up and down, his face wrinkled in thought. I asked no questions, of course, but after the Spider and Senhor Affonso returned I soon learned what was the matter.

They had found the jaguar, and brought with them his great, glossy hide, which Senhor Affonso proudly showed to the girl and her father.

"It shall go back to Rio with us," he said, looking at Flora, and there was that in his face which added: "And some day, beloved, it shall be in our home."

She smiled and blushed a little, dropping her eyes.

I do not know why I did it, but I glanced at the Spider to see if he watched this. I saw he did and that a nasty expression crossed his face. The *coronel* saw this, too, and his mouth tightened. When the others started into the house he said —

"Senhor Schwartz, I would speak with you."

I turned to go away. But, as I have said, my leg was stiff, and I had to walk slowly — and I will admit that I did not try very hard to hasten, for I knew the *coronel* was about to say something worth hearing. Before I had gone far the old gentleman spoke:

"Senhor, you have now made me quite a long visit. I have greatly enjoyed your companionship and I am grieved that in this poor home of mine I have been unable to offer you better entertainment. I trust, however, that the little I could do to show you the workings of the estate has been of some assistance to you, and that on your departure you will carry with you many pleasant memories."

The Spider said nothing. So the *coronel* added —

"It is with sorrow that I learn that you are to leave us on the next boat."

After a pause the Spider said:

"Ya, I see. It is because I lost that bag mit my papers."

"Pardon, *senhor*," said the *coronel*, "but the *Aurora* was here yesterday, and as you are my guest I asked the captain if any trace of your black bag, of which you told me, had been found. He told me, *senhor*, that you had no black bag whatever — only the brown one which you brought here, and that nothing had been taken from you. No doubt there is some mistake. Yet I have known this captain for years, and I know him to be honest and truthful."

There was another pause. Just as I passed out of hearing the Spider said —

"He is a goddam liar, but I will go."

I heard him walk into the house.

As no boat was expected for a time, things went on as before. I said nothing of what I had overheard and I know the *coronel* did not tell the others, for he is the very soul of hospitality and it had cost him an unpleasant struggle to do what he had to do. The Spider went out into the bush a few times alone and returned and talked of various things he had seen. Then one morning he and Senhor Affonso went out together, to look at something or other this blackhearted man said he had found.

I watched them go and I became more uneasy than ever before. I wanted to follow, but my leg was not yet good enough to let me travel easily and noiselessly; so I looked about, and my eye fell on young Pedro, the droll fellow who used to pretend to devour spiders. I beckoned to him and whispered to him to follow the pair and keep out of sight. He did so at once.

TIME PASSED, and a sort of drowsiness had crept upon me, when there came a sound — a sound like a shot, some distance away and muffled by the bush. I sprang awake and listened. Suddenly I remembered that Pedro had not taken his rifle — only the machete he always carried at his belt. Senhor Affonso, though, had a gun with him and he might be shooting at some animal.

Before long there came two other shots. These were nearer than the first and sounded like the spiteful crack of the Luger. I got up and went to my quarters to get my rifle. Senhorita Flora who had heard the shots too, come out and called to me —

"Lourenço, what is it?"

But I made no answer and went on as fast as a lame man could.

I was just coming out with the gun when Flora's name was called from the edge of the forest. There stood the Spider.

"Come quickly, *senhorita*," he said. "Affonso has met with an accident."

She started running toward him. I called —

"Do not go, *senhorita*! Wait!"

But she kept on, and I began to run, too. Then the Spider stopped us both. He fired at me.

The bullet missed me so narrowly that I felt it pass my face. I dodged, my clumsy stiff leg twisted, and I fell sprawling. When I looked up the girl had whirled and was running back to the house.

The Spider, who thought he had killed me, was running after her with all his spidery speed. My rifle had fallen from my hand, and while I was getting it he caught her. He dragged her back toward the jungle. She struggled to escape, and he struck her so hard that he dazed her. Then he picked her up and ran, but I had my rifle now.

I fired from where I lay, aiming low, trying to hit his crooked legs and so avoid injuring Flora. But I shot hurriedly and missed him. Still, my shooting stopped him, for when he saw I was alive he swung the girl toward me and, using her as a shield, fired at me again.

As you perhaps know, a man lying down is hard to hit, but his bullet ripped across my shoulders and tore the shirt from my back and burned my skin. I could not shoot again without striking the *senhorita*, so I did not try.

Then came a burst of fire from the house, where the *coronel* had seized weapons. Now he came bounding out like a jaguar, with a pistol in each hand spitting flame and lead as he ran. Somewhere behind me, too, a rifle barked, fired by some man about the place.

Of course, both the *coronel* and the workman shot high, lest they kill Flora. But the Spider, thinking only of himself, had no time to realize this. Finding himself under fire from two directions and hearing yells of rage as other men ran for their guns, he suddenly dropped the girl and ran, diving into the bush.

I shot at him again as he fled, but again I missed. Then we all hastened to Flora, whom the *coronel* had caught up in his arms. For the moment we forgot everything but her. Then, still stunned by the blow of the Spider, she moaned —

"Affonso!"

We all started and looked at one another, and I said —

"Yes, Senhor Affonso must have been shot — and Pedro, too."

I explained how I had sent Pedro to follow. The *coronel* snapped:

"Go, men, and find them! And find that — that Schwartz, too!"

We growled. The Spider would not come back alive if we found him. But we did not find him, for he had vanished. We pressed on to find our own people. I could not keep up with the others, but I was not far behind when they met Pedro. He came staggering down an old *estrada*, his face twisted with pain, and he bore the body of Senhor Affonso.

At first we believed that body to be dead, for it hung limp and there were two bullet holes in it, but while we were cutting down branches to make a litter Senhor Affonso stirred and moaned. Pedro cried out joyously:

"He lives! The *senhor* lives!"

Then he dropped, did Pedro, fainting from loss of blood, for he, too, had been shot by the Spider, and his wound was bad, near the shoulder. So now we had two men to carry home.

As I learned later, this was what had happened:

The Spider had told Senhor Affonso he had found a trapdoor spider's nest which was quite the most wonderful thing he had ever seen, and the *senhor*, greatly interested, went with him into a place where no men were working. There the Spider pointed to a hole at the base of a large tree, with thick spiderwebbing across it, and said that was it.

If the city gentleman had been better acquainted with spiders he would have known that no trapdoor spider would ever make such a nest, but that it would be concealed so that it could not be seen at all. But he went up to it, and then the man Schwartz said —

"Look closely, Affonso, and see how a spider acts when he is cornered!"

Then he shot him in the back.

The only thing that saved the *senhor* was that, even as he bent to look, he sensed something treacherous in the Spider's words and turned to see his face. The bullet struck him before he had turned halfway, but he had twisted so far that, instead of going into his heart, it went through him sidewise and came out under his right arm. The shock threw him forward and his head struck hard against the tree, knocking him senseless.

The Spider, thinking him dead, swiftly robbed him of everything valuable — though he did not get so much as he probably expected, for the *senhor* had put most of his money in the *coronel*'s safe soon after his arrival. Then he dashed back to carry off the handsome Senhorita Flora, but on the way he met Pedro.

Pedro, not wishing the pair to know he was there, had followed at some distance and, though he heard the shot, he did not see the shooting and could not be sure of what it meant. So, with his machete ready, he sought to stop the Spider and question him. Without a word the Spider shot him, too, firing twice. The first bullet knocked him down in the thick bush and the second missed. When he struggled up again the Spider was gone. Since the first thing to do was to find Senhor Affonso, he went and found him.

For some time it seemed that both Pedro and the *senhor* would die. But both were strong, and at last they recovered. While they lay there we hunted the Spider, but found nothing at all; he had disappeared as if he never had been there. It was during this time, too, that we learned what he meant by his double-tongued advice to Senhor Affonso to see what a cornered spider would do, for there came a boat, and with it two quiet, common-looking men who talked with the *coronel* and went out into the bush with our men. They finally left without telling their business to anyone except the *coronel*. When they had gone we learned with surprise that they were police. We also found that they sought the Spider, and that he was wanted in Para for murder, and at Manaos for — worse than murder.

So you see that though he could not know the law was so close behind him, he did know he could not go back down the river on the next boat. He had reached the last place where he could live among men, and now there was no place left for him but the jungle.

My leg was well long before the *senhor* and Pedro were, and I went back to work. I heard, though, that Senhor Affonso vowed he would stay there until he had hunted down the man who had shot him and assailed the lady Flora, if it took the rest of his life.

The *senhorita* was even more bitter against that man than Affonso himself — not so much because he had attacked her as because he had nearly killed her sweetheart. That is the way of women. Yet she pleaded with him not to seek the Spider, as he might be killed in doing so. The *coronel*, too, pointed out that he was city-bred and not fitted for man-hunting in such terrible country as ours, that the Spider must have perished in the jungle, and that even the police had abandoned the idea of looking for him. Pedro, for whom the *senhor* now had much affection, also urged him to change his mind, and said:

"Leave him to me, *senhor*. He is mine as well as yours, and I know the forest far better than you. If ever I find him, he dies."

And so he was dissuaded, and finally he and Flora went back to Rio.

WE HAD long given up the Spider as dead, for he had not much ammunition and no way of getting more. Thus his weapons would soon become useless, and then he could kill no game to eat. We had decided he was dead, I say, when strange things began to occur. The first of these was the disappearance of Custodio Barros.

We were working far out from headquarters at the time, in new rubber land, and we needed more supplies. Custodio was sent down the river in his canoe to get them. A long time went by, and he did not return.

Then we sent another man. Before he had gone far he met two boats coming up from headquarters, and when he asked what ailed Custodio, the men in the boats were astonished, for they thought he had returned to us. They said he had come, got his supplies and started back; since then nothing had been seen or heard of him. Their own action in bringing more supplies had nothing to do with him, but was the usual arrangement. They said they would keep a sharp lookout on the way back to see if any trace of him could be found, but they discovered no trace at all.

This, of course, caused much talk and argument among us. Custodio was an honest fellow and even if he had not been he would hardly have run away with a few supplies. He might have gone ashore and been killed by a snake or a jaguar, or he might have been drowned, or devoured by alligators or *pira-nhas*. None of those things, however, would have destroyed his canoe, and the empty canoe would have been seen by someone. It might be that Indians had killed him and taken all he had, but this did not seem likely. Each of us had his own idea of what might have happened, but none of us knew anything more than the fact that he was lost.

Gumercindo Penna was the next. He was a steady, thrifty man who had worked among us for a long time and had never gambled. He had accumulated a large account with the *coronel*. He had a little family at a place well down the river, and now the longing for home had grown too strong in him, and he was going out.

The *coronel*, who is always very kind to those who serve him well, not only paid him his due but gave him a handsome present besides, so that he was quite rich for a man of this region. Yet, partly because he was so thrifty and partly because the home fever was burning strong in him, he would not wait for a regular boat and go home as a paying passenger, but started at once in his own canoe.

Since he was going downriver, the *coronel* asked him to bear a message to some of our men working some distance below headquarters, telling them to come in, as he had decided to send them into another place. Gumercindo gladly promised to do so.

The men did not come in, and, after waiting awhile, the *coronel* sent another man with the same message. This time the men came promptly. They said, *senhores*, that Gumercindo not only had given them no message, but he had never passed their camp!

At this the *coronel* was much perplexed, and after turning things over in his mind he sent two men all the way to Gumercindo's home to see if he had arrived there. He had not. Nobody knew anything at all about him. Nowhere between the headquarters and his home was there any sign of him. He, too, had disappeared.

This alarmed and angered all of us. Searching parties went out with orders to find the lost man or some trace of him, and they hunted all along both banks and sent word far down the river to seek him. But nothing was found; neither Gumercindo himself, nor his canoe, nor even his hat.

After that no man traveled alone. We felt that some terrible thing was on the river, though what it might be we could not guess. We made note of one thing, though — that both of these men had disappeared with something of value. Custodio had vanished with some supplies; Gumercindo with money. Men who had nothing were not molested. Still, the fact that both of those lost men had been alone when they were destroyed made us want to travel in pairs, whether we had anything or not. For a time this worked well. Nothing happened to any of us, except the usual accidents and hazards of our work.

Then came something that struck dread deeper into our hearts. Two men disappeared together, and with them a whole boatload of valuable supplies. One of them, Lucas Maciel, was a rather simple fellow and slow of thought, but the other, Saldanha Saraiva, was a man of quick wit and much experience on the river, whose only weakness was a fondness for women. They were bound upstream when they were last seen, and somewhere between that point and our workings the mysterious Death which haunted the river reached out and seized them, their boat and all they had. As before, no trace was left behind.

While we were searching along the banks and back in the jungle for any sign of what had happened to these mates of ours, a fifth man was swallowed up. Antonio Maciel, he was — a brother of Lucas. This time the Death struck not on the water, but in the jungle.

Antonio was one of several men who were beating through the bush, strung out in a long line with wide spaces between them, and he was at the end of the line nearest the stream. After a time the man next to him found that Antonio was not answering his calls. He cut his way toward where Antonio should have been. He was not there, nor had he reached that place. There was no trace of him. He was gone, as if the ground had opened under him and closed again. The last sign of him was a place where he had slashed some vines with his machete.

This was too much. Men now feared to work — to go in canoes — to do anything. They were not cowards, these comrades of mine, but the mystery and silence of this awful Death that left no trace was more than they could stand. Some crossed themselves and said it was no mortal thing, but a demon. No man knew when or where it would strike him down, for it had seized Antonio, who was on land and had nothing but his weapons, just as it had devoured the men on the water who had money or supplies. Though our work went on, we toiled always with a cold feeling on our backs, and went always by twos or threes. There was not one of us who did not shudder at the mention of this mysterious Death.

NOW PEDRO had recovered from his bullet wound and was back at work with me, we had many talks about this thing which we called the Death, but none of them got us anywhere. Yet, through these talks, we got into the habit of being together, and where one of us went the other went, too. So when I was told to go to headquarters and fetch back some things that were needed in our work, Pedro came with me. At the headquarters I got what we had been sent for and, as the things were few, I gave them over to Pedro to put into the canoe while I told the *coronel* how all was going at our *tambo* up the river. When I came out and saw our canoe I was astonished. It seemed to be full of supplies.

"What is this, Pedro?" I asked.

He smiled his odd smile, and answered:

"It is bait. The boxes and bags are filled with trash." And as I stared at him he added: "The Death strikes at men with full canoes, Lourenço. I would see what this Death looks like."

"Are you mad?" I cried angrily. "Is there not danger enough without inviting more?"

"Perhaps so," he said, his brown eyes dancing. "If you are afraid, we will leave this bait behind."

Of course that silenced me, as he knew it would. We pushed off and paddled away with our worthless cargo. After we swung into our longdistance stroke some of his recklessness crept into me, too, and I began to look forward to meeting the Death and fighting it.

The only thing we did meet, however, was far from what we half expected. At a place where a slow, quiet creek flowed into the river, a soft call came to us, and as we looked we saw standing there an Indian woman. We held the canoe steady and stared at her.

She was a magnificent woman, for she was tall and shapely, deep-bosomed and full-hipped, and she looked as strong as a man; her face, too, was really handsome. She laughed and beckoned to us. Pedro laughed back, waved his hand and asked her what she would have of us; she made some answer, but we could not understand it, for we did not know her tongue. Then she waved to us again to come ashore.

Pedro, who was in the bow, drove his paddle into the river to do so, but I backed water and held the canoe where it was, for, though the things we had been sent for were few, they were badly needed at our *tambo* and we were under orders to waste no time. When Pedro scowled at me I reminded him of this and told him I had had enough of his foolishness and that we would go on at once. Still, we stayed there a few minutes, out on the water, while he and the woman talked back and forth without understanding each other at all. Then we went on, paddling fast to make up for lost time.

The sight of this woman had surprised us much, for we knew of no Indians along that stream — their country was farther west and south. Had she been a man it would not have seemed so strange, for the savages are rovers and hunt for long distances away from their homes; but a woman, all alone on the bank, was something to be wondered at. We puzzled about her as we went on and concluded that a band of the Indians must be living near the stream for a time, as she certainly would never be there unless some men were about. As I have said, she was the only person we saw on all our trip. The mysterious Death never molested us. So, when we neared our journey's end, I said:

"Let us now throw this bait overboard. It has caught no fish."

"Very well," said Pedro, and we drew up to the bank to do so.

But suddenly, as he reached for the first bag, a strange look dawned in his face, as if a great thought had struck him.

"Lourenço!" he said hoarsely. "That woman — I wonder if

she too was bait!"

I frowned at him, wondering what he meant, but he did not explain. Instead, he said:

"We will not throw away our bait. We will hide it and use it again. Say nothing of the woman, Lourenço. I have an idea, and later you shall know what it is."

So we hid all the trash beside the water, and marked a tree so that we could find it again, and went on to the *tambo*.

Now in this gang of ours there was a silent, surly man who had been a lone rubber-picker in very wild parts of Peru and Bolivia, and who knew Indian tongues. He was said to be a refugee from both countries because he had killed men there, and most of us left him alone as much as possible.

Now I observed, however, that Pedro was with him a good deal. Pedro was the sort of man who can make friends with anyone, and even this sour, suspicious killer liked him. What they talked about Pedro did not tell me, and I asked no questions. This went on for a time, and then one night Pedro took the gang-boss aside and talked with him. After that he came and told me to clean my rifle and prepare to go downriver, and in the morning we went.

At the place where the marked tree stood we got our bait again, and arranged it so that it looked much different than before. Then we went on downstream, ready for anything that might come, but nothing came.

When we reached the place where we had seen the woman, we held the canoe, and Pedro gave an odd cry like a bird. I recognized the call as one he had been practicing since he began talking with the Peruvian outlaw. We listened, but neither heard nor saw anything, so we went on. At intervals he called again, and at last there floated back the same call from the jungle. We stopped the canoe where it was. Pedro called again, and again came the reply. Soon a figure appeared among the trees, and we saw the savage woman.

"Hold your rifle ready, Lourenço," he whispered.

I seized the gun and cocked it, watching the shore. He began to talk to the woman, using strange words which meant nothing to me, but which she evidently understood, for she responded at once. Now I saw why he had spent so much time with the man from the west who knew Indian languages. He had been learning how to speak the savage dialect himself.

She laughed, that woman, and chattered eagerly to Pedro and waved to us to come to her. But that we did not do. Pedro shook his head, and once he pointed upstream and said more things.

After a time he began to paddle again and went on down the river and left her behind. We passed around a bend and then another, and when we were well out of sight, he turned the canoe toward the shore — across the river from the bank where the woman had stood. At a good place we landed, and there he arranged our cargo again to suit himself. He laughed at all my questions and made no answer, but his eyes sparkled, and his face was alive with his thoughts, though at times he looked a little puzzled and doubtful, too.

When he was ready we went back upstream. This time he gave no call, and we paddled steadily until we reached that place where first we had seen the woman. There he turned toward the little creek, and as we neared it I saw her again. Pedro had made tryst with her and now he stepped out on land and went boldly to her. I stayed in the canoe.

"I think there is no danger here, Lourenço," he said, "but be alert."

He talked more with her while I watched them and everything around them. As before, she chattered and laughed with him, and I could see that she admired him much, which was not strange, for men admired him, too — he was so tall and straight and strong.

I saw also that he was questioning her, and that she was not answering all his questions. Once she wanted to look at the stuff in our boat, but I warned her off, and Pedro himself held her arm and stopped her.

Finally he stepped back into the canoe, and we went on upriver until we were out of sight. There we picked a place to camp and stayed there that night, lighting no fire.

Before we slept, he told me that the woman was living in the jungle with a man, but what sort of a man he was or where he lived she would not tell him. This man, she said, was away somewhere that day, and what he was doing she did not know. When Pedro asked her if she would lead us to the man's camp she refused. Then she asked what we had in our boat, and he told her they were supplies for a new camp. It was then that she tried to look at them and we prevented her. After that she asked where this new camp was, and he told her at a certain place well up the river, where there really was no camp and where none was intended. In leaving her, he told her he would not work the next day because it was his birthday, and he would come to meet her again at the same place.

"I ask you again, Pedro," I said, "what is the meaning of all this? And why are you so interested in this savage woman?"

"Lourenço," he answered, "we are now not very far from headquarters. All of our five friends whom the Death has struck have disappeared not far from headquarters — or so I believe. The place where we first saw that woman is not far from headquarters. The place where she answered my call today is still nearer to headquarters. More than that, she answered from a spot very near where Antonio Maciel vanished. Now there is a riddle for you to puzzle over. I am going to sleep."

IN THE morning we took out all our bait and put it into the bush. Pedro sat awhile and watched the creeping shadows, and, when it was time, we went down the river again. As we paddled along I said:

"Pedro, if this woman has anything to do with the Death, as you believe, then we are fools to meet her again where you agreed, for we are likely to go into a trap and never come out."

He laughed and replied —

"If the Death is what I think it is, it is now up the river seeking that new camp of which I told her, and so it can do us no harm."

He seemed to be right, for the woman awaited us, and they talked again for some time, and nothing at all happened. I could see that she was very much taken with my handsome

companion, but, as before, he could not make her answer all
his questions. After we left her he said:

"She is no fool, Lourenço, for all that she seems so simple.
Still, I think that in the end we shall learn what we want to
know."

When I suggested that we hasten matters by going
straight to the place where she had answered his bird cry and
searching the jungle there, he snorted and replied:

"Oh, yes, surely. That was just what Antonio was doing —
searching the bush at that place. And there were more men in
his party than in ours. Have patience, comrade, and do not
jump in the dark."

This silenced me.

We hid for the rest of that day and that night, and then we
went to meet her again — for the last time, as it turned out.
She seemed sulky, and when he tried to put her in better
humor she answered crossly, and we saw that something had
happened since we left her. Yet Pedro finally coaxed her into a
cheery mood and she began to smile and give him soft looks.

Later I learned that she had blurted out that he was lying
to her because there was no camp where he had said. Of
course, that instantly showed him that his shrewd guess had
been right, and that she or her man had sought that camp. He
was not foolish enough to let her see his thought, however, and
he told her that the plans had been changed and the new camp
was being made at another place. After that they talked on for
some time, and he told her how handsome she was and so on.

I was crouched in the canoe, as usual, watching everything like a cat, and listening. All at once my ear caught a tiny
sound in the bush — a soft rustle as if something had brushed
stealthily against some leaves. Pedro and the woman were
talking low, and I put all my attention on that little sound. It
might be only a wandering breeze, a crawling snake or some
other natural thing, but I had to be sure. Soon I heard it again,
very soft, and I knew something was creeping nearer to us.
Then, at a place where the tangle was very thick, I saw a slight
movement caused by something about the height of a man.

"Take care, Pedro!" I shouted.

Like a flash he dodged and leaped forward, landing several feet away. Like a flash an arrow sped through the place where he had been. I threw up my rifle and fired straight at the spot where I had seen the movement; but even as my finger pressed the trigger I knew the bullet had missed, for a violent shaking of leaves showed that the man there had thrown himself sidewise. Then, while I was throwing another cartridge into the barrel, the killing of that man was taken out of my hands.

The woman sprang at the bush. In one hand she held Pedro's machete, which she had snatched from his belt. With that weapon she hacked and stabbed in a fury that was terrible to see. I caught glimpses of a body writhing under her and heard a snarl, a broken scream and a groan. Then the body lay still and we heard no sound but the slash of the long knife through the leaves as the woman struck and struck and struck.

For a moment Pedro and I were paralyzed. Then Pedro seized her and twisted the dripping machete from her hand. I jumped ashore, and while she stood shaking and sobbing with rage we dragged the body out and looked at it.

"Por Deus!" muttered Pedro. "The Spider!"

Yes, *senhores*, it was the Spider. He was a frightful thing to look at, but he was the Spider — the man whom we had thought dead and who now truly was so. Even in death he looked the Spider, for his arms and legs were crumpled up as if something had smashed him. From his belt hung a narrow bag made from a skin, and in it were several arrows. Stepping into the place where his woman had killed him, we found his bow — a short, clumsy but powerful weapon that could drive an arrow clear through a man at close range.

While we were looking at this we heard a dragging sound and stepped out in time to see the last of the Spider. With one hand the woman was hauling him to the river. There she picked him up as if he were only a monkey, swung him and threw him out into the water.

He struck and sank with a soggy splash. A moment later the water began to seethe and boil. We knew the *piranhas*, those ravenous cannibal fish, were swarming upon him and chopping him into fragments. So thick were they that some of them were crowded up into the air, snapping their jaws like traps. A red stain grew on the surface and slowly drifted down the current with that hellish boiling going on under it. Before long, though, the water grew quiet again, and the red stain floated out of sight.

Then the woman looked at Pedro. The hatred faded out of her face, her fierce eyes softened and she took his hand and led us away into the jungle. We traveled for some distance and stopped at length in a place where Pedro looked about and said —

"This is where Antonio disappeared."

We could not see anything strange, though at one spot the tangle of vines and bush was very thick and matted together, as it may be anywhere in those forests. The woman saw we were puzzled and she walked up to that tangle — and suddenly she was gone. But she called, and we followed her. And as we reached the matted vines a part of them moved outward like a door, and there she was, laughing like a little girl playing a game.

Senhores, that was the Spider's nest — a lair made from the growing bushes and vines so cunningly twisted and woven among themselves that a man could stand within ten feet of it and never suspect that it was a shelter and hiding place. If ever there was a great trapdoor spider's nest, that was it.

The man Schwartz had followed the trapdoor spider's example inside his den, as well as outside.

That spider, as you probably know, not only makes a door which swings shut behind him, and covers that door with things that grow around it, but he also makes a secret pocket at the side of his nest, where he can hide if any enemy discovers his lair. And the Spider had done this also.

At one side of his den the ground rose, and there he had dug a hole and covered it over with the growing things so that nobody would ever know it was there. It was not meant to hide in, though, but to conceal the things he took from murdered men. In that hole, when the woman showed it to us, we found all the property of Custodio, Gumercindo, Saldanha and the brothers Maciel. There was Gumercindo's money, the supplies taken from the others and their weapons and even their clothes. But of the men themselves there was no sign anywhere.

When Pedro asked the woman what had become of the men, she said that after the Spider killed them and stripped them of all they had, he did with them just what she had finally done to him — threw them to the *piranhas*, which quickly destroyed them.

Their canoes, she said, he hid until night, when he took them far up the quiet little creek where we had first seen her, and there, where neither flame nor smoke would be seen by anyone, he burned them — all except the light, fast canoe of Custodio, which he concealed very cunningly and used himself. In this he made his spying trips, going at night and staying away for a day or two. No doubt he had been almost beside us more than once, lying low, watching and listening with that spidery patience of his and learning whom he might kill with profit.

In all these murders, the woman said, he used the bow and arrow which was silent and easy enough to handle at close range. In all the killings except that of Antonio Maciel he made her lure the men ashore at some place where he lurked, ready to strike them down. To Custodio, Lucas and Saldanha she had called and showed herself, just as she did to us, and they came to her and so to their death. Gumercindo was caught in another way, for he was a shrewd man and was hastening home and thus was not so likely to tarry for any savage woman. The Spider had had her stay out of sight, though near the water, and scream as if in great danger. Gumercindo, like a brave fellow he was, sped to shore and dashed into the bush to save the one who was in such distress. He was shot in the back for his pains.

Antonio Maciel was killed because he was coming straight at the Spider's nest with his machete ready to cut through what he took for a natural tangle. Through a small opening in the side of his den the Spider shot him and dragged him swiftly inside, so that when the other men arrived they found nothing but the last place where he had cut his way. That was some distance back from where he died.

We learned, too, that Pedro and I were to have been the next victims, if we had come near enough. The Spider had a place downstream where he could watch what went on at headquarters across the river, and he saw Pedro load up the canoe with what looked like many supplies, and so hastened back and made the woman run to that place at the creek and play her part when we passed on our return. While she tried to bring us ashore he lurked ready to kill us, but when we refused to come he was too wise to attack us at a distance, so he let us go.

So Pedro's foolish bait caught something after all, though even he did not suspect that the Spider still lived. He carried that bait to see what might come of it and later he believed that the Death was some Indian.

When we came back and Pedro had given the bird call of her people, she was alone, for the Spider was away somewhere spying, and she wanted us to come ashore only because she was hungry to talk with the man who could speak her own tongue.

After she left us at the creek she told the Spider, on his return, of our new camp and all our new supplies. He went seeking it, came back angry and beat her. From that time on she told him nothing more of us but met Pedro secretly. She did not know that the Spider had followed her on that last day until Pedro jumped, and the arrow flashed by him. Then her hatred of the Spider, which had long been growing in her, flamed out in the fury that destroyed him.

She had no love for him, but had been sold to him by her people, whom he had met by chance in the jungle before he came back to the river and made his lair. He gave the headman his rifle for her, she said, and, though he had used up all his cartridges so that the gun was useless, the headman made the trade because women were plentiful in his tribe but guns were very scarce, and he might be able to get cartridges.

She told us also that her people knew where there was

gold, and that the Spider had planned to get much of this gold in trade for the supplies he took from our men. Thus, in time, he hoped to become very rich, and then, perhaps, would make his way into Peru, where he was not known, and where he could enjoy the wealth gained through the deaths of honest men.

So you see, *senhores*, it was as I told you at the beginning — this man lived like a spider and he died like one. If you know spiders, you know that the female is larger and stronger than the male, and that often she turns on him and destroys him. The thing that destroyed this Spider was the fact that he did not know this big, handsome woman's heart.

Though I do not claim to know much of women, yet I have observed a few and I have noticed that when a man treats a woman as something bought and paid for, the time may come when he had best beware of her. I have noticed, too, that when women meet men for whom they care, it makes little difference whether they are fine ladies from Rio, or humble maidens of the village, or savage women of the jungle — at heart they are all the same.

THE PECCARIES

PARDON ME, *senhor*, but I think you are mistaken. Those peccaries which attacked you while you and your companions were exploring the headwaters of the Javary must have been those with the white lips and jaws, not those with the white band across their chests.

You say there was a big drove of them, and that they were large, black, and ugly. Yes, those surely must have been the white-lipped peccaries; for the white-collared pigs do not travel in such big bands, and they are not so large or so dark, nor so likely to attack a man if they are let alone. Those with the white chest-band, though, are dangerous and bad.

For that matter, all peccaries are wicked fighters if they are aroused, and it is best to avoid them if you can. But, bad as they are, they are not so bad as the cruel band of human Peccaries who, not long ago, ravaged the rubber-lands where I and other men employed by old Colonel Nunes were working. Perhaps you have heard of them. No?

Then I will tell you about them, while we sit safely here on the deck and the mighty Amazon bears us on toward our homes; and when you *senhores* arrive at last in your North America you will have one more tale to tell to the pale-faced folk who dwell in the cities, and use our rubber, and know nothing of the hardship and torment and death that go into the gathering of it.

It is an old saying among us Brazilians that "each ton of rubber costs a human life," and it is true — too true; for there is many a ton that means not only one death, but several. And the rubber which the Peccaries took from us was measured not by tons but by pounds, and it was stained red with our blood, and with theirs too.

These men were not the wild people of our own Brazilian jungle. They were wild and savage enough, it is true; but they came upon us from across the Javary, which, as you know, is the boundary between Brazil and Peru; and they were not merely *barbaros* who killed for the joy of fighting or because they ate human flesh, but an organized band of desperate men who hunted plunder in the form of rubber, or gold, or women, or whatever else they valued.

They were merciless, and were led by a yellow devil more pitiless than they. And nothing could stand before them until they met another band of human Peccaries, brought upon them by a man who escaped them after torment. I was that man.

We first heard of them from our fellow workmen down the river, who had the news of them from other men who brought supplies. We ourselves were toiling in a rubber district which was very rich, but very far out from headquarters, so that we had to go a long distance through the jungle at intervals in order to renew our food, which was brought up in boats to a large *tambo* where another of the *coronel*'s gangs was working a number of good *estradas*.

On our trips to this *tambo* we always carried out with us some rubber to be sent down-stream, but there was much more of it which we left behind; for the journey through the bush was so long that it had been decided to pile up the rubber we made until the flood-time drew near, when a large band of men were to be sent in to take it away. So we had many balls of it, worth much money, waiting out there in the forest when we heard of the Peccaries.

Our friends told us the Peruvian side was being raided by a large band of marauders whose leader was a yellow half-breed, and who painted their jaws a whitish color like the white-lipped peccaries; and from this, and their savagery, they got their name. That was all that our men knew of them at that time. So we went back to our district, talking about this new peril of a region that is always perilous enough, but fearing it not at all; for none of us thought those robbers would ever come into our place, so far away from the hills of Peru.

Now, as you have been among peccaries, *senhores*, you must know the fetid smell that comes from them, especially when there are many of them together. It comes from a gland in their loins, and if you kill one for his meat — which you probably will not do if you can find anything better — you must cut this thing out at once.

And one day some time after our trip outside, while we were lounging around the *tambo* in the heat of noon, this smell floated to us from the thick forest round about. It grew strong and rank in the heavy air, and we looked at one another and arose to get our rifles. But the beasts that burst out upon us were not what we expected.

A voice snarled an order, the bush rustled, and we were surrounded by a score of evil-looking men. They were Indians and half-breeds, almost naked, armed with rifles, revolvers and knives, and smelling most foul. We saw at once that they were Peruvian *caboclos*, for they had the slanting eyes and high cheek-bones. Then I grew cold inside, for I observed that their lips and jaws were daubed a dirty white; and that and their peccary-smell told me who they were.

Shots crashed out, and I turned to see two of my men fall dead, killed because they had seized their rifles. Then the yellow-faced, black-mustached leader of the raiders strode before me and snarled in Spanish —

"Who commands here?"

"I do," I snarled back.

He grinned a mocking grin, and said:

"Then, *señor el capitan*, tell your men to make no fight, or they will all go the way of those two dogs on the ground. We are the Peccaries — you know of us, yes? Then you know what we do to those who oppose us. But we would spare you for a time, because we can use you."

"For what?" I demanded.

"For beasts of burden, illustrious *señor*. You have much rubber, which will be carried out for us. And you will do the carrying."

As my rifle was not near my hand I leaped at him with my machete drawn. He sprang away from before me and hissed something through his yellow teeth. A sudden shock smote the back of my head, and I fell.

When I came to myself the fight was over, and of my

eleven men only two were left alive. One was Jorge Tourinho, who was very ill with fever; and the other was Paulo Pereira, a big fellow who was very powerful but rather slow of thought and action. All the other nine lay where they had died fighting those devils who would not only rob us but enslave us too.

And though they had been outnumbered, surrounded, and caught by surprise, they had fought well, those mates of mine. Among their bodies lay those of six dead Peccaries, and four more of the raiders were shot and slashed so that they would soon die. The yellow leader, however, was unharmed, and as I started to rise he sprang and kicked me down. And then, grinning that cruel grin, he said:

"Stay where you are, dog, until I tell you to get up. And look around you and see what has come to your men. If I had not decided to make you sweat blood before I finish with you, and so had you struck down from behind, you too would now be meat for the vultures, which are gathering for their feast."

And I looked up as I lay there, and saw that he spoke truth, for the black *urubus* already were settling into the trees around us.

Swiftly I rolled over and sprang up and attacked him again in fury — with my bare hands this time, for my machete was gone. I got his throat in my hands and throttled him. But another blow smashed on my head, and for the second time I was knocked senseless. And when the light came back to me I could not fight more, for I was sick — sick from a terrible headache caused by those blows, and sick because I had been brutally kicked in the stomach while I lay there.

And as I looked around I grew yet sicker from what I saw. For those *demonios* were mutilating the bodies of my comrades in a manner such as I can not tell you about, and such as only fiends could ever have thought of.

I looked at Paulo, who lay near me, and saw his face was gray-white. As I moved he caught my eye and said hoarsely:

"Do not fight more, chief, or they will do to us what they are doing to the dead — and do it while we are alive. Their yellow *caitão* has said so."

I made no answer, but my face may have shown my

thought, for he added:

"Do not look so at me — I can not fight. See, my right arm is broken. And I was struck down from behind even as you were, and I am sick."

Before I could say anything, if I had wanted to, a voice arose in a babble of meaningless words. The sound came from the *tambo*, where Jorge lay racked with fever, and I knew it was he, raving in his illness. The Peccaries turned and looked toward the noise, and the leader went to the hammock where Jorge lay.

"Ah! The fever?" he purred. "That is very sad, my friend, that you have fever. If you were well you might be a beast of burden for us, but you are far too weak to be useful. And since I am very tender of heart, and it grieves me deeply to see you suffering so, I will cure you at once."

Then Jorge's babbling burst into a sudden scream, and after that he was silent. And the yellow man came out grinning, and carrying a red-stained knife.

The foul-smelling *caboclos* laughed harshly at his murderous humor. A cold, deadly rage filled me. I ached to kill them all. Yet I saw how hopeless my position was, and swiftly determined what I would do. Though I would rather die fighting than be their pack-animal, yet I would not fight, nor die either; for if I were dead I would be of no use to myself or anyone else, while if I lived and awaited my chance I might find a way to destroy this band, or at least some of them, and avenge my mates.

So when the chief murderer ordered me roughly to get up I did so meekly, though with some difficulty because of my aching stomach. And when he called me dog again, and told me that if I made more trouble he would cut out my bowels, I answered:

"I will make no trouble, *senhor*. You have won, and I am no fool. I fought for my rubber and my friends, and you can not blame a man for that."

"You have it right," he answered. "And you have sense also, and you are a good fighter. If you serve us well we may not treat you so badly. Perhaps you may even become one of us, for we need fighting men. If you do become a Peccary you shall have much gold, and women.

"But first we shall see how you act. If you try treachery, you will scream for death a long time before it comes to you."

"Gold and women?" I asked as if that bait tempted me. "Where do you get your women, *senhor?*"

He laughed then, a vile laugh, and stared at me with glittering eyes so evil that I secretly felt ashamed that any man should think of me what he thought. And he said:

"So you are interested, yes? We get the women wherever we find them. There are handsome maidens in the Indian villages here and there — yes, young and strong and beautiful — and when they have come to us they love us so much that they never leave us — until they die."

And he laughed again, cruelly; and the white-jawed men laughed too, so that I shivered, picturing to myself what the fate of those women must be. But I concealed my feelings, and when they ordered me to the rubber *tambo* I went, with Paulo trailing silently along behind.

There the Peccaries loaded themselves with the rubber, cursing and growling because there were not more men to carry it. They loaded me and Paulo, too, until we could scarcely walk under our burdens.

The yellow man scowled at Paulo's broken arm a minute before he was loaded up, and fingered his knife as if half-minded to kill him because he was crippled. But then he looked the yellow man all over, and saw how big and strong he was, and decided to keep him alive because he would be able to carry much weight when the broken arm should mend; so he had that arm tied up roughly with creeping vines.

When we had all we could carry, the raiders took the weapons from the dead and hid them in the forest, where they could get them when they came again with more men. Then they started westward, driving us like beasts.

For two days we marched, Paulo and I plodding on silent and sullen. Paulo was suffering much from his broken arm, but our captors showed him no mercy. Because of this he soon developed a fever, and between this and his pain he could not sleep at night, but turned and groaned so that I could not sleep much either.

Of course, I did what little I could for him, and whispered encouragement, telling him we would live to repay these murderers for all they had done to us and our comrades. But he said:

"Chief, I shall not live. I feel that I shall see few more dawns, and I am glad."

And he was right. For whenever the band paused to drink from a stream they always let us drink first, and waited a while before taking water themselves, which puzzled us somewhat. And on the third day Paulo drank heavily from a little brook while I lay where I dropped to snatch a moment's rest, too tired even to creep to the water. And very soon after that be began to writhe and squirm, while the Peccaries looked at him with gleaming eyes and nodded to one another as if they had expected this.

I went quickly to him, and said —

"Comrade, what is it?"

He gasped —

"Poison!"

And soon he died in great pain.

I turned on those *caboclos* then and cursed them. But they only laughed, and the leader said:

"Why waste your temper? He was only a cripple. Do not curse us, but the Indians who poisoned the water because we took some of their women and made them happy. We have been very polite, and have always allowed you to drink first; is it not so?"

Then he cackled his hideous laugh, and I burned to kill him. But there was nothing I could do, and so I swallowed my hate and went on with them, trying to comfort myself with the thought that now Paulo was at peace.

WE REACHED a river, and they drew out canoes from concealments under the bank, and we went downstream for quite a long distance. Then we landed on the western shore, hid the canoes again and kept on westward.

Though I staggered on under my load like an unseeing brute, I was really using my eyes all the time and remembering our course, so that I could use it again by myself if the chance came. And at last, when it seemed I could go no farther, we came into a village which was the lair of the Peccaries.

It was a filthy little town with *barracãos* built much like ours, except that these houses did not stand high on poles as ours do; for the place was in hilly country, far above the reach of the floods. There were few men about, but quite a number of women — Indian women, all young, some not bad-looking, but all seeming sullen and hopeless. The men were as hard-looking and foul-smelling as those with us, and they had the same white-daubed jaws.

I soon learned from their talk with our leader, whom they called El Amarillo — probably because of his yellowness — that there were more robbers, but that they now were out on raids of their own, led by sub-chiefs. And during the next few days these bands came in, bringing some rubber, and a large amount of raw gold which they had won by murders somewhere in the hills.

In all, there were fully fifty of them, and I doubt if such a brutal crew ever was gathered before in any place. They were beasts — beasts that walked and talked like men, but had no human hearts.

Nobody paid much attention to me, except to curse me or throw vile jests at me, and see that I did not escape. This I made no effort to do, for two reasons: I was so worn down by my hard march that I wanted rest above all else, and besides I hoped to work out some way to destroy them, which was really what I had undergone all that hardship for.

But I could see no way to do this, for I was one unarmed man among half a hundred cutthroats, and all I could think of was to set fire to their *barracãos* at night. This idea I discarded, for there was little chance that I could do them much harm by burning their houses. And so for the time I did nothing but watch and listen.

I saw that the rubber they had brought in from their raids was taken away again by a gang of stolid Indian porters, commanded by a villainous *caboclo* with one eye, who probably delivered it at some place where it could be sent to a market and sold.

I saw also why these men smelled so; for they killed peccaries in the forest, and ate their flesh, and smeared themselves with the musky fat from those pouches in the pigs' loins; and as they never washed themselves this odor quickly became most vile. Besides this, I saw something of their treatment of women.

As ten of them had died in the fight with my men, and all of them had had women, the Yellow One now decided to give these girls over to other men. He had them brought out and lined up before him like cattle, and picked the best-looking for himself, although he already had two others of his own. Then he gave each of his sub-chiefs one, and those who were left he handed over to men who had none.

The girls made no protest, but went dumbly with the men who got them — all except one. She was one of the youngest, and she turned from the bandit to whom she was given and begged El Amarillo not to make that man her master. He snarled, and told her to go as he ordered.

Then she broke away and fled very fast, trying to escape; and the big brute who now owned her ran after her, cursing. He caught her by the hair, and his knife flashed, and she fell; and then he picked her body up and threw it out to one side for the *urubus* and came back, muttering with rage.

The Yellow One grinned his beastly grin, and the others said nothing, but walked off as if such things were common. And I went away and sat down by myself, sick at heart.

Soon after that a dozen more Indian carriers came in, and the chief took them and me and four of his fighting-men, and we started back to my old *tambo* to bring out more of the rubber. Before we went the Yellow One ordered that large boats be kept waiting for us at that place on the river where we had first taken to the canoes, as several trips through the bush would be necessary to clean up all the loot.

At first it seemed strange to me that he should go back himself instead of sending a lesser man and devoting his own time to new work elsewhere. But as we marched back to the river I learned from his talk with his fighters that it was not alone the rubber that took him back, but that he planned another raid in my country, and a foul one.

For he was not satisfied with the three women he now possessed, but wanted more; and he knew of an Indian tribe who lived in the Brazilian bush in a great *maloca*, or tribal house, and who were lighter in color than most Indians and had among them many handsome young women. So, after our rubber should be all brought out and sent down the river, he intended to lead his men against this tribal house by night, when the Indians were asleep, burst in its single door, and, in the darkness and confusion of the sudden attack, to seize a number of girls and drag them swiftly away to a fate which I knew only too well.

I learned, too, from their talk that this would not be the first time they had assailed those Indians and carried off their women, and that in a previous raid they had captured, among other girls, the one whom I had recently seen murdered.

Now, though I had been unable to help that girl, because she had fled and met her death so swiftly that I could not interfere, I had noticed her particularly among the women, and had wondered whether she came from a certain tribe of Indians whom I knew. Some time before this I had roamed the jungle with a man from your North America whom I called the Jaguar, because he was a terrible fighter; and we had been captured by Indians said to be cannibals, but had not been killed and eaten by them because the Jaguar dared the chief to fight him barehanded, and killed him; and then a cunning old man who wished to use us for his own purposes made the Jaguar chief of all the tribe, and finally we seized our chance and escaped.

And though we had been among those people only a short time, quite a number of their faces stayed dimly in my memory, and it seemed to me that the girl murdered by the big brutal Peccary had been among them. So now, when I heard this talk of a woman-stealing raid, I became sure that the tribe these men were about to attack was the same one which had held me prisoner.

And though those Indians meant nothing to me, the knowledge of what these beasts were scheming to do made my hatred for them all the more bitter; for it brought back to me burning memories of a time when I had a girl for whom I cared much, and lost her when she was carried away by a fiend even worse than the Peccary leader. And, brooding over this, and the deaths of my men, and the brutality from which I myself had suffered, I resolved that from this journey either El Amarillo or I would not come back.

We reached the river, and took the canoes upstream, and resumed our march through the jungle. The Yellow One walked near me several times leering at me and calling me beast and dog, and taunting me with the fact that I should soon look upon the torn remnants of my brave comrades who had died fighting.

I bit my tongue and kept silence. But from the corner of my eye I studied his weapons, as I had done a number of times before. He carried a rifle in one hand, a machete and dagger at his left side, and a revolver at his right.

The thought of snatching one of these grew in my mind. I wanted one of the knives, which would do its work quickly and surely if I once got a grip on it; but somehow he always walked at my left, in such a way that the knives were on the other side of him and out of my reach.

The rifle, too, he carried usually in his left hand, and I knew that if I seized it there would be a struggle, and that probably one of the other Peccaries would kill me before I could wrench it from his grasp. Thus the revolver would be best, for I could get it more easily, and perhaps kill the other robbers with it as well as their leader. Whether the Indian carriers would attack me I did not know, nor care.

Then came my chance. The yellow man came up beside me once more — on the left, as before — and jeered at me, and stepped ahead. In a flash I swooped at the revolver, caught its butt, yanked it from his belt. He whirled like a cat. As he faced me I pointed at his body and pulled.

The hammer snapped down, but no explosion came. I pulled trigger again — and again and yet again. The weapon only clicked. It was empty.

Then, swift as a striking snake, the Yellow One's rifle-barrel hit my hand and knocked the revolver from it. And the Yellow One burst into a shrill, screeching laugh, and I saw I had been tricked.

I sprang at him. But he jammed his rifle into my stomach, stopping me in my tracks and knocking out my wind. Four men seized me and held me powerless.

"So at last you have come to life, my illustrious pack-animal!" he mocked me. "I have been testing you, waiting to see if you would not seize that unloaded weapon which I brought near your hand. You were so slow about it that I began to think you could be trusted to become a Peccary — but you bit at the bait, yes!

"And now do you remember what I told you, señor — that if you tried treachery you should scream for death long before it came to you? I see you do. And since my conscience is so tender that I could not rest if I failed to keep a promise, I am compelled to see that you receive what I pledged you."

Though I wrestled and kicked and bit, the men holding me dragged me to a big tree and held me there while their leader went into the bush seeking something. When he came back he carried a double handful of long thorns, as hard and sharp as nails.

At sight of these the other Peccaries chuckled as if they had seen them used before and knew what was to be done with me. More of them grasped me and held me against the tree so that I could not move at all. They twisted my hands up behind me and around the tree-trunk, and the Yellow One picked up the revolver he had knocked from my fist and held it by the barrel like a hammer. Then he stepped around the tree behind me. A moment later a sharp pain pierced one of my hands.

Yes, *senhores*, that is how I received these ugly scars on my hands and arms, at which I have seen you glance more than once, though you were too polite to ask me about them.

And these are not all, for there are other scars all down my body and legs, made in the same way. With those thorns the grinning Amarillo nailed me to that tree so that I hung in torment, unable to escape.

"There, *señor*, you will not have to carry any more burdens for us," he jeered when it was done. "You will have nothing at all to do but to hang here and scream curses after us when we are gone. When we come back we will let you watch us eat and drink, for you will have hunger and thirst by that time.

"Oh no, dear, friend, you will not die before then, for I have been very careful not to break any large blood-vessels, which would let you die too soon. You will last for some days, unless a wandering jaguar should happen to find you. In that case — well, a jaguar must eat; is it not so?"

And all the Peccaries laughed. But I kept my jaws locked and made no sound. After watching me a minute he added:

"The thorns hurt, yes? That is very sad. Perhaps I can find something that will take your mind off the thorns for a few hours to come."

He went away again, and returned with a folded leaf. Keeping it closed, he shook it violently. Then he flipped it open and snapped it at me.

Out from it flew several ants, maddened by the shaking they had had — and they were the *aracaras*, the fire-ants whose bite gives keen pain that is felt for hours afterward. The instant they struck my body they bit me, and ran over me biting furiously, until I groaned in unbearable pain.

Then those beast-men laughed again harshly, and one of them went and caught a couple of *tucandeira* ants — those terrible black ones which are more than an inch long. He would have thrown these on me too, but the Yellow One struck them from him and destroyed them with his rifle-butt.

"Fool!" he snarled. "Bitten as this man is already, those black ants would kill him. Would you spoil all the enjoyment we shall have with him in the next few days?"

The man muttered something and turned away. And after spitting in my face the bandit chief turned away too, saying:

"We have more important things to do than to stay longer

with you, you Brazilian dog. But we shall return, and then you shall have new things to think about."

And soon they were gone in the bush.

How long I hung there, *senhores*, I do not know. It seemed eternity. Burning with the torment of the fire-ant poison and the thorns and my wrenched and twisted muscles, I know I raved and screamed after those men had gone. I know, too, that if it had lasted much longer I should have gone stark mad, and that when the Yellow Man returned he would have found me only a yelling idiot. But before my mind gave way a new thing happened. Without a sound two men suddenly stood before me.

They were Indians. For an instant I took them for a pair of the Peccary porters who had sneaked back to torture me anew. But then I saw that they were lighter in color, their faces were shaped differently, and they carried big bows.

They were men of the cannibal tribe in the big *maloca* where I had once been assistant chief, and their faces showed that they knew me. They had little love for me, I felt, for when the Jaguar and I had been among them we had killed their chief and five others of their men. Still, a quick death at their hands would be a mercy to me now; and as I had learned some of their language during the time I spent among them, I begged them either to kill me or set me free.

They grunted to each other, and one asked me how I had come there, nailed to that tree. I made them understand that a band of human Peccaries had left me there. At once they flew into a rage, and I knew my guess had been right, and they were of the tribe whose women the beast-men had stolen.

They gritted their teeth, and beat their chests, and acted as if about to start off in pursuit. But I managed to tell them they were much outnumbered, and their foes had firearms, and so they must have more men before attacking the bandits.

They scowled, but talked it over between them and agreed that I was right. And then they laid down their bows and set to work taking out the thorns.

Though they were wild, fierce fighting-men of the jungle and eaters of human flesh, they handled me as gently as they could; and when the thorns were out they laid me down and brought me water in big leaves, and gave me to drink. They did even more; they got certain herbs from the forest, and crushed them, and placed them on my wounds; and before long the cruel pain of those hurts grew less, so that I could lie still and not twist and writhe. Then they swiftly made a crude bed of branches and vines and leaves, and put me on it, lifted it, and started straight away through the bush.

They marched a long time — so long that once when they paused to drink I asked them what they had been doing so far from their village. They said they were hunters, and had been following a tapir's track. Then they lifted me and were off again.

It was nearly night when our journey ended at a cleared place, in which stood a great round house about forty feet high, its sides made of palm-trees and its roof of palm-leaves — the *maloca* where my rescuers and some two hundred other Indians made their home. There my carriers laid me down and left me while they crept through the one low door of the house to report to their chief.

Men and women and children crowded around me as I lay there, and I thought how different was my first arrival among them. Then I had come fighting, hating and despising them as eaters of men.

Now, after what I had just gone through, they seemed friends and decent people; for I knew they ate only their enemies, and that the eating was due not so much to savagery as to some obscure religion; and I knew also that they washed themselves daily, and that a man who allowed himself to stink like the Peccaries would quickly be punished or banished. I saw, too, that they seemed sorry for me in my present condition, and felt that they would be kind to me. And it was so.

Soon the hunters came out again, and with them their chief and two lesser chiefs, painted red and black, and wearing blue and red feathers bound on their heads, shoulders, and loins. The chief, who was a powerful young fellow, I did not remember; but one of the sub-chiefs was the crafty old man who once had saved my life, and the only one in all the tribe who spoke any words of my language.

This old man looked at me and nodded and talked to the other two. And I was lifted again by the hunters and carried in through the little door and put in a hammock, where women soon brought me a gourd of broth that strengthened me much. And then I told my tale to the head men of the tribe.

They listened in grim silence, except when I told of the murder of the young girl. Then a growl ran among the men around me, and the three chiefs snarled in rage. When I was through I felt sick, and my wounds burned again, and I gave no more attention to the chiefs or anyone.

But soon an old woman came with two younger ones, and they put a thick, dark liquid on my injuries which stung like fire for an instant, but which soon eased my pain wonderfully; and then they gave me a drink of some sweetish stuff, and before long I fell into a deep sleep.

When I awoke the sun was glaring down through the big smoke-hole in the roof, and women were cooking at their little fires scattered through the *maloca*. At once I was offered food by the old woman, and as I ate it I noticed that the tall young chief was gone.

The old sub-chief was there though, and he came and sat by me and told me that the Peccaries already were being hunted down. The big chief and twenty of his best fighters, with the two hunters to guide them, had taken the trail at the first light of dawn. He added with a frightful grin that to-morrow much peccary-meat would be eaten here, and that if I did not care to taste it I should have the head of the Yellow One to kick about when my legs healed.

He was not quite right; for the wild men were gone two days instead of one, and when they came they did not bring the head of the yellow *demonio* nor any other part of him. But they did bring with them the hands and feet of all the rest of that brutal gang — even those of the Indian carriers.

They had ambushed the raiders in the act of carrying my *coronel*'s rubber to their boats, and in a swift fight had killed them to a man — except the leader. How that cunning devil had escaped they did not know; he had been there, and then he was not there, and they could find no trace of him after that.

They were angry over this, and all the more so because before he disappeared he shot three of their mates; and the chief asked me to tell them the way to the headquarters of the Peccaries in Peru, so that he could lead a war-party there before the Yellow One should bring his men to attack their *maloca* with their guns and bullets. This I could not do — I tried, but they could not understand me well. So then I told them that as soon as I could travel again I would lead them there myself, and we would kill all the Peccaries in their own homes.

At once he became more cheerful, and promised to make me strong as quickly as possible; and he gave orders to the old woman who seemed to know so much about curing hurts, and she nodded. Then everybody prepared for a great feast to celebrate the victory they had already won. All the men, and the women too, painted themselves anew with curving stripes of black and red, and the chiefs put on their finest feathers and squirrel-tail belts, and the others wore necklaces of the teeth of animals. The women took the hands and feet brought back by the fighters, and stripped the flesh from the bones, and fried it in tapir-lard or boiled it in reddish pots.

Much monkey-meat also was cooked, and parrots, and fish and other things; and all that day there was much eating and drinking, and a sort of ceremony that I could not understand and did not try to. They offered me none of the man-meat, and I was glad, for it angers those people to refuse any of their food. I ate some monkey, and then tried to sleep and forget what they were doing.

For days I lay there while my hurts healed — and they did heal with surprising swiftness. For the old woman was by me day and night, brewing different things in jars over a little fire and putting some of them on my injuries and giving me others to drink; and I grew strong and well much faster than I could have done otherwise.

While I was recovering the Indians were not idle. Some got plants with blue blossoms and small pods and yellow roots, and crushed the roots into pulp, and went away into the jungle;

and the old sub-chief told me that with that root-pulp they were poisoning all the streams for a long distance around, except those which they themselves used.

Others went out and made man-traps, such as pits and spring-guns, to kill anyone approaching the *maloca*. And those who did neither of these things worked on their weapons, fitting new cords to their great bows, or fastening barbed stingray bones on three-pronged spears, or testing the sharp jaguar-teeth set in big war-clubs, or dipping arrows and blowgun darts into that brown poison which swiftly paralyzes and kills anything scratched by it.

And while this went on the young war-chief sat with me at times and had me tell him about the Peccary village, so that he could get a clear picture of it in his mind and know what to do when we should reach it.

Then came the time when I was whole again. I asked for weapons, and the war-chief gave a command, and men brought in all the guns and cartridges and knives taken from the Peccaries they had killed. From these I took the best rifle, and two revolvers, and cartridges, and a machete.

I tried to have other men take the rest of the guns, but the chief would not have it so; for he said they were not skilled in the use of such weapons, and would do the expedition more harm than good with them. They did take the knives and machetes, however, for these they could use. And that night we all slept early, for we knew we had before us a long, hard journey with a death-struggle at the end of it.

Before we slept, though, the fighting-men painted themselves once more. I noticed that this time they added a new stripe — a broad whitish curve around their chests and collarbones; and from the way they grinned at it I thought they were not used to it. So I asked the old man what it meant, and learned it was a savage joke.

Since the Yellow One's band painted themselves like the white-lipped peccaries, he said, the wild men would make themselves peccaries of the other kind — those with the white collars; and they would soon show that their teeth were sharper than those of the stinking pigs of the hills.

At dawn we were up and away. There were fully sixty of us, all hard, relentless men. I would have turned northward, whence I had come, but the war-chief shook his head and led the way straight to the west. When we should reach the river, he told me, we should find there the Peccaries' own boats, which the Yellow One had intended for carrying away my rubber, but which now had been brought upstream for us. And when I asked about this he said he had sent men to get the boats, and that they would not fail.

I found that he spoke truth; for when we did reach the river there were the boats with a dozen more wild men in them — and with bloodstains on the wood which showed what had become of the Peccary boatmen.

Though we filled those boats dangerously full, we went down the stream swiftly. Neither on the water nor on the Peruvian shore did we meet any man, nor even on our way through the hills to the lair of the beastly men-pigs. It seemed that they never suspected Brazilian Indians would come against them or could find their place.

Still, we went quietly and carefully, lest we either fall into a trap or allow our enemies to learn we were coming. When at last we did come upon one of the guards they always kept out we were traveling so silently that he did not hear us at all.

I saw him first, for I was the guide; and I recognized him as one of those who had thrown filthy insults at me when I was a prisoner there. Hot with the memory of those things, I lifted my rifle.

But the chief, at my heels, caught my arm and shook his head; and I read his thought — that the explosion of the cartridge would be heard. So I lowered the gun, and he whispered something to those behind.

A bowman crept up to us. His cord twanged. A war-arrow whirred. A gasping groan broke from the outlaw, and he fell on his face. We moved forward again.

Soon after that I halted, and told the chief we now were near the village. As I have told you, I had described this place to him before we started, and he knew there were three trails to it — one from the east, where we were now; one from the

north, by which the robbers' loot was taken out to some market; and one from the southwest, which they often used in
starting on a raid toward the high mountains. Each of these
trails was always guarded.

I knew the chief planned to attack from all three trails at
once as well as from the thick jungle around the clearing where
the *barracãos* stood; so that now it was necessary to creep
around the town, kill the outposts on the other two trails, and
arrange the warriors so that all could sweep into the place at
the same time.

It was late in the day, but there would be time to attack
before darkness dropped on us; and the chief quickly divided
his forces into three parties. One, which he would lead himself,
was to go to the northern trail; another, under the younger
sub-chief — for the old sub-chief, unfit for fighting, had stayed
at home — would take the southwestern path; and the third
division would remain with me.

Two orders were given — that no man should attack until
the chief himself began the fight; and that if the Yellow One
was there he must not be killed, but taken alive. For an instant
I was angered by that last command, for I had long thirsted to
repay that yellow devil for what he had done to me and my
mates.

But then I saw the hard gleam in the chief's eyes, and
knew that what I might do to that Peccary would be merciful
compared to what the Indian intended. So I determined that
neither I nor any other man should kill him quickly if I could
help it.

The chief and the sub-chief went their ways, and we crept
forward on our own path. Before long we heard sounds of life
that told us we were almost at the edge of the clearing; and
after I spied ahead and found the end of the trail clear I sent
my men into the bush. Most of them were bowmen and blow-
gun men, and I gave them no orders, knowing they well understood what they were to do — stretch out along the edge of the
jungle and be ready for action.

Those who were clubmen and spearmen stayed with me —
six of them, each powerful enough to crush the life out of two

ordinary men. The spearmen stripped the grass sheaths from the points of their weapons, and I saw that each of the terrible barbs was dark with poison. To them I gave one command: that they walk last, with the spearheads turned backward. And then we slipped up to the clearing and waited.

The Peccary lair was on a hillside, and our path ran along that hill, so that we now were lurking at a point about opposite the center of the town, with houses above us and below us. We could see into the middle of the place, where stood the *barracão* of the Peccary chief; and we saw that the men of the bandit gang were gathered at that house.

Then, in the darkness of the doorway I spied the sickly yellow face of the man who had nailed me to the tree and who now, no doubt, was putting some fresh deviltry into the heads of his followers. And for the first time since my comrades and I had smelled those peccaries in the bush, *senhores*, I laughed as I thought that even while that merciless band plotted more murder and torment, death was creeping silently around them, and the fate they planned for others soon would burst upon themselves. And the savages, understanding, grinned back at me a sharp-toothed grin of death and hate.

The time dragged. We knew that in the forest around the clearing our men were slipping into their places, that the guards on the other trails were dying or dead, that we should soon spring out on our enemies. But it seemed that night would come before we moved. I could feel my heart pounding as if it would break my ribs, and hear the wild men grind their teeth with the lust for battle, though they made no other sound or movement.

And then the waiting ended. From the north rose a deep, roaring yell — the war-cry of the chief.

Instantly a rain of arrows whizzed into the Peccaries grouped at the *barracão*. And as they yelped and jumped under the shock, and some fell dead, out from the northern forest burst the fighting-chief and his spearmen, and up from the southwestern trail rose the shrill yell of the sub-chief's men breaking cover.

My own six savages surged forward; but I sharply ordered

them back and opened fire with my rifle. I shot fast, but I shot straight, and at each explosion a Peccary staggered and fell.

And then, dropping the rifle, I drew my two revolvers. And with a frightful roar my men dashed forward with me.

As we ran a burst of arrows and poisoned darts whirred around us and over us into the bandits. And as we ran we saw that most of the Peccaries were running also — running for their rifles — though some stood and shot with their revolvers. Already the ground was littered with dead, and more than one of those who ran for guns never lived to use them, because of the poisoned blow-gun darts that had struck them.

And now behind us and all around us rang the screeches of the bowmen, who came charging to closer quarters, lest they hit their own men closing in. The air was full of yells of hate, cries of fear, screams of dying men, the snarl of arrows ripping into bare flesh and the smashing reports of guns.

Shooting with both hands, I ran straight for the *barracão* of the Yellow One, who had suddenly disappeared. A few men who still stood in our path and answered my fire went down quickly. Others, terrified by the ferocious charge of my club-men and the long spears, fled from our path.

So fast did we run that we reached that *barracão* just as the Yellow One came bounding out of it with a rifle. He shot instantly, and one of my wild men coughed and fell dying. Then I leaped at him, dropping my revolvers, and caught him by the throat so savagely that he went down, losing his rifle in the fall.

As we struck the ground I clamped my legs around his hips so that he could not draw his revolver or knife, and then I sank my fingers deep in his throat. Surprise and fear flashed across his face as he recognized me.

Then he squirmed like a snake and fought like a jungle-cat, so that I had all I could do to keep my grip. But I kept it, and as I crushed the breath from him I forgot the chief's orders and my own resolve not to kill this man. I throttled him, *senhores*, until his face was black and his struggles grew weak. And then I remembered, and let go, and started to rise.

His right hand went to his revolver. But I grabbed one of

my own revolvers from the ground and struck him on the head with it. He fell back senseless.

Swiftly I disarmed him, and looked about for something to tie him with. Finding nothing, I bounded into his *barracão*, where his three women were huddled in a corner in fright; and there I found ropes, and ran out again, and bound him so that he could not move when he should get his senses back, and dragged him to the side of the house and threw him down there. And then, with his revolver and my own, reloaded, I turned back to the fight.

By this time the battle was raging all over the village. Near me stood the war-chief, roaring his war-cry to his men; and around him a little knot of clubbers, spearmen, and blow-gun men were rushing back and forth, killing Peccaries as the chance came, but never going far from their leader.

But now a solid group of Peccaries came charging straight toward me, probably intending to free the Yellow One. The chief and his men sprang into their path. Shots cracked out in a ripping volley, and several of the wild men fell. Then the Peccaries closed in on them with swinging machetes.

The spearmen drove their weapons into the bellies of some and tore them out again. The clubmen attacked with terrible blows, their tooth-studded bludgeons smashing men's heads and tearing out their brains. The chief himself swung one of those clubs, and I saw him crush the skulls of four men. The blow-gun men seized machetes from fallen foes and slashed throats open with them. And I stood where I was, snapping a bullet into any Peccary I could hit without shooting one of my Indian friends. It was a bitter fight, and a fast one. Soon the charging Peccaries were only mangled corpses.

Then I knew the fight was won. For the crash of gunfire died out, and only a few scattered shots cracked out here and there as some cornered wretch fired his last bullet and went down under club or arrow.

Then from all around rose the exulting yells of the savages. And suddenly the sun dropped behind the mountains, and darkness swept around us.

Somewhere a man set fire to a *barracão* and quickly the

others burst into flame. By the red light the wild men dragged
the bodies of the dead bandits into a heap, and attended to
their own hurts, and brought all the women before the chief.
And there we found that one of the Yellow One's three women
was a girl of this same Indian tribe — a girl who once might
have been handsome, but who now looked thin and old from
the abuse he had given her. In her own language, which I did
not understand very well because she spoke fast, she told the
chief her story; and the Indians growled and hissed as they
heard her and glared at the Yellow One, who now had his
senses back and lay with his yellow face a very pale yellow
indeed. But the chief ordered that no man touch him, and set
me and a clubman over him as a guard through the night. And
you may be sure, *senhores*, that we gave him no chance to
escape.

Once in the night El Amarillo asked me in a whining tone
what would be done with him. This I did not know, but I did not
tell him so. I told him to remember what he had done to me and
to others, and that he would be well repaid for all his kindness
to helpless prisoners.

At the thought of enduring himself what he had done to
those in his power he groaned and squirmed and struggled to
break the ropes. When he tired of that he offered me much gold
if I would free him. I ordered him to be quiet, or I would make
him so. And he said no more, though he tried again and again
to loosen his bonds as the night wore away.

At sunrise the ropes were taken from him, and he stood up
in a circle of Indians, and the chief sat and looked at him with
eyes hard with hatred. And whether he was desperate with
fear and hoped to anger the chief so that he would be killed at
once, I do not know; but he began to sneer and boast. The
woman who had been his and who was of this tribe repeated
what he said, so that all the wild men understood.

He boasted of his evil deeds, of robbery and murder and
worse, and called himself King of the Peccaries, who feared no
man. If he sought quick death he came near getting it, for the
savages, hating him bitterly already, were maddened by this.
But the chief spoke sharply, and nobody touched him. And

then the chief answered him.

"So you are King of Peccaries!" he said. "We shall see whether peccaries know you for their king."

He laughed then with all his pointed teeth, and we wondered. Not even his own men knew what he meant. But he said no more to the Peccary, but turned to me and asked me what I would like to do with that man.

And thinking of Paulo and his broken arm and of my own toil under a burden, I replied that I should like first to drive him many miles under a heavy load and make him "sweat blood." He grinned again, did the chief, and said it should be so.

When he understood that he was to be made a beast of burden the Yellow One snarled and tried to fight. He only got himself a terrible thrashing. The *barbaros* beat him with the flat sides of machetes until he could hardly stand. Then they looked about for something to load him with.

The Indian girl came forward again and told us that under his burned *barracão* was buried gold which his gangs had brought in from raids. And since gold is very heavy, and also because it pleased them to load him with the yellow dirt for which he had committed so many crimes, the wild men forced him to dig up his treasure, and made rough bags from the scanty clothing of the dead Peccaries, and lashed these bags on him with ropes and vines.

And they got large balls of rubber which had been scorched in the burning of the town, and fastened these on him too, until he was bent far over by the weight — as Paulo and I once had been. Then they drove him eastward toward their own land.

Before we departed, though, the chief proved himself a wise young man as well as a good fighter. For instead of forcing all the women to come with us he told them they might go wherever they wished, and make their way back to their own people if they could. I saw he understood a thing which some men never learn — that a woman taken and kept against her will is not worth taking, because she will surely make trouble when she can.

And so the women did as they pleased. Some came with us, but more took weapons from the dead men who had been their masters and went away in a band, seeking their own homes.

And then, with two wild men yanking the Yellow One along by a rope around his neck and others jabbing him from time to time with machetes, we men from Brazil took the trail by which we had come.

In the next few days El Amarillo learned what it meant to be a pack-animal. He carried that load at all times; he slept with it on him at night, and was never free from it for an instant.

And he carried more than that — the weight of the death and misery and agonized curses of the men he had tortured and killed for that rubber and gold, and the knowledge that for him there was no escape, and the terror of the unknown death that finally should come to him. And that, *senhores*, was all of my own revenge on him — driving him like a beast. In what came to him later from the wild men I had no hand.

As we went down the hills to the river, and up the river in the boats, and on through our own jungle, all of us remembered the chief's puzzling words about the peccaries knowing the Yellow One for their king; but none of us knew what he meant by them, and he did not tell us. The only time he spoke of peccaries was soon after we started, when he ordered his men to watch for the wild pigs on their hunts — for of course we had to hunt as we went, and kill game to eat.

Twice there came hunters who told him they had found peccaries in the bush, and then he asked what they were; and when the men said they were few and white-collared he shook his head. So most of us saw none of the pigs until we were nearing the maloca and the long march was nearly done.

Then came men hurrying through the forest and told their chief they had sighted a herd of the white-lipped peccaries. At once he gave orders to a number of others, and they went into the bush with the hunters who had seen the pigs. He also called two more savages, and I saw they were the same ones who had found me hanging in torment; and after a word from him they went into the bush by themselves.

With a knife he then cut the ropes around the Yellow One, and the gold and rubber fell from him. He had been bent under that crushing weight so long, *senhores*, that when it dropped he dropped also, falling forward, unable to keep his balance. But he was up again soon, rubbing himself and scowling at the savages. Fear showed in his eyes, though, as he glanced around him.

And when the two wild men came back and gave something to the chief the Peccary glanced at it, and his face turned sickly white. I looked too, and my recently healed wounds seemed to burn again as I saw what the chief held — a handful of those terrible long sharp thorns.

With a yell of terror the bandit sprang away and tried to dash into the jungle. But men caught him, threw him down hard, and dragged him to a tree. And there, faced at last by the fate he had made more than one victim suffer, he screeched and whined and sniveled for mercy — the mercy he had never shown to his prisoners.

It did him no good. The wild men only growled in disgust, while their chief stood before him holding the thorns for him to look at. I shivered, *senhores*, but I could do nothing for him even if I tried; they might seize me and nail me up again too, for those people are easily angered, and their anger is deadly.

Then the chief ordered all but those who held the yellow man to climb trees. And while we climbed he fastened the Yellow One's hands to the tree — yes, only his hands; he did not use the thorns elsewhere on him. Then the chief himself and the other men followed us into the branches, so that nobody except the evil Peccary remained on the ground. Shouts came to us, and the sound of bodies crushing through the tangled forest, and the grunts of pigs. Soon a huge white-lipped peccary trotted out, followed by others. From his perch in the tree over El Amarillo the chief bellowed at the animals, and the first ones stopped, looking around them, while the rest of the herd came running in from the bush until more than forty of them were crowded under us.

The chief roared again, and answering calls came from the hunters he had sent out to drive the beasts here. We heard sounds of climbing, and knew they too were taking to the trees. And then the chief spoke to the man below him, at whom the pigs were staring wickedly.

"Here are peccaries. Show them you are king. Make them take out the thorns!"

The Yellow One broke into horrible cursing. He howled the vilest words I ever listened to, raving until froth was on his mouth. And he kicked out at the stinking pigs.

His voice and his movements maddened them. Suddenly they surged at him.

They took out the thorns, *senhores*.

The weight of their charging bodies tore him from the tree. He fell, screaming. But so thick were the beasts about him that he fell not on the ground but on their backs, and fought to his feet again. Yet when he had risen he could not escape; he was wedged among them and knocked back and forth.

Squealing with rage, the devil-pigs seemed to boil up around him, climbing on one another's backs and leaping upward to strike. With their knife-edged teeth they chopped and slashed his body and arms and legs into ribbons.

Then he went down again, and rose no more. His body was thrown on the heaving mass as it was struck again and again by the furious animals. Then it rolled down among them, and his ghastly yellow face disappeared.

Long after he was dead the peccaries tore him and trampled him into the dirt. And other pigs dashed at the gold-bags made from Peccary clothing, and ripped those also into tatters, and scattered the gold all about.

Some leaped up against the trees where we perched, their vindictive black eyes fixed on us and their teeth clashing together. But as we made no move, but only stayed beyond their reach, they soon abandoned us.

And at length, grunting among themselves, they all moved slowly away, their white lips now stained deep red, and leaving behind them only a torn thing that had been a man, fragments of cloth that had held gold and their own disgusting smell.

We came down again. The savages fell into line and started away as if nothing had happened. But I felt sick, and I wanted to see no more of these men. So I told the chief that now

I would leave him and go back to my own people and tell them how he and his brave fighters had destroyed the foul pig-men of the hills.

He nodded, pointed the way I should go and strode away. And without a farewell word or a backward look the whole band of wild men passed on into the forest, and I was left alone.

So, *senhores*, that is the tale of the Peccaries. Up in the hills of Peru the vines are creeping across the place where once stood their village, and where now remain only sodden ashes and scattered skulls. Out in the pathless land beyond the farthest rubber-workings, where only wild men and wild animals prowl, lie the bones of their leader and the blood-stained gold he gathered.

And soon the great green jungle, which has swallowed many better men, will blot out every trace of them, and only their evil name will live on for a little time at the headwaters of the Amazon, to die out at last and be forgotten. For that is the way of the jungle.

THE FIREFLY

BEAUTIFUL BUT false, *senhores*, is the firefly. Beautiful as a flashing jewel floating in the darkness of the jungle night; false as flame without heat, which will neither comfort your body nor cheer your mind.

When the cold southwest winds blow and the *tempo da friagem* sweeps across this upper Amazon, you may cover yourself with those brilliant insects until you blaze with light, but does the chill leave your bones? No. And if the gleam of the firefly in the gloom moves you to follow after and reach for it — beware! You may sink suddenly in sucking mud whence there is no escape. False fires they are, *senhores* — false and cold.

In your own North America, you tell me, the firefly is a weak and tiny thing compared to the big beetle which glows so bright in our Brazilian jungle. That does not surprise me, for the United States is a colder country — is it not? — and so the little light-bugs can not grow so big and strong.

But I am much astonished to hear you say that the fireflies flash their lanterns so that they can recognize comrades and friends, just as men use lights to see one another in the dark. You tell me, too, that the reason why other beetles which have no lights make noises in the night is because they know one another's voices, as we do and in this way they find their friends whom they can not see.

It may be so. I have noticed that you two explorers know many odd things about living creatures — things which even we rubber-workers who live among those creatures do not know. We are too busy keeping ourselves alive among the dangers of the deadly Javary region to study deeply into the lives of beasts and birds and bugs.

Yet as the months pass by we too see strange things, *senhores*. And I sometimes think that the most strange and wonderful thing in all the world is life itself — that unseen power and impulse within a creature which makes it move and act in different ways under different conditions.

Why are we what we are? Why do we do what we do? Why do some men hate each other at sight? Why can some women be trusted and others not? I do not know. I know only that we are wrong as often as right, and I think perhaps we are little better than those lightless beetles of which you spoke, struggling along in life, making a noise as we go, and doing the best we can.

What is that, *senhor*? You say I am a philosopher? I do not know what sort of thing a "philosopher" may be, for I am only a humble *seringueiro* of the Amazon headwaters, and those big words mean nothing to me.

You will pardon me if my talk is tiresome. But perhaps now I can speak of something more interesting as we float on down the great river and those fireflies flash over yonder on the black shore. Listen, and you shall hear of a firefly far more beautiful than they.

In the time of the great floods, when all work in the swampy rubber-forests of old Coronel Nunes was stopped by the high water, I had gone out on an adventurous canoe-trip with another seringueiro — a handsome, happy-go-lucky young comrade of mine named Pedro. We had paddled far into hilly country on the frontier of Brazil and Peru, and, after using up most of our food and cartridges, had started back to headquarters.

On this return trip I had gotten into a bad fight with some *caboclos* while helping a young fellow to rescue the girl he loved from a cage where she was shut up by her drunken father; and in this fight I had been pounded so severely that every muscle in me was lame. So now, paddling on down the river the next day, I found myself so stiff and full of aches that it was hard for me to keep at work.

I shut my teeth and said nothing, hoping that the pain would work out as my muscles loosened up. In this I was disappointed. True, my arms did not hurt so much after a while, but the ache in my legs grew worse, as they were cramped by the canoe. Besides, I had wrenched my back, and the swing of paddling seemed to give me a sharp stab every time I stroked.

So, though I choked back the grunts and groans boiling up inside me and tried to do my share of the work, Pedro soon felt the difference from my usual power. He stopped paddling and looked back.

"Let us go ashore, Lourenço, and rest today," he suggested. "You are too lame to keep on. I will give you a good rubbing now and another tonight, and tomorrow you will be yourself again."

He spoke sense. But I was feeling sour, both from pain and from vexation at myself, and I would not quit.

"I am not an old woman," I growled. "And you know very well that we can not waste time in resting now — we have hardly any food left, and very few cartridges. I will not go ashore at all today, even to eat. I will push this canoe until dark."

He laughed.

"If you are not an old woman do not talk like one," he advised me. "You speak like a cross old grandmother. What if we have only a little food? The time to worry is when we have none at all. But if you enjoy torturing yourself do not let me interfere with your pleasure. Let me see you do this."

And he twirled his paddle over his head and around behind him in a way that would have made me yelp with pain if I had tried it.

"Let me see you do this," I retorted, shoving with my paddle so hard that the canoe jumped and he nearly fell overboard.

It hurt my aching back, but it showed him that I was in earnest. He laughed again, then settled down to his regular long-distance stroke. And all that day we swung on down the river, covering considerable distance with the aid of the current.

At last, when night was nearly on us, he moved his head toward a cove at our left.

"Unless you wish to paddle all night, *senhora*, perhaps we had better go ashore there," he said. "We must make camp soon if we are to make it at all, and we are not likely to find a better place."

I knew that as well as he did, and I was more than ready to

stop. I was rather ashamed of myself, too, for having answered him so sharply that morning. But now he had spoken as if to an unreasonable old woman and even called me "*senhora*" with a mocking grin that made me cross again. So I only grunted as I turned the dugout up the cove, and after we went ashore and made camp I kept my mouth shut. He was in a teasing mood, and I was not in the humor to be plagued.

We slung our hammocks, ate and smoked. Night came before our cigarettes were burned down. I intended, after finishing my smoke, to curl up in my hammock and sleep. But that intention, like some others I have had, was not to be carried out.

Lights came into the darkness — spots of light twinkling above us and all around us there in the bush. They floated out over the black water too, looking very beautiful as they rose and dipped and drifted in the gloom. Watching them, I forgot my aches and pains.

"We have come into a bay of *cucujus*," I said. "They will swing their little lanterns over us while we sleep."

"I hope they will not show us to some hungry jaguar," laughed Pedro. "I am tired tonight, and I expect to sleep soundly. It would be unpleasant to wake up in the morning and find myself trotting around in the belly of the big cat."

Before I could answer there came a sound. It made us sit motionless, breathless, staring in wonder at each other. It was not a noise of the jungle, nor even the voices of men. There in the darkness, somewhere out beyond the gliding fireflies, a woman was singing!

Soft, sweet, low but clear, the music of her voice floated to us along the water. In that wild and savage place, far from where any woman should be, it seemed a voice from another world — an impossible dream, which presently would flit away like wind-blown smoke. Yet, dream or not, it held us still as men of wood while it sang on. After a time it died out of the air.

"*Nossa Senhora!*" whispered Pedro. "Are we awake, comrade, and in our right minds? A woman, singing in this black hole where only fireflies live! A white woman, too — for no Indian could sing so sweetly, or would even try to. We have not seen any human thing in all this day, and the last persons we did see were only *caboclos*. Did you too hear that voice?"

I made no answer for a time, and we both strained our ears for some further sound of human life. None came. At length I said:

"Pedro, I do not know what this thing may be, but I shall not sleep well tonight unless I find out. A sound drifting along the surface of the water is hard to place, but this singing seemed to come from the right, at the end of this *enseada*. We have not been down there, and it must be that someone lives there. Let us go and see."

We had some trouble in starting, for the night was so black that we could hardly find the canoe, though we knew just where it was. We had been sitting beside our little fire, you understand, and at first our eyes would not see in the dark. But after we left the shore behind us we began to make out the things near us, though faintly. Very slowly and carefully we felt our way along the murky water toward the head of the flooded bay.

Though the distance was not great, we took some time in covering it. The darkness seemed to grow even more dense as we moved, and the fireflies which before had looked so beautiful now confused us — for in thick gloom a man's gaze will follow a moving spot of light in spite of himself, and where his eyes turn his body is likely to turn also.

Yet they helped us too, those tiny lanterns, for we knew most of them were on the land, and so by keeping away from them we avoided running aground. Finally, however, the canoe bumped softly into the shore and stopped.

"We are at the end," said Pedro, up in the bow. "I do not see anything new. Do you?"

I saw nothing at all but the flaming insects. We stayed there for a time listening. No sound came, except a few of the usual night noises of the bush.

"We had best go back —" I started to say, when I was struck dumb. Near us, ahead of us in the unseen bush, the voice broke out again in song.

"Glitter, glitter, pretty firefly!
Born but to dance and flash and die!
Blaze ye the way through the dark night's span;
Leading me back to the love of my man!
Back to the lights on a far-off shore,
Back to the laughter I hear no more —
Floating along like a star above,
Show me the road back to life and love!"

For long minutes after the song ended we crouched there, motionless and wordless. Somehow I felt chilly, and the skin of my back prickled. The thing was so weird that I wished I were back beside my fire, where I could see Pedro's face and my hammock and the other things to which I was accustomed. And while I was thinking of this, a thing occurred that made me doubt my senses.

Some of the fireflies drifting about in the bush before us suddenly disappeared. They vanished as if seized by a swift, silent hand. Then they blazed out again, but now they were not floating along as before, but resting on something — something that moved. It was too small to be a man, but still it acted like a man. It snatched at the flies and put them on itself. Yet, though the cluster of insects grew larger and their combined light increased, we could not see the thing that did this.

Before us grew the outline of a small head and shoulders, and at times I thought I could catch the glimmer of little eyes, but that was all. It made no sound. It seemed alive yet not alive, human but not human, an uncanny creature made of the darkness itself.

Then we found that this thing was real. It coughed. The noise told us instantly what it was.

"A monkey!" marveled Pedro. "A monkey as big as a child, lighting himself with fireflies like a village belle! Did you ever see such a thing?"

At the sound of his voice the creature stood very still. We knew it was looking at us. Then instead of jumping away and hiding, it moved straight toward us.

It came rather slowly, stopping now and then, but advancing each time. We kept very quiet. Finally it halted at the bow of our dugout and stood watching us. Some of the light-bugs had jumped off it and others had been brushed away by the leaves as it came, but enough remained to let us see its head quite plainly.

As my partner had said, it was as big as a child. It seemed as unafraid as a child, too. Soon it swung itself up into the boat, and I saw a shadowy arm reach out toward Pedro.

"Welcome, *compadre!*" chuckled Pedro. "You are a friendly fellow. I am glad to find that you are flesh and blood — I almost thought you were a demon. Now sing again for us."

Senhores, I should not have been greatly surprised if that monkey had done so. He had already amazed me much, and he seemed to be the only living thing there besides ourselves and the bugs. But he made no sound at all. I could not see him well, because Pedro was between him and me, but it seemed that he was pulling at my comrade. Soon I found that this was so.

"He is trying to take me ashore, Lourenço," said Pedro. "He wants me to go somewhere with him. And I am going."

Stepping out on land, he added to the monkey:

"Take my finger, *compadre*, and lead me where you want to go. 'Show me the road to light and love.'"

I got out, pulled the canoe farther up on shore so that it would not drift off, and followed. It was quite easy to see the little animal and my partner stooping to give him a good hold on his hand, but I could not see much else.

As I trailed behind the pair I marveled. I have been guided through the bush in odd ways, following sights and sounds and even smells, but never before nor since have I followed an illuminated monkey through blackness, seeking a voice. Yet I could not ask for a better guide than that wordless beast proved to be. Perhaps he did not know where we wanted to go, but he knew exactly where he wished us to go, and it came to the same thing.

The ground under foot was firm and fairly dear of bush, feeling like an old path nearly grown over. We followed, our queer guide with no difficulty and with little noise. Presently Pedro halted.

"A house!" he whispered.

Peering around him, I saw close beside him a section of mud wall showing in the light from the monkey's fireflies. It looked old; it was cracked, and vines grew on it. Somehow I felt that the house was empty. This proved to be true.

The monkey tugged at Pedro, and we went on. I passed my hand along the wall until it struck a window. There I looked in and sniffed. The place was black and had an odor of decay. Nobody lived there.

Beyond this house the monkey pulled Pedro to the right. My comrade made a soft noise in his throat, I looked again. A few strides ahead of us a faint light came out through the window of another house.

Under this window the monkey stopped. Strong wooden bars ran across the opening, but they were meant only for safety, and it was easy to see between them. We peered in, and stood amazed by what we saw.

The room beyond those bars was well lit, but the light was not made by fire or oil. It came from two large hanging cages, out of which shone the lights of many fireflies. This use of the insects was not new to us, for we had sometimes seen little cages of them in other parts of our river country, so that we were not much surprised now. It was the woman under them that held us silent and still.

She too was ablaze with fireflies. They were fastened in her black hair, on the dark-red gown that flowed down around her, and even on her bare arms and her throat. She was slender and shapely, with big dark eyes, a pouting scarlet mouth, and a skin as clear and white as the waters of a brook falling over a cliff.

Facing us, she was looking at something near the window where we stood, smiling a little as if she saw something that pleased her and holding her head to one side in an alluring way. With the silent lights of the caged night insects shining softly down on her and the other beetles flashing from her hair to her knees, she was so beautiful that she seemed more than human.

She moved toward us a little, still looking at the same

spot, and slowly moved her round bare arms out to the side and overhead. I saw how she kept the fireflies on her smooth skin — they were fastened into narrow bracelets and a necklace made from small vines. Gradually her arms came down until her hands rested on her shoulders, then sank to her sides. Her lips opened in song.

> *"Come through the night,*
> *O heart of my heart?*
> *Speed o'er the leagues that hold us apart!*
> *Clasped in your arms I will —"*

We lost the rest. A black hairy thing rose into our faces, startling us so that we jumped back and poised to strike at it. Then, seeing what it was, we withheld the blow. It was the monkey, which we had forgotten and which now had swung himself up to the opening. Grasping the bars, he chattered through them to the woman. She broke off her song.

"You — you little beast!" she scolded. "You frightened me. Stop shaking those bars. Go to the door, and you may come in."

She passed to one side, and at her movement the monkey dropped to the ground. We followed close behind him. A bar dropped and a door opened, letting out a vague path of light. The monkey swung himself inside. We stepped into the light and halted.

"Good evening, *senhorita*," Pedro greeted her, sweeping off his hat and bowing. "Do not fear. We are friends."

With a startled gasp she sprang back. One hand leaped to her breast, rose a little, and stopped. Below her fingers we caught the glint of a half-drawn dagger.

"If we frightened you, *senhorita*, pardon us — we shall go away at once," my comrade added. "We are here only because we heard a wonderful voice singing in the night and could not rest until we found the singer. Our camp is down the *enseada*.

"But before we go, will you not sing once more for us? It is not often that travelers in the wilderness hear the voice of an angel."

Though I did not glance at him, I knew he was smiling at

her. I knew too what a winning smile this handsome young partner of mine could give a woman if he would. An answering smile came into her face, and in her eyes dawned the look of admiration I had seen in the eyes of other women when they gazed at him. The knife slipped out of sight.

"Perhaps I may," she said. "First tell me who you are."

"Pedro, *senhorita* — Pedro Andrada. I have with me a cross old lady named Senhora Lourenço Moraes. She is very lame, and really ought not to be out at night, but I dared not leave her behind for fear she would fall into the fire."

The Firefly Lady laughed at that, looking much more lovely than before. I grinned, though I did not like to be made fun of before her.

"Your old lady needs to shave," she answered. "Her beard is terribly black. You must have traveled far; is it not so?"

Now I saw my chance to repay Pedro. At the place where we had recently fought the *caboclos* he had led the people to think we were scouts of a big company which dealt in medicinal herbs and bark. So now, to plague him, I spoke up and told her the same tale, intending then to enjoy his efforts to carry out his part.

"We have traveled far, indeed, *senhorita*," I told her. "We have been seeking sarsaparilla and Peruvian bark and such things among the Indian towns above here for the markets in Europe. A big new company of Englishmen at Tabatinga, on the Solimoes, has sent us out as scouts to find where good trade is, before beginning to send in boats for these medical things. We are now on our way back."

She smiled again, very graciously this time, and said she could see we were honest men. Would we not come in? We would, and we did.

As we stepped inside I glanced at the place near the window where she had been looking when we first saw her. I expected to find someone sitting or lying there. But there was nobody at all. Wondering what she had been looking at, I kept my eye on that spot as I advanced. Then I saw. The thing she had been smiling at and flirting with was her own face.

On the wall hung a round mirror half as large as my head,

with a handle that looked like silver. It must have cost considerable money somewhere, and it looked out of place there against that old dingy mud. Yet as I looked back at the Firefly Lady it did not seem so strange, and I did not blame her for wanting to see her own pretty face; for the rest of the room was very ugly, and there was nothing at all worth looking at. I wondered, though, that she should deck herself with fireflies and pose and sing when there was nobody to see her except that black monkey. Still, women do queer things.

In the farther wall I noticed a door standing partly open. Beyond it was darkness and silence. Nowhere was any sign of another person. She seemed all alone.

"Have you hunger, *senhores?*" she asked. "I have not much food, but you are welcome."

"Do not trouble yourself, *senhorita*," Pedro declined. "We have eaten. It is not food we hunger for, but the sound of your voice — and the charm of your companionship."

She laughed lightly again, and her eyes spoke very kindly to my comrade.

"Tell me more of your company of Englishmen," she said. "They are at Tabatinga? They have not been long in this country! They are rather old men?"

Pedro gave me a queer look. I bit my tongue to keep from laughing and spoke no word. After an instant of hesitation he answered easily:

"You have it partly right. They have not been here long, but they are young men, not old. They are very rich too, *senhorita* — three young men, handsome and wealthy."

"So? And married?"

"No. At least I do not think so. I have not seen nor heard of any wives."

She glanced at the mirror. Then she lifted her arms and floated around for a few steps, her face alight with some pleasant thought. But as she again faced the open door through which we had entered she started and fear flashed into her eyes. We whirled.

Nothing was there. Only the blackness of the night met our gaze.

"What is it?" I asked.

"There!" she whispered, pointing. "By the door! Has he — has he come back?"

We jumped through the doorway, seeking whatever might be lurking outside. We found nothing.

"Is this a joke, *senhorita*?" demanded Pedro, as we came in again. "There is no danger."

"No, no!" She still looked frightened. "I thought — I thought I saw the terrible face of — of Carlos Guimaraes. If he should find you here he would kill us all."

"Why?"

"Why? Because you are men and here with me. He — he keeps me here as his prisoner."

"Oh! So that is why you are here alone! Let him come," Pedro said grimly. "Killing is a game which more than one man can play. I should much like to meet this Carlos. But he is not there now. Who is this man, and who are you, and how came you here?"

Still seeming nervous, she asked him to shut the door. He closed and barred it. Then, glancing at the other door, he asked where it led. She said it was only the door to her sleeping-room, and so there was no danger from that direction. Then she smiled again.

"It is very comforting to have two strong men here to protect me," she said. "Now come, let us sit by the table, and I will tell you all."

She sank into a rough chair beside a small bare table, directly under the light-cages. There was one other chair, and we looked at each other but remained standing. She rose and sat on the table itself.

"Now there is a chair for each of you," she said. "See, the table holds me easily — I am so much lighter than you big men. Sit, *senhores*."

"We are not '*senhores*,'" said Pedro bluntly. "We are but plain men. Call us 'friends' or by our names, *senhorita* —"

He paused and looked a question.

"My name is Francisca."

He bowed, glanced swiftly around him and sat down in the

chair she had used. I lifted the other and set it against the wall where I could watch her face, the window, or the door to her room, all with a mere turn of the eyes. As I sat down. I thought I heard a small sound from that other room.

"Is there a window in that room?" I asked.

She looked quickly at me, her eyes narrowing.

"Yes, surely. Why do you ask?"

"I heard something."

"It is nothing," was her swift answer. "There is a — a sick monkey in there — a poor little baby monkey which seems hurt. I found it yesterday and have made a little bed for it, where I can feed it and no snake or other evil thing can harm it."

"That is truly kind of you, *senhorita*." I told her, and said no more.

For a little time none of us spoke. No further noise came from the other room, and the only sound was the continual clicking of the *cucujus* in their cages as they tried to leap up and fly. We men watched the big black monkey which had guided us there, and which now had climbed up on the table and squatted beside her. A few of the fireflies still remained on him, and he picked them off one by one and put them on her.

Knowing how a pet monkey will imitate people around him, I could easily see how he had learned this trick — he had seen his mistress fasten fireflies on herself, and had caught the habit of doing the same thing and then bringing the insects to her. She laughed now as she took them from him, and I thought that she did indeed feel safe with us there.

Soon, though, she grew very serious and began to tell her story.

She was not a Brazilian girl, she said, but the daughter of a wealthy Italian. This surprised me a little; for, though I had noticed that she did not speak Portuguese in our own way, she did not seem much like the few Italian people I had seen. Still, different kinds of people may come from the same country, and the Italians I had met were rather poor, while it was easy to see that she was accustomed to the things of wealth. My eye went to that expensive mirror as I thought this, and I was all the more curious to know how she had ever come there. She soon told us.

Her father, she said, had become interested in reports of immense wealth waiting in the Amazon Valley for men who would develop it — lumber, rubber, medicinal herbs and other things — and had decided to come to Brazil and see for himself whether these stories were true. As she was his only child and anxious to see something of South America, he took her with him to Rio, where he intended to leave her with friends to enjoy the society and fashion of the capital while he made his long trip. But after staying for a time in Rio she felt that she would be lonely there during the long weeks when her father was gone; and so she coaxed him into taking her with him.

All the way up the great river, even to the headwaters, these two journeyed together. They stopped at towns along the river, saw what there was to see, and talked with men who were in business of various kinds. Then, as they were nearing the upper reaches and thinking that soon they would turn about and travel back seaward, they became acquainted with a man who had recently come on board — a Senhor Azevedo, who was developing a large rubber estate for some rich men living in Rio. This man invited them to visit his headquarters for a time and see how the work was done. They accepted.

Leaving the steamer, they traveled up into the Javary region in the private boat of Senhor Azevedo. He was a courteous host, and all his men took much interest in showing her father about.

One of these men — Guimaraes, a sort of foreman — showed much interest in Francisca also. Indeed, he was so attentive that she had to complain of it to her father, who told Senhor Azevedo. This resulted in a sharp rebuke for the man Guimaraes, and for a time after that he did not trouble her.

Then death struck her father. A snake bit him, and in an hour he was dead. And that very night Guimaraes managed to get into her room, struck her senseless before she could cry out, carried her silently to the river, put her into a canoe, and fled up the river in the moonlight.

He paddled hard until dawn, and for several days after

that he kept on, until at last they came to this place. What place it was she did not know — it was a town without a name; a few old mud houses, totally deserted except by bats and snakes.

Since coming here she had seen nobody but the man who had stolen her; and even he deserted her at times, going away somewhere for days and leaving her with only the black monkey for a companion. He was away now, and she was alone in this wild jungle with no way of escape.

I heard this with wrath growing hot within me. I wished this Guimaraes would come back now and give me a chance at him. Pedro perhaps was thinking the same thing, for, with a hard note in his voice, he asked —

"Do you think he will return tonight?"

"I do not think so," she said, looking at the door as if frightened by the thought. "He went only yesterday, and he usually stays away for days. Yet I never know when he will come."

"I wonder, *senhorita*, that you can sing when you are alone and a prisoner," said Pedro.

"If I did not I should go mad!" she cried. "When the night comes — the blackness and the loneliness and the cries of animals killing in the jungle — oh, you do not know!"

Jumping from the table, she held out her arms to him.

"Oh, take me away!" she pleaded. "Take me out of this awful place — to Tabatinga, to any place where I can find people who will be kind and help me to get home. Your employers, the Englishmen — surely they will help a girl in distress."

Then, *senhores*, I felt meaner than ever before in my life. I had lied to her — there were no Englishmen, nor were we going within many miles of Tabatinga. But the thought came to me that this did not matter so much after all; for we could take her to the headquarters of our kindly *coronel*, who has a daughter of his own in Rio and would surely do everything possible for the poor little Firefly Lady.

Pedro spoke.

"Truly, *senhorita*, we shall do our best for you. We go on down the river in the morning, and you shall go with us. We will take you to someone who will gladly help you."

"Oh!" she cried joyously.

With a swift movement she threw her arms around his neck and kissed him. Then, glowing, she turned toward me. I got up rather hastily.

"Will you not sing for us now, *senhorita?*" I asked.

She laughed, a clear, ringing laugh.

"Are you afraid to be kissed?" she teased.

"Remember that I am a cross old lady with a terrible black beard," I grinned. "Wait until I am shaved. Pedro has had his kiss, but I can look forward to mine. Now sing — sing something in your own tongue."

Again her eyes seemed to grow narrow.

"Do you know Italian?" she asked.

"No," I said truthfully, "I do not. But I should like to hear a song of your own land, even though I do not understand the words."

"And so you shall," she promised.

Breathing deep, she began to sing in a foreign tongue.

As she sang she seemed to forget us, and into her eyes came a far-away look as if she were gazing across the jungle and the ocean at her homeland, to which she would soon return. What she sang I do not know; but it was gay and lively, showing the joy she felt over her coming escape from this dreary cage. Soon she began to dance also — swift whirling steps in time to the measure of her songs, which carried her around the dingy room in a flashing swirl of fireflies until she was breathless. Then she stopped, panting, her white skin flushed.

Glancing at Pedro, I was puzzled to find on his face a thoughtful frown. But as she turned to him this disappeared, and he gave her many compliments on her voice. Then he suggested:

"We start at dawn, *senhorita*, and it would be well for all of us to get some sleep. We will lie down on the floor beside that outer door, if you wish, and see that nothing disturbs you."

"But no, that is not necessary. You will be more comfortable at your own camp, and I shall be safe enough — Carlos will not come so late as this, and I shall bar the door. I — I would rather be alone, my friends, this last night here."

"As you will," my partner bowed. "We shall come for you at daybreak."

We turned toward the door. She slipped in front of us.

"You will not forget? You will not go and leave me?"

"There is no danger of that," we assured her. "Sleep well, and have no fear."

She gave us each a little white hand, and we passed out.

"Por Deos!" grumbled Pedro. "How black it is! We shall have to feel our way back to the canoe."

I said nothing. We crept back the way we had come, guiding ourselves along the wall with our fingertips. As we went we heard the door close and the bar go into place.

We found the next house, felt our way along that, and reached the corner where we should turn. There Pedro stopped. I bumped into him.

"What is it?" I whispered, thinking he must have made out something in front of him.

"I am thinking," he whispered back.

"Then think fast. I want to sleep."

Softly he turned around and spoke in my ear.

"Lourenço, I think there is more here than we have seen. It might be well for us not to hasten away. Did you hear that thing move in the back room of her house?"

"Yes. The baby monkey."

"If it was a baby monkey it was the biggest baby I ever heard. It moved only a little, but it was heavier than even a full-grown monkey would be. And here is another thing: She said she feared that this Carlos would come and kill us, and so she had us bar the door. Then she sat down under those light-cages and had us sit beside her. All of us were in plain sight from the window. If anyone had come, could he not have shot us through the window? Certainly."

"I thought of that too, and sat where I could watch it," I reminded him.

"I know you did. I saw how you placed your chair. But I doubt if she really fears this Carlos. Perhaps there is no Carlos at all. And do you remember her story of Azevedo, a developer of a big rubber estate in this Javary region? We are rubber-workers, and I never have heard of any big estate run by a man named Azevedo. And here is one thing more: She did not sing in Italian."

"Are you sure?"

"I am sure. Some years ago I knew a man of Italy and learned enough of his language to recognize it when I hear it. What tongue she used in those songs I do not know, but it was not Italian nor English nor Portuguese. She said she would sing in her own language, and I believe she did so. If she deceived us about one thing, why not about others?"

"But surely she stays here only because she must," I objected. "A woman like her would never pick this forsaken place to live in, or even find it. And she is mad to get away."

"True. But — Lourenço, I want to know what is in that back room. Let us go back softly and look and listen."

Very carefully we stole back to the barred window where the light showed. Even before we reached it I knew Pedro's suspicion was well founded, for we heard a voice — not the voice of Francisca, but that of a man.

It was a low voice and seemed weak. We could not make out the words until we stopped at the window and put our eyes and ears at the openings. The room which we had just left was empty now, and the voice came from beyond the door in the farther wall.

"But you will not leave me to die!" it pleaded. "To starve and die here alone like a sick rat in a hole! You would not do such a thing to a man who has ruined his life for you!"

Then came the voice of the woman. It was so cold and cruel that we hardly knew it.

"If you die I can not help it. I did not give you the fever, and neither can I cure it. If you think I intend to throw away this chance to escape from this place you are much mistaken. These men are traveling fast and hard — they are gaunt and un-shaven — and they will not wait. I shall go with them, and there is an end of it."

"An end of me, you mean," said the man hoarsely. "An end

of the idiot who sacrificed everything to go with you to the end of the earth — who stole for you and even killed for you. I saved you by knifing that police agent who trailed us all the way up the Amazon — and this is your reward! This is the love you promised me! To leave me dying, starving, screaming at the empty blackness —"

"What else can I do?" she cut in. "You yourself say you are dying. You are as good as dead already. You can not go out. Even if you were well you could not go out. The police —"

"Yes, the police!" he cried. "I would rather die in the hands of the police than here alone. They would at least be human toward a dying man. And what do you think the police will do to you? You, the enemy of their country — you, the Austrian singer who spied during the war — you, the woman who married a Brazilian for the protection of his name and then poisoned him and fled with his money and the jewels he gave you? Your record is far blacker than mine. What do you think will happen to you?"

"I do not care!" she cried wildly. "Anything is better than staying here in this place where only snakes and monkeys live, and where the only jewels I have are fireflies! Fool! You do well to speak of jewels! You made that blunder in Rio that set the police on us and destroyed our chance of escaping to Europe.

"When that servant of my husband found you taking the jewels you only tied and gagged him instead of making him silent forever, and so he was able to talk when he was found and freed. That made the police seek both us and Azul, and they found him too — dead. And when we had fled up the Amazon you let yourself be robbed — robbed, fool, of all our fortune!"

"That is true," he admitted. "But I could not murder that poor old servant. I was never a criminal until love for you made me one, and I am no cutthroat."

"The old story!" she jeered. "'The woman beguiled me.' No, oh no, you are no criminal — you are not clever enough! But your stabbing of that man who trailed us makes your record black enough, Manoel *meo*, to send you to death."

"I killed him for your sake," he insisted. "And I killed him in fight — he was drawing a revolver. An instant more and we would both have been prisoners. I never poisoned a fond old man as you did — I did not even know you had killed him until you told me. And I am glad I did not slit the servant's throat. A killer I may be, but not a cold-blooded murderer."

"Bah! It makes no difference. You must die if you go out. You will soon die here. Death here or outside — what does it matter? You deserve to die alone after the blunders you have made, and so you shall. And I shall find a way to escape your Brazilian police. You Brazilians are all alike — stupid fools!"

Pedro drew in his breath softly, and I heard him mutter —

"I think you are mistaken, my lady."

The sick voice came again, stronger with wrath.

"Yes, I know your way — a way of falsehood. False to your husband — false to me — you will be false to these men and to the Englishmen also. You are a good actress, with your pretended fear of an imaginary Carlos Guimaraes. You are a fine liar, with your wild tale of abduction and an Azevedo who never existed and a wealthy Italian father — Italian! Ha!

"You have made these strangers swallow your story, and you are trying to lure them also — yes, I heard you kiss one of them! But you will forsake them as soon as they have served your purpose.

"Then you will play on the hearts of those young Englishmen as you have played on mine. You will try to set them against one another, to rob and ruin them as you have done to other men. Or you will tell them you are French, perhaps, and persuade them to help you reach Europe.

"If you are caught, you will swear that I was the one who poisoned your husband and that I forced you to come with me. Otherwise you will think no more of me whom you leave to perish."

"Since you are so wise," she replied, her voice harder than ever, "I will tell you that you are nearly right. I shall make the Englishmen send me to Europe, and there I shall go home to Austria and find again the one man I love — Karl, my Karl, captain of hussars.

"And you are right, too, when you say I shall forget you

and your whines, and the fat old fool I married in Rio, and all the rest of your accursed country. And I shall be happy —"

"Ha-ha-ha!" The man burst into a terrible laugh. "Happy! Yes, you will be happy! You will be happy in a Brazilian prison! I am not dead yet, and we shall see!"

"What do you mean?"

He laughed again in a crazed way.

"I am not the only fool! You are one also! Those men return at dawn for you. I shall see to it that they hear me and come into this room, and I will tell them who you are and what you have done. Then you will charm the Englishmen — oh yes — ha-ha-ha!"

For a moment she made no reply. When she did speak her voice sounded like the hiss of a snake.

"So! You will do that! Then you must become silent before they return!"

"*Deos meo!* Put away that dagger! Will you stab me?"

"Hold!" shouted Pedro.

Seizing the wooden bars, he tugged at them. They bent, but stayed in place. I grabbed them with both hands and we heaved together. The whole frame flew outward and I tumbled on my back. As I jumped up I saw Pedro go squirming through the opening.

The instant he got through I followed him, landing on hands and knees inside. As I rose I saw the Firefly Woman leap into the doorway beyond. Fear and anger both showed in her face. In her right hand glimmered her dagger.

Seeing Pedro bounding toward her, she realized instantly that her scheme had failed. With a scream of fury she sprang at him like a jungle cat. She stabbed at his stomach. He slipped aside and the thrust missed him. His rifle-barrel smacked against her wrist. The knife flew from her hand to the floor.

Swiftly she stooped to recover it. But he blocked her, grabbed her, swung her up off the ground. She fought, kicked, tore at him with both hands; but he twisted his face downward, shielding his eyes from her nails. I was beside him now, and I caught up the dagger.

"I have it," I told him. "You can drop her."

But before he put her down he strode into that other room. There he caught her hands and held them, and as he let her down he commanded:

"Be still! You will only get yourself hurt. You can not harm us nor get away, and you had best stop trying."

She twisted and tugged, but could not free herself. So, though her eyes still blazed, she ceased struggling and stood breathing hard.

"Welcome back, friends!" cried the man's voice from a dim corner. "You come just in time to save me from being butchered."

We made out the gleam of teeth, the glint of eyes and the pallor of a sick white face. I turned back into the outer room, cut the hangings of one of the light-cages and brought it in with me. By the new light we saw a tall, fever-thinned young fellow lying on a rough bed. We saw, too, that he had not long to live.

"You came back and listened, is it not so?" he asked.

We nodded.

"Then you know us, and it is useless to try to deceive you further. A little while ago I dreaded to have you find me. Now I do not care. I am Manoel de Mello, of Rio, and this gentle companion of mine is Frances Andravery — or Senhora Francisca Azul, widow by her own deed. You know, of course, of the murder of her husband, Ailonso Azul."

We nodded again. The truth was that we never had heard of this Azul or his murder; for Rio was many hundreds of miles from us, and the news of that city is not likely to reach the ears of jungle-workers at the head of the Amazon. Yet we knew he spoke truth, for we had heard him accuse her of the crime while we listened at the window, and even now she did not deny it. So, as I say, we let him think we knew all about it.

"And now what will you do with us?" he asked.

We looked at him thoughtfully. A few months ago he must have been a strong, active, handsome fellow. Now he was a wreck, too far gone to have a chance for life. We had no medicines, and we knew he would die before we could reach the headquarters of the *coronel* with him. More than this, our canoe was a light two-man craft, and it never would carry all four of us.

"Where is your canoe?" I asked.

He laughed as if the question were a ghastly joke.

"Canoe? Gone, weeks ago! We stole it when we were hard pressed on the Amazon, traveled in it until we found this dead town, and stopped here to hide and rest. Then one night when the water rose it floated away. We never found it. We have no canoe. I ask you again, what will you do with us?"

"I do not know," said Pedro slowly. "If we take you out it will be only to death. We are not police, and it is not for us to punish you. We are not doctors, and we can not cure you. We are not priests, and we can not save you. And I am much afraid, friend Manoel, that you will see few more dawns."

"You have it right," agreed Manoel. "There is little hope for me. And I am not afraid to die — I am glad to die, now that I know how cruel and false this woman is. But I do not want to die alone and deserted."

The woman spoke.

"It is as I said. It is useless to take you out. But these men will take me out, if only to punishment. Even that will be better than staying here."

Looking keenly at her, I guessed her thought: that in some way she would yet succeed in saving herself — perhaps by charming the young Englishmen, who we had said were our employers, and convincing them that we were liars and that she was a much wronged girl. So I decided to kill that idea.

"Perhaps we will take you out, *senhorita* — I mean *senhora*. But not to Tabatinga. We stay here until we have done all we can do for Manoel. Then you go with us to the headquarters of Coronel Nunes, our employer.

"The tale I told you was a joke. There are no young Englishmen at Tabatinga — at least none that I know — and we are not scouts but rubber-workers of the *coronel*. And the *coronel* is no young fool. He is old and shrewd, and you could neither beguile him nor deceive him."

My guess had been right. Her face writhed. With a sudden wrench she twisted her hands from Pedro's grip and sprang at me. I slipped her dagger into my belt at the back, where she could not reach it, and held her off. After fighting me a minute she stood still and began to curse me.

I had heard rough talk from women sometimes in the past, for the women of the frontier are not always choice in their language, especially when angered; but never, *senhores*, have I listened to such words from a woman's mouth as I heard then. No man could have called me such names and lived. But, since she was not a man, I could only stand and let her rave.

At length she choked with rage and could say no more. In keeping her away from me I had moved about so that my back was toward the sick man. Now I heard his voice again, and to my astonishment it was almost at my ear. Turning, I found that he had managed to drag himself up and stood supporting himself against the wall. His sunken eyes glittered.

"A sweet, dainty, lovable woman for men to throw away life and honor for, is she not?" he said. "Yet I have loved her — God, how I have loved her! Now I have nearly reached my end, and there is no escape for me. But for you, Francisca, there is still a way to avoid the prison and the shame awaiting you down the river. It is very simple."

His voice grew weak, and he swayed.

"Since this is the last thing I can do for you, Francisca, I will tell you —"

We could hardly hear him now. He seemed about to drop. But he moved his head, beckoning her closer.

"You will tell me what? Speak quickly."

Eagerly she stepped close to him. He straightened. His teeth flashed again. Something else flashed too — cold steel.

A scream broke from her. She staggered back and fell.

Swiftly on the breast of her red gown spread a deeper red. Her white face grew whiter.

She lay utterly still.

We whirled on Manoel. As we did so he too dropped. Whether he stabbed himself before falling or collapsed from weakness and fell on the knife I do not know. But he struck on his face, and when we turned him over we found the dagger in his breast, driven into the hilt.

It looked like Francisca's own dagger. I threw a hand to my

belt. Her weapon was gone. Then I realized what he had done.

While my back was toward him and both Pedro and I were looking at the furious woman, he had drawn on his last strength to rise, slip the knife from me and stand against the wall until he could lure her within reach. The dagger with which she had intended to silence him forever had done its work — but had found her own heart first.

"The simplest way," Manoel gasped. "No prison. No lonely death. We lived together — we die together. I go out with her blood on my hands. Yet I have been through hell for her. Perhaps the good God will have mercy on me."

"Perhaps he will, Manoel, " Pedro echoed. "Truly, there is no hell like the one into which a woman can drag a man."

Manoel twisted once and was still. We rose and gazed down at both of them. In Francisca's black hair, on her red gown and her white arms and throat the fireflies still gleamed bright and cold. From Manoel's haggard face the lines of pain and weakness were gone. Both slept the long sleep, freed forever from the fear and struggle and disgrace which were the only things left them in life.

"As he said, it was the simplest way," mused Pedro. "It is best for them and best for us. They themselves have finished what they began. Now there is only one thing we can do for them."

Stooping, he lifted her. I straightened Manoel and laid him back on his bed Pedro lowered the girl beside him.

Then taking with us the firefly cage, we went to the door, pulled it shut behind us, crossed the outer room and crawled out through the window. Back down the path we went, found our canoe and silently paddled back to our hammocks.

At dawn we returned. As she had said, there was a small window in that room where she and Manoel lay. Across it ran wooden bars like those at the front of the house. With our machetes we cut vines and creepers, wove them into the openings until they were tight, and plastered the whole frame thickly with clay.

Then we repaired the broken frame we had torn from the front window, put that also in place, and clayed it like the other. With its outer door still barred and its windows sealed, the last refuge of the Firefly and her lover had become their tomb.

One long look we gave at the dreary, silent town half buried in the bush. Then we went down the path for the last time. As we stopped at our canoe Pedro whirled, his rifle up. Then he lowered it. Behind us was the black monkey.

"Adeos, compadre," Pedro said soberly. "I am glad you did not get walled into that house, for we had forgotten you. Now we go. This is your town. We leave you here to live your own life as we go out to live ours. Farewell. "

We pushed off and paddled away, leaving the queer fellow watching us.

He may be there tonight, that monkey, snitching at fireflies in the gloom at the head of the cove and putting them on himself as he once saw his mistress do. But neither he nor I nor any of us will ever again hear that voice singing in the night.

> *"Glitter, glitter, pretty firefly!*
> *Born but to dance and flash and die."*

Nor will any of us ever again see that woman, driven from the lights of a far off shore by her crime, decking herself with the only jewels left to her — the natural jewels of the jungle And it is as well. For all fireflies, beautiful though they may be, are false, *senhores* — false and cold.

THE TAILED MEN

THOSE are true words, *senhor*, though spoken in jest. You say that if men were shaped to fit their natures some would find it hard to wear hat and trousers, because they would have horns and tails.

I have met men who should have been so marked, and who ought also to have had claws instead of hands and split hoofs instead of feet; for, though their bodies were human, they were fiends at heart. True, in time their malice became known, and at last their own evil deeds caused their deaths, but not until they had brought much misery to others. How much blood and tears could be saved if only *Deos Padre* would make men — and women too — so that their natures could be seen at once.

Yes, that is a useless wish. But your remark, *senhor*, brings to my mind a memory of the strangest creatures I ever saw — creatures so queer that perhaps you will not believe me when I tell of them. Yet the tale will pass the time while we lounge here on the steamer's deck, and anything which kills the tedium of this long journey down the Amazon is worthwhile.

Now you two North American explorers, if I am not mistaken, have been adventuring in the country along the river Javary and westward in Peru toward the Ucayali. Then you have not visited the river Jurua, east of the Javary? It is well. If ever you return to Brazil and go far up that river, be prepared for trouble.

I have been there — and I am not going back. If the floods had not been very heavy that year I should never have gone there at all. With my comrade, Pedro Andrada, I had recently been out on a long rambling trip through the wild jungle along the border of Brazil and Peru, and there we had met with hardships which made us satisfied to stay in idleness at Remate de Males, a Javary town where we rubber-workers gathered in the rainy season. But now, loafing one day at the store of a trader with nothing to do but smoke and watch the dirty waters swirling past, we grew restless again.

"Lourenço, too much idleness is worse than too much work," said Pedro, yawning and stretching his powerful arms. "I feel stupid, and you are getting fat. If the flood does not go down soon you will get such a big belly that you will grunt like a sloth every time you tap a tree."

This was only a joke, for, though I am broad and had grown heavy from inaction, I had not swollen up along the belt-line. But I felt sluggish, as he did, and so weary of lounging that I wished someone would start a fight, or anything else that would quicken my blood. Lazily I tried to think of something we could do, but the only ideas that came to me were old ones and not worth trying. So I only grunted and sat still, looking up the river.

Something was floating down toward us and I watched it because there was nothing else to look at — drifting trees were so common that I hardly ever noticed them. As this thing came nearer, though, I saw that it was not a tree but a small canoe. It swung slowly around on the current, seeming empty and useless.

"There is something we can do," I said, nodding toward it. "A short paddle will stretch our muscles and give us another boat."

He yawned again and untied our own canoe, fastened to a post of the store. I got up and splashed toward it — the water was so high that, in spite of the tall poles on which the store stood, it flowed over the platform — and we were about to step in when Pedro started.

"Por amor de Deos!" he cried. "Look!"

The drifting boat was quite near us now. Above its edge something had risen and was moving weakly in little jerks; a thing like a skinny claw, or the hand of a man almost dead from starvation or fever, trying to attract attention and bring help. As we stared it dropped out of sight.

Without a word we leaped into our canoe and drove our paddles in deep. We were both old in the ways of the bush, and we knew what to expect. Yet the man we found out there on the river was in such a condition that even we, who had looked on many hard sights, turned cold as we stared down at him.

He seemed dead. His eyes were fixed and glassy, his mouth open, his chest motionless, his body shrunken to a skeleton. This did not disturb us, for we who work in the jungle of Javary see much of death. He was totally naked, and scabbed from head to foot by the bites of thousands of *piums* or *carrapatos*. Yet this did not shock us either, for any man who travels the Brazilian bush will be badly bitten at times by insects, and if he loses his clothing he will suffer much. The things that chilled us were two — the fear stamped deep in his ghastly face, and the marks of torture.

The scars were not new, but they were plain. They were the marks of fire and knife. And the worst of all was that he had been not only burned and cut, but mutilated.

Gripping the edge of his canoe, we went drifting down the current, looking at him and at each other. It seemed useless to take him ashore, for there was nothing to show who he was or whence he came, and the water was so high that we should have some trouble in finding a good place to bury him. Yet we nodded to each other, and were preparing to tow him in, when we jumped as if a snake had struck at us. He moved!

We had fully decided that he was dead, and that the fluttering movement of the hand we had seen was his last struggle. And when you see a dead man move, *senhores*, you are likely to recoil from him. We twitched our hands away from his boat. Before it could float off, though, we grabbed it again and hung on. His movement had been slight, only a quivering of the arms and a rise of the chest, with a low moaning sound as he breathed. Now, seeing that he still lived, we swiftly fastened his craft to ours and bent our paddles in hard strokes back to town.

Other men loafing at the doors facing the river had been watching us, and some of them were coming in their *montarias* and dugouts to see what we had found. Warning them out of the way, we drove ahead at full speed straight to the small *barracão* where we lived. There we put him into a hammock and poured brandy into his mouth.

He strangled, shivered a little, and coughed. We rubbed his cold hands and feet, raised and lowered his arms and legs, and gave him more brandy. Soon he began to breathe more deeply, and his eyes moved and stared at us. But no light showed in those eyes; they were as blank as those of a fish.

"You are safe now, friend," said Pedro. "Lie still and rest, and you will soon be strong again." Then he turned to the men who had crowded into our house after us.

"Do not stand idle!" he commanded. "Do you not see that he is naked and starving? Meldo, your woman is a good cook — go at once and have her make some broth. You others, go to Joaquim's store and get more brandy — this is gone. And bring clothes."

They went, all except Domengos Peixoto, a surly sot whom nobody liked. I asked him what he waited for, and he answered that there was no sense in rushing about for a man who would soon be dead. This angered us both. Pedro roughly grabbed him and shoved him toward the door, and I kicked him out into the water. He scrambled out, got into his *montaria*, and went away cursing.

After he was gone, though, we had to admit that he probably was right when he said this man would not live. Not only was he at the point of death from sickness and suffering and starvation, but he was crazed. Staring straight ahead, he was whispering and muttering, and his look of fear was even stronger than before.

We bent over him, listening. His talk was broken and confused. The terrible mud was dragging him down, he said. The jungle was black, black, and a jaguar was snarling under his tree. A huge snake was coiled beside his canoe, and if he could kill it he would eat it, but he had no weapon. *Thepiums* were a torment as bad as fire. Something with a long black tail was grinning at him. Oh for a machete or a rifle! These things, and many more, he mumbled.

"Poor fellow, he raves of the terrors of the unknown jungle where he has been," said Pedro. I nodded, for I too had seen men whose brains were twisted by hardship. But before I could answer, the man screamed out:

"The tailed men! The tailed men! Devils of hell, they — ah! Drop that knife! I will do it; I will do it; yes, yes, but put away that knife!"

He cringed and shivered miserably as he screeched.

"Have courage, comrade!" Pedro soothed. "We will protect you. There are no knives or — or tailed *demonios* here."

But the human wreck lay whimpering and moaning, and we could make nothing of his words. Then Meldo came hastening in with a bowl of hot broth, and the other men arrived with clothes and more brandy, followed by still more men who had come to see what was going on. We raised the sufferer in his hammock and began to feed him the soup.

The smell of that food seemed to give him strength, and he sucked it up so greedily that we had to restrain him from seizing it and burning himself. When it was gone we pulled shirt and trousers on him and laid him back. He grew stupid, like an animal which has starved and then gorged itself. Our hopes rose a little, for we thought he might sleep and gain power to live. So we drove everyone out, and, though some would not go away but stayed outside in their boats, the house became quiet. We sat in the other hammock, silently waiting.

All that afternoon we waited. The sick man seemed not to sleep but to doze with eyes partly open. It was nearly night when he breathed deep and the eyes opened wide. As we rose and stood beside him we saw two things: that the gray shade of death was on him, but that he had become sane.

Under his matted black hair his eyes gleamed hollowly first at me, then at Pedro. A light came into his scarred face, and a weak smile grew on his bearded mouth.

"Pedro!" he whispered.

My partner stared down at him.

"Yes, I am Pedro, friend," he said. "But I do not know you."

"Luis Pitta," breathed the other.

"Luis Pitta! *Deos meo!* Are you Luis?"

The dying man nodded slightly.

"Luis. I die."

He lay breathing a moment, then went on:

"I am glad — to die and be at peace. Keep away — Jurua."

"Luis Pitta!" repeated Pedro in a shocked tone. "Luis — Luis, old comrade, who has treated you so? You were a strong man, and now —"

Luis shivered. Fear shot back into his face. As he answered his voice rose to a scream.

"The tailed men! The black men with tails! The demons of the Jurua! O God, save me from —"

He went limp. His jaw dropped. He was dead.

Again I felt cold. From the door, where other men heard that awful cry, came a low mumble of whispers and exclamations. Over the dead man Pedro made the sign of the cross. Then he began making a cigarette, and his hands shook. When it was lighted he began pacing up and down. His face grew hard and his eyes burned. Stopping suddenly, he demanded —

"Who remembers Luis Pitta?"

Nobody answered. The men outside had left their boats and edged in at the door, where they stared at the dead man as if trying to remember him, but none seemed to know him. The name of Luis Pitta meant nothing to me either, so I kept silence.

"We were boys together in Santarem, long before we came into this cursed Javary country," said Pedro. "Luis went to work as a *seringueiro* at the rubber estate of Senhor da Costa on the Branco, while I worked for Coronel Nunes. I have not heard anything of him since two years ago, when a man of the da Costa *seringal* told me Luis had grown restless and homesick for the open *campos* and clean sandy beaches of Santarem, and, in the time of high-water, had left for the East. He intended to paddle through flooded lakes and channels until he reached the Jurua, go down that river to Fonteboa on the Solimoes, and there get an Amazon boat which would carry him home.

"He was a strong, merry-hearted, fearless man, was Luis. Now look at him! A broken, tortured, fear-ridden wreck who raved of demons on the Jurua. *Por Deos!* Demons they are, the things which have done such work on my old comrade. But, demons or not, they shall pay!"

He choked with rage and struck one fist hard into the

other hand.

"Who will go with me?" he roared. "Who will go to the Jurua and fight these fiends? Luis was a *seringueiro* like ourselves. Who goes to avenge him?"

Still no one spoke. The men glanced at one another, stared at the dead Luis, shuffled their feet, but made no answer.

"Pah! You sicken me!" Pedro growled. "You are not men of the bush, but potbellied town loafers. Get out! The air around you stinks!"

Then up spoke a man shamed by my partner's scorn.

"Pedro, you are mad. From the mouth of the Javary to the mouth of the Jurua is more than four hundred miles, and from there to the upper reaches of that river is at least six hundred. Shall we go a thousand miles to avenge a man we did not know? No. And this man Luis said the ones who broke him were devils — *demonios* with tails! Any of us will fight men, but we will not go far away to attack things spawned in hell. So long as they stay where they are we will let them alone."

The others grunted their approval of this. After glaring at them a moment, Pedro slowly nodded.

"You have it right," he admitted. "This is not your business. What is more, I do not want any of you now. If you would travel a thousand miles to get to a place that can be reached by paddling a hundred miles in another direction, you have not brains enough to be worth taking with me. I will go alone."

He motioned for them to leave the house. They went, shaking their heads and saying he was crazed. Then he turned to me, and found me squinting down the barrel of my rifle.

"I am not asking you to go either," he told me.

"You do not need to," I said. "Where is the oil? This barrel is rusty again."

He laughed out suddenly.

"Good old Lourenço! I should not have said that. The oil is there behind that *cuya*. But first let us bury Luis while it is yet day. We have not much time."

After some difficulty, we found a place where the dead man could be laid at rest. Then we went to the store, where we found men growling because we had buried Luis so quickly instead of burning candles over him all night and giving the townsmen an excuse to sit up and get drunk, as is usual when someone dies. They hushed, though, when we gave them hard looks and then bought many cartridges.

"Are you indeed going on this wild trip of which men talk?" asked Joaquim, the trader. When we said we were, he added:

"Then talk with my old father, who traveled much in his younger days and knows something of the Jurua. You will find him in the family-room behind that door."

In the room to which he pointed we found an old man lying in a hammock and smoking a long pipe.

"Greetings, *compadre*," said Pedro. "We go to the Jurua. Joaquim says you can tell us something of that river."

The old man blinked up at us, took out his pipe, and cleared his throat.

"And so I can, my sons," he answered. "What do you seek on the Jurua?"

"We know not, father, whether we seek men or beasts or demons; they may be all three. We would find things with tails which have tortured my old friend, Luis Pitta. The tailed men of the furua, he called them."

"*Si.* I have heard of the death of Luis."

He began puffing again, gazing through the smoke as if seeing something far off. We said no more, but waited. After a time he spoke again.

"The Jurua is bad. It is long and more crooked than a snake, and on its banks live evil things. I would advise you not to go there, but I see that your eyes are hot and your heart burns for your friend, and I am not so old that I have forgotten my own youth. You will go. But I hope, my sons, that you will not find those things you seek, for if you do you may not come back.

"I have not seen those *demonios*, but I have heard of them. They are far up the river and they are beasts which walk like men. To reach them by going up the river would take many days and you might not live to enter their country, for the Arauas would murder you if they could. These Arauas live eight days' journey from the Solimoes and they are not to be trusted.

"There are also the Catauxias, but these are not so bad. Above these were the Canamaris, but the Canamaris have nearly died out through war with the Arauas. And much farther up are the Culinos and Nawas, of whom I know little, for it takes two moons to reach their region from the Amazon. Above all these are the Uginas. They are the tailed men.

"Yet you can avoid the tribes lower down the river, and shorten your journey to the Ugina country, by paddling up the Tecuahy and following a *furo* to the south."

"That was our plan," Pedro nodded. "I know there is a *furo*, but I do not know where it begins."

"It is in the Red Jungle. Far up the Tecuahy you will find it — a great forest of *massaranduba* trees. Soon after you have entered it you will see opening at the left a long *enseada*. Go into this bay and you will find it narrowing to a *furo* which will run almost straight for a time and then will become more winding. Where it ends I do not know, but it leads toward the land of the tailed *demonios*. *Adeos*, my sons. Go with God."

As we strode out Pedro turned and looked back at him. And when we got into our canoe he said:

"There, Lourenço, is the first real man I have seen this day, except yourself. Did you notice how his old eyes followed us when we came away? He has been an adventurer in his day, and even now he hungers to go with us. It is a pity he is so old and feeble."

Back to our *barracão* we went, stowed our equipment in our canoe, cleaned our guns, curled up in the hammocks, and slept. As soon as the black night turned to gray day we rolled out again, ate, and started.

DAYS OF paddling followed. On our first night out we found ourselves very tired, for the loafing at the town had softened us and shortened our wind, and the next morning we were sluggish and stiff. After that, though, our muscles hardened, and we swung along at a stroke that put the miles steadily behind us. We talked little, for Pedro brooded on the fate of his old friend Luis, so that for a time he was not the lighthearted fellow I had usually found him. He did not seem like himself again until we reached the Red Jungle.

Late on a day of rain we found it. The dense green wall of jungle along the banks of the Tecuahy thinned out. Then the huge reddish trunks of *massarandubas* began to slide past us, their lofty crowns matting together so thickly that they seemed to make a solid roof. Soon we were in the midst of them. To right and left and up ahead they towered out of the flood waters. Through them we paddled on fast, looking to the left. And before long, as the father of Joaquim had told us, a long *enseada* opened out toward the southeast.

In among the giant trees we pushed until we reached a hill where we could land. There Pedro took from the canoe his *machadinha* — the little hatchet which we use in tapping rubber trees — and cut into a big trunk until milk came pouring out. As you know, *senhores*, the *massaranduba* is a "cow-tree," and its milk is good to drink if taken fresh, though it soon thickens to a tough glue if exposed to the air. We were hot and thirsty, and each of us drank a cupful of milk. Then, much refreshed, we made camp between the root-walls of that tree and ate our evening meal.

Though the day had not quite ended when we finished, it was very dark under that thick roof of branches and leaves. But the rain had stopped, and now the low sun suddenly flashed out, shooting its long rays in from the bay and making the wet reddish trunks glow like dull fire.

"This is a solemn place," I said, gazing at the great columns standing out against the farther gloom. "It seems weird and unnatural. No Indians would ever live in such a place; they would believe it to be the home of the Caypor, that great jungle-demon with the flaming red hair."

He nodded and opened his lips to answer. But no words came. His eyes widened, then narrowed, as if a strange thought had come to him, and he looked sharply at the nearest tree. I looked too, but saw nothing odd.

"What is it?" I asked.

"The women —" he said slowly, "the women of the *caboclos*

make red dye from the bark of the *massaranduba*."

"Yes. But what of that?"

Still he studied the tree. Then, for the first time since Luis Pitta came floating down the river, he laughed. But why he laughed he would not tell. So, knowing him well, I asked no more questions.

As suddenly as it had come, the sun left us. At once it grew so black that we could see nothing at all. Tree frogs and crickets burst out into their usual nightly hammering. Their racket made us feel more at home here, and we soon slept.

In the morning we drank again of the tree-milk, and before we left the hill Pedro cut off chunks of the rough *massaranduba* bark. These he stowed away in the canoe. Seeing my questioning look, he grinned.

"Perhaps I will make a red dye and paint the tails of the Uginas with it," he joked. "Who knows?"

"If we find them, I think we will paint them with red from their own veins," I replied.

His face hardened, and he grunted agreement. We left the hill, paddled away through the trees to the open water, and went on until we found the *furo*.

IN THE next three days we journeyed far and fast. The *furo* was narrow, but straight and deep, and there was neither current nor low-hanging bush to hold us back. The Red Jungle still rose around us, and its thick roof prevented the usual small stuff from growing around its trunks. In the dim shadows among those tremendous trees we saw no living thing, and heard no sound except that of frogs and bugs.

Then the big trees ended, and again we met the tangle of undergrowth and hanging vines. Here we had to travel more slowly. In some places we had to use poles instead of paddles. Snakes dropped down around us from branches overhead. Swarms of *piums* and *motucas* attacked us and bit until blood dripped from us. At night we heard jaguars roaring near by, and once we had to sleep almost buried under our supplies to protect ourselves from vampire bats. But we made good speed along the narrow canal in the daytime, and at length we shot out into a clay-colored water which at first we took for the Jurua.

We soon learned, however, that this was not even a river. It had a slight flow, but it was only a winding maze of flood waters in which we wandered for days. And in this wandering we lost the *furo*. When we found that we were not on any river we sought it again but could not find it. But we did find a small river flowing in from the south, and up that stream we went.

Before we had gone far on this river we were attacked. Shrill yells sounded in the bush, and arrows dropped around our boat. We snatched our rifles, but could see no men — only the heavy arrows rising slowly from the farther shore, curving in air and plunging straight down. Several struck in the canoe.

"Drop as if you were hit," snapped Pedro. Even as he spoke an arrow fell down my back, scratching my shoulder muscles and catching in my shirt. I slumped forward, thinking that now I was a dead man in truth — for if that arrow was poisoned I could not live long. A second later Pedro gave a groaning cry and flopped backward.

At once the arrows stopped. The yells became screeches of savage joy. We lay quiet, our boat drifting downward, until Pedro gave the word. Then we popped up and found naked wild men in plain sight on the bushy bank. Before they realized we were alive our bullets were striking them down.

At the belch of our guns they screeched again — this time from fear. They jumped away, but not before three of them had fallen dead and a fourth had tumbled into the river. We slammed several more bullets into the jungle, and heard their yelps grow fainter as they fled. Then I yanked that arrow out of my shirt and looked at its point. There was no stain of poison on it, and so the scratch across my shoulders meant nothing.

"Let us get that man," said Pedro, and I saw that the Indian who had fallen into the water was alive and trying to crawl out. We drove the canoe at him, caught him, and dragged him in. Then we crossed the river again and hung to bushes while we questioned him.

He had been shot in one leg but he paid no attention to the wound. He was more afraid of what we might yet do to him than of what we had done. His face was dull and stupid but his beady eyes showed his fear. We took care that he should keep on fearing us and tried to make him talk.

It was hard to make him understand. We spoke in Tupi, the *lengoa geral* of the Amazonian Indians, but he seemed to know only a few words of it. From this we judged that he belonged to one of those small tribes often found far away from the Amazon, who have lived in one place so long they have almost forgotten the language of others.

Yet we learned a few things. We had been attacked because we were strangers, and these people feared all strangers. They would not assail us again, because now they would be too much afraid of our guns. The river we were following came out of a chain of swamps, and at the other end of that chain another stream ran south. This was what we most wanted to know, for it meant that we were on a route that would bring us out on the Jurua. We tried to find out something about the tailed men, but he could not — or would not understand; he seemed to think we spoke of monkeys. So, having learned all we could from him, we let him go.

Back across the river we took him and put him out on the bank, knowing the others would find him there when they came back for their dead. Then we continued up the stream.

Our prisoner had told the truth; perhaps he was too stupid to lie to us. At the head of the river we came into great dismal *lagos*. After crossing these dead waters we found a flowing current which took us down another small stream to the south. This widened into a good-sized river, and at length it carried us out into a big, slow, dark water which was wider than anything we had seen since leaving Remate de Males. We had reached the Jurua.

"The Jurua is long and more crooked than a snake, and on its banks live evil things," said Pedro, gazing out across the dreary river. "So spoke the father of Joaquim. In truth, this looks to be an evil water. Now shall we go up or down? We do not know where Luis was held prisoner."

"Up," I judged. "We were told that these Uginas live higher up than the other tribes. And Luis, in escaping, would naturally go down the river so that the current would aid him. The place where he was held must be above here."

So we turned to the right and journeyed up the dark water.

For two days we found nothing. By day we stole along through flooded swamps, keeping near shore, watching the bush and listening. By night we hid our canoe and slung our hammocks at the top of some hill, lighting no fire. We shot no game, made no noise we could avoid, and slept lightly with our guns beside us. But we neither saw nor heard anything except the usual animal life.

Then came a storm. The sky had been dull for days, and rain had fallen often, but not hard. Now, as we scouted along a steep bank rising several feet above us, Pedro stopped paddling and looked behind him. I too looked backward, finding that the sky was swiftly growing black. As we held our paddles there came to us a dull roar of wind.

At once we snapped into swift strokes, seeking an inlet. Before we found one the wind had struck us, and the storm-waves were slapping heavily against our boat. But as we sped onward the bank grew lower, and then a small cove opened. We swerved into it. As we tumbled out on shore the storm broke.

Blinding lightning, crashing thunder, and drowning rain came all at once. We dragged the canoe up as high as we could, then squatted beside a tree until the squall should pass. But it did not pass as soon as expected. The wind and the deluge of rain swept onward after a while, but the thunder and lightning continued. So we stayed where we were, our eyes nearly closed to lessen the glare of the light-flashes, and waited.

Suddenly I felt Pedro's hand on my wrist. His lips moved, but a roar of thunder swallowed his words. He had come out of his squat and was sitting straight up on his heels, and his eyes were wide-open. Following his stare, I saw, peering at us from behind a tree, a face.

It did not move. It hung there as if it grew from the tree, and the swift lightning lighted it up time after time. It was the face of an animal, but yet the face of a man. Heavy black hair hung down over its low forehead. Little black eyes glimmered at us. The nose flared so that it seemed a snout. The thick lips were drawn back, and yellow teeth gleamed in a soundless snarl. The whole face was bestial — such a face as a man might see in a bad dream.

The rapid flicker of lightning suddenly stopped. With the end of that winking glare the jungle seemed black. Pedro pushed me, and I lost my balance and toppled sidewise. He shoved me again, and then I caught his idea — that we should move away from that spot. We crawled several feet, got behind a tree, and stood up with rifles cocked.

Another flash whitened the bush. We saw the beast-man again. He too had moved, though only a little. He had slipped out until his arms and shoulders were clear of the tree, and he held a bow with the arrow aimed at the spot where we had been.

Though that space now was empty, he loosed the arrow before he realized we were gone. In the same instant he fell with two bullets through his head.

The lightning vanished, but we jumped through the gloom to his tree. Beside it we found him huddled as he had fallen. While other flashes came and went we squatted there, peering around to learn whether this man had companions. Seeing none, we dragged him out to the canoe.

There we looked him over. We had dropped him face upward, and we saw that he was small, scrawny, filthy, and totally naked. Now Pedro took one arm and flopped the body over. We both recoiled.

"Deos meo!" cried my comrade. "It is true! Look! The tail!"

Yes, *senhores*, that dead man-animal had a tail. It was a long, naked, blackish tail like that of a great rat. It was not a thing fastened to him by rods or glue, either, but a real tail that grew from his body. And in spite of the dying screams of Luis Pitta, in spite of what the father of Joaquim had said of the Uginas, the sight of that bare, repulsive thing hanging from the dead man struck us dumb.

We stood staring at it until Pedro stooped, grasped it, and

lifted. The body rose from the ground and dangled in air like that of a monkey. Dropping it, my partner rubbed his hands on his breeches as if to get rid of a snaky feeling.

The thunder died to a dull mutter before we spoke again. Then Pedro said:

"We have sent one of Luis' *demonios* down the road to hell. But yet this thing is no demon. It is hardly more than a *bicho do mato* — a beast of the forest. Either of us could kill two of these creatures at once with our bare hands. I wonder that a strong man like Luis let such things overcome him."

"They must have caught him asleep, or trapped him in some way," I reasoned. "And any one man, no matter how strong, can be overpowered by many others. You know how it is when we meet a horde of ants — we can crush a score of them at one step, but the others will swarm upon us and bite us horribly. And an ant is a tiny thing compared to this brute."

"True," he agreed. "I should not have spoken so of Luis. Let us see how bad the bite of this misbegotten creature would be."

We went over to the arrow sticking in the ground, pulled it up, and examined it. It was poorly made and had no barb, seeming to be only a straight stick with one end badly notched and the other fire-hardened and scraped to a point. Looking closely at that point, we could find no sign of poison.

"They are so ignorant that they do not know how to make poison," said my partner. "Yet we must not make the mistake of holding them too lightly. This arrow was shot hard enough to kill one of us. And no doubt they are cunning, like an alligator or any other low beast. Ah, the sun shines again. Let us see where this man came from."

As he said, the sun had blazed out. By the new light we went back to the tree where the man-beast had lurked, and there we found a few more arrows and his bow. The bow was as poorly made as the arrow we had inspected, but was strong enough to kill. Working away from the tree, we sought a path, but found none. In the mud, however, we spied the tracks of the dead man's feet. This trail we followed back through the bush.

It was not easy to track his course, for the footmarks were

few and scattered, and he seemed to have rambled in a winding, purposeless way. But when we lost it we always managed
to find it again, and gradually it led us back some distance
from the river.

We judged that he had been hunting, for we found spots
where he had stopped and stood, making several marks in one
place as he shifted his feet. On and on we crept, watching
everything, saying nothing, until we came into what seemed a
very faint path. There the wet earth was pressed down more
firmly, and by looking along its edges we found a few marks of
human toes.

Along this vague track we went with our heads up, glancing at the trail only now and then to make sure we did not lose
it. All at once I stopped and threw up my rifle. Ahead of us a
dark shape was swinging down along vine hanging from high
branches.

But I did not shoot. The moving thing was only a big
monkey. It showed no fear of us, but came down until it could
get a good view of us. There it stopped, gripping the vine with
all four of its paws and swinging slowly, watched us. We stood
still, staring back. After a time it climbed deliberately up again
until it reached the tangle of limbs. Then we saw it go jumping
and swinging away through the trees.

"He goes toward the place where this path leads," whispered Pedro.

"A pet monkey, perhaps," I guessed.

"Perhaps."

He smiled oddly, then motioned for me to go on.

We advanced for some distance before we saw or heard
anything more. Often we stopped to listen; and it was at one of
these still moments that we caught a sound ahead — a low
mutter like a man's voice. At once we slipped aside into some
thick bush and squatted.

Soon we heard a slight rustle of leaves. Then a man came
stealing past. Another followed, and another — four in all.
They might have been brothers of the one we had killed on the
riverbank, for each had the same low, brutal sort of face. I
thought I saw tails too, but could not be sure, for their bodies

were partly hidden by the undergrowth. All were armed with bows and arrows, and all were peering ahead as if hunting something.

When the last man had passed I started to creep forward, intending both to look after them and to see whether more were coming. But I stopped where I was. High up over us broke out a noise.

Glancing upward, I saw the big black monkey which had watched us and gone away. He was hanging from a branch, looking down at us and chattering loudly. Low grunts came from the path where the savages had disappeared.

"Do not shoot!" whispered Pedro. "Use your machete!"

Silently we drew our bush-knives. With our legs tensed under us, ready for a spring, we waited. In the path a man reappeared, scowling into the tangle on both sides of the trail. On his heels crept another. Before we saw the other two, the first man spied us.

The instant his eyes met ours we leaped up and at him. My machete chopped him across the neck, and as he reeled I heard the cutting crunch of Pedro's heavy knife killing the savage next to him. Clutching my man about the body, I swung him around as a shield as I faced the two left alive. It was lucky that I did this, for one of those *barbaros* had drawn an arrow to its head, and now he shot. The arrow plunged into the body I held. Throwing the dead man from me, I jumped at my enemy and, before he could put another arrow to the bow, struck him down. Then I turned toward the fourth man.

He was stabbing at Pedro. My comrade jumped back like a cat, and his red machete whirled up sidewise against the other's wrist. A snarling grunt sounded in the throat of the Ugina. His knife flew aside. An instant later his whole body rose from the ground as Pedro drove his machete into his stomach and lifted.

A short, gasping wail burst from him. After Pedro threw him to the ground he writhed a moment, then lay still. We looked all around us, but saw no other man. Except ourselves, the black monkey overhead was the only living thing in that place.

We kicked the dead men over on their faces. Each had a tail.

"Four more gone to whine to Luis for forgiveness," said Pedro grimly, as he wiped his machete on a leaf. Then he stood scowling thoughtfully at the one he had just killed.

"He had a knife," he went on. "I chopped his bow, and then he drew — See! He wears a belt! A black leather belt and a knife-sheath! Where could such an animal get a knife, belt, and sheath? Where is that knife?"

Searching the undergrowth, we found it. It was long, with a sharp point and an odd handle — a handle of white bone, carved to fit the hand, with a knob at the upper end.

"It is as I thought," said Pedro, nodding. "This is Luis' own knife. I remember it well. It is a North American knife, and was given him by a man from Nova York who stayed for a time at Santarem collecting birds and insects for a great *museo*. He was very proud of it, for there was not another like it on the Amazon. Poor Luis!"

"These are the fiends who tortured him. This one must be the very man who cut him with his own knife — the one of whom he screamed as he died. I am sorry I did not know it sooner, for then this beast would have died more slowly."

He glowered down at the dead Ugina. Then he plucked big leaves from the bush, wrapped up the knife, and tied the bundle with bush-cord.

"I do not want the belt and sheath, now that this vile creature has worn them," he said. "But the knife Luis loved so well shall stay with me. Now let us throw these brutes out of the way."

We did so. After that Pedro turned back toward the river.

"Come," he said, "I have a plan which is better than going straight ahead now. And we had best get more cartridges."

It was not until then that I realized we carried no cartridges except those in the magazines of our rifles. So, picking our guns from the undergrowth where we had hidden them, we returned as we had come. We took no care to conceal our trail, for our feet were bare and made no strange marks in the path.

In the riverbank Pedro stopped short, staring at the

ground.

"Lourenço!" he muttered. "We killed that *demonio*, did we not?"

I looked for the dead man. He was gone.

Our canoe was there, and nothing in it had been touched. There was no sign that other men had come while we were away. The bush around us was silent and empty. Yet that tailed thing with the top of its head blown off had disappeared.

The sun had gone under clouds again, and the light was dim. Stooping, we scanned the ground where the Ugina had lain. Then we saw signs that something had been dragged from the spot. The signs led toward the water. In the mud at the edge of the water was the trail of a big alligator.

"Ah, that is more natural," Pedro said in a relieved tone. "I was almost ready to believe that the man-devil had stuffed his brains back into his head and walked off. I think I am losing my own brains. Let us go somewhere else for the night. It is too late to do anything more today."

So we left the inlet, paddled back downstream, crossed to the other side of the river, and camped there.

As you may suppose, we argued that night about the tailed men. We agreed that they were not much more than animals, but the question was how they got tails. They might be monkeys turning into men, or they might be men becoming monkeys; but still they did not seem monkey-like, except that they were hairy and had the tails and faces of brutes. Their feet were the big flat feet of men, not monkey paws; and their tails seemed useless. Finally Pedro said:

"The things of which we are sure are that they have tails and that they are vile and cruel. They have no human hearts. And my idea about them is that they are men, but so low that they breed with monkeys.

"You remember the *barbaros* who attacked us before we passed through the swamps, and what a stupid fellow that one was whom we caught. He was not much higher than these Uginas, though he had no tail. You know how some of these small tribes who live in one place breed among themselves until their brains become hardly better than those of animals.

They sink lower and lower until they are beasts, living only to eat and sleep and do vicious things. And you remember that black monkey we met, which looked at us and then brought those four men to seek us. He was a *coaita*, the tallest and most knowing monkey in our jungles — you have seen *coaitas* kept as pets along the Solimoes. Why, then, should a tribe so low as these Uginas not breed with *coaitas*? And why should not that breeding give them tails?

"Who knows where men came from in the first place? Who knows whether the first men on earth did not have tails? If they did, would it be strange that such people as these, by mixing with monkeys, should grow them again? Lourenço, I think this is the true reason why these tailed men exist.

"I believe that *coaita* who spied on us was not only a pet, but a blood-brother — or perhaps a father — to some of those creatures who came to hunt us! And I believe that when we enter their town — if they have a town — we shall find other *coaitas* there."

"You may have it right," I admitted. "Now that I think of it, I remember something I once heard said by a college professor from North America — Senhor Grayson, who stayed at the *coronel*'s place for a time to study jungle creatures, and whom we named the Jabiru because he looked so much like that bird.

"He said there had been a time, far back in the early days, when men lived in trees like monkeys. He did not say they had tails, or even that men and monkeys ever were the same. But if they lived like monkeys perhaps they were like monkeys in other ways — I do not know any reason why they should not be.

"But the question now is not so much where these men got their tails as what we shall do to them tomorrow. What is your plan?"

"My plan now is to sleep," he said. And sleep he did, so that I could do nothing but wonder a while and then sleep also.

In the morning Pedro made the first fire we had lighted since reaching the Jurua. The place where we had slept was up a narrow creek concealed by thick bush, and we could find no sign of human life near it. My partner set water to heat in a cooking-vessel, broke up the *massaranduba* bark he had cut in the Red Jungle, and put that also into the pot. Then, leaving me to watch the fire, he went away.

He was gone for some time. When he returned he brought an armful of light-colored strips of thin bark and a number of small springy withes. While I kept the water boiling he untied the knife of Luis, which was more thin of blade than his machete, and with this he shredded the light bark into fibers hardly bigger than hairs.

At this work he spent most of the forenoon. When it was done we pulled the boiled chunks of *massaranduba* bark from the pot. The water in that vessel now had become a red dye. Into this we stuffed the hairy fibers, leaving them in until they became red, then taking them out and putting in others, until at last all were dyed.

All this time I had asked no questions, for Pedro had plagued me many times in the past when I sought reasons for what he did, and had always found that behind his actions was an idea. But now I could no longer keep still.

"If it is not a great secret," I said, "may I ask what you are making?"

"Hair," he grinned. "Red hair. Is it not beautiful?"

"It is red enough, if anyone loves red hair. But what has this to do with killed tailed men?"

"I am surprised that you have not guessed it," he mocked. "We shall make ourselves so handsome that when the Uginas see us they will drop dead from admiration."

I said no more. When he took some spare clothing and rubber-covered pack-sheets from the canoe, however, and began to shape them over withes bent and tied into the shape of a large head, I caught his idea. Back came the memory of my idle remark in the Red Jungle about that demon of the Indians — the Caypor. Now I saw why Pedro had brought along the red bark and why he made red hair. At once I went to work helping him.

Over the frameworks of springy branches we built up trunks, shoulders, and heads, weaving bush-cord through holes in the cloth and rubber and tying them into the right shape. Around the great heads we bound that red hair which we had just made. On the dark rubber we made awful faces, using bits of fungus, daubs of clay and streaks of red dye, and cutting slits for mouths, into which we fastened bits of wood like jagged yellow teeth. When we lifted the things and set them on our shoulders we became the most horrible monsters I have ever seen, except in nightmares.

We seemed misshapen giants whose arms grew from our waists, whose hair had been dyed in blood, and whose huge red-smeared mouths were stretching open ready to tear men into mangled corpses. Even a civilized man would have started with fear at first sight of us. And we believed that such low-brained creatures as the tailed Uginas would take us for real and deadly fiends.

Making sure that the frameworks fitted well over our shoulders and that the holes cut for our eyes would not slip aside and leave us blinded, we took them off again and emptied our canoe. After hiding our equipment where nothing could disturb it while we were away, we ate and smoked.

"Our arms are stained red from that dye," I said.

"They will be more red before we return," Pedro answered. And he spoke truth.

No rain was falling, but the light was poor. This suited us well. Carrying with us only those weird false bodies, full cartridge-belts, and our weapons, we slipped the canoe down the creek to the river, crossed over, and stole along up the northern bank until we reached that little inlet where we had shot the first Ugina. A short scouting trip proved that this time no enemy lurked there. So we bound on our terrible masks, looked again at our rifles to make sure they were full, and took the trail toward the lair of the tailed men.

We soon found that, though our towering masks were not heavy, they were awkward and uncomfortable. Before long we were dripping with sweat, and we had to walk in a stooping posture and step carefully to keep our false heads from butting against low branches.

But we knew that unless the Uginas lived in different fashion from all other tribes their village would be in a cleared space, and there we could stand erect. We knew, too, that they probably would be dozing now, for it was midday and the muggy air was sweltering hot. Our plan of attack was very simple — to walk in among them and start shooting.

At the place where we had hidden yesterday and fought the four men led by the monkey, we found signs that other men had been there since we left. The bush was beaten aside and broken, and fresh footmarks showed in spots where the soil was soft. Though we stayed in the path, we knew the bodies which we had thrown aside had been found and taken away.

"We had best go slowly," I advised, "or we may fall into a trap. They must be hunting us, now that they have found those bodies."

But he snorted.

"You forget that we are demons," he objected. "Who ever heard of a demon slinking along cautiously? We must go in with a roar. If a few lurk in ambush, they will run when they see us. And I do not believe they are waiting for us — they have no reason to expect us to return, and it is so hot now that they are probably sleeping in their dens."

He was not wrong. We saw no man until we opened our fight. Abruptly the jungle ended and we emerged into a clearing. Trees grew there, but they were few and large and scattered, and the smaller growth had been hacked or burned away. We saw no houses of any kind. Surprised by this, we halted.

Then out rang a scream, so near us that we jumped. From the base of a huge tree close at hand sprang a naked figure which ran shrieking down the open space. We threw up our rifles, but did not shoot; for the long hair flying out behind that form showed it was a woman. Later I remembered that she was not a tailed creature. Now we glanced at the place whence she had jumped, and saw that it was a tangle of sticks with a door-like hole in it.

Out through that hole scrambled two other figures. One was a big *coaita*, which looked at us and then fled up into the tree. The other was a squat, scared-looking beast-man who rose to his knees and threw a spear at us. Pedro's rifle barked, and the Ugina flopped on his face.

Then we saw the others. From the butts of those big trees they came popping out like ants. The woman was still running, still screaming, and as they saw us they too began to jabber and yell. In our deepest tones we roared an answer. Then, our guns spitting death, we advanced on them.

For a moment it seemed that they would run for the jungle. I hoped they would stand and fight, for I would dislike to shoot even such beasts as these in the back. But I need not have troubled about that. They ran only to get weapons. If they had known we were merely men they probably would have swarmed on us. As it was, they bunched around their trees and shot arrows and threw small spears, fighting as a beast fights — because he is too much scared to do anything else.

We stopped before we came too close, bellowing as fiendishly as we could and moving from side to side while we reloaded our guns. Arrows fell around us, some striking fire-charred stumps and bouncing off, some slithering through the grass, some chunking down into pools of water. Many of these might have hit us if we had stood still, but by our irregular movements to the side we evaded most of them. Besides, the Uginas were shooting and throwing with the hurried aim of fear, and their spears fell short and their arrows flew high. No doubt those who took any aim at all shot for those terrifying false heads of ours. At any rate, the few missiles which hit us went into the hollow framework of our masks, leaving our own heads and bodies untouched.

Shooting swiftly but carefully, we poured another magazineful of lead into a knot of snarling savages around the butt of the nearest tree. Some yelped as they fell. Others dropped silently. One or two squirmed on the ground, then lay still. The note of terror in the yells of those still standing became sharper. And when, our guns once more emptied, we began advancing toward them as we reloaded, panic swept them into howling flight.

A couple of dropping arrows had caught in my shirt and stuck there, scraping my skin but doing no harm. From our false heads and shoulders several other arrows protruded. And the Uginas, seeing this and finding that we showed no signs of hurt, must have believed it was impossible to kill or even wound us. Yelling hoarsely, they turned and ran for the bush.

But it was only the first tree that was deserted. From the other butts more Uginas ran out and joined those seeking cover, but these seemed to be mostly women and children — or, perhaps, monkeys. The men stayed, bunching together and sending a few more arrows at us. One of these, falling slant-wise, pierced my left foot.

I was glad then that those arrows had no barbs, for it was easy to pull out that one and throw it aside. I tried to do this carelessly, as if it did not hurt. But I must have shown some sign of pain — perhaps I had jumped when the shaft struck me — for the shouts grew louder and arrows came more thickly again. We paid no attention to these, moving on as if we scorned them until we came into the shelter of the big aban-doned tree.

There, partly covered by the huge trunk, we shot steadily into the knots of savages around the other trees. We divided these between us, Pedro taking those to the left while I attacked those to the right. And now we did not concentrate on one spot alone, but shifted our fire from butt to butt, striking men down here and there so rapidly that it must have seemed we were killing the whole tribe at once. Yet the Uginas fought on, though their fight seemed to be weakening and their noise died down.

If they had known enough to keep quiet we might have died suddenly. Nothing had threatened our backs, and our enemies were in front, so that we never glanced behind. But now new cries began to come from the line of trees, and we saw the beast-men looking beyond us. Wheeling, we found several stealthy forms crawling up on us among the stumps.

They were on hands and knees, partly hidden by stumps and grass, but we could see their heads well enough. Into two of those heads I sent bullets. Then my hammer snapped down without an explosion. Dropping the empty gun, I yanked my machete and jumped at the rest of them.

But they did not wait. Their only weapons were short spears, and as we bore down on them they rose, threw their weapons, screeched, and ran for their lives. One just ahead of me fell over a stump, and another tripped over his outflung arms. I got both of them with slashing blows across the back of the neck. Pedro, too, caught one of the fleeing creatures and killed him, and later I found that he had shot another as he charged at them. Only two were left, and they went bounding away, howling fearfully.

We turned back, sweeping the line of trees with our eyes to see whether other Uginas meant to rush us. But none did. Instead, more were sneaking for the bush.

"My cartridges are running low," said Pedro, as we reloaded. "Let us advance on them before we use up all our bullets."

With our deepest yells we left our tree and advanced at a trot. The beast-men could stand no longer. A few sprang out from each butt and fled. The rest wavered an instant and followed. Halting, we shot fast and straight, downing several more of them. Then the clearing was empty.

"Now that they have quit, they will keep on running until they think themselves safe," said Pedro. "To help them on their way I will scream a little."

And scream he did, horrible wailing screams that sounded as if some wounded man were being torn apart and devoured by those yellow teeth in our false faces. They made me cold, even though I knew who made them and why. And the fear-ridden fugitives must have fled deep into the bush on hearing them, for we saw none of them again.

Roaring and screaming by turns, we passed along the line of big trees, seeking any living thing that might remain. We found only two. In the doorway of one of the miserable hovels built between the root-buttresses we spied a wounded savage. As we stepped toward him he gave one snarl of terror, lifted a spear, and plunged it into his own heart. In another hut we found a sick coaita monkey which squatted and watched us without moving. Nothing else was under those trees except bodies.

Some of the dead men, we noticed, had no tails. But, tailed or tailless, all had the same brute faces. We paid little attention to them, except to make sure they were dead and could not kill us from behind. When we reached the end of the open space we stopped yelling and stood looking at each other.

Pedro's mask was pierced in several places, and one arrow jutted out only a few inches from his eyes.

"Are you hit?" I asked.

"No. This arrow scraped my head and may have torn my scalp, but it is nothing. Your foot wound is much worse than that. Let us finish our work and go."

Out from a pocket he drew a small package carefully wrapped in rubber, and from this he produced matches. We pulled a few dry sticks from inside the stinking hut nearest us and set fire to them. Soon we had all the shelters around that tree going up in smoke. Then we passed back as we had come, firing the filthy hovels until each tree was ringed with flame.

After leaving the tree where we had made most of our fight, we stopped a moment to look down at the bodies of those whom we had shot while they were creeping up on us from behind. They lay face down, and they were tailless and had long hair.

"Nossa Senhora!" exclaimed Pedro. "They are women!"

I shoved one over with my foot. It was true. The other two whom we had shot were women also. Their faces were as vile and their bodies as scraggy as those of the men, but women they were. Wondering whether the others also had been females, we went on and looked at the three whom we had killed with our machetes. We found them to be men.

"That explains it," nodded Pedro. "I wondered how they dared to come so near us. The women were the leaders. Perhaps we had killed their mates. The men had sense enough to fear us, but a woman crazed with fury loses all fear and all sense. I am glad we did not fall alive into their hands."

Remembering the scarred body of Luis Pitta and looking into the faces of those she-devils, I grunted agreement.

We left them there and went our way. At the edge of the bush, where the faint trail began, we turned and looked back. The dismal clearing, with its blackened stumps and its few gaunt trees, now was blue with low-crawling clouds of smoke through which glared the belts of flame eating up the habitations of the *bichos do mata*. Around those fires, we knew, lay the bullet-torn corpses of many tailed creatures who never again would torture a prisoner. The jungle around us was empty and silent, and the only sound was the sullen crackle of the fires. We had come as demons to fight demons, and we left behind us a death-strewn hell. Our work was done.

Back along the vague path we passed to the river. There we cut off our monstrous disguises, pitched them into the canoe, and breathed deep of the damp air.

"Luis, old comrade, we have done our best for you," Pedro said soberly. "So far as two men could destroy these fiends we have destroyed them; and into the others we have put fear that will abide. Now sleep in peace, Luis *meo*."

And we got into the canoe and paddled away toward the creek where our supplies were hidden.

THE TRUMPETER

DEOS PADRE! Hear that war-horn!

Hand me your field glasses quickly, *senhor*! Something is happening over there on the southern bank of the river, and I can not see it plainly. If it is an attack there will be rifle shots, unless the settlers are overpowered at once. Listen!

Ah, it is nothing. Only a celebration. I can see Indians with great false heads doing a devil-dance before the house of some planter, who stands there with his woman and laughs. Probably he is their *patrao*, and has given them a holiday to keep them in good humor.

If the harsh blast of that *turé* had not struck my ear so suddenly I might have realized that it was blown only in merry-making, for the days when hordes of bloody *barbaros* attacked settlers here on the Amazon are long past. Past, I mean, on the Amazon itself. Up the great wild rivers which flow in from the south there are still plenty of savage killers, and we Brazilians who rove the unknown jungle know well what the *turé* means. It is the voice of death.

You can not blame me, then, for leaping up so suddenly just now. That jarring note made me forget for an instant that I was safe on the deck of a steamer instead of back in the wilderness of the Javary. Moreover, it is not many months since I heard the *turé* blown in deadly earnest, and I have not forgotten what followed.

Certainly, *senhor*, I will tell you the story if you care to hear it. Wait a moment until I make another cigarette. The one which I was smoking must have dropped overboard when I sprang up.

Now this thing of which I speak came about while the waters of the great yearly flood were sweeping over the lowlands of the Javary region, where I was a rubber-worker for Coronel Nunes. As you know, there are really two floods each year here on the upper Amazon, but only one of these is the great rise. Then the water overwhelms all except the highest places, and our work in the swampy forests must stop until it drains away to the far-off ocean. And it was at this time that I met the Trumpeter.

With my comrade, Pedro Andrada, I had paddled southward through flooded channels to the upper reaches of the river Jurua. We were in no hurry, for we thought there would be nothing to do when we should reach our journey's end. But two days after leaving the river, as we were looking about among the half-drowned trees for a solid spot fit to sleep on that night, Pedro spoke in a tone of concern.

"Lourenço, we had best paddle a little harder tomorrow. The *enchente* has ended and the *vasante* has set in."

As he said, the great rise had reached its height. On the trees around us were wet stains showing that it was beginning to ebb. From now on the waters would drop steadily until they were fifty feet or more below their present level. We had never traveled on this *furo* before, knew nothing of its depth ahead of us, and were not even sure that it ran all the way to the Javary region. So, though we did not worry, we knew it would be well to waste no time and take no chance of finding ourselves stranded in unknown country.

When we found firm land and went ashore to sling our hammocks I nicked a tree with my machete, making a mark just at the waterline. The next morning that mark was more than the width of my hand above the surface. And all that day, as we swung on homeward, we saw the wet stains lengthen on the big trunks towering around us and knew we were sinking toward the thick bush submerged far below. So we talked little, ate without delay, and kept going until darkness was near. When we landed again we were tired.

"A good day's work, comrade," Pedro said. "I do not know where we are, but we are nearer to the Javary than last night. It is good that the dull skies of the rainy time have gone and the sun shines steadily. Now we can tell better which way we are traveling."

"Yes," I agreed. "And now that the sunny *verao* has come we should hear birds calling more often. This country has been too still to suit me. I should like to hear the sweet song of the *realejo* — the organ-bird — or the long piping of that fifer, the *uira-mimbeu*."

Just then, as if in answer to my wish, a long clear call came floating through the forest. It died so softly that it seemed to hang in the air when we could not hear it more. As we stared at each other it came again. Three times in all it sounded, neither rising nor falling — just the one note, long and slow. Then we heard nothing further.

"That is not a fifer, and it certainly is not the *realejo*," said Pedro. "It must be a trumpeter. You have heard that bird, of course."

I nodded. I had not only heard it, but I had seen it. The trumpeter is that blackish bird which the Peruvians call *trom-petero* — a creature about the size of a big hen, but with longer legs and neck. It is a fast runner but a poor flyer, and the Indians sometimes tame it. I had known one *caboclo* who kept such a bird, and when it died I carefully cut it open to see how it made its trumpeting cry. I found that its windpipe was very long, running down under the skin almost to the tail, then doubling around and rising again to the chest, where it went inside the breastbone to the throat.

The sound which had just come to us was much like the call of that bird I had known, and yet it did not seem quite the same. If I had heard it anywhere else I should have said it was made by a man with a horn. But here in this desolate region such a thing seemed not possible, unless the man were an Indian; and a blast from an Indian trumpet would never have such smooth sweetness.

"Yes, it must be the trumpet bird," I agreed. "If it would only stay where it is until tomorrow we might see it, for it is over to the westward. But probably we shall not even hear it again."

I was wrong. We were to hear it once more that day, and several times in the days to come.

WE BUILT a little fire, ate, got into our hammocks, and lay

back smoking. Around us it was quite dim; but high up overhead, where were scattered openings in the tangled roof of
branches, the sunshine still glinted. Then suddenly it was
gone. Darkness swallowed everything but our tiny fire.

With the passing of the sun the distant trumpeter spoke
again. And this time the sound was not one unchanging call.
Slowly, sweetly, it rose and fell, going higher on each long note,
quivering on the highest, and then sinking to the one on which
it had begun. There it died away. And we lay there silent,
senhores, silent with surprise, and silent with a feeling of loneliness and sadness which that strain left in our hearts.

At last Pedro spoke.

"That is no bird, Lourenço. It is no wild man of the bush,
either. Then what can it be?"

"I do not know," I said. "Some things happen in the jungle
which can not be explained. But listen. Perhaps it will come
again."

We listened long, but heard only the usual night sounds.
After a time these noises blurred and faded into nothing. I
slept.

MORNING BROUGHT the trumpet call again. While we were
making our coffee we stiffened into listening. The sound was
the same one we had first heard — three slow notes in the
same tone. But somehow it seemed to us that this time they
were weaker than before, and that in them was a note of
despair.

We said no word. We only looked at each other. But we
hastened our meal, rolled up our hammocks speedily, and paddled away with swift strokes. As we went we searched the
jungle with sharp glances. The *furo* was leading us straight
toward the place whence those sounds must have come.

After a time we halted. We had heard nothing more, nor
seen anything alive. Yet we knew we must be near the spot we
sought.

"It can not be a bird or a beast," said Pedro. "If it has a body
it can be nothing but a man." Then, breathing deep, he roared

out the call we give in our own region when approaching a house —

"*O da casa!*"

For a moment no answer came. We heard only the slight sucking sound of water around the tree trunks. Then, not far away to our left, the trumpeter answered. And now the notes were not long and slow. They were quick, urgent, discordant — as if a man were blowing a horn in a frenzy of hope and fear lest we go past and leave him.

We yelled together, swung our dugout, and passed in among the trees toward the noise. Soon we found land. We called again, but no voice answered. Several small sounds came to us, though, and we stepped ashore and moved toward them.

Suddenly we stopped, staring at the ground.

A man was dragging himself along toward us. His head hung down so that we could not see his face — only a thick mass of long blond hair. He moved on both hands and one knee. The other leg dragged behind him as if useless. At each forward lift of his knee he grunted as if the movement cost him a mighty effort.

"Stop, friend," I said quietly. "We are here."

He stopped. His arms quivered under him, then suddenly bent and let him slump down. But as we dropped on our knees beside him he turned his head and, lying quiet, peered up at us. We looked into blue eyes gleaming in a tanned face overgrown with short yellow beard. The face looked drawn and pinched.

"Howdy!" he said hoarsely. "Got any grub?"

"We have plenty of food, *senhor*," Pedro said. "Have you hunger?"

"You said it. That's all I've got — hunger and a busted leg. For the love of God, slip me some eats!"

"*Por amor de Deos*, we will do so," smiled Pedro. "Lie still." And he arose and strode back to our canoe.

While he was gone I looked the man over more deliberately. His speech and his dress — pocketed shirt, khaki breeches, knee boots, web belt and flat pistol — showed him to be American. The clothing was not so badly worn and stained as it would be if he had been long in the bush. The right leg was unbooted, and rough splints were tied to it below the knee. Glancing again at his face, I saw that his teeth were set and the sweat of pain was on his forehead.

"You have hurt that broken leg by your crawling," I said. "Why did you not lie still and let us come to you?"

"Because that would be the sensible thing to do." His voice was weak, but he grinned gamely. "I never show any sense. If I did I wouldn't be here at all. Besides, I've been on my back for a week, and I've learned what it is to be lonesome."

"What! You have been lying here a week?"

"Yep. Not here, but back in my tent."

Before we could talk more, Pedro came hurrying back with a gourd of *chibeh*. At sight of it the man tried to scramble up, but groaned and sank back. I scolded him, telling him to keep quiet. Then we fed him.

It was not until the gourd was empty that I thought to ask him how long he had been without food. He said it was three days. Then I wished we had fed him more sparingly at first. But since chibeh is only a mush of *farinha* and water, I decided that it would not hurt him. This proved true.

"Now if I only had a bucket of coffee and a smoke I'd be all set," said the stranger. "Got a cigarette on you, buddy?"

I quickly made a cigarette for him, and we promised him coffee as soon as we could make it. But first we decided to take him back to his tent and make him more comfortable. So, when he had finished his smoke, we lifted him as gently as possible and carried him back through the bush.

The distance was short, but the traveling was not easy, and in spite of our care we knew we must be hurting his bad leg. Yet he made no sound. Keeping his teeth locked, he stared straight upward until we brought him to his camp.

Beside a huge *itauba* tree we found his little tent. Inside this his hammock hung. On the ground lay his mosquito net. We laid him down easily and picked up the net to drape it over him again. On the earth under the net we found a battered bugle.

"So it was this we heard, not a bird," I said, picking it up and glancing it over. "At first we thought you were a trumpeter."

He lay quiet a few minutes, his teeth still set. Then, as the pain in his leg grew easier, his jaws unlocked and he grinned in a tight-lipped way.

"I am," he said. "Been fooling with tin horns since I was a kid. Maybe it's my name that makes me that way — Horner. Folks used to call me Little Jack Horner, though my first name really is Jerome. How about that coffee, buddies?"

"You shall have it," I promised. We left him there and returned to our canoe, where we got our coffee and other things and started back.

"A brave fellow, Lourenço," said Pedro, as we neared the tent. "No fuss, no groan or whine, though he is broken and starved and has been alone with no help in sight. *Por Deos!* Look there!"

On the ground were jaguar tracks. They were more than tracks — they made a path, showing that the beast had circled for hours around the tent. The marks seemed fresh.

"You were not alone last night, *senhor*," I said, entering the little cloth house.

"Huh? Oh, you mean the big cat. Sure, he did sentry-go around here most of the night. He wouldn't come in, so I kept still and let him prowl."

"Your tent saved your life," Pedro told him. "He could smell you, but he did not know he could force his way through these strange cloth walls. If he had —"

"If he had I'd have eaten him," Horner cut in. "Did you bring the coffee?"

We made the coffee, and we made it strong. The hot black liquid gave him new vigor. When he had swallowed all he could hold he gave a long sigh.

"Oh boy!" he said. "That's better than a bushel of that sawdust you fed me. How do you guys live on that *farinha* stuff, anyhow? It takes pork and beans or ham and eggs to put hair on a fellow's chest. Now say, while I'm feeling husky I wish you'd straighten out my leg. It feels twisted."

It was twisted. Working carefully, we reset the broken bone as well as we could and bound new splints on it. As before, he made no sound. When the work was done he calmly asked for another smoke. And then, with the cigarette glowing, he told how he had come there.

HE HAD been a soldier of your United States in the great war in Europe. When the war ended and he returned to his own country, he said, he made the same mistake that many other released soldiers made — he lingered in the vast city of Nova York, quickly spent all his money, and then found himself unable to get work. So, when a chance to make money came unexpectedly to him, he grasped it eagerly.

While he was sitting with other penniless soldiers in a place called Union Square, a tall bony man with strange eyes passed by several times, looking sharply at him and his mates. Then this man asked him and four others to come with him. Being curious, they did so. He led them to a big hotel some distance away, took them to his room, and there made them an odd offer.

He wanted trusty and fearless men to go with him into South America and help him seek something of which he would tell them later on. They would be handsomely paid, and if he found what he sought they would all be made quite rich. There might be danger, he said, but they would be well armed, and the reward would be worth any risk. He had already obtained the promises of other war veterans to go, and he intended to get more. All they had to do was to come along, obey orders, ask no questions, and take their chances of success.

With nothing to lose except their lives, all five of them accepted. Soon afterward they sailed southward with more than a dozen other soldiers whom the bony man had got in the same way. They came up the Amazon and turned into a smaller river, where Indian paddlers in long canoes carried them southward for many days. And in all this time their queer leader never told them where they went or why.

He had been acting oddly for some time, and naturally the men had been talking much among themselves. Now at last they demanded the reason for this long journey into dismal and flooded jungle. Still they got no satisfaction. They were told that they would soon know, but the time had not yet come. Quarreling followed.

The men said they would go no farther. Finding them determined, the bony man suddenly began to rave and shriek. He screamed that he was somebody named Midas, and that he could turn all things to gold by touching them. Then he jerked out a revolver and began shooting at the men.

His bullets killed two soldiers before they downed him. Somebody fired back, and he toppled overboard and never came up again.

After that the men disputed among themselves over what they should do now. None of them had a clear idea as to where they were. Some were for going back as they had come, while others believed that by keeping on they would soon reach the Andes and could then cross the mountains and so reach the western ocean. Before they could settle the question their paddlers brought them to a small Indian settlement where the people gave them welcome. And since all were tired of so much boat travel, they agreed to stay at that place for a few days while they rested and determined what should be done next.

Two days of this were enough for Horner. In spite of much argument, his mates could not yet agree, and he grew too restless to stay idle any longer. So, quietly taking a small canoe, a tent, a little food, his guns and his bugle, he slipped away by himself on an exploring trip to the eastward.

He did not intend to desert his comrades, but only to see what he might see and then return. But he found it so pleasant to be alone that he traveled onward for five days before he tired of it and decided to turn back. Then he became confused among some winding waterways, and before he could find the right one again he met more misfortune. He lost his canoe and broke a leg.

The boat drifted away in the night. While seeking it, he tripped among some vines and snapped his leg over a projecting tree root. Then he could do nothing but crawl back to his tent, lie there, and blow his bugle in the hope that some of his comrades might seek him.

He knew well that his chance of rescue was slight, for he had left the settlement without telling anyone where or why he was going, and the other men probably would think he had gone along the river. And yesterday, he said, his courage had almost failed.

"It's the loneliness that gets you," he added. "Being hungry and busted up is no joke, but knowing that you've got less than one chance in a million of coming through is a lot worse. I've lain out in No Man's Land for two nights and a day, with five shrapnel holes in me and all hell rip-roaring around, and I thought I was out of luck. But I'd rather be there than here any time. A fellow has lots of company out there. Last night I got so down in the mouth I blew taps over myself."

Seeing that we did not quite understand, he lifted the trumpet which we had laid beside him and blew the sad, sweet song we had heard at sunset.

"That's Taps," he explained. "They blow it over dead soldiers. I didn't know but I might go west before morning, so I did the honors beforehand."

"But how could you go west without a canoe, *senhor?*" I asked.

He laughed, and explained that by "going west" he meant dying. So then I told him he was going west indeed, but not as he had thought.

Whether we should be able to find the Indian town over to the west we did not know; but if we did not find it, I told him, we would carry him with us all the way northwestward to our own country, where our old *coronel* would do everything possible for him. And since it was best for all of us that we lose no time, we would get underway at once.

Carrying him and his hammock together to the canoe, we left him there while we took down his tent. On our return we folded the canvas to make a bed in the bottom of the boat, stowed our supplies differently, and helped him in. When he was comfortable he gave a long yawn.

"Guess I'll rip off a few yards of sleep," he said. "I'm about all in. Haven't had a real solid snooze since I cracked my shin." His eyes closed.

After we had paddled a while Pedro said:

"He spoke truth when he said he would rip off his sleep. Hear him snore!"

I grinned, for the blond trumpeter certainly was a noisy sleeper. But as I thought of the long black nights of pain and hunger and hopelessness that lay behind him his snorts and gurgles did not seem funny at all. Indeed, I marveled that he had not gone mad or ended his torment with one of his bullets.

All the rest of the day he slept while we paddled on. Near night, as we were seeking a sleeping place, he opened his eyes and blinked at us, the canoe, and the trees.

"Aw shucks!" he grunted. "I'm back here again!"

"Where have you been, Senhor Trumpeter?" laughed Pedro.

"I was back home, playing ball and cussing the umpire because he called me out when I never even offered to swing. Home was never like this. I'll say not! Say, when do we eat?"

"As soon as we land," I told him. "Are you ready to eat more of our sawdust?"

"I'll eat anything, buddy. If you don't get ashore pretty quick I'll start chewing your leg."

Then, lifting his bugle, he blew a loud, lively air, much different from anything we had heard before.

"That's reveille," he said. "It means 'wake up — snap into it.' Put a hop on your stroke and land me before I get violent."

"Calm yourself and spare my leg awhile longer, and we all shall eat," I promised. "But I would not blow that trumpet again, *senhor*, until we reach some place where we know we are more safe. We are few, and it would not be well to let any savage Indians know we are here. Did you blow a bugle in the war?"

"Nope. Not so anybody could hear it. I knew all those army calls before any war came along. Then I wanted to fight, and the only way you can be sure of fighting these days is to make the personnel sharks think you don't know anything."

"How is that?" I wondered.

"If you can do anything they try to make you do it in the army. If you're a mechanic they keep you tinkering on bum motors. If you're a newspaper man they make you a censor. If you know a shirt from a sock they shove you into quartermaster work. If you're a cop they make you an M.P. — and then you're popular, I guess not!

"It's the same way all along the line. So when my turn came I didn't know a thing. If they'd learned I could blow a horn they might have made me a bandmaster or something. But seeing I was dead from the neck up, they gave me a gun and let me in on the big show."

This seemed very queer to us, for we had always thought that in an army everybody was expected to fight. He grinned as he talked, and it may be that he did not mean just what he said. But we spoke no more of the matter, for then we spied a good camping spot and went ashore. And after eating and smoking, we all slept soundly.

THE NEXT day Horner found himself. Without realizing it, we strayed off the *furo* into another channel, along which we paddled for some distance before the slant of the sun-thrown shadows warned us that we were off our course. Then, as we slowed and told each other we must go back, the Trumpeter spied an oddly bent tree leaning out over the water ahead.

"Say, this is the way I came!" he told us. "I know that tree. There was a big snake on it. I shot him off, and he kicked up such a riot he nearly upset me. Gee, he was a regular whale! Keep on going, and you'll hit the burg where the rest of my gang hangs out."

So we kept on, and as we went he recognized other things along the way.

Two days later we came out into a rather large river flowing northeastward. And there our passenger blew again that dancing reveille tune.

"Home again!" he laughed, when the last note had pealed away through the jungle. "Injun Town is only about half a mile upstream, and the rough old tough old bunch is waiting for us up there. Snap into it, buddies!"

We snapped into it. We knew how eager he was to meet his comrades again, and it had been some time since we ourselves had talked with white men. So we went upstream fast.

The Trumpeter was much stronger now after the long sleeps and hearty meals of the past few days, and as we surged on up the river he sat leaning forward, grinning and waiting for a sight of his mates. But as we swung around a bend his smile faded and his jaw dropped.

A little way ahead, under tall trees where little bush grew, a number of Indians were standing at the water's edge. Several small canoes also were there. But we saw no large boat nor any white men.

"Hell's bells!" groaned Homer. "The gang's gone!"

It was so. Only the Indians waited for us there. They held weapons, and at first they seemed unfriendly. But when we came near and they saw Horner clearly they grinned at him, and as Pedro and I stepped out on shore they greeted us cordially.

A tall, grave man who seemed to be chief spoke in a Tupi tongue, saying they were glad to see again the blower of the horn, and that they had thought him gone forever. I explained why he had left them and why we now came with him, and asked where the other white men were. He said they had gone two days after Horner disappeared; that they believed he had gone up the river, and so they had decided to go that way also. He added that he was sorry to know the blower of the horn had hurt himself, but that a broken bone would soon mend, and all of us were welcome to his village.

"When you guys get through making a noise with your mouths maybe you'll give me the lowdown," said the Trumpeter. "It don't make sense to me."

So I said it all over to him, and asked how he and his fellow soldiers had been able to talk with these people if they knew no Tupi. He said the talking had been done through one of their canoemen. The thought came to me that if he could not speak their tongue he might find it hard to get along with them after we left, and that we had best take him on with us. But I said nothing of this just then. We helped him out and followed the Indians.

They led us only a short distance back from the water, and then we found ourselves in a small town of little low houses. The chief took us to one of these, ordered a man and woman living in it to go elsewhere, and told us it was ours. Then he went away, and his men with him. But before he left us he looked shrewdly at our guns and asked whether we could make them speak many times.

Of course we told him yes, we could make them spit death at a whole tribe. This was not true, for we had used up many of our cartridges in a fight with some beastly *barbaros* back on the Jurua, and now we had not a great number left. But it is not wise to let Indians think you to be weak, even though they are friendly; so we were prompt in our answer. He said it was well.

After we put up our hammocks I told the Trumpeter he had better come on to the Javary with us. Before this he had been one of a score of fighting men, I pointed out, but after we went he would be alone among these Indians, and perhaps he would not be so well-treated as before. So, though the journey to the Javary might be hard, he might come out better in the end than by staying here. But he only laughed.

"Oh, they're good skates," he said. "They wouldn't pull anything raw. You don't know 'em as well as I do."

"Perhaps not," Pedro answered him. "But we have ranged the bush far more than you, *senhor*, and my comrade here speaks sense. It takes more than a few days to know Indians well; and the ways of Indians toward twenty strong white men and toward one broken white man may not be the same. And these people came to meet us with weapons and their leader just asked us how strong our guns are. True, they seem peaceable, but — you had best go on with us."

"But I tell you they're all right," he insisted. "They're only a bunch of hicks, and they don't want trouble with anybody. They raise crops and kids and take it easy, and they're regular fellows. Walk around and look 'em over. Me, I like 'em fine."

STILL RATHER doubtful, we did walk around and look over the place and the people. And we found that it was as he said: the Indians here seemed to be quiet and honest, happy in the peace of their town and content to toil on the plantations beyond it, where the trees had been thinned to let the crops grow. Still, we noticed that here and there were men with weapons, watching the women work and occasionally scanning the thick bush beyond.

Stopping beside one of these armed men, we talked for a time about hunting and such things, and then asked why he and his mates stood guard in this way. In a quiet, respectful manner he replied that they watched lest the place be attacked. And when we asked further about this, he said they had heard that a band of fierce savages was somewhere in the region round about.

Who the bad men were he did not know, nor whether they would come this way. This flood season was not the time for such attacks, he said, for usually those roving bands of warriors were not boatmen and so were more likely to come at the time of low water; but of course one could never know when creatures of that sort would take it into their heads to run wild and kill. He spoke of them as if they were jaguars or other beasts — dangerous animals against which his people must guard themselves but which they considered unworthy of any respect.

Thinking this over, I saw why the chief had asked about the strength of our guns. I thought, too, that this might be one reason why we were so welcome here — three men with rifles would be a great help to him if an attack should come, even though one of us was crippled. I wondered, too, why he had not planned to keep the other Americans here until he knew whether the *barbaros* were coming this way. So I asked the guard whether they had warned the white men about these savages before they left.

He said no. They themselves had not heard of the wild men until yesterday, he said, and the white men then had been gone for days. He added that he hoped the whites would meet the marauders somewhere up the river, because then there would be a fight, and of course the men with guns would kill all those brutes.

I had some doubt about this, for I thought the soldiers would find fighting in thick jungle to be far different from what they had been accustomed to in Europe. But I told him the white men would surely kill every one of the savages if they met them. Then we went back to Horner, much better satisfied with these people than we had been at first.

"Sure, I knew you'd like these brown boys after you got their range," said the Trumpeter, when we told him we had changed our ideas. "When you thought they were sneaks you were overshooting. I'm satisfied to stay here until I'm ready to go down river. So you guys needn't worry about me, and if you want to move on don't let me block you."

We urged him again to come with us, but he flatly refused. Then we went to the chief and asked him whether he had any real reason to expect an attack. He seemed a little surprised that we had learned of this; but he said there was nothing to show that their enemies were coming here, and his men were watching only because they always did so when they heard that bad men were near. So, since the blond American would not go with us, and since we could not dally here long, we decided to continue our homeward journey the next day.

BUT THE next day brought squalls. Soon after our morning meal, while we were talking with Horner and the chief and preparing to go, the sunlight was blotted out. Thunder crashed and sheets of lightning dazzled us. A flood of rain fell, driven slantwise by a fierce wind. And when the storm had passed, the chief advised us to stay over for another day.

He said such sudden storms were not uncommon here at this time of year, and that a squall so early in the day would be followed by others. If we went on now we should meet worse weather before long, he told us, and if we were not swamped by some sudden blast of wind we should at least sleep wet and uncomfortable that night. He added that the rains today would make the waters rise, so that we should gain rather than lose by waiting. So why not remain here and be comfortable and visit his people, whom we might never see again?

This sounded sensible, and we were pleased by his honest way of speaking. So we decided to stay until the next morning, and then start early. And we were glad we tarried.

For one thing, we found that he knew the weather. More squalls did come, and they were heavy. Besides this, the people were agreeable companions, and they brought us fresh food, which was a welcome change from the rations we had recently been eating. So, between watching the lightning, eating huge meals, listening to the Trumpeter's bugle, and talking with the chief and others, we spent the day very pleasantly.

While we talked we cleaned our rifles, which had grown rusty. The chief was much interested in these weapons, partly because he knew little about them and partly because Pedro's gun and mine were different from that of Horner. Ours were the American repeating rifles generally used in our region, with the lever behind the trigger and a bore of .44 caliber. The Trumpeter's gun also would repeat, but it looked much different and its action was not the same. The wood under the barrel ran almost to the muzzle, and it was cocked not by a lever but by a sort of handle on the bolt. The bore was much smaller than ours, but Horner insisted that the power of his gun was far greater than that of our big-bulleted weapons. We did not believe him until he told us his was an army rifle. Then we knew it must be high-powered.

The bony man who led him and his comrades here, he said, had managed to get enough of these rifles to arm every man in the party, as well as the flat pistols to which they were accustomed. He added that besides these guns he had something more deadly than any bullet. Then, twitching from his belt a long knife which we had taken for a sort of machete, he snapped it onto the gun under the muzzle.

"That's the real killer," he said. "A guy can get all shot up and still live, but when you slide this little old toothpick into a man he's through. Hot lead is all right, but the cold steel is the stuff that mops 'em up."

Dropping the blade into a line with my stomach, he made a

playful jab upward. I fell over my own feet and knocked Pedro down in dodging away from it. Then Horner chuckled, the chief grinned, and I laughed rather foolishly.

"Don't feel very good to see that thing start for your lunch basket, does it, even though I'm only a one-legged crip sitting down?" asked the blond man. "Then figure out how Fritz felt when he saw hundreds of 'em coming over. He sure made himself AWOL, and then some."

After he explained what AWOL meant, I said I did not blame Fritz for going somewhere else without orders. I added that in this thick jungle of ours such a weapon was likely to be more useful in a fight than a far-shooting gun. His answer disturbed me a little.

"Yep, and if I hook up with any tough nuts before I hit the Amazon I may have to use it. The gang carried off all the ammunition with them, and all I've got left is two clips for the rifle and one for the pistol. But when I get my legs under me again I can show anybody that wants a row some wicked bayonet stuff."

Pedro and I glanced at each other, but said nothing. Our cartridges would not fit his gun, so that even if we could have spared any they would have been useless to him. We could do nothing to help him — or so we thought. Yet before we were many hours older we were to help him much.

With one final ripping squall the day ended. Before the rain stopped the light had gone. A moonless night followed. As we intended to start early the next day, we soon got into our hammocks. Before we slept the Trumpeter blew again, loud and clear, that song of Taps.

"Why do you do that, *senhor?*" asked Pedro. "There are no dead soldiers here."

"Right. But Taps isn't just a dead man's tune. It means 'good night — sleep tight — all's well.' I'm just saying good night to that bunch of gorillas that beat it upstream while I was away. They can't hear it, but they're getting ready to snooze now somewhere up there, and maybe they're thinking about me."

Though he spoke lightly, we could see that his heart was

lonely for the companionship of those "gorillas." We said no more. Soon we slept.

BEFORE DAYBREAK Pedro and I awoke and arose. Around us it was very dark, but not silent. Horner was trumpeting through his nose, and from other little huts near by the snores of sleeping Indians came back like echoes. Outside we could see nothing but the vague loom of the jungle against the star-spattered sky. So, since it was too dark to take down our hammocks, we sat down in them again and smoked, waiting for the shadows to lift.

Soon a wan light dawned on the clearing. The trees became trees instead of a black blot. The sun was not up, and a thin mist blurred the air, but day had come. We snapped our cigarette butts through the doorway, and stood up.

Then came war. A long harsh trumpet-blast tore across the gurgling chorus of snores. A roar of yelling voices followed. Out from the edge of the jungle sprang naked warriors. Through the mist they came bounding toward the huts, howling and brandishing spears and clubs and bows. Other cries answered them: shouts of men springing awake, screams of women terrified by that awful trumpeting — the deadly blare of the *turé*, war-horn of brutal murderers.

We swooped up our guns, sprang outside, opened fire. The leaping brutes nearest us swerved and fell. Others screeched sharply in shocked surprise and stopped. They had not expected to find men with guns here. For an instant they wavered. While they hesitated we dropped several more of them. Then our hammers snapped down on empty chambers. But as we turned toward our door, the *barbaros* also turned and ran.

It was only those fronting us, though, who fled. The rest, though they slowed and looked toward the roar of our rifles, came on. But now they ran into a rain of arrows shot by the Indians who had sprung from their houses, and more of them fell. We saw nothing further just then, for we dashed into our hut to get more cartridges.

The American was sitting up, and he asked no questions — he was a soldier. As we swiftly reloaded and shoved our remaining cartridges into our pockets he said with a tight-faced grin:

"Go to it, buddies! Blow 'em wide open! Get around behind the house! I'll handle anything in front."

He was sitting on the edge of his hammock, with his crippled leg resting in it and the other foot on the ground to steady him. On his lap he held his rifle, pointing toward the door, and the long hungry-looking knife gleamed at its muzzle. We saw this in a flash, and then we were outside again.

Even as I left the door I met a big savage running toward it. He hurled a short spear, but I ducked and shot him in the stomach. Pedro's rifle cracked twice, but I did not look around, for I knew he had killed his men. The American's order to get behind the house was a good one, and I followed it. At a rear corner I halted and looked about.

The *barbaros* had swept in from all sides at once, and fierce close fighting was going on everywhere. A few arrows darted out from the houses, but the combat was mostly hand-to-hand. Stabbing, clubbing, choking and clawing and breaking bones, small knots of men struggled desperately for mastery. Caught by surprise and perhaps outnumbered as well, the townsmen seemed to be getting the worst of it; but they fought furiously to protect their women and children, who kept screaming as if they were already being murdered.

Picking my men, I fired again and again into the battling *barbaros*. Behind me, on the other side of the hut, sounded Pedro's gun. Then from the house itself came a shot — a sharp crack not like the blunt bark of our own weapons. Twice more that army gun cracked, and then it was still.

When my gun was empty again I shouted to Horner, asking if all was well. In answer his bugle rang out. Above the screams, the fighting yells, and the hoarse bellowing of the savage *turé* it sounded — quick, sharp blasts on the same note, lifting suddenly to two higher ones, dropping back then to the same tone as before. And it did not stop. Over and over it blared defiantly, hammering away at our ears until the men defending their homes seemed to gain fresh strength from it.

Whether the urge of that trumpet really did give them new power, or whether it and our bullets together brought fear into the minds of the wild men, I do not know. But I do know that soon the fighting died. While I was emptying my gun once more I saw that the attackers were giving way toward the bush and our friends were battling harder than ever. Before I had filled my magazine again the savages on my side of the town were gone.

Running around to the front, I found that there too the space was clear except for the townsmen and a few men grappling on the ground. The battered defenders pounced on these small groups, and when they turned away the *barbaros* who had been fighting there were dead.

The war-horn had stopped blowing. The cries of the children too had ended, and the yelling men were still. Only the bugle sang on in the same quick tune. Then, with one long flare, it became silent.

"Pretty slow stuff!" grumbled the Trumpeter as we stepped into the hut. "If that's the best your South American badmen can do I don't think much of them. All I had to do was to pot two or three out front here and then toot my horn to pass away the tune."

"You did not see much of the fight, *senhor*," Pedro reminded him. "You are inside, and the walls shut out most of it. Yet it was not such close work as some I have seen — at least not for us three. Our friends had their hands full beating them off."

"Slow stuff," Horner repeated, yawning. "Did the chief come through all right? If so, tell him I'm hungry."

We laughed, went out, and looked about for the chief. But we did not see him anywhere. Some of the Indians were picking up their dead and wounded, while others stood watching the jungle where their enemies had disappeared. We passed along among these, glancing at the bodies and noticing that there were more dead townsmen than savages. The wounded, of course, were defenders, for the injured attackers all had gotten away into the bush or been killed when their mates retreated. Without trying to count the dead, we could see that without our bullets to aid them our friends would have been quickly overwhelmed and butchered.

We could not find the chief among either the living or the dead there in the clearing, so we asked men what had become of him. They told us he was hurt and now was in his own house. They said also that, armed only with a club, he had killed three of the *barbaros*; and they showed us the bodies, each with its head crushed.

When we entered the chief's hut we found that he had not fared any too well. His left shoulder was badly torn by a spear-thrust, and a long arrow stuck out from one leg. A little old man whom we had not seen before was working to pull out the shaft, but its head was buried so deeply in the muscles that he was only hurting the chief, who sat silent but with lips drawn tight.

Looking up and seeing us, the chief motioned for me to draw that arrow out. I did so, but I had to pull hard, with one foot against the leg to brace it. When it came away the chief rocked in his hammock with pain, though he still gave no whimper. A look at the arrowhead showed me why it had stuck so stubbornly. It had double barbs, pointing both forward and back, which tore the flesh when they went in and when they came out, and which would prevent the shaft from being removed by pushing it on through the wound instead of draw-ing it out backward.

It was one of the most cruel weapons we had ever seen, and the sight of it angered us. Until now we had not felt any great hatred for those wild men; we had fought only because we were attacked, and so must kill or be killed. But those barbs, deliberately placed so that they would torture a man wounded but not killed, made us hot.

"If the brute who made this is still alive I hope he has one of my bullets in his bowels," I growled.

"And I wish I could shoot a few more of them," said Pedro.

We talked in our own language, but the chief was watch-ing us while the little old medicine man worked on his wounds, and perhaps he understood. He spoke, telling us to keep our guns ready for quick use when the time should come. The *barbaros*, he said, probably would attack again.

Somewhat surprised, I said we thought the fighting had ended. He shook his head, saying that it was not the way of those fierce men to quit while many of them were left alive. They had expected to overpower him and his people by attacking while the town still slept, but our prompt and deadly fire had surprised and confused them so that they could be fought off. But now they were preparing for another assault, and when they were ready they would come in spite of our guns, and the next fight would be to the death.

He added that unless we and our guns were strong the wild men would win. Many of his best men were dead or hurt, and he himself could not fight so well as before. He spoke very calmly, as if only saying that it might rain before night; but his eyes went to his two small children, who stood close by and watched the medicine man. We too looked at them — chubby little fellows with round faces and wide eyes — and shut our teeth. And though we knew our cartridges now were far too few, we told him our guns were strong enough to wipe out those beasts of the bush if his people would fight as bravely as before. He answered simply that they would fight until they died.

Soberly we went back to the Trumpeter, taking with us the bloody double-barbed arrow. We told him all there was to tell, and gave the arrow to him. As he studied it his face hardened.

"Dirty mutts!" he said. "If they'd shoot a thing like that into a man what would they do to the women and kids? Blast 'em, I hope they do come back — I want another crack at them! And say, if they come don't stick around this shack. Pick a couple of places where you can get a crossfire and make your bullets count. I'll take care of my end of the riot."

Then he grinned.

"Gee, but wouldn't the gang be hopping mad if they knew they'd missed a regular row! By this time they must be halfway to Borneo, or Bolivia, or whatever you call that spiggoty country down south, and wishing something would happen. And here squats little old Jack Horner, the poor crip, with a real rough-house coming off and not another Yank to see it. If I ever

meet up with that bunch of gorillas again won't I rub it into
'em! Say, when do we eat?"

We did not eat at once, but after a time food came to us.
Armed men watched ceaselessly, and nobody went close to the
bush, but otherwise life went on much as usual in and around
the houses. We breakfasted heartily, talked more with Horner,
and tried to pick places for that crossfire he wanted. But this
we could not do with any certainty because we could not guess
how the next attack would be made.

All around the clearing rose the jungle, and the *barbaros*
might burst out from any part of it. They might come as they
had come before, from all points at once, or they might divide
into parties and charge from several different quarters. If we
fixed any particular spots for our firing we might find ourselves in the wrong places when we were needed. So, after
some argument, we decided simply to take things as they came
and do our best to meet whatever plan our foes had.

"One thing is pretty sure," said Horner, "and that is that
they won't come just the way they did the first time. They
attack by trumpet signal, and that shows they've got some idea
of teamwork. Fighting men with any brains don't pull the same
stuff twice running, and you've got to watch out for a trick this
time. Tell the chief not to let all his men go piling into the first
bunch that shows up, but to hold some in reserve until he sees
where he can use them best."

That was sense, and I took the message to the chief while
Pedro stayed and watched. I found the tribal ruler now sitting
quietly with his leg and shoulder bandaged with pads of bark-
cloth, and talking with several of the older men. He agreed
that the advice of the white soldier was good, and gave orders
to those with him that certain men should be held back for a
time. He asked me also whether I would direct the fighting of
those men. But I refused, for I wanted nothing to think of but
my own work, and I knew his men would understand their own
leaders better than me. Then I returned to our hut.

A LONG time dragged past. The sun rolled high and hot in an

unclouded sky. We talked little and smoked much — I do not believe I had ever smoked so many cigarettes in one morning. Around the other huts hung the strained silence of tense waiting. At the edge of the jungle no life showed, and from it came no sound. Between houses and bush the only living things were the vultures that had swooped down and were stripping the bones of the dead wild men.

"Ho-hum!" yawned the Trumpeter. "This is the hardest part of war — waiting for the other guy to start something. I'm getting sleepy. Might as well have a little music. Guess I'll give those roughnecks out yonder the reveille and wake 'em up."

As his rollicking tune ended Pedro leaned forward, listening. A confused noise, muffled by the bush, sounded and died.

"The *barbaros!*" I said.

"Perhaps so," he replied doubtfully. "It seemed like the voices of men shouting together, but I did not think our enemies were so far away."

Again we listened, but no further sound came. We settled back into waiting.

"Lourenço," my partner said softly after a time, "do you see something climbing in that tall slim tree over yonder?"

Following the line of his pointing finger, I glimpsed a dark body moving upward at the edge of the bush. The leaves between it and us were so thick that I could notice it clearly, and soon I lost it altogether.

"Yes. I saw it. But I can not see it now."

"I can. It has stopped and is resting on a limb. Perhaps, Senhor Trumpeter, your music has made the blower of the *turé* jealous. If that is he, I will play him a tune on this little steel pipe."

Lifting his rifle, he rested it against the side of the doorway and stood aiming steadily at the thing in the tree. And soon his joking remark proved truth.

Out from that tree broke the bellow of the war-horn. Pedro's rifle spat. The blare of the *turé* ended abruptly. The dark form felt crashing down through the branches.

Yells sounded behind our hut. Pedro and I jumped around

the corners. A mass of savages was charging straight at us.

As we threw up our guns the mass split into three bodies. One swerved to the right, one to the left, and the third came on. At the head of this middle force ran a huge brute smeared with red paint, wearing a belt of human hair and a necklace of human teeth, howling like a madman and carrying a tremendous club.

We both shot him at the same instant. He pitched on his face and lay quiet. Over his body the others jumped, and we fired so fast that we killed some while they were still in the air. A small heap of corpses grew between us and the dead leader. Other warriors stumbled over these bodies, falling themselves and tripping more men behind them. By the time our guns were empty the force of the rush was broken.

But we got little time to reload. I managed to get two more cartridges into the magazine before the first *barbaros* reached me, and I fired these straight into their faces. Then I swung my gun, braining one man with the barrel, and dropped the empty weapon. Seizing the warrior I had just killed and holding him up before me as a shield, I pulled my machete and set my back to the wall.

Just what happened after that I can not tell you. It was stab — slash — dodge aside — stab and slash again, always holding that dead man in front and keeping the wall behind. All I can remember is snarling faces, stinking breath, grunts and groans and screeches, blood and brains and entrails. At last, gasping and dizzy with exhaustion and half-blinded with blood from a gash on my forehead, I leaned against the wall and found no man attacking me.

On the ground near me four men were heaving and wrenching, and out of the tangle a red machete rose and fell. By the time I got my wind and stood away from the wall their fight was over. Up from among the bodies rose a half-naked, red-smeared figure which reeled toward me. I lifted my machete to attack it. Then I recognized the bloody man as Pedro.

He stumbled against the wall and slouched there, sick from fatigue and blows. When he could breathe naturally again he twisted his split lips in a grin.

"Drop it!" he wheezed, looking at the dead savage still clutched in my left arm. After a glance at it I dropped it. Its head was no longer a head but a crushed pulp, battered in by club blows aimed at me. Its trunk, too, was full of gaping wounds, and several short spears stuck out from its ribs.

We picked up our guns and reloaded. The cartridges were our last, and so few that neither of us could fill his magazine. We looked at each other and at the fighting around us. And Pedro said —

"We must keep these for our last stand."

It was so. The townsmen were being beaten down. Near us no man lived, but we knew our turn would come again all too soon, and that then our rifles and machetes would not save us long. The women and children were screaming again, and the yells of the savages spoke brutal exultation. Already some of them had stopped fighting and were butchering the wounded.

Behind us the army rifle cracked twice. Horner still lived. Dimly I remembered hearing him shoot several times while we fought. Now we ran back to the front of the hut, and there we found another fierce fight going on all along the line. The wild men had charged from the bush on this side also, and only the American's foresight in providing for reserves had prevented them from catching the chief's men from behind. These men, held back from meeting the rush at the rear, had stopped the one in front. But here too they were being killed faster than they were killing.

The end of all of us was close at hand, and we two stopped at the corners and held our fire for our last fight. But then a pair of red-streaked brutes went plunging into a hut close by, and out from that house a long scream rose high over the other cries around us — the shriek of a woman in an agony of fear. It was too much for me.

I dashed down to that place, shooting down a savage who got in my way, and attacked the murderers inside, who had seized a woman and a child. Two more of my bullets were gone when I came out; but the woman and child still lived, while their assailants did not.

As I left the doorway another wild man came bounding at

me. Firing from the hip, I shot him in the body. He fell, writhed, clawed the ground, went limp and was still. The downward yank of my lever brought up only an empty shell. My last shot was gone.

A thrown spear thudded into the wall. Several more *barbaros* were coming at me. I sprang back into the house, where, with machete drawn, I waited just inside the door. But most of those killers never reached me.

A sudden crash of gunfire ripped out. Two of the charging savages toppled sidewise. The others stopped, faced to their left, poised there staring. At the same instant the wild yelling ceased. It seemed still as the grave.

Crash! Another volley.

One of the wild men before my door doubled in at the middle and dropped. Another fell backward, the top of his head gone. Only one was left standing. He whirled about, looked this way and that, and bolted for the shelter of the hut where I stood. As he came I saw that now his face was drawn with fear.

I stepped aside. As he plunged in at the doorway I swung my machete hard to his throat. He flopped down, his head cut almost off. The woman and child cowering behind me screamed again, but I gave no attention to them. I popped out into the open.

No more volleys came. Instead, the firing now was a steady crackle. Naked men were dropping dead. Other savages were running — some toward the bush, some toward houses, some straight at the place where the shooting sounded. That place was near the river, and there among the shadows I saw gleaming steel, spurts of flame, yellow shirts and broad hats.

The Trumpeter's "gorillas" had come back.

Shouting in wild joy, the desperate townsmen sprang again on their confused enemies. With spears, clubs, bare hands, they fought as if suddenly given new life. Then a whistle shrieked, out — one long blast — and at once the firing ceased.

With the end of the shooting, wild men who had taken cover came running out again and rushed toward the yellow shirts. They thought — and so did I — that the bullets were used up. But the riflemen had not stopped fighting. They had only begun.

With a roar they came lunging forward, the long knives on their guns flashing in the sunlight.

Then, while I stood there staring like a fool, I saw what those knives could do in the hands of men trained to their use. I had thought the bayonet must be a slow weapon, but I learned otherwise. Those grim-faced Americans seemed hardly to be really fighting, but only to be jabbing and dancing about; yet the savages swarming at them dropped, dropped, dropped, and the soldiers kept coming on.

But they came more and more slowly, and soon they were stopped. Heaving, hacking, stabbing, spearing, white and brown men were locked in a solid mass. And then, with the *barbaros* jamming together, the shooting started again.

The shots sounded dull and muffled now. Later I learned that this was because the muzzles were almost against the skins of the *barbaros*, and also that each of those bullets tore through two or three men. The firing did not last long, but it seemed to blow the wild men off their feet. So many fell dead at once that they blocked and bore down the others, and what had been a tangle of raging warriors became a heap of flesh.

Out of that pile squirmed men yelping with terror, who tried to break loose and run. And into that pile plunged the soldiers, reaching the struggling *barbaros* with tremendous long thrusts and spearing them like fish. Here and there a savage managed to pull himself out of the welter and run, but none of these ran far. The townsmen cut them off and slew them before they could reach the shelter of the jungle.

"Lourenço! To the rear!" called Pedro's voice.

I started, looked around, could not see him, and got around the hut quickly. I had forgotten all about the fighters on the other side of the houses. There too I found white men battling hard, and these had not overcome their foes. There seemed to be fewer soldiers and more savages on this side, and the two forces were not locked together but broken up into scattered groups, every white man fighting his own battle against a number of copper-skins.

Pedro, after his shout to me, had thrown himself into this fighting and was swinging his machete on wild men who were swarming on a lone soldier. As I ran I picked another group doing the same thing, and a few seconds later I was hacking at their necks. For a while I was very busy. Then I found a limping townsman helping me with a spear, and between the soldier in front and us two in the rear we cleaned up that group.

Shots cracked around us as the last wild man fell at our feet. New yells rang out. *Barbaros* ran for the bush. The soldiers and village Indians from the other side of the town had swept in here to finish the battle. With their coming the wild men had bolted, and they found nothing to do but stand and shoot rapidly. When the crackle ceased no living enemy was left in sight.

"HOOEY! 'Tis a hot day for workin'!" panted the soldier whom I had helped, mopping his broad face with a sleeve and grinning at me. "Thanks for carvin' up them guys the way ye done. I been gittin' fat, and me wind ain't what it was."

"And I thank you, *senhor*, and your comrades, for coming when you did," I said. "My last shot was gone."

"Was it so? I wouldn't think ye'd need a gun anyways, feller. Ye sure can sling a wicked knife."

Then up came another soldier — a long, lean, easy-moving, red-spattered man.

"Howdy, mistuh," he drawled, looking at me. "Have yuh seen a good-fo'-nothin' rapscallion named Hawnuh — a li'l cuss with a brass hawn an' a lot o' gall?"

"He is in that house, *senhor*," I nodded. "My partner and I found him with a broken leg and brought him back here."

The tall man lifted his brows slightly.

"Laig busted, huh? Reckon we bettuh mosey ovuh an' see how he come through this li'l pahty. Nawthin' mo' to do heah — these town boys will do the moppin' up. Come on, Mike, yuh fat Dutchman."

"Dutchman!" snorted the broad-faced man. "Ye slab-sided

skeleton of a down-South hookworm, if I'm a Dutchman ye're a greaser."

The lean man grinned a slow grin, but made no answer, and we moved toward the Trumpeter's hut. Other soldiers joined us on the way, looking curiously at me.

"Friend of mine," said the man Mike, noticing these looks and moving his head toward me. "Who he is I dunno, but he's there wit' the rough stuff. Anybody cashed in?"

"All present or accounted for," answered a stocky soldier with bow legs. "Tim Moran is busted up some, and so are Chicago Tony and Scotty McLeod, but nobody's gone."

"Arrugh!" grunted Mike. "Tim and Scotty need a swift kick for mixin' in at all — they're both rotten wit' fever. And that little fightin' fool of a Chicago wop — Holy Mother! Whaddye know about this!"

We had come around to the front of the house of the Trumpeter, and we stopped and stared. Its doorway was choked by a heap of dead *barbaros*.

"Hey, you Jack Horner!" some man snapped. "You all right?"

"Sure, I'm all right," came the Trumpeter's cool voice. "Kick that stuff out of the door and come on in."

We threw the dead aside and entered. Horner stood on his one good leg, with the other knee supported by the hammock. His rifle-butt rested on the ground, and the long bayonet sticking up near his shoulder was dyed red.

"Who gave you guys any license to horn in on my party?" he complained. "Here I'm getting a lot of good bayonet practice and you bust in and shoot up the whole works just when I'm going good. What you doing here, anyhow? Did the spiggoties down in Borneo give you the gate?"

"Listen at him, will ye!" rumbled Mike. "Talkin' like he was a growed-up man! And him blowin' the guts out of his tin horn a while back, tryin' to git reinforcements!"

"Not by a jugful!" Horner denied. "I blew the Charge, but I did it just to make a racket and give these boys out here a little pep. Where were you guys, anyway?"

"Upstream a ways. We found it bum goin', so we turned

around and come back. We camped above here last night, and heard ye play taps. When yer Charge come to us this mornin' we took our foot in our hand and come on. Didn't ye hear us yell when ye blew reveille?"

"I heard shouting, *senhor*," said Pedro. "But we thought it must be *barbaros*."

"'Twas a bum guess — there ain't a barber in the gang," said Mike. "But now listen here, Kid Horner. We got to slide right along downstream before anymore of the bunch kick off wit' fever. Eb Peabody, that New England feller, cashed in a couple days ago, and Tim Moran and Scotty are gittin' bad too. I hear they come ashore here wit' the rest of the gang and got mauled, and that won't do 'em no good. So we'll move as soon as we can git them lousy paddlers back — they was that scairt of the wild guys they beat it acrost the river as quick as we landed. I'll go git 'em now. When we're ready we'll give ye a yell. Slim, stay here and help Jack frog it down to the water. Fall in, the rest of ye."

He turned and went, followed by all except the lean man with the slow drawl, who stood calmly chewing tobacco and spitting in the eye of a dead savage who lay face upward.

"Yuh li'l hawn-toad, yuh!" said Slim. "Yuh sho' did tickle these felluhs' ribs some. Whyn't yuh jab 'em lowuh down? Yuh might of busted the steel on them rib-bones, an' then whah'd yuh been?"

"Had to take 'em any way I could get 'em, Slim," replied Horner. "They rushed the place after Pedro here left, and if I hadn't plugged a couple and sort of choked up the door with them they might have got me. Then I jabbed straight and withdrew quick. You can't do any footwork when you've got a dead leg. Ho-hum. I sort of hate to leave this town, it's so quiet and peaceful."

Slim grinned, and we laughed. After looking at the dead men a minute Pedro strode out, crossed the clearing, and disappeared into the bush. Soon he returned with a long tube.

"Perhaps you would like a remembrance of the peace and quiet of our Brazilian forests, *senhor*," he suggested. "Here is the *turé* of the *barbaros*."

"Say, that's mighty white of you!" cried the Trumpeter, reaching eagerly for it. After turning it over and examining its wooden barrel and crude mouthpiece he unfixed the bayonet from his rifle and passed the gun to Pedro.

"It's a fair swap," he said. "You guys will likely need a gun before you get home, and yours are no good with your ammunition all gone. The gang will give you plenty of shells. I won't need the gun anymore."

Knowing we were indeed likely to need a gun before reaching the Javary, we took the weapon thankfully. Then came a yell from the river, and Slim came in, took Horner's arm around his shoulders, and started with him to the stream. We took down the hammocks and followed.

At the house of the chief we stopped to say farewell, and from him we learned that about a mile down the river we should find a channel which would take us on toward our own country. Then, with a final wave of the hand to the townsmen who had been our hosts and fighting mates, we went on to the water.

There we found two, big *ygarités* — long canoes with arched cabins — manned by stocky *caboclos*. And there we found waiting for us another of those heavy army rifles and many of the queer bottle-necked cartridges that went with it. The gun, we learned, was that of the man Peabody who had died of fever, and we were welcome to it. After big Mike had shown us how to work the bolt action and explained what he called a "safe" and a "cut-off," we got into our own canoe and took up our paddles.

"All set back there, Brazil?" someone called.

"All set, North America," we answered.

Our little fleet pushed off and swung away toward the far-off Amazon.

Though our canoe was lighter and faster than the big *ygarités*, we had to stretch our muscles to keep up with them. Perhaps because of the sick men aboard, but more likely because they themselves were homeward bound, the *caboclos* heaved their craft along with swift, hard strokes. It seemed that we had gone much less than a mile when we spied at our left the channel of which the chief had told us.

"Adeos, senhores!" we shouted then, and swerved toward the bank. But a roar of protest followed. The big canoes stopped, and the soldiers yelled to us to come on. When we did so they told us they had thought we would camp with them a few times, and urged us to continue on with them for a day or so. But we said no, the water was ebbing and we must cut across country here.

One by one they shook our hands, slapped our shoulders, and wished us well. When the Trumpeter's turn came he said less than any of them, but there was that in his eyes and his grip that spoke louder than all the jovial voices of his mates.

"So long, buddies," he said simply. "I want to take back what I said about that sawdust grub of yours. And any guy that I ever catch knocking Brazilians is going to get one stiff clout in the jaw from little Jack Horner."

I grinned, but my thoughts were back in the jungle behind us. Somehow I seemed to see him again as on that first day — hunching himself along on hands and knee, sick and starved and broken, yet unflinching and brave clear through. And, though I too said little, when my hand left his it was numb.

With one final chorus of farewells the big boats moved away. We wriggled our fingers to bring back the blood driven out by those parting grips and paddled back to the place were the *furo* opened. And there, as we turned into the bush, we heard our last of the Trumpeter and his comrades.

Out broke the hoarse, menacing blare of the *turé*, now blown only in fun by some homeward-bound soldier. As its growl died, the clear, smooth notes of the bugle rang again in that swift "charge" which had brought the fighting men of North America that morning to pull us out of the jaws of death. Finally, when the bugle in turn was still, there came to us a roaring, rollicking song.

> *"HAIL! HAIL! The gang's all here!*
> *What the Hell do we care?*
> *What the Hell do we care?*
> *HAIL! HAIL! The gang's all here!*
> *What the Hell do we care now?"*

THE BARRIGUDO

HAVE you noticed, *senhores*, the big, slow-moving monkey which that oily-faced trader over yonder is taking down the river with him?

It is a *barrigudo* — the "bag-belly" monkey — and one of the largest I have seen, though I have met many of those big fellows during my years of service as a rubber-worker in the Javary jungle. From the end of its solemn nose to the tip of that strong tail, which it can use as a fifth leg in the trees, it must be more than four feet long.

The trader tells me that he intends to sell it as a pet in Para. But unless he is very lucky his monkey will be dead long before the end of his journey. For the *barrigudo*, *senhores*, is a creature of this upper Amazon alone, and when he is taken away from his own country he dies.

Why this is so I can not tell you. Looking at his bulky body, you would think he could endure almost anything. Yet he is *mortal*, as we Brazilians say — delicate, not hardy. It may be that in his silent way he grieves himself to death because he has lost his own land and his old friends. You can not always tell, by looking at either monkey or man, what sort of heart is hidden in his breast. And, after all, the heart is the only thing that really counts.

This may seem, *senhores*, like idle talk, but it is not. I have a tale to tell you — a tale of the most surprising *barrigudo* I ever met.

I CAME upon this creature at the time when the great yearly floods had passed their crest and were going down again. Indeed, they had gone down so far that I was worried; for I was far from where I ought to be, and in strange country where I might soon find myself stranded in the midst of unknown jungle.

With my comrade Pedro Andrada, a fellow workman on

the big rubber estate of old Coronel Nunes, I had paddled across country from our Javary region into the upper reaches of the Jurua, a low-lying and very crooked river to the south and east. Then, after meeting with queer experiences and traveling some distance down the river, we had turned homeward, journeying along a flooded *furo*, or natural canal, until we met a number of roving North American soldiers who saved us from death at the hands of a horde of fierce savages. Now these men had left us and gone back toward the Amazon, whence they had come; and we were trying hard to reach our own territory before the ebbing waters should leave us trapped in some blind flood-channel.

As I say, I was worried. If we had known where we were I should not have cared so much, for then we should have been able to judge our course. But neither of us had passed this way before, our only guide was the sun, and we had to trust to that and to luck to carry us through the maze of twisting watercourses opening around us on all sides.

The *furo* itself, which had been fairly plain, now was becoming harder to follow, winding here and there in a confusing way; and already we had blundered off it more than once and lost much time in learning our mistake. Besides this, our food supply now was none too plentiful, and we found little game to shoot. And inch by inch, day and night, the thick tangle of bush was rising steadily around us as the waters slipped away.

Yet these things, serious though they seemed, suddenly became nothing at all. They were swallowed up by something far more grave.

Pedro fell sick.

It must have been the Spotted People who gave the disease to him. We came upon them in the morning of a sweltering day when no breeze stirred. We were stripped almost naked, breathing with mouths hanging open, gasping now and then for the air which it seemed we could not get, but shoving steadily onward. All at once my comrade, up in the bow, held his paddle and called sharply:

"*Quem vai la*? Who goes there?"

No answer came. No sound of any kind followed his hail.

He was peering at a tangle of trees rising from the water at his left.

"Do you see anything, Lourenço?" he asked.

"Nothing," I replied.

"Yet I thought I heard — Let us go and look."

We turned the canoe into the trees. As we neared them a figure rose behind a big blown-down tree-trunk. It held a bow and arrow. Instantly we backed water and snatched up our rifles.

For a moment we hung there, the man menacing us with his arrow but not daring to loose it with our gun-muzzles covering him. He was a naked Indian, and seemed to be standing on the water.

"*Baah derekoh*? What is the matter with you?" he growled sullenly in the Tupi tongue.

"*Anih baah*. Nothing," I answered in the same language. "Put down that arrow if you would not be shot."

He lowered his weapon in a surly way.

"What are you doing here?" Pedro snapped.

For answer the man stooped and held up a spear, on which a fine big fish hung quivering.

Laying down our rifles, but keeping them within instant reach, we pushed up to him and found that he was in a small canoe hidden by the prostrate tree. He still held the spear, and the water on its shaft showed that he had plunged the barb into the fish just before Pedro shouted. We saw that he was peaceable enough, and that he was a very ordinary-looking fellow except for one thing. His face was blotched with hard, rough, black spots.

After telling him we meant no harm to him or to any other man who did not attack us, we asked him whence he came. In a slow, heavy manner he replied that his people lived close by, up on a little hill above the reach of the floods. We asked him if they were many, and he said no. Then, without questioning us in turn, he dropped spear and fish into his canoe, picked up a paddle, and began to move away.

"Wait," said Pedro. "Will you sell that fish?"

He stopped, squinted at the fish and at us, and said he

would barter for beads. But we had no beads, for we were not on a trading trip. We offered him some empty cartridge shells, though, telling him they were lucky bells which would keep demons away. He hesitated so long that we thought the fish was ours. But then he grunted, "No," and started on.

"Wait," Pedro commanded again. "Is there fruit at your town?"

The fellow said there was much fruit. So then we told him that if he would give us fruit he could have the lucky bells. At once he consented. We followed him a short distance through the watery forest to the hill where his village stood.

It was a miserable little place of a few scattered huts, and the people in it seemed as wretched as the town. When we walked boldly in among them, following our guide, they gathered around us in a sluggish way and looked us over without saying anything. Their eyes were dull, their expressions blank, their movements lifeless and their skins spotted with those same black patches which disfigured the fisherman. Everyone of them — men, women, children — was spotted.

The older they were, the worse they looked. The children had only small spots, with lighter rings around each blotch. But the grown people were crusted with hard patches, and among them I saw a withered man whose face was one great black scab. And not only the people, but the town itself, seemed sick; for there was a smell in the air — a heavy, depressing odor of disease which made me wish we had not come.

"Let us get our fruit at once and go," I muttered. "I can not breathe well."

"Nor I," my partner agreed. "But I want something fresh to eat, and I will have it. Here, stabber of fish! Fetch the fruit quickly, or we will go and keep our demon-bells."

The fisherman grunted, moved his head for us to stay there, and went away. He was gone for what seemed a long time. We stood still, and all the others stood still, staring without a blink. And the odd thing was that they stared not so much at our guns and breeches as at our skins. After a time it dawned on me that they marveled because we were not blemished as they were.

"Por Deus!" muttered Pedro. "When we leave this place I shall take a bath. These people make me feel slimy."

"I feel the same way, and the smell here makes my stomach squirm," I said. "But here comes our man."

The fisherman was returning, bent forward under a long *atura* basket which hung down his back. We turned at once toward the water. He followed, and at the canoe he put basket and headline and all into the bottom.

Handing him the empty shells, we pushed off and away, leaving him jangling his "demon-bells" in his palms. No doubt he thought we were great fools to give such a charm for a simple basket of fruit. And the time was not far off when I was to believe we had indeed lost our luck at that place.

We paddled away fast and traveled some distance before we either ate of the fruit or took the bath we had promised ourselves. Somehow the sickly smell of that village seemed to stay with us long after the town itself had disappeared behind us. A thin mist had hung over the place of the Spotted People, and the same vapor was crawling along the water and keeping up with us. Not until we finally got clear of it and breathed clean air once more did the odor fade away.

"Phew!" whistled Pedro, his nose wrinkled. "What an unwholesome hole! Now that we are quit of it, let us bathe and eat."

So we found a firm bare spot where we could stand and pour gourds of water over ourselves. We wanted to take a swim, but the water did not look inviting and we knew well that under its surface might be lurking death in the shape of fish or reptile, so we bathed on land.

When we felt clean again we ate heartily of the fruit, which tasted very good. And as we paddled onward after that we munched now and then at other fruits taken from the basket.

That night neither of us ate well. Our stomachs did not want the usual ration of dried *pirarucu* and *farinha*. So we devoured the rest of the fruit and were satisfied.

Before dawn I awoke to hear Pedro moaning softly in his sleep. He had a bad dream, I thought. So I yelled and roused him, grumbled that he was disturbing me, turned over in my hammock and shut my eyes again. He said nothing, and I slept almost at once.

When next I looked around me it was day, and my partner was sitting up and holding his head in his hands. He only grunted when I spoke.

I got breakfast, but he would eat none. This was so uncommon that I looked sharply at him, finding his skin pale and his face drawn. But when I asked him what ailed him he said only that he had not slept well.

We paddled away as usual, and all through the hot, sunny morning he said no word. His stroke lacked its regular power, and several times he stopped work and bent forward as if to favor his stomach. I grinned, thinking he had a touch of colic from eating too much fruit and was too stubborn to admit it. At last I snickered outright.

"Poor little man!" I mocked. "Does his little belly ache? Perhaps he needs a little drink —"

I did not finish. He groaned, wavered dizzily, and slumped into the bottom of the boat.

This scared me. He was not the man to let anything overpower him as long as he had an ounce of fight left in him, and I realized that he must be very sick.

As quickly as possible I got the boat to shore. There I found that his illness was not a mere ache of the stomach.

He had fever. And it was not the ordinary jungle swamp-fever — which is bad enough — but a deadly sickness which burned and froze and griped and turned him inside out. When at last his spasms ceased he lay so limp that I thought him dead.

He could not even whisper. He could not move. He lay like a corpse and he looked like one, and only the feeble throb of his heart and his shallow breathing told me that he still lived. And there was not a single thing that I could do to help him, for we had no medicine — not even a mouthful of rum to strengthen his heart.

Squatting beside him, I tried in a dumb, dazed way to think of something I could do.

He was more to me than anyone else in the world. He was far closer than a blood brother — he seemed a part of myself. A handsome, happy-hearted, boyish man, strong of hand and quick of thought and action, he had been my comrade in fair weather and foul, in times of merriment and times of deadly fight. Either of us would throw away his own life to save the other — yes, or endure torment worse than death, if by it the other might escape.

And at that very moment I was in such torment of mind as I hope will never come to me again. I could not let him die, but it seemed that I could not aid him to live.

At last I thought of a thing, though it seemed of little use. If I could find some *pajemarioba*, a bitter medicinal herb some-times used by the Indians to make a sort of tea, it might start him to sweating and drive the fever out. The *pajemarioba* grows wild in many places, and some might be there.

I started at once and hunted all about the spot where we were. But I found none.

I came back to him just in time. He lay on the ground as I had left him, limp and motionless. And halfway out of the water, crawling up toward him, was a big alligator.

I leaped at the beast in fury. It slewed and slid back under the surface. Then, lifting my partner, I laid him in the canoe and stroked swiftly away from that accursed place.

As we went onward I watched along both sides, hoping to see a patch of *pajemarioba* on some point of land. The chance of finding it was poor, I knew, but it was all I could do, and at any rate I was doing something. So, hunting desperately for some sign of that herb, I kept on for I know not how long.

At length I came into a place where the water widened out and met open shores covered with fine *matupa* grass, beyond which grew ferns and slim *assai* palms. I paddled slowly near one bank, thinking that here I might land and seek again for the *pajemarioba*. And while I looked around and thought it over, an astonishing thing came about.

On the empty shore, a few feet from me, a voice spoke.

"*Ko tam baheh?* What is that?"

I started, looked at the spot whence the words had come,

and saw no man. Nothing was there except thick tufts of grass, and the grass was not tall enough to conceal anyone unless he were lying down. Yet I was certain the voice had spoken at that place. Watching it steadily, I turned the canoe straight at it.

But just as the bow touched shore the voice came again from another spot.

"*Bihpende hoh?* Where are you going?"

The question came from a small bush standing a foot or so above the grass and a few feet to my left. As before, no living thing was there — no living thing with a voice could be there. The bush was so thin that I could see through it, and beyond it was nothing except grass and trees.

I felt a little chilly. Then I grew angry. If some man was there and making sport of me I would spoil his joke. Picking up my gun, I stepped ashore into mud that rose over my ankles, and through this I plowed straight to the bush.

I found nothing at all. No man was there and no man had been there, for the mud held no tracks but my own.

Then, as I scowled around me in wonder, a new thing came. It was a sound of singing.

It seemed to be far away, yet very near — almost over my head, a clear, sweet song without words, up in the blank air above me. I stared upward, and, seeing that nothing but the sky was over me, I grew chilly again. Was I going mad? Was I, too, about to become delirious with fever? Was this a place of demons, where grass and bushes spoke and the air sang? I did not know. But I did know I wanted to get out of there. Turning, I sloshed back through the soft mud to the canoe.

As I got into it the voice spoke once more. From the water near me rose the same question the spotted fisherman had asked:

"*Baah derekoh?* What ails you?"

For the first time I answered. With my eyes on Pedro I growled in Tupi:

"*Heraku.* Fever."

Then I shoved off. But a reply came that stopped me.

"*Ehe ahrahm. Che ahoh apuh ayuk.* Wait. I will cure the sickness."

This time the voice seemed to be heavier, more like that of a man; and it came from a place near the edge of the trees. I looked sharply at that spot, but saw no man there. For that matter, I did not expect to see anything human, after what had happened.

But this weird voice had said it would cure Pedro, and if the great horned devil himself had risen beside me and given me that promise I would have embraced him. Holding the canoe still, I told the Thing to come to me.

It answered that it could not come, for it had no body but was only a spirit. But if I would go and find a man who now was sleeping on the shore of a narrow neck of water beyond us, and would follow him, the fever should be driven out.

That was all. I asked the Thing just where this man was, but got no reply. No sound of any kind came to me. The *matupa* grass, the bush, the water, the trees — all were vacant and silent. I drove my paddle into the water and heaved the dugout ahead.

Pedro moaned, squirmed a little, and lay still. Looking at him, I shut my jaws and began watching along shore for any narrow water such as the Thing had told about. And soon, *senhores*, I found it. And I went into it, and under a tree I found a sleeping man.

He was half-lying, half-sitting with his back against the tree trunk. His mouth hung open, and from it came a gurgling snore. But after I looked at him, I came near turning about and going away. No such creature as he, I thought, could ever cure Pedro.

He was a greasy, bag-bellied *barrigudo* of an Indian. Hairy as a monkey he was, too, and the black hairs of his whole body were matted with clay, plastered on thickly to keep biting bugs from reaching his hide. The long, stringy hair of his head hung down over his face so far that I could see little of it, but what little I could make out looked blank and stupid.

As I have said, I would have welcomed the devil himself if he had offered aid to my comrade; but the devil, *senhores*, has brains, while this creature looked as if he hardly knew enough to scratch an itch — a mere mass of fat, hair, and dirt.

I grunted with disgust, and half-moved my paddle to push out and away. But just then the queer voice spoke again.

"Hemba eah hy," it reminded me. "You are sick."

It came from the tree, a little above the sleeping man. I looked first at the tree trunk, on which was nothing alive. Then my eye swerved again to Pedro. And instead of going away I drove the dugout to shore, stepped out, and prodded the human *barrigudo* with my paddle.

His snoring ended. I caught the glint of eyes staring through his hair. He grunted, and the sound seemed to come from the depths of his belly. Then he sluggishly pushed himself up higher against the tree, yawned with a wheezing noise, and growled —

"Baah derekoh?"

"My mate has fever," I answered, pointing at Pedro.

He sat bunking. Then he yawned again.

"Hembara ahreteh. I am very tired."

And his head drooped as if he meant to go back to sleep.

His callousness angered me. In one long stride I was at the canoe. In another I was back, with my cocked rifle in his face.

"Get up, you filthy beast!" I snarled. "Get up and take care of my comrade, or the next alligator that comes here will find a fat feast awaiting him."

He got up. Slowly, as if afraid he might touch the gun and discharge it, he rose and stood against the tree. When I lowered the weapon he waddled past me and stared at Pedro. Then, with a sour grunt, he pointed a thick finger and moved his head to show I was to pick up my partner and go somewhere with him. After scowling at him I did so.

He led me for some distance back into the bush — so far that before we stopped I was breathing hard, for Pedro was no lightweight to carry. Yet I would rather carry him myself than have that dirty Indian do it, even if he had offered to.

As I look back at that time I wonder that I followed him at all, for in spite of the promise made by the queer voice I had faint hope of any real help from him. But I kept on, and presently we entered a cleared space where were huts and people.

The *barrigudo* man, striding along easily in spite of his

size, went straight to a hut set off at some distance from the rest. Half-blinded with sweat, humped over under the burden of my partner's hot body, I trailed at his heels.

We passed through the doorway into a dim room of shadows, where a tiny fire smoldered in the middle of the dirt floor. There the Indian pointed to a sort of legless bench or bed of woven sticks, which hung like a hammock but was straight and flat. On this I laid Pedro.

Pedro squirmed again and kicked about, and for a minute I had to hold him to keep him from rolling off. When he quieted I straightened up and turned toward the *barrigudo*. But he was gone.

Puzzled, I stared around. He could not have gone outdoors, for I was between him and the spot where he had last stood, and I should certainly have known it if he had passed me. Yet there was no other opening in the house except a small smoke-hole in the roof ten feet above me, and he surely could not have gone out there. But he was not in the place. The huge creature had vanished into air.

Peering at the walls about me, I found no sign of any door except the one where we had entered. The walls were made in basket fashion of tightly woven sticks and creepers. On them hung strange and horrid things — skins of deadly snakes and huge lizards; great black poison-spiders; skulls of ugly beasts and of fish with terrible hooked teeth; a vampire bat, and other things of the sort. But all these were dead. No living thing was in the room but ourselves.

As I gaped around I thought I heard a slight chuckle somewhere, but whence it came I could not tell — indeed, I was not sure that I really heard it. Then came a thing that made me forget it. Behind me sounded the hiss of a snake.

I whirled, looked, and saw on the farther wall the head of a big boa. Yes, *senhores*, only its head — a head as dead as the skins and skulls near it. But as I looked at it its mouth slowly opened; and out of that mouth came a hissing voice that told me to go.

The head closed again and hung silent as before. Feeling rather prickly, I stood watching it until a slight rustle near me drew me around again. There beside Pedro stood a great figure muffled in a garment of bark-cloth.

Senhores, I was now so confused and bewildered that I recoiled and leveled my gun at the thing. If it had moved toward me or touched Pedro I would have shot it. But it did not move. It only stood there, and though I could see no eyes on it, it seemed to be watching me with no fear whatever.

As I scowled back at it I thought it must be the *barrigudo* man, but then I saw that it was much taller than he had been — so much taller that it could not be he. Moreover, it seemed not even to be human. It was armless and headless.

The cloth hanging over it showed no sign of a man's head underneath. It hung as if from a pair of shoulders whence the neck and head had been sliced off. Seven feet high, shapeless and silent and still, it loomed up in that dim and smoky room like a specter born of fog and fever and nightmare — a thing which the eyes saw but which could not exist; a thing which had taken shape as silently as the *barrigudo* had vanished. And again there came to me the thought that I was crazed: that I had fever or worse, and all this was delirium.

Then the Thing spoke. Out from the folds of cloth rolled a voice, deep and powerful, unlike any voice I had yet heard here.

"The dead live. The living die. The blind see. The seer is blind. This man dies, yet shall live. You live, but you shall die. Go, but remain."

Without realizing it, I let my rifle sink. Stupidly I stared at the thing before me and tried to make sense of its words.

"Go!" came the voice, deeper than ever. "Three suns shall set, two shall rise. When the third sun sinks low this man shall walk again. Until then, go and stay."

"I will not go," I growled. "I stay with my comrade while he lives or until he is surely dead. Whatever you are, help him if you can."

"Go!"

"*Vive Deus,* I will not!"

The thing and I fronted each other for minutes, neither of us moving. Then it said:

"You would help your comrade? Then take from the wall that vampire bat, which shall draw the fever from him."

Glancing around, I saw the dead vampire bat, which I had hardly noticed before. I went to it and tried to take it down.

But it was fastened tight. So I pulled harder, then yanked at it. Suddenly it came away, and from behind it a quantity of dusty powder fell into my upturned face.

The dust stung my nostrils and choked my throat. I coughed and turned back toward Pedro, carrying the vampire bat. But I did not reach him.

A swift chill ran down my back. My muscles stiffened. The house whirled. The headless figure swelled to a huge blot. I felt myself falling. Then I was floating in some place far, far down, where all was still.

*   *   *

AFTER A long time I found myself lying on a bare dirt floor. Above me was a roof, around me were walls, beyond me was an open door; but they were not those of the house where I had fallen. The walls were bare mud, and in this house was no fire, no sick comrade, no shapeless monster — not even my rifle. As I realized that my gun was gone I reached to my belt for the machete which usually hung there. That too was gone.

I started up. As I reached my feet I turned dizzy and nearly fell again; but soon the place stopped whirling and I became steady. At once I strode toward the doorway.

But before I reached it, it was blocked. Two men jumped into it from outside and stood with spears leveled at my stomach. I stopped and peered at them.

They were tall, well-muscled fellows with clean faces which looked good-humored but rather determined. Presently one of them smiled slightly. But they held their weapons ready.

"What is this?" I grunted. "Drop those spears and step aside."

They stood their ground. The one who had smiled answered:

"Sit down and be still. You can not go to the House of Voices until it is time."

"I do not understand," I told him. "What house is that? And what house is this?"

"The House of Voices is the one where the other stranger lies. You will stay here while he stays there. Make no trouble, if you are wise."

I asked where my gun and machete were, and why I was held here. They looked at each other in a puzzled way, and one said they knew nothing of gun or knife. I was here, he added, because Pajé ordered it. I would remain here until Pajé gave the word to free me.

Now I knew that the *pajé* of a tribe is its medicine man, but never before had I heard Indians speak the word with such respect. This man had used it as if it meant God. And I saw that what this Pajé had ordered would be done. Yet I growled again, told them to get out of my way, and advanced on them.

Their faces tightened, their arms tensed, and their shoulders swayed forward a little. They were in deadly earnest. Unless I stopped they would plunge those spears into my body. So I halted, laughed as if I had only been joking, squatted, and rolled a cigarette.

They relaxed, though they still watched me closely. Studying them through my tobacco smoke, I thought the wisest plan would be to pretend friendliness and talk of other things, meanwhile watching for a chance to spring and snatch the spear from the nearer man. For I was very uneasy about Pedro, and I did not intend to wait here longer than necessary.

Giving no sign of my thought, I began to talk of our journey from the Jurua. They listened with much interest. When I told of the Spotted People both nodded quickly, and the taller one spoke.

This town too, he said, was once a place of black-spotted people. He himself had been spotted from boyhood, and the black patches had grown until he was repulsive and useless. But then Pajé came to them, and with him came demons of the air who had no bodies; and by the magic of these air-devils and strange-tasting water he had driven out the black sickness and made them strong.

I smoked up my cigarette and slowly made another while I thought about this. Their *pajé* was far more powerful than any I had met in my jungle wanderings. Those whom I had seen before now were good enough at healing wounds or setting broken bones, and some of them were wise in the ways of poison; but when they had to deal with a pain or sickness whose cause was not clear they all worked in the same way.

The medicine man would make a huge cigar, and with great ceremony he would blow the smoke from this thing on the place where the sick man's pain was worst. Then he would suck that spot for a time, and at length he would stand up and take out of his mouth a long whitish thing looking much like a worm. This evil worm, he would say, was what had caused all the trouble, and now that it was out the sufferer would get well. The truth was that the white thing was no worm at all, but a soft plant-root which he had hidden in his mouth before beginning work.

Did this Pajé of theirs draw worms from their bodies? I asked. They looked puzzled and a little offended. The taller one replied that Pajé did nothing of the sort, and that he and his people were not wormy. I asked them what sort of man Pajé was. And who was the fat, dirty man who had led me to the House of Voices? Surely he was not Pajé?

Both grunted scornfully at this. No, the fat man was only a lazy drunkard and the servant of Pajé. Yet he was valuable to them because he was the only one who knew how to call Pajé when his help was needed in time of sickness. He could talk with the air-devils, too.

So the men of the town watched over him carefully when he was drunk, and saw to it that no alligator or snake or other evil thing should destroy him while he was helpless. If they should lose him they would have no way of reaching the ear of Pajé.

For Pajé was not a man like themselves, but a demon-spirit who came there when summoned and took the shape of a great headless creature without arms. When he did appear it was always inside the House of Voices. This house once had

been that of an old medicine man who had little power and who
finally had died suddenly in the night, leaving the people with
no medicine man at all.

Then, many moons later, a drifting canoe had brought
them the fat hairy man, who at that time was not fat but
almost dead from starvation. They had fed him and put him in
the empty house of the dead medicine man to recover his
strength if he could. And he had grown strong, and after a time
he had found a way of calling the air-demons, and after that he
had brought Pajé himself to cure them.

As you may suppose, I did some more thinking and puzzling about this. Then I asked how Pajé worked on wounds or
hurts if he had no hands. They said they did not know — even
the men whom he cured did not know.

A man would be taken to the House of Voices, they said,
and the fat servant would take him inside. Somehow the hurt
man would always fall into a deep sleep before anything was
done to his injury, and although he might stay there for days
he would remember little or nothing of what went on around
him while he lay there. Only a few had ever seen Pajé himself,
and those few could tell only that he was a monster with a deep
voice that made them quake with fear.

In driving out the spotted sickness, they added, Pajé had
not been seen. The fat man had gone about and ordered certain
ones to come later to the House of Voices. When they obeyed,
much afraid but not daring to remain away, they had found the
house empty of life.

But the air-devils had spoken around them, saying queer
things and singing as if far off, and finally commanding them
to drink deep of strange water in a big gourd on the floor. The
same persons had to go each day for a time to the house and
drink of the same water, and at length the sickness and the
spots had left them. And this kept on until all in the town were
well.

They asked me what had come to me in the House of
Voices, and I told them. When I asked them in turn how I had
reached this place where they now guarded me, they said that
while they watched the House of Voices from a safe distance —

for nobody ever went near that house unless called — they saw me tumble out of the door as if thrown. Then a loud voice had come, telling them to take me away and guard me. And they intended to guard me well until further orders.

WHILE WE talked the sun sank low. It glared in at the doorway, half-blinding me. I moved aside, and instantly my guards grew tense. There was small chance for me to jump them now or later — they were too wide-awake, and probably expecting me to do that very thing. Watching the path of light lengthen across the dirt floor, I remembered the words of the headless giant:

"Three suns shall set, two shall rise. When the third sun sinks low this man shall walk again."

The first sun now was sinking. Forty-eight hours must pass before I should know whether the promise was true or false. To remain here in useless idleness was all against my will.

Yet, even if I did break out of my prison, what could I do to help Pedro? Nothing. Against his fever I was helpless as a babe.

"How far is the House of Voices from this house?" I asked.

They looked suspiciously at me. Then one replied:

"Not far. Why do you ask?"

"If Pajé should call to you from there could you hear him?"

"We could hear him."

I nodded and said no more. If the House of Voices was within easy call I too could hear any cry coming from it; and the voice for which I would listen was not that of the misshapen Pajé but of Pedro. At the first sign that he was not being well treated I would fight my way to him somehow. Otherwise I might serve him best by waiting.

So I settled myself to wait the sinking of the third sun.

Before night came other guards arrived. One of them brought my hammock, which I slung inside my prison hut. Women also came, bringing food — a big pot of thick stew which seemed to be partly of fish and partly of sweet turtle-meat. The savory odor of it put so keen an edge on my hunger that I completely cleaned out the pot.

Lying back in my hammock to smoke after eating, I spied a little smile on the face of one of the new guards. All were watching me intently. Before my cigarette was half-smoked a heavy drowsiness came over me. And as the darkness of night fell on the jungle town, the darkness of sleep numbed my mind. The vigil of the jailers had been made easy by some drug in my food I think, *senhores*, that I was kept drugged most of the time for the next two days. I know that I felt dull and sluggish, that sleep came very easily, and that it was hard for me to keep awake long at a time. There was no chance for me to walk outside and shake off the drowsiness, for I was not allowed to leave the hut. Always guards were there to block me with ready spears.

Suspecting that my lethargy came from something in the food, I refused to eat anything the next noon, but this did no good; for I had a great thirst, and the water I drank must also have held some sleeping-powder. Both nights I lay like a dead man, and both mornings I woke with difficulty, long after the sun was up. The time slipped away in a sort of daze, and it was not until after noon of the third day that this feeling left me.

Then, rousing myself from a *siesta*, I found that once more I was wide-awake. In the doorway squatted the same two guards whom I had first seen there. As I arose they also stood up.

"What is the word?" I demanded.

"No word has come."

"My comrade — does he live?"

They lifted their brows as if to say that was a question which no man could answer. When I insisted on a reply the tall one said:

"Only Pajé or his servant can tell. Pajé has not spoken, and the fat drunkard has not been seen. The House of Voices is closed. What lies within it we know not."

"And no sound has come from the House?"

"Yes. On the night of the day when you came a hoarse voice babbled broken words as if struggling in fever. That is all.

We have heard nothing more."

I chewed my lip and looked at the sun-shadows outside. The third sun had not yet sunk low, but it was beginning to slip down the western sky. The time of which the monster had spoken would soon come. And then — what?

The next two or three hours, *senhores*, were the longest of my life. I tried to sit still and talk about other matters; but my eyes always were on the creeping shadows, and at times I had to stride around the room to keep from springing at the sentinels. When at last the light began to glare in at my doorway and crawl across the floor I could no longer hold myself back.

"The time has come," I said, stepping toward the men. "Stand aside."

But they fronted me with weapons low.

"When Pajé orders it —" the taller one began doggedly.

I growled. My toes gripped the floor. But just as I was about to leap at them there came a shout outside.

"The House opens!"

We hung there as we were — poised, watching each other, but listening. And then sounded a thundering voice.

"The closed door opens. The open door shuts. Slave of fever, thou art free. Guards of the free man, your task ends. Go forth, ye two, but go not hence."

Slowly, as if not quite certain that they understood the words, the watchmen at my door lowered their weapons and glanced out. At once I walked between them into the open. My gaze darted to the House of Voices. Outside it, staring around as if bewildered, stood Pedro.

"Pedro!" I called, running toward him.

"Ah, Lourenço!" he answered, smiling in a relieved way. "So you are here."

He walked to meet me, but his step lacked its usual lithe swing. His face was drawn, his eyes and cheeks hollow, his skin pale. But he was alive and free of fever. I nearly seized him and shook him in my joy, but restrained myself in time.

"What place is this?" he asked, glancing at the Indians who were gathering. "Who are these people? How came we here? What has happened?"

"You have been sick."

"Yes, I know I have been sick, and I must have been crazed — I thought I was dead and roasting in hell with some huge headless devil watching me. I feel now as if I had been through purgatory, at least. But what —"

He stopped, staring around him again. I saw that he swayed on his feet.

"You are safe and sound now," I said, slipping an arm around his body. "Come and rest in my hammock, and you shall hear all about it."

And I drew him on toward the hut which had been my prison.

Indians, men and women, crowded beside us and behind us as we went, muttering among themselves but smiling at us. At the doorway I halted and spoke to them.

"My sick comrade is well again but very weak. Will you, my friends, bring food to make him strong?"

Several at once answered that they would do so.

"And do not put into it the thing that makes men sleep," I added. "I have slept overmuch."

At this most of them looked blank, but two of the older men grinned in a knowing way. We passed into the house, which now was unguarded, and Pedro slumped into the hammock.

"My legs are water," he muttered wearily, "and my head is a whirlpool."

Squatting against the wall, I waited for his weakness to pass. Soon his eyes opened and he repeated his questions. I told him all I knew.

"So I was not so crazed as I thought," he mused. "There is a giant without a head. And singing voices. I heard them too. I thought they must come from heaven, and wondered why I was in the other place."

His brow wrinkled, and I saw he was puzzling over what I had told him and what he had seen and heard. Presently he added —

"Are you sure we are in our right minds?"

"No, I am not," I grinned. "But we are alive, and that is

something. Tell me what you can remember."

"It is not much. I became horribly sick while paddling. My head split and my body burned. Voices came and went, some singing, some speaking.

"At last I felt that I was awaking from a frightful dream. I looked around and saw fire, awful things back in the shadows — snakes and skulls and spiders — and a demon without head or arms. I was sure I had died and gone below. But I felt no pain — the demon did not torment me. Then he was gone —"

"How did he go?" I cut in.

"I do not know. I saw no opening anywhere, no light except one small fire. The monster was there and then was not there. It must have been night, and I must have slept a long time after that, for the next thing I can remember was just before I came out and saw you.

"The place was lighter then, and there was a small hole up overhead where brightness showed — the sunshine outside. Not a living thing was in sight anywhere. Then a door slowly opened and I looked out into the daylight.

"And, Lourenço, nobody opened that door. I looked straight at it and saw both sides of it as it swung, and nothing touched it. It opened itself."

We stared at each other. I shook my head, for I could make nothing of it.

"And then?"

"Then a voice came. A queer little voice that seemed to come from a jaguar skull. It told me to arise and go. And I got off a strange flat hammock — it went out from under me as I did so, and I fell on the floor. I crawled through the door on hands and knees, fearing it might close again before I could reach it. While I was scrambling out another voice sounded behind me — a deep voice that said — 'The closed door opens — the open door shuts?'"

"Yes. So you heard it. As soon as I was outside I stood up. Then I saw you."

We were silent for a time, thinking.

"Here is another odd thing, Lourenço," he added then.

"The deep voice spoke in the Tupi tongue. But the odd little voice from the skull, telling me to go, used our own language — Portuguese."

"*Deus Padre!* That is strange!" I muttered. "No man here except ourselves speaks Portuguese —"

"Here is food," announced an Indian voice at the door.

A man and two women stood there. The women held bowls. The man was the taller guard who had watched me during the day. He held no weapon now, and as I went to the door he pointed to each of the bowls in turn.

"This broth for him — this stew for you," he said.

Moving his lips close to my ear, he went on in a whisper:

"In his broth is a little of that which makes sleep. Sleep gives strength. It is the order."

"Whose order?"

"It is the order," he repeated.

"And is my meat also heavy with sleep?"

He grinned.

"No. You have slept enough. Now make your own sleep."

"Who watches us tonight?"

"There is no watch. But it is the order that you stay here until the man with you is strong. Until then your canoe is hidden."

I scowled at him, but he had spoken sense. Pedro must gain strength before we went on, even though the water was ebbing steadily away.

"Where are our guns?" I demanded.

He turned away without reply. The women put down the bowls and left us. Saying no more, I took Pedro's broth in to him. He sniffed at it, tasted it, and drained it to the last drop.

I ate my own stew more slowly. When I set down the empty vessel and glanced at Pedro I found him sleeping as peacefully as a tired child.

A woman carrying a bundle came to the door, dropped her burden, and went away. The thing she had left was Pedro's hammock, brought from our canoe.

As I picked it up I saw another figure come lurching along from the direction of the House of Voices. It was fat and hairy — the *barrigudo* man who had led us there.

With the hammock under my arm I stepped out to meet him. Frowzy and filthy he might be, but he had guided my dying partner to the spot where death's hand was warded off, and now I would say my thanks and offer him reward. Yet I did nothing of the kind. For as he came near me I saw why he staggered. He was drunk — stupidly, disgustingly drunk.

His bloodshot eyes were glazed and set, staring straight past me. His heavy mouth sagged. He breathed thickly, and he hiccoughed. He reeked of liquor as if he had spilled a quart of it down over himself. His look, his reeling gait — and his smell — were those of a man who had wallowed in drunkenness for days. Sickened, I stood back and let the sodden brute stumble past, then swung on my heel and returned to our hut.

There, as I threw another look after him, I noticed that he was being trailed by two armed men. The words of our guards came back to me — that this bleary creature was the only one who could summon the great Pajé, and so he was always protected from danger while drunk.

Perhaps, I thought, the monstrous Pajé was the devil himself, and this servant of his had bartered his hope of heaven for unlimited drink. If ever I saw a man who seemed to have sold himself, body and soul, to the king of all rottenness, the Barrigudo was that man.

But the Barrigudo's future was nothing to me, and I gave him no further attention. After slinging my hammock I curled up in it. And all that night Pedro and I slept peacefully side by side.

I awoke late, but earlier than Pedro. The morning light showed that his color was better and his face did not look quite so hollow. He had rested almost twelve hours when at length he stirred, yawned, blinked at me, and lazily demanded a cigarette.

"Do we go on today?" he asked between puffs.

I shook my head.

"Not until you can swing your paddle again."

"I can swing it now."

"For a time, yes. But not all day."

I did not tell him that our canoe had been hidden and that we were under orders to remain here. That would only have made him determined to go at once and to fight anyone trying to stop us. And he was in no condition for fighting.

"So you are afraid you would have to do all the work?" he laughed. "Perhaps you have it right. I feel lazy this morning. Yet we should start onward soon. The water must have sunk while we stayed here, and we are far from the Javary."

"There will be water enough. And I like the cooking of these Indian women."

"Oho! So that is it! The broth they gave me last night was delicious, it is true. I could eat more now, and meat with it."

"You shall have it."

Calling an Indian boy near the house, I told him to get food. He went away, and soon the same women and the same guard came with the clay bowls. The man looked at Pedro, smiled in a satisfied way, and went out.

After he had gone I thickened my comrade's broth with some of my turtle-meat, and we both ate our fill. When he had smoked again he arose and stretched himself.

"I am going to walk and see the place," he said.

And he went out, lounging along languidly but with far more sureness in his step than he had shown when last he walked. I followed.

Outside we stood and looked long at the House of Voices. For the first time I noticed that it was round. The wall curved away in a circle, and its high pointed roof also was round. An odd thought came to me — that the demon's house was bigger outside than inside; for my memory, though somewhat hazy, told me that its one room was rather small. But as I thought again I could see why it might have seemed small — because of the things that were in it: the heads on the wall, the fire in the middle, the flat hammock, the body of Pedro, and that giant figure looming up in the smoke. And then I forgot it, for again the *barrigudo* man appeared.

He shambled up toward us, heading for the demon-house, followed by the same men who had trailed him last night. He looked even more sodden than when I had last seen him, but not so drunk; the look of a man who had slept off some of his liquor but was stupid from the sleep and from the drink still working in him. His guardians were heavy-eyed, and it was easy to see that they had been awake all night.

I expected him to pass as before, but this time he halted near us and stared at Pedro. And Pedro stared back with disgust plain in his face.

"Phew! What an animal!" my partner sniffed. "The rest of these people look clean. Why do they not wash this beast or throw it to the alligators? An alligator will eat anything — and the fouler the better."

"This is the noble gentleman who brought us here. The Barrigudo, of whom I told you. Embrace him and give him thanks."

"Ugh!"

Pedro gulped as if sickened by the thought.

"I would rather touch a corpse that had lain in the sun. He is worse than the Spotted People. But I can thank him, unless the wind changes and blows his scent this way."

Changing then from Portuguese to Tupi, he spoke to the man.

"You are he who brought me here and called your Pajé to heal me? I am grateful for my life. If I have anything which you or Pajé want, speak. You shall have whatever I can give."

The Barrigudo made no reply. He only stared stonily at us both. His eyes, though, held an expression I did not like — a look that seemed anger. Yet why should he be offended? Such an uncouth creature surely could not understand what we had said of him in Portuguese, and he would scarcely resent Pedro's offer to reward him.

But, as I say, he made no answer. He gave one sour grunt and plodded on.

"You said you had to put a gun in his face to make him guide you," said Pedro. "I can believe it. We owe him no gratitude."

And we forgot the drunkard as quickly as we could, not even watching to see where he went.

Strolling slowly, we walked among the little houses of the

Indians, who received us with a quiet dignity which increased our liking for them. Before long we found with us the tall guard who had told me of the orders and had come each time with the women bearing food.

"Are we still under guard?" I grumbled.

Looking slightly surprised, he said no; I knew the orders and of course would heed them, and he came only because his father wished to see us. When we asked who his father was, he astonished us by replying —

"The chief."

Somehow we had not thought of a chief in this place, and still less had we thought that a chief's son was one of our guards. I did not know whether to consider this an honor or an indication that the real ruler here was Pajé. But I said nothing on this point. To make talk as we crossed the clearing I remarked that the dirty servant of Pajé was drunk again.

He nodded, as if I had said the sun was hot or water was wet. Pedro, still disgusted, asked him the same question he had asked me: why they did not make that man keep himself clean. The Indian said they could not do so without treating him roughly, and in that case he might sulk and refuse to call Pajé when needed.

"And no one else can call Pajé?" I asked.

"I have said so."

"But in time he will rot himself to death. Then how can you reach Pajé?"

"We can not. But he is strong and will live many years."

"Perhaps. Yet he might leave you at any time and go to another tribe."

The Indian's face grew grim. The fat man would not go away alive, he said. And I saw that the *barrigudo*, though he did as he pleased, was not much better than a prisoner.

We found the chief to be old, thin, but clear-eyed and shrewd-brained. He asked us many questions and answered none of ours. When we left his mud house we had learned nothing new, and we felt that, so far as he was concerned, we were neither welcome nor unwelcome here. The servant of Pajé had brought us to the place, and if he and his headless master wished to amuse themselves with us it was nothing to the head of the tribe.

Outside, as we stood a moment talking with the young chief, a man came up with three fine fish. One was a splendid *surubim*, as long as my leg, beautifully spotted and striped. The others were *tucunares*, with the big eye-spots on their tails. The man laid them down respectfully before the young chief, who glanced at them, then picked up the *surubim* and started away toward the House of Voices.

"The finest fish goes to Pajé," said Pedro as we strolled back to our hut. "Let us see whether he comes out to receive it."

We saw nothing of the monster, but we soon heard something from him. At the doorway of the round house the tall young savage stopped, spoke, laid the fish down, and backed away; then stopped again, seemed to listen to a voice, backed once more, swung on his heel and came straight to us.

"At the sinking of the next sun the *gamba* drums will beat," he told us.

"What does that mean?" Pedro yawned.

"It is the night of the full moon, when demons are restless. Many voices will be round about. Demons of water and air and earth will be near. No man may stay in his house, lest a devil seize him in the dark. All must gather around the House of Voices, where the drums will beat and Pajé himself will protect us. Sleep well tonight, for tomorrow night there will be no sleep."

With that he strode off toward his father's house.

"Demons seem to rule this place, Lourenço," my partner said. "Voices in the air — a monster without a head — devils who seize men in their houses when the moon is full — I shall not be sorry to leave it all behind me."

He spoke half in jest, but he expressed my own thought. We had already been delayed too long, and I had seen more than enough of this devil-ruled village.

Since there was nothing to do, we did nothing but eat, sleep, and argue about Pajé and his fellow demons until the night of the full moon came. In that time Pedro's strength flowed steadily back into him. And when the sun dropped low and we saw men carrying the long log drums to the House of Voices, the old reckless twinkle was in his eyes as he said:

"Since we must sit up and evade the devils, let us start a *pira-purasseya* fish-dance with some of these good-looking girls while the drums beat. Ask the young chief to bring out some *cachassa*, too, and we can make a real night of it."

"Playing with girls and rum is no way to dodge the devil," I told him.

"But if you have a handsome girl and plenty of drink, why care if the devil does get you?"

I knew well that he cared little for women or liquor. But I retorted:

"Your friend the Barrigudo has plenty of rum. See what it has done for him."

"Ugh!"

He wrinkled his nose as if I had put something offensive under it.

"I hope I shall not meet him again tonight. He spoils my appetite as well as my thirst."

"Have courage. I have not seen him since yesterday, and he probably is sleeping off more drink. We are not likely to be near him."

I was wrong. We were soon to be much nearer to that Barrigudo than we expected. And before we parted from him — Well, *senhores*, you shall hear.

THE SUN slid down and was gone. Fires sprang up around the House of Voices. The thunder of the big *gambas* filled the jungle, each beaten by a man astride the log, pounding the skin head with his knuckles. The clatter of *caracasha* rattles broke out. And all the Indians, big and little, hurried to the round demon-house where they could be safe. Walking more slowly, we followed.

The fires surrounding the House were many but small, none being very close to the curving wall. We found that there were really two rings of these fires, with a fairly wide space between the inner and the outer circle; and in this space the people arranged themselves.

As we approached, the young chief came out to meet us and pointed to a spot where we were to squat. When we had settled ourselves we found the old chief himself beside us, staring at the ground. The young chief sank down on the other side of us.

Nobody spoke. Talk would have been useless in that booming, rattling uproar. Patiently we waited for Pajé to walk out, or for something else to occur. But we waited long and nothing happened. The drummers and rattlers kept up their work without a pause, and everyone else squatted or sat motionless while the bright moonlight flooded the clearing. At length I tired of it and arose to go back to my hut.

At once the young chief sprang up and blocked me. Other men also arose and moved toward us. Shouting in the tall fellow's ear, I told him I did not want to stay here, and that I would risk being carried off by devils. I wanted to get into my hammock.

But he yelled back that the danger was not mine alone. If a demon got me, that demon would keep coming back each night and taking others. And when I still insisted on going, he added that no man could be allowed to imperil the rest in that way, and that anyone trying to leave the fire-circle would be killed at once.

I sat down again.

Then came a sudden break in the drumming. The door of the House had swung open. Out from it came the *barrigudo*. He lifted a hand. The racket of the *caracashas* ceased. With the end of the tumult the place seemed still as death.

"Pajé, master of demons, has come," he said in a throaty tone. "Be still."

We were still. And in the stillness we heard whisperings and squeakings in the air above and around us. The air-devils also had arrived.

Thin voices spoke from nowhere — in the grass, up overhead, at the very walls of the House. And they spoke one word only:

"*Hewy!* Blood!"

A singing voice answered them:

"*Ehe ahrahm! Ehe ahrahm!* Wait a while! Wait awhile!"

Another singing voice, high and sweet, played around in the air over us, saying nothing — only singing without words. But then, from the smoke-hole at the peak of the House, a harsh little voice croaked:

"*Hewy! Hahmbuya heh!* Blood! I am hungry!"

And another voice, sharp and squeaky, cried:

"*Heyimbeh! Kunyimuku!* A heart! A young girl!"

Fear showed plain in the faces of the Indians near me as they heard the demands of the dreaded demons. All stared at the roof. I too looked up there; but, seeing nothing, dropped my gaze and glanced along the line of terrified eyes gleaming in the light of fire and moon.

For a moment all was very still. Then out rolled the sonorous tones of Pajé himself:

"Seek ye the blood and hearts of beasts, not of my people. Begone from this place!"

The command came from within the House. The Barrigudo was not in sight. The door stood partly open, and in the dimness beyond it I saw a giant figure — tall and thick and headless — standing in smoke. Others saw it too. Pedro drew in his breath sharply, and the old chief gave a startled grunt. Slowly the door swung shut.

Queer snarling noises sounded on the roof, as if the hungry demons raged at the command to go. Silence followed. When it had lasted for the space of a dozen slow breaths, Pajé spoke again.

"So ye would snatch at the lives of young girls, the mothers to be? Ye would drink the blood of the strong men? Then I, Pajé, will give my people to drink of that which will not harm them but will burn you if ye touch them. Slave, take this bowl and give to all except the two strangers."

Again the snarls sounded above, with broken cries of rage. The door opened, and out came the Barrigudo, grunting under the weight of a tall clay jar of liquid. This he set down beside the old chief.

"Three swallows," he growled. "Then pass on. Do not step

outside the fire circles. You and you" — looking at Pedro and me — "stand inside the inner ring. You get none of the drink of Pajé."

Wondering, we obeyed and stood watching. The Barrigudo tilted the jar. The old chief drank three times from it, arose, and made room for his son. When the young man had taken his three swallows he also moved on. And one by one, in their turns, men and women and children stopped at the jar, drank, and passed along between the fires.

At length the old chief returned, having walked all around the house, and sank into his place facing the door. Everyone in the circle except Pedro and myself had taken of the drink, and the jar was almost empty.

"Let the drums beat," muttered the Barrigudo.

The old chief cried out shrilly. The thundering of the logs broke out again. Pedro and I, not knowing what else to do, squatted where we were. When we tired of squatting we lay down on our backs and watched little clouds drift across the big white moon.

For some time the drumming went steadily on, and I became so used to it that I began to grow sleepy. If this was to last all night, I thought, I might as well take what rest I could there on the ground. So I shut my eyes, and was dozing away when I noticed that the drumming seemed to be growing weaker. The drummers were tired, I thought, and should be relieved. But I did not bother to look at them until Pedro softly gripped my shoulder.

He was wide-awake and grinning. He moved his head toward the nearest drum. I looked and found that its drummer was no longer astride it, but lying beside it. He seemed asleep. Beyond him another drummer was swaying drowsily, and soon he slipped off his log and lay still. Only two of the dozen drums now were booming, and soon there was only one. Then that one stopped.

But the place was not silent. Now that the drums were quiet we could hear a chorus of snores. All around the circle lay Indians sound asleep, and others were drooping forward and slumping down on the earth. Both the old chief and his son lay as if dead.

By ones and twos they all slipped down and remained where they dropped. We heard a short, hard chuckle from the door of the round house. In the opening, his teeth gleaming in his dirty face, stood the Barrigudo.

As we looked at him he walked away from us, around the house. Returning to the door, he went in, remained a moment, and came out with an *atura* basket on his back. In his hands he held our guns and machetes. Straight to us he came.

"Come," he grunted.

He was sober, or nearly so. He walked away with a sure, steady stride. We arose and trailed behind him.

"Get your hammocks," he ordered, pausing before our hut.

Swiftly we untied our beds and slung them over our shoulders. Across the moonlit clearing he swung then to the edge of the deep jungle shadows. There he halted.

"A torch. In the basket."

I dipped a hand into his *atura* and found at the top a fagot of twigs and bark. Pedro lighted it. The Barrigudo took the flaming bundle and started on. I walked along behind him, Pedro coming after me. Under the trees it was very black in places, but our leader never hesitated. Before long we reached water.

The fat Indian held his torch out, and we looked down into our own canoe. He dropped our weapons into it and motioned for us to get in. Throwing in our hammocks, we did so. As we picked up the paddles he turned away.

"Wait! What does this mean?" I demanded.

"Wait! You shall see what it means," he retorted.

His torch moved a few yards along the bank, dipped, wavered about, then stood still. In a moment it moved outward. A paddle dipped. The *barrigudo* also was afloat.

Along the narrow inlet the boats moved until they entered a wider space where the moonlight shone down. Here the barrigudo pulled the torch from its fastening at the bow, plunged it hissing into the water, dropped its charred stub into the bottom of his canoe, swerved to the right, and slid on along the wide *furo*.

For hours we worked steadily westward, saying nothing. To me, after the days of inaction, it was a joy to feel my muscles loosen and stretch, to be going somewhere, even though I knew not where or why.

Pedro too, though not so strong as before his sickness, moved with his usual swaying stroke. The *barrigudo*, however, with his big belly and his weight of fat and his muscles rotted by rum, soon found his task harder and harder.

Often we heard him gasp and grunt as if driving himself beyond endurance. But he kept on doggedly, though splashing more and more, until we marveled that he could still move. Not until the sinking of the moon made the channel very dark did he quit.

Then he dropped his paddle noisily into his canoe. Wheezing and groaning, he slumped forward, clasping his huge stomach. We drew alongside and waited. After a time his distress passed and he straightened up.

Beside us opened another narrow cove. He swung his head toward it, lifted his paddle, and shoved his boat into it. When well away from the *furo* he stopped again.

"Keep awake," he said hoarsely. "I must sleep. If anyone calls do not answer. Wake me at sunrise."

Exhausted, he laid himself down in his canoe, gave a long sigh, and slept.

"What do you make of this, Lourenço?" my partner asked.

"Nothing, unless he is escaping with us," said I. "Yet for us it is not really an escape — we should soon have been freed. But we shall see."

"Would soon have been freed?" Pedro puzzled. "Were we not free to go at any time after I left the House of Voices?"

"No."

And for the first time I told him of the hiding of our canoe and the orders of the young chief.

"I wish I had known that," he grumbled.

"Yes, and you would have made trouble for yourself. We are out of the place now, so forget what is past. You had better sleep a little too. I will keep watch."

He retorted that he was no child and could watch as well

as I. Yet after he smoked a cigarette he did curl up on our hammocks, and soon I was the only one awake.

When the sun had burned away the morning mists I touched Pedro and prodded the *barrigudo*. Pedro sat up a little stiffly, but with a smile. The slave of Pajé and of liquor had hard work to sit up at all, but after several attempts he managed it. He scooped up some water in his hands and drank it thirstily. After blinking a minute he again took up his paddle.

"*Por Deus!* Your *barrigudo* now drinks water!" Pedro laughed. "What marvel shall we see next?"

The *barrigudo* gave him an ugly look through his hair. I began to suspect that the man did know Portuguese. So I spoke to him in that tongue.

"Let us eat."

He only grunted as if he did not understand and did not want to, and shoved his dugout toward the *furo*. We did not stop to eat, but pushed out in his wake.

Again he turned westward. And all through that hot forenoon, *senhores*, he kept going. Sweating, breathing hard, groaning at times, but always pulling away at his paddle, he drove onward until noon. By that time his strokes were so weak that his boat merely crawled, and we were so hungry that we were ugly.

"Are you trying to kill yourself and us with work and hunger?" I complained. "What does all this mean? Where are you going?"

Slowly, looking us straight in the eyes, he answered:

"*Eheh ahoh putare heretamo koteh.* I am going away to my country."

So that was it. Somehow it seemed strange that this creature could have any country other than the place where we had found him. Yet I did not despise him now as I had. His grim fight to keep going in spite of his clumsiness and his rum-rot made me respect him a little. I was about to ask him, in a more civil tone, where his country was, when Pedro broke in.

"So are we. But we have eaten nothing today, and I am going ashore now to eat and rest a while."

The *barrigudo* watched him a minute, then stooped, drew

something out of his basket, bit off a piece, and threw the rest to us. It was a flat cake of pressed leaves and bark, wet and sticky as if it had been soaked.

"Chew that," he said. "Swallow."

Seeing that he was already chewing his own, we each bit off a chunk and ground it between our teeth. It tasted both sweetish and sour, quickly filling our mouths with water. After we had swallowed a few times our hunger left us and we felt refreshed.

"What is it?" Pedro asked.

"*Petema.* Tobacco," he replied with a slight grin. "*Yahoh uahn.* Let us go now."

And he resumed paddling.

"It is no more tobacco than my foot," Pedro snorted in Portuguese. "But I will not let that bag-belly outpaddle me."

And his shoulders also began to sway again and we moved on.

IT WAS sundown when we stopped at last. Up another inlet we went, around snake-like curves, and into a large, rounded pool.

"Here we are safe," panted the hairy man.

Picking a shelving spot, he drove his dugout ashore, high and hard. As the canoe struck he tumbled forward and lay wheezing. When he was able to get up he crawled out on hands and knees, looking more than ever like a huge monkey.

While we landed he sat in the soft mud by the water, his head hanging, his eyes closed; and he stayed there until we had put up our hammocks, made a fire, and prepared our meal.

"Come and eat," I called.

Wearily he lifted his head and slowly he got up. But he did not eat. He looked at the fire, then stumbled over to it and flopped down beside it.

"*Anih hahmbuya heh.* I am not hungry," he sighed — and went to sleep sprawling on the bare ground, with the smoke creeping over him.

We let him lie. We did not feel hungry either at first, but after the first few mouthfuls we ate like starved men. When we were full we were stupid from fatigue and heavy eating. After building up the fire so that it would burn slowly and long, we tumbled into our hammocks; and I fell asleep at once.

When I opened my eyes on a new day the *barrigudo* was gone.

My machete also was gone. The rifles were there, however, and nothing else was missing. And when I looked at the water's edge, there was his canoe, just as he had driven it up at sundown Of the man himself, though, there was no sign — no blood on the ground, no fresh tracks near the water. He had not been killed or carried off, and he seemed not to have walked away. He had simply vanished.

Wondering, I made breakfast and awoke Pedro. We called, but got no answer. So, after some talk and argument, we ate and smoked, intending then to search the bush. Before our cigarettes were finished, however, a deep voice spoke behind us.

"Good morning!"

The words were English. The voice was not that of the *barrigudo*, yet it was familiar. And the man we saw as we whirled and looked was not the *barrigudo* either — not the *barrigudo* we knew; but it was such a man as the *barrigudo* might be if, by some miracle, he should become clean.

A broad, heavy white man stood there. Yes, *senhores*, a white man — burned to a coppery brown by the sun, black-haired of body as well as of head, but a white man for all that. His whole body glowed as if it had been scrubbed and scraped and scrubbed again. His hair was not long and greasy like that of the *barrigudo*, but cut close to his broad skull; and his scalp, too, was rosy as if rubbed almost raw.

Under his black brows a pair of deep brown eyes looked straight at us without wink or waver. His mouth was not loose-lipped but set in a resolute line. His head was up and his shoulders back; and, though he was overfat, both face and body were those of a man strong and self-reliant.

Open-mouthed, we stared until he spoke again.

"Understand English?"

"Y-y-yes, *senhor*," Pedro gulped. "We both speak it. But — but are you — the *barrigudo*?"

"I was. Yesterday. Today I am — somebody else."

He talked slowly, halting for words as if it had been so long since he had last used his own language that it did not come easily to his tongue.

"Now that I am fit to do so," he went on, "I will eat breakfast. Been cleaning up at a little pool back in the bush."

Calmly he advanced and handed me my machete. In a dazed manner I took it.

"Yours," he nodded. "I used the back to scrape myself and the edge to saw off my hair. Overdid the haircut a bit. Shall have to make a leaf hat now. What have you to eat?"

Dumbly I arose and got out more *farinha* and dried fish. With the *farinha* I tried to make some *chibeh*, but I paused to stare at him again and spilled half of the water.

"Never mind the *chibeh*," he said, gnawing off a chunk of the *pirarucu* fish. "I will make it myself. Sit down. You seem upset."

A little vexed, I put my mind on my work and made the *chibeh* as it should be. Placing the gourd on the ground, I made a new cigarette and watched him eat.

"Roll me a smoke too, if you please," he added. "Haven't had one for four years. Now that I have quit boozing I need a smoke to steady me."

"You have stopped drinking?" I repeated as I reached for my pouch.

"I have. It's gnawing at me now, but I'm through with it. Damn the stuff! It's been my curse. I'll beat it or die trying. And I'll not die."

He bit savagely into the fish again, and chewed it as if grinding up with it his craving for drink. He ate his *chibeh* in the same fierce way. When that was gone he drank heavily — of water. After that he swiftly lighted the cigarette I had made, sucked the smoke into his lungs, coughed, choked, tried again, and made better work of it.

"Got to learn to smoke all over again," he grumbled. "It makes me dizzy and it tastes rotten. But it helps some.

"Now you fellows are bursting with questions, I suppose. Shoot them quick. We've got to move."

"Anything you wish to tell us, *senhor*, we shall be glad to hear," Pedro replied. "We ask no questions about matters that do not concern us."

"Thanks. Mighty decent of you. Then I'll say this much now, for it does concern you: About another day's paddle from here we hit a rambling sort of river running northeast. Are you hunting for a way to the Amazon?"

"No. We seek the Javary, in the northwest."

"Oh. I see. Probably this *furo* continues northwest after we reach the river. Not sure about that, though. We'll see. If you go northwest I leave you at the river. I travel northeast."

"To the Amazon?"

"To the Amazon. Then to the Atlantic. Then to America — North. Three A's in a row. They spell 'Home' to me. Let's go."

He heaved himself up, winced from the pain of stiff muscles, clamped his jaws, and marched to his canoe. As soon as we could gather up our hammocks, weapons, and food we entered our own craft, and again we were off.

ALL DAY we kept on his wake. All day he drove himself to keep his paddle going, eating nothing, only chewing a few mouthfuls of that "tobacco" of his which banished hunger and subdued fatigue. And as mile after mile crept past and the sweat continued to roll off him he seemed slowly to shrink — shrink to firm muscle and slough off his gross fat.

Whether or not this was only my fancy, I know that when we stopped that night on the far side of his rambling river — for we did reach it late that day — he was shaped more like a man and less like a monkey. And his face, with new lines eaten into it, was that of a man, fighting a hard but winning fight.

That night, too, he bathed himself again, though so tired that he could not stand steadily. And he ate and smoked before he lay down by the fire.

"Take my hammock," I urged.

But he would not. And when I spoke of snakes, he retorted:

"Any snake that bites me will die of delirium tremens. There's a lot of bad booze in my system yet. I'll take the chance.

Good night!"

So, as before, Pedro and I slept in our hammocks and he on the ground. And, as before, he was up first in the morning.

"Now," he said after breakfast, "we have time to talk.

"You're wondering, of course, how I came into this part of the world. Briefly, then, I was a surgeon. I was a good surgeon. But I drank. More than once I operated when I was nowhere near sober. That meant trouble ahead.

"The trouble came. There was a delicate operation — a young woman — and I was shaky from the effects of a wild night. I had to quit in the middle of the job. Another doctor finished it, but the damage was done. She never recovered consciousness. It was just as well that she didn't.

"That botch broke me. I lost my grip. I drank harder — slid downhill fast. Lost my practice and about everything else, including self-respect and hope. Never committed any crime, though. I'm clean in that way if in no other.

"Drifted into Brazil as 'doctor' of a crowd of wealthy bums who came up the Amazon on a steam-yacht, calling themselves 'explorers.' Lots of money and fool ideas, but no brains. Only thing they explored was every known variety of Brazilian booze. I was the best explorer in the bunch when it came to that.

"Had a drunken row and got put ashore at some Indian town and left there. Thought I had hit the bottom then, but there was still some distance to slide. Yes, there was.

"I kept drinking. Quit everything else — even quit wearing clothes — but I kept drinking. Went from one place to another with Indians — only friends I had left, and some of them not very cordial. I was a no-good white, down and out.

"Just how I got into that place back yonder I don't remember. Drifting around, drunk whenever I could find booze — finally got lost, starved nearly to death, woke up in a place of scabby spotted folks who had fed me and then dumped me in a medicine man's hut.

"I got well, looked for more booze, and couldn't find enough. But I fixed a way to get plenty. Then I stayed with it until you fellows came."

He paused, scowling out at the river flowing past, as if he saw the last four years of his life floating by him on its surface. We said nothing. After a time he went on.

"There is more than one way of getting booze. Buy it, make it yourself, get others to make it for you. When you're lazy and broke there are objections to all these ways. Making it yourself means work and waiting. Buying it means paying for it. And folks won't make it for you unless they receive something in return.

"Of course, a man who won't make his own and has no means of buying it has two ways left — to beg it or steal it. But there are places where even these ways won't get you much. And I was in one of those places.

"There was a little booze in that town, but only a little. The reason why there wasn't more was because the people were too sick and sluggish to work and make it. What little I could get was only a teaser for a two-handed rum-hound like me. I grew desperate. And in my desperation I got a big idea.

"I had bummed many a drink — and many a drunk — among Indians who gave it to me because I could do surgical and medical work for them. I had knocked around in this country long enough to pick up a knowledge of your jungle dis-eases, and also of the medicinal virtues of your native roots, herbs, leaves, barks, and so on. I had seen that scabby, spotty skin disease before, and I knew how to cure it.

"But I was tired of begging drinks; I wanted to command them. And while I was in that dead medicine man's house I got the idea. I began to play God.

"I mean just that. God created men. I had to create men too. Those spotted Indians were nothing but living corpses, and I had to take those dead-alive people and turn them into healthy folks. Otherwise they wouldn't make booze for me.

"So, for the sake of rum, I became a creator and a savior of bodies. Their souls didn't interest me. My own didn't interest me either.

"Worrying along with what rum I could get and driven by my idea, I worked like a beaver inside the round house until it was ready. Then I made the air-devils talk and sing. After that

I built Pajé.

"Pajé was just the boy to handle those Indians, both before and after they were cured; and I saw to it that he never botched things as I had botched that operation back home. So everybody got well, and as the servant of Pajé I lived on the fat of the land and was soused to the collar most of the time.

"And then you chaps came along and woke me up. That's all. Make me another cigarette, please."

"But *senhor*, that is not all," I protested. "What was that work which you did in the round house? How did you make air-devils and Pajé? What is Pajé? How did you —"

I broke off and glanced upward. Above our heads sounded a sweetly singing little voice. Nothing was there; the air was empty. As I dropped my gaze again to the *barrigudo* I found him grinning.

"The singing voices follow us," he laughed. "And so does Pajé."

Without moving, he suddenly boomed out in resonant tones:

"You have eyes but you see not. You have ears but your brain is deaf. I am Pajé, master of demons! I am the air-devils! I am the whole damn works! Give me that cigarette!"

It was the voice of Pajé himself.

"But how —" I gasped.

"Oh, give me the makings and let me roll my own smoke," he said impatiently in his usual tone.

When his cigarette was lighted he explained.

"I built an inner wall to the house. A false wall, with space between it and the real wall for me to move. Fixed a blind doorway on a slant in a dim spot at one side. Kept the house dark and smoky all the time to conceal it. Could appear and disappear in no time that way.

"The great Pajé was hidden between the walls. He was nothing but a light framework fitting over my shoulders, with dark cloth draped over it. Had a very thin place in the cloth so that I could see through it. Trickery and a change of voices did the rest."

"Por Deus!" muttered Pedro. "You fooled us with our own

trick. We ourselves used such frames and great false heads to terrify Indians back on the Jurua. But yours was headless and armless —"

"And you were sick, and I kept up the demon stuff, and the Indians firmly believed I was an infernal monster and told you so. As for the air-devils, I happen to be good at ventriloquism — throwing voices around, you know.

"I had a bag of tricks inside the house too — strings which would open and shut the door or the jaws of heads on the wall, and so on. You saw some of them, Lourenço. Remember the boa's head that ordered you out and the vampire bat that put you to sleep? That dust that fell into your face when you pulled down the vampire bat was a sure-fire knockout powder.

"There were other things which you didn't see because I didn't need to use them on you. I had a very complete workshop there."

"I believe you," I agreed. "But if you yourself are the air-devils, how did you throw those voices all the way from the place where we found you to the spot where I first heard them? How did you even see us through all that bush? Why, *senhor*, you were asleep!"

"No more asleep than I am now," he chuckled. "Wasn't far from you, either. I was right at the edge of the bush, squatting and grubbing around for a certain kind of root, when you hove in sight.

"Happened to have just enough rum in me to make me feel good. Kept out of sight and tossed voices around just to see what you'd do.

"Then, finding you had sickness aboard, thought I'd look it over. While you were paddling downstream and then going up that cove looking for me I took a shortcut, lay down under a tree where you couldn't miss me, and pretended sleep. After that I had to be surly and carry out my role. Anything else?"

"Yes. What ailed Pedro, and how did you cure the Indians of spotted sickness, and —"

"Not so fast. I am not going to tell you all I know. But if ever you become diseased with that spotted ailment, make strong sarsaparilla and drink it. Very strong, plenty of it.

"Pedro had malignant fever, which kills in a few hours. You brought him to me barely in time, and I had a job to pull him through. Didn't touch a drop of rum in all the time I was working on him — didn't sleep a wink either. The minute he was out of the house, though, I gulped about a gallon of jungle lightning."

I nodded, remembering his appearance when he passed me an hour after Pedro's release from the House of Voices. After being sober and sleepless for forty-eight hours, it was no wonder that he had become drunk so swiftly and completely when the tension ended.

"Now that I know what I know," Pedro said slowly, "I am sorry, *senhor*, that I said what I did when I saw you the next day."

"You needn't be. It was exactly what I needed — a look at myself through another man's eyes. It jolted me into realization of just how much of a beast I had become.

"When I had shut myself up inside the round house and knocked out my hangover with a little homemade bracer I sat down and did some real thinking. Didn't have to meditate much concerning my exact social status — your disgust showed me where I stood.

"But I had to figure out a way to get out of there quick. Knew I had to go quick or I'd lose the ambition to go. Knew the Indians would never let me go if they could stop me.

"So I fixed them so they couldn't stop me. Scared them with the air-devils and then fed them that Pajé-drink, which was doped heavily enough to knock them cold for twelve hours. So here I am."

"And now that you are here, what will you do?" I asked.

"Go home, I told you. When I reach home I'm going to atone for sacrificing that young woman's life on the altar of Bacchus. I'm going to save a good many other lives in its place.

"No, not by surgery — I doubt if I shall ever operate again. But, as I said before, I've learned a good deal down here about native medicines, and I've experimented a lot and worked out new remedies of my own. Had to do it in order to keep up my bluff. The result is that I know powerful drug combinations of which North America knows nothing. But North America is going to hear about them soon. See that basket?"

He motioned toward the *atura* which he had brought from the House of Voices on that last night, and which now lay in his canoe.

"It's full of leaves, bark, roots, twigs, pieces of vine — stuff which you'd call rubbish. But every one of them has a big value in medicine, and I know exactly what each is good for.

"In the next few years there may be good jobs here for men who will collect those things for the North American market. Want a job like that?"

We laughed.

"Thank you, *senhor*, but we are *seringueiros*," Pedro told him. "We collect nothing but rubber, mosquito bites, and danger. Those three things keep us so busy that we have no time for anything else."

"Suit yourselves," he said, and arose. "You say you go westward from here. But you haven't found the *furo* yet, so we'll travel together until you think you've hit it.

"Now let's move. My Indian jailers may be coming this way, and I'd rather make a clean getaway than have to fight them."

He planted his big body in his dugout and pushed out and downstream. Half a mile below our camping place he slowed.

"Looks like a channel there, running west," he said. "Your *furo*, perhaps. Going to chance it?"

After studying the quiet water opening out on the left bank we decided that it was what we sought. We urged him to come with us to the headquarters of our *coronel*, who would send him home as a gentleman. But he shook his head.

"I'm through with bumming," he snapped. "I'm working my way home. Glad to have met you, gentlemen. Goodbye."

"Wait!" cried Pedro. "You must take a gun. Here is one given me by an American soldier back toward the Jurua — he and his comrades had come here on a treasure-hunting journey, led by a crazy man, and when they went back toward the Amazon they gave us each a rifle. We have another, and plenty of cartridges. Take it, *senhor*, and some of our food, and my clothes — I shall not need them."

"I'll take the gun and some cartridges if you insist. Been wondering how you chaps got those Army Springfields, but didn't like to ask. Nothing else, thanks — not a thing. I can handle myself in the bush. Thanks again, and goodbye."

He held out a hand, and we grasped it in farewell. Then he slapped his paddle into the river and heaved his boat downstream. Holding our own craft steady, we watched him until he passed out of sight. Not once did he look back.

"If he holds that pace to the Amazon he will grow much thinner than he is now," said Pedro as we turned into the *furo*.

"He will be hard as *itauba* stone-wood and free from all drink-craving when he reaches the great river," I agreed.

"Do you honestly believe he will win his fight with himself? He has far to go, and he may find Indian villages on his way."

"He will win. He has something to look forward to now. I have seen such men before. At first he drank as you and I drink when we feel like it — for the fun of carousing with others. Then he drank to drown the memory of the girl he had killed. Here in the jungle he drank to forget that he was, as he said, 'a no-good white, down and out.'

"But now he has before him the thought of home and the knowledge that he can wipe out his past. With that to draw him on, the rum of Indian villages will not snare him."

"You have it right," my comrade admitted. "A man's life depends on what is in his own heart. Yet you named him rightly when you called him *barrigudo*. Do you know what happens to a *barrigudo* when he leaves his own country?"

"He dies."

"He dies. And this man, leaving his own land, died and became a beast."

"But now the *barrigudo* is dead and a new man lives in his place."

"*Si*. It is as it should be. Now let us lean on our paddles, for we have many miles to go and the water ebbs."

We shot away along the *furo*, homeward bound.

THE BOUTO

NO, SENHOR, that loud snort which sounded from the river just now was not made by an alligator. I do not wonder that you thought so, for this upper Amazon is full of alligators big and small — *jacaré uassú, jacaré tinga, jacaré curúa,* and others not so common — and the alligator, like other beasts, has his night call. But the sound which you heard was made by a river animal far more graceful and less dangerous — a dolphin.

Look! Over there you can see its back fin glisten in the moonlight. Ah, it is gone. It has dived, and by the time it rises again this steamer will be so far downstream that we shall see it no more.

What is that? You would like to take a shot at one? If you will pardon me, I would urge you to do no such thing. You might be so unfortunate as to kill it with your heavy bullet. Have not you and your companion learned, while exploring our Amazon headwaters, that to kill a *bouto* is bad luck?

Indeed it is true, *senhores.* Everyone on the river knows that. If you do not believe it, tell some Indian that you want dolphin oil to burn in your lantern and that you will pay him well to harpoon one for you. He will answer that blindness creeps on those who use the oil of the *bouto* for light, and that even worse fortune falls on him who slays the fish.

He may tell you, too, the legend of the Bouto Woman, which you perhaps have heard before. No? At our river towns the tale is told that sometimes the *bouto* turns itself into a handsome girl whose hair is so long that it sweeps on the ground behind her when she walks. Leaving the water at night, she strolls about until she meets a man. She smiles on him and coaxes him to walk down to the riverside, saying that there they will be alone. And if he goes with her he goes to death. For at the edge of the water she seizes him around the body and leaps with him into the flood, and he is gone for all time.

Yes, it is an odd tale, as you say. But, *senhores*, an odd story is not always untrue. I will not say that I believe the *bouto* itself does this, yet — well, you North Americans have a saying, have you not, that "where there is smoke there is fire"? And queer things sometimes come about on this Amazon of ours and on the jungle rivers which flow into it — happenings which the great world outside never knows. I myself, a rubber-worker of the Javary region, have seen some such things. And now that we speak of the Bouto Woman I can tell you of something which I saw not very long ago.

The great annual flood, which turns nearly one-third of our Brazil into a vast tree-choked sea, was nearly at its end. Indeed, the flood itself was long past, and in many places the wet land had risen once more above the water. To me and my comrade Pedro, urging our canoe northwestward through the jungle toward the river Tecuahy, this reappearance of the muddy earth was both welcome and unwelcome. Welcome, because it meant that the time was near when we could return to our rubber-work in the forests of old Coronel Nunes and earn more money. Unwelcome, because we had not yet reached the river we sought, and the rising of the thick bush from under the flood had made our travel slower and harder.

We had been on a long journey to the upper reaches of the river Jurua, off to the southeast — a trip with which our work for Coronel Nunes had nothing to do, for it was made in the time of high water when neither we nor any other men could labor in the flood-swept lowlands of his *seringal*. We had gone in burning rage and hate to avenge the death of another *seringueiro* captured and tortured by a tribe of beast-men — and we had avenged it well. Then, drifting down the Jurua while I recovered from a wound, we had at length turned off westward on a flood-channel through the forest, hoping by this to return to the Tecuahy and then go down that river to the Javary town of Remate de Males, whence we had started.

On this channel, which we never had seen before, we had met with delays. Most of them were due to losing our way, but a few had arisen from more serious causes. The latest of these was an attack of malignant fever which had struck my partner suddenly and nearly swept him across a river wider even than this Amazon — the river which runs between the worlds.

But he had been saved by a white medicine-man who was at once the ruler and the prisoner of an Indian tribe; and when Pedro was strong again this man had arranged our escape and himself fled with us to a wandering river running northeast, where he had left us and struck off alone toward civilization. And now, days later, we were still driving our canoe onward, guiding ourselves by the sun and holding as true a course as we could in the maze of thick bush and blind channels.

At length, late one day as we were watching ahead for a place to make camp for the night, we saw rising ground at the right. We slowed and scanned it as our dugout floated by, but found that between it and us was mud too thin to walk on but too thick to paddle through. So we continued on, curving around a bend in the channel, until a sudden brightening of the light and widening of the water drew our eyes to the left. We found ourselves just entering a river.

"*Por Deus!* Have we reached the Tecuahy at last, Lourenço?" cried Pedro, both joy and doubt in his voice.

"It is time we did," I growled, squinting in the glare of the low sun on the wide water; "but from what I can see I fear it is not. It seems to run almost east."

"True. But this may be only a turn. Let us go down it and see."

He stroked hard and the canoe jumped. But after a swift glance at the sun I dug my paddle in deep and held back.

"Not today," I disagreed. "We must get ashore soon if we are not to be caught by black night. The sun is dropping fast."

He grumbled something, but he too began looking again at the right bank. Then he nodded sidewise and edged the bow shoreward. I swung the stern, and we floated into a little natural port. Above us were firm ground, tall trees, and only a little of the low bush growth.

Landing, we threw up a small *tambo* to keep off any night rain, slung our hammocks, built a fire and ate. Night fell. The sky was clear, but we knew the moon would be late, so, though we spoke of paddling downstream a little way by moonlight, we decided against it. The river would not disappear overnight, and we were tired. Before long we slept.

Bright moonlight, breaking through openings among the treetops and shining on my face, woke me. I blinked, glanced at Pedro, turned in my hammock and let my eyes droop again. But just as they were closing they flew open. Something had moved.

I had heard nothing except the usual nightly hammering chorus of frogs, seen nothing but the dark mass of jungle sprayed with moonlight. Yet something had come between me and the moon, for its light had dimmed. And as I lifted my head and peered toward it I started. Framed in the glare were a head and a pair of bare shoulders.

They did not move. They stood out against the moonshine as if they belonged to a dusky statue with a neck nearly as thick as its body. For minutes I hung there squinting at it, and it stared straight back at me. Then the moon, rising fast, rolled up past the gap at the back of the creature; the light became more evenly balanced, and the face and form of the phantom grew more distinct. And I was more astonished than before, for I saw that it was a woman.

A woman, quite young, but with the plump shoulders and full bosom of maturity. A woman whose hair hung unbound behind her to her waist, where it was looped around her body like a belt. I saw now that she was not thick-necked, for with the change in the light her face and throat glowed pinky-brown against that black cloud of hair which at first had made her look so misshapen. And as I continued to stare I found that she was far from bad-looking.

She smiled, lifted a hand, and beckoned. I dropped my feet to the ground and sat up. At my movement she turned and began to fade away into the murky bush, still beckoning. Profoundly puzzled, I arose and took a step toward her. And just then Pedro, lying back in the shadows, cried out.

He was still asleep, but struggling with a bad dream. At his smothered yell both the woman and I jumped. For an instant she poised as if startled. Then, with a swift movement, she was gone.

Pedro yelled again and awoke. Seeing me standing there, he snatched his machete and leaped up and at me.

"Drop it!" I snapped.

"Oh, it is you, comrade!" He laughed nervously. "I am not quite myself — I have just been fighting with some cannibals. Why are you up?"

"Because you were howling so hard that I was looking for a rope to choke you with," I grumbled.

"Sure you were not sneaking out to make love to some lady monkey?" he chuckled.

"Not to a monkey. But I might have gone walking with a handsome young woman if you had not scared her away."

He stared, then grinned.

"So you too were dreaming — a more pleasant dream than mine. Pardon me for waking you. Were you in Remate de Males, or back at your old home below Manaos?"

"Neither. I was here. And if I dreamed I am still asleep."

Again I looked out at the bush. The woman was not there. Pedro, wondering, said nothing, and I listened. As I was about to speak again I heard a slight splash. No further sound came.

"Did you hear that splash?" I muttered.

"Yes. A fish jumping."

"Perhaps. But it came from over yonder, not from the river. In the morning I shall explore this place."

With that I sat down and told him of what I had seen. He grunted in disbelief.

"Moonshine!" he scoffed. "I have heard that men with weak heads should not sleep in the moonlight. You say the moon was shining in your eyes when you awoke. Your mind is full of moonbeams and moon-dreams. Unless" — and he laughed again — "you had a visit from the Bouto Woman of the Amazon. If it was she, beware! You know what comes to men who follow her. Did her hair drag at her heels?"

"No, but it might have done so if she had let it down. It was wound around her waist and hips like a *tanga*. Laugh if you like, but this was no dolphin-woman. Besides, a dolphin turned to a woman would be black, unless it changed color as well as shape."

"But no, it would not," he disputed. "Some of our river dolphins are entirely black, but others are black-backed and pink underneath, and some are pink all over. Have you never seen flesh-colored dolphins? They are not uncommon."

He spoke truth. It had been some time since I had seen a dolphin, and still longer since I had heard anyone tell the tale of the Bouto Woman. Now, thinking about them there in the dark mystery of the jungle, I half-believed that the old legend might be true. But I said no more, and soon my partner lay down again.

"If your fishy lady comes back before dawn wake me," he yawned. "I should much like to see the famous Bouto."

And with another derisive chuckle he went back to sleep.

I lay awake for some time, listening to the night noises but hearing nothing strange. Several times I sat up and stared long at the place where that moon-born woman had stood. But whatever might have been there before, nothing human was there now. So at length I too drifted off to sleep.

PEDRO'S HAND on my shoulder roused me. The sun was up in the sky, the smell of wood-smoke and boiling coffee was in the air and excitement was in my partner's face.

"Wake up, old lady-charmer, and receive my apologies," he said. "I knew well you were a fascinator, but I never suspected that fish would turn into women for your sake. The Bouto Woman was here last night! Come and see!"

A few feet east of our *tambo* he pointed to the ground. There in a soft spot was the print of a bare foot.

We had worked barefoot in building our hut at sundown, but this track could not have been made by either of us. It was much too small. In another place a couple of yards farther off Pedro pointed out another footprint of the same size. Working back through the bush, he showed me more of them here and there. The trail brought us to water.

"This is an *enseada* — an inlet," he explained. "It must run in from somewhere downstream. Your woman seems to have walked out along that fallen tree and plunged into the water. There is no track anywhere else along the shore."

As he said, the trail began and ended at the base of a tree stretching out into the quiet water. I stepped out along the floating trunk and on its rough bark I spied little dabs of earth scraped off the feet which had passed along it.

Fifty feet out from shore, at the point where the first branches jutted upward, I halted and scanned trunk and limbs. They showed no sign that a canoe had been tied there. And the *enseada* itself, as I looked along it, held no indication of life. The woman had come from the water and gone back to it, leaving nothing but a few scattered footprints.

"Before you jump in after her," Pedro called, "come back to the fire and have some breakfast."

"I am not jumping after her or any other woman," I retorted, turning toward shore.

And we hastened back to our boiling coffee.

When we had eaten and stowed our few belongings in the dugout we pushed off downstream, keeping near the right bank. The hill on which we had camped stretched along the river for perhaps a mile, rising steep from the muddy waters and seeming unbroken by any cleft. Yet we had already found one dent in it — the small port where we had spent the night — and we looked for another opening where the *enseada* began. And before long we found it.

It was so narrow and so overgrown that if we had not been hugging the shore and watching for it we should have passed it without a glance. And even when we forced our way through the half-drowned bush choking it up we were not sure that it was what we sought, for it turned to the left and seemed to end. But as we paddled on we found that it did not stop there but looped sharply back around a point. Turning the point, we held our paddles and stared.

Before us rose a wall of thin, straight palm-logs standing on end in the water. The posts stood close together, yet not too close to let the water flow through between them. They were lashed to one another by loop after loop of tough woody vines and bush-rope, and the whole wall looked firm enough to last for a lifetime. It extended up the steep banks on either side, rising to a height a little above the topmost flood mark. In it we could see no gate, and no path showed around either end. It seemed made to let water in but keep all else out.

"Por Deus!" Pedro said softly. "This is a queer thing to find in uninhabited jungle. No dolphin-woman made this, nor any other woman. It is the work of a strong man."

"I do not like it," I muttered. "It looks like a trap."

He nodded. But instead of answering he held up a hand for silence. Beyond the barrier sounded splashing.

Softly, silently, we stroked our canoe up to the poles. Pedro, in the bow, leaned forward and peered through one of the narrow openings.

"Nossa Senhora!" I heard him whisper. Then, turning his head and shielding his mouth with one hand, he added, "The Bouto!"

Quickly but quietly I worked my end of the boat around until I too could look through. And there in the water, some distance away but unmistakable, I saw the woman who had beckoned to me in the moonlight.

In truth, she seemed a dolphin woman. She was swimming and playing about with the smooth ease of a fish, disappearing sometimes below the surface, staying under until it seemed that she must have drowned, then gliding into sight again at some place a long way from the spot where she had vanished.

After floating quietly a moment she would splash water upward with both hands and go down backward, her feet kicking a white lather as they sank. And then we would see her pink toes peep out somewhere else, followed by her hands and then by her flushed face, above which her black hair was piled in a cone resembling a dolphin's snout.

She turned over with a gleam of sleek arms; she swam on her right side and then on her left; she even went feet first, her toes held above water. And we clung to the poles and marveled.

"She is better than the dolphin itself," Pedro murmured. "I have never seen a fish that could swim backward as she is doing."

It was not only her skill that held me quiet, however, but

her fearlessness. Neither of us, though we could swim if we had to, would think of sporting about as she was doing — there are too many perils waiting for a swimmer in our waters. Alligators, huge water snakes, bloodthirsty *piranhas*, barb-tailed *araya* devil-fish, electric eels which shock and stun, and other deadly creatures too foul for me to speak of — all these lurk under the surface that looks so harmless to a stranger, and we were too old in the ways of the jungle streams to expose ourselves to them. Yet this dolphin woman seemed to give them no thought, and she suffered no harm.

At length she tired of her play and came swiftly toward us in a final dash. Swerving toward the left bank, she reached upward and caught at something we had not noticed — a little platform on poles, like the *moutás* which our Indians set up in the waters of the jungle pools when shooting turtles. One of the posts supporting this was notched to form a ladder, and up these notches she climbed to the platform.

There she sat breathing a moment. Then she arose, unbound her cone of hair, pressed the water from it, and shook it loose to dry.

Senhores, that hair was longer than she herself. It hung down below the *moutá* on which she stood, and her head tilted backward a little as if drawn down by the weight of it. Against its blackness her face and figure glowed far more clearly than when I had last seen her, back in the dark jungle under the wan light of the moon. Plump, smooth-skinned, unclothed except for a tight-drawn *tanga*, glistening with the water-drops rolling down her shapely form, she still seemed the Bouto Woman of the old tale — a dolphin such as Pedro had mentioned, black of back and fair of body.

Yet her face, as she stood with chin upward and gaze fixed on the jungle beyond, did not seem that of a woman nimble-witted enough to lure men to destruction. Somehow it looked rather blank, and the eyes seemed to stare as unwinkingly as those of a fish.

A choking sound from Pedro drew my attention away from her. He was struggling to hold his breath. His effort failed. He burst into a snorting sneeze.

Muttering a curse, he looked again through the palm wall. So did I. The woman turned sharply toward us, watched the logs a moment and probably saw our canoe through the openings. With a leap she cleared the space between her platform and the land. There she stood still again, frowning. Then, instead of running away, she calmly came toward us.

While she was balancing herself along the abrupt slope we pushed the canoe to shore and waited. Her head rose over the wall and hung there, peering down.

"Boa dia, senhorita," Pedro greeted her. "I hope we have not disturbed you."

She made no answer. Her steady stare rested long on his face, then passed to mine. A slow smile came on her full lips, and I knew she recognized me. But still she did not speak. Presently a hand rose over the wall and beckoned. And the invitation was not to Pedro but to me.

I sat still, for this was most astonishing. Never before had a woman ignored my handsome partner for me. As you *senhores* can see for yourselves, I am so plain that women are not likely to notice me at any time, and certainly not when I am with such a tall, graceful fellow as Pedro. Now, with this attractive woman preferring me to him, I was as much surprised as if our canoe had suddenly grown legs and started to walk up the slope.

Watching me, she laughed quietly and continued to beckon. Pedro turned to me.

"Why do you not go?" he demanded. "Must your lady come down here and carry you? Use your legs."

I stepped out on the bank. But there I stopped, glancing again at the wall.

"Come with me," I said in an undertone. "As I said before, this place looks like a trap. Perhaps no harm is near, but we had best make sure. Here you are walled in on three sides, and the way out is not easy."

"So you think there may be a reason for trying to separate us?"

"I do not know. But I do know that two men can be killed more easily when apart than when together. And, as you have said, no woman built that barrier."

He nodded, fastened the boat to a post and followed me, rifle in hand. The woman frowned, but still said nothing. After a slippery climb up the bank we crossed the wall at the point where the last and shortest stakes joined the steep earth. By that time the woman had started away, and we trailed in her footprints, balancing ourselves with difficulty on the wet clay. When we came above the *moutá*, however, we found a path where the soil was packed into a narrow shelf, and from that point we trod more easily and could look at other things besides the ground.

The woman, I noticed, had again looped her hair around her waist. Then, as I glanced beyond her, I noticed something else. A couple of hundred yards farther along the ravine the top of another wall of poles showed above the water. Now I understood why the woman could swim here without fear.

These barriers would keep out *araya*, *piranha* and all other evil creatures except those so small that they could do no serious injury. True, a great snake or alligator might come into the place from the land, but this was hardly probable. Walled in at both sides by abrupt declivities, barred at both ends by the posts, it formed a long pool where a good swimmer could play unharmed.

The path twisted upward and began to zigzag back and forth. We dug in our toes and mounted to the top. There, under big trees, the ground was nearly level and almost free of undergrowth. Still silent, we three walked onward to the base of a great prostrate *massaranduba* tree which at some time had come smashing down and which, though lying on its side, still loomed high over our heads.

We had seen such prone giants often before, and now we only glanced at it and would have passed on. But at a spot some ten feet beyond its towering roots the woman halted, pointed and stepped straight into the tree itself.

"Por amor de Deus!" exclaimed Pedro. "A house cut in the virgin wood!"

It was so. We stared at the strangest house we had ever seen. Above us that huge trunk rose for nearly twenty feet, and from its lower side had been hollowed a home about eight feet high and fifteen feet long. The enormous weight of the tree had driven its underside solidly into the soil when it struck, and the space between its lower curve and the ground had been filled in with smaller logs and clay, forming a nearly straight wall at each end of the cavity. From the roof to the earth an outer wall of small palm-logs had been built, with a window and a door. The inside of the place was very dark.

"No woman made this," I mumbled. "It took more than one man and many days of chopping."

"Perhaps not," he disagreed. "See how black the bark is at the ends and up above. It was not chopped out, but made as we make our canoes —burned out and then finished with the ax. One strong man could do it easily."

"True. But let us look at the man who made it."

Then, raising my voice, I called gruffly:

"Ho there! Come out!"

No one came out. The woman appeared in the window and stood there, a question in her face. No other creature showed itself.

"Is no man here?" I asked.

With her slow smile she shook her head. Her beckoning hand appeared at the window. And, as before, she motioned to me, not to Pedro.

"The strangeness grows," said my partner. "A woman who swims better than a fish is rare. A woman who lives alone in manless jungle is unheard of. But a woman who will not talk — it is a miracle!"

Without reply I walked in at the door, rifle ready. But no man lurking in the shadows menaced me. She had told truth — no man was there. Yet, as my eyes grew accustomed to the dimness, I saw that a man had been there. Not only one man, but three.

From pins in the wood wall hung the clothing of three men. And in a corner stood rusty rifles and machetes.

"Where are those men?" I demanded, pointing.

With a wave of the hand she signed that they had gone away.

Peering again at the rusty weapons, I thought their owners must have been gone for some time. And they had left clothes and guns behind.

"Are they dead?" I snapped.

She nodded.

"How? What killed them?"

Her cool brown eyes did not waver — nor did she speak. Another calm movement of both hands and a shake of her head told me that she did not know how they had died.

Her unbroken silence irritated me. I asked rather sharply whether she had no tongue. Smiling again, she stuck out her tongue and wriggled it impudently at me. It looked as good as my own. I growled, seized her shoulder with my left hand and tried to scare her into speech.

"Talk, or I will thrash you!" I threatened, trying to look ugly and brutal.

It did no good whatever. She laughed in my face, lifted a hand, raised my fist with a smooth strength that astonished me — and then drew my arm down around her waist.

I twisted my hand free and stepped back hastily.

"Pedro!" I yelped. "Come in here!"

His chuckle sounded at the door.

"I have been watching," he told me. "But why call for me? She is yours without a struggle."

"Er — ah — look at those things!" I stammered, hot-faced, jabbing a thumb toward the weapons and clothes.

"Yes, I saw them. That was what brought me to the door — your question about men."

His face sobered and his eyes narrowed as he looked from the guns to the woman.

"What killed those men?" he barked.

She pouted, shook her head again and then motioned for him to go.

"Very well," I said. "We shall both go. *Adeos, senhorita.*"

But she caught my arm again and held it, and once more I was surprised by the power of her grip. As I paused she moved her mouth as if eating, then nodded to each of us in turn.

"Yes, we will eat with you if you like," I consented. "But I stay in no place where my partner is unwelcome."

She released my arm, pointed to a hammock slung against the far wall and motioned for us to rest there. Then from a stool under the window, where we had not observed them, she picked up a pair of trousers with belt and machete. Stepping into these, she buckled the belt around her and started out.

"A queer way to prepare a meal for visitors — to strap on a machete and leave them," Pedro remarked.

"This whole matter is too queer to suit me," I said. "I am going with her to watch her. Stay here and look over those guns — and anything else you see. Our tongues and ears are useless, so we must depend on our eyes."

And out I went after her.

She was walking along the trunk of the *massaranduba*. I made no attempt to sneak and spy, but followed openly. She looked back, waited until I reached her, then went on toward the head of the tree, glancing at me now and then in a way which was neither bold nor shy but very friendly. As I usually do when with women, I kept my mouth shut. And thus, wordless, we passed around the great sprawling treetop and walked on into the forest beyond.

Past other tremendous trees, towering so high that their heads were lost beyond the roof of branches above us, we went. Around a dense mass of thorny bamboos we made a circuit, and then we came among trees of medium height, corded and draped with vines, which hung from above and mingled with other vines matted on the ground. Here the woman slowed and looked searchingly at the vines. Presently she stepped to a liana, drew her machete and cut off a piece about a yard long. With this in her hand she turned toward the *enseada*.

Down the bank, which here was far less steep than at her swimming place, we went to the edge of the water. There, concealed in a small hollow, lay a short canoe in which was one paddle. Entering this and lifting the paddle, she motioned for me to squat in the bow. I did so, facing her.

She pushed the craft out, turned it to her left and sent it gliding down the inlet. Around a double curve we floated. Looking over one shoulder, I saw that the *enseada* now became wider and straighter; and a gunshot beyond us I spied a tree lying far out in the water, its butt on shore. Studying it, I knew it was the trunk on which I had walked out that morning, trailing this woman.

We did not reach that tree. She swung the canoe into a small cove at the left, and we got out on shore. There she held the piece of vine against a tree, pounded it with her machete until it was well mashed up and threw it out into the still water of the cove. After that she sat down at the base of the tree and motioned for me to sit beside her.

More puzzled than ever, I scowled at her and at the crushed vine. The vine floated almost motionless, and the dark water around it looked slightly milky, as if some whitish juice from the wood were soaking out of it. As I looked back at her she raised a hand toward the sun, moved it a little westward, dropped it and pointed at the drifting vine, lowered it again to the place beside her. I took this to mean that in about half an hour the vine would do something, and that meanwhile I was to keep her company.

So I squatted against the tree — not so close to her as she had indicated — and made a cigarette, which I offered to her. She took it, and when I had rolled another I lit them both. She puffed at hers as if she had smoked before, but not recently. And then for a while we sat there burning tobacco.

While I sucked smoke I remembered that we had not given her any account of ourselves. Perhaps if I did so she would break her stubborn silence. So I told her my name, where we worked, and as much of our recent history as seemed best. Her eyes showed interest, but she never spoke. And when I questioned her as to who she was, whence she came, and how long she had lived here, into her face came that blank look I had noticed before, and she stared straight before her.

Then she leaned forward, looking at the water. There on the placid surface was something more than the vine — the glistening side and light belly of a small fish.

Its gills were wide-open, and it seemed dead. I was quite sure that it had not been dead long — some other creature would have devoured it. And in another few minutes I became certain of this. Without splash or struggle, three more fish came drifting up from the depths. And, one by one, others appeared here and there on the surface. And not one moved so much as a fin.

The woman rose and stood looking them over. None was large, but there were enough to make a meal — if they were fit to eat. Yet she stood quiet as if waiting. And before long the water showed its first sign of life. Wriggling weakly, a fine big *pescada* came up, gasped a few times and was still.

At sight of that creature I sprang up, thinking only of getting him before he should give a twist of his tail and disappear. Then I stopped short as the meaning of it all flashed on me. The woman was fishing with the *timbo*.

I had heard of this before, but never had seen it. The *timbo* is a poisonous liana, and if it is crushed and thrown into still water its juice will stupefy and kill the fish near it. Yet the flesh of the fish is unhurt — the creature seems to be stifled rather than poisoned — and it can be eaten without harm. And there was no need for me to hurry about capturing that *pescada*, for he never would move again. He was as dead as if his backbone had been severed.

With a motion of the head the woman stepped into the canoe, and I followed. A few strokes brought us to the *pescada*, and I lifted him in. The dugout moved around among the other fish, and I spied a couple of rather small *tucunarés*. These also I gathered up. The rest we left behind us.

Around the double twist in the winding water we returned, to the little cove and thence to the dug-out house. When we entered it Pedro was lying lazily in the hammock, seeming half-asleep.

"Our friend is a witch," I told him with a slight wink. "She dropped a vine on the water and the fish arose to feed us. It is magic."

The woman looked pleased. He winked back to me. As she picked a small knife from where it stuck in the wall and went out again to clean the fish he swiftly arose.

"The men who died had money," he whispered in my ear.

Somewhat surprised, I glanced at the clothing on the wall.

It looked as poor as our own. And my surprise almost became disbelief when he added —

"Twelve thousand *milreis!*"

"Deus meo!" I muttered. "Are you sure?"

"Sure. It is all in one great roll, tied with busk-cord, lying there in the corner under those rifles as if it were a mere lump of dirt. The guns are Winchesters, forty-four, such as we use. The machetes are Collins, like ours. The clothes are the same as we should wear. And I believe the men were *seringueiros* like ourselves."

"But three *seringueiros* — where would they get twelve thousand *milreis?*"

"Perhaps by gambling with others. Or perhaps more than three men have died here, and the guns and clothes of the rest are lost or thrown away. And — hush! Let us go outside."

We lounged out, meeting the woman coming toward us. She entered the place, but came out almost at once with a piece of that queer stony stuff which sometimes is found floating down our streams and which our Indians believe to be hardened river-foam[1]. We watched her return to her fish, lift the knife and scrub rust from the blade with the foam-stone. She gave us the same slow smile as she passed, and in her gaze we saw no suspicion.

Strolling idly away, we acted as if only looking about us. I noticed that between her house and the edge of the bank no small growth stood, and that we could see for some distance up and down the opposite hilltop. Perhaps the light of our small fire had glinted through the jungle last night and caught her eye, or its drifting smoke had been borne to her on a breeze, to arouse her curiosity and send her to spy on us as soon as moonrise gave enough light. We walked on until we could continue talking.

"Twelve thousand *milreis!*" I muttered. "And this woman led us straight to her house and left you, a stranger, there with

---

1   Pumice from Andean volcanoes.

that money while she went fishing with me. She certainly is not sly — at times she looks as if her mind slept — and yet she is not simple either. She shows us everything and tells us nothing. I can make neither head nor tail of it all."

"Nor I," he admitted. "What do you think her to be? White, or only partly white?"

"A *mameluca*," I judged. "Like ourselves — white, with a little Indian blood. Beyond that I can not guess what she may be."

"We can only watch and wait," he said. "Asking questions is useless. Let matters shape themselves."

But as we idled back to her I thought of one question which she might answer, and which meant much to us. When we were beside her again I pointed toward the river and asked —

"Tecuahy?"

She nodded.

"Praise God!" I rejoiced. "Our fight with the bush is over. What part of the Tecuahy is this? Where does the Branco flow in — above or below here?"

At the word "Branco" she started. A sudden wild light flared into her eyes. Then she dropped her head and went on with her work.

We glanced at each other. On the Branco, a river three hundred miles long which enters the Tecuahy from the west, are a few *seringales*. Where *seringales* are, there must be *seringueiros* to work them. The clothing and weapons — and perhaps the money—in her house were those of *seringueiros*.

We began talking of the Branco and of rubber-workers from there whom we had met at Remate de Males. But it did no good. She only arose, made a fire and began cooking the fish.

We shrugged our shoulders and gave it up. As Pedro had said, talk was useless.

While we ate of the fish — which she had cooked very skillfully — and while all three of us smoked again afterward, Pedro and I were as silent as the woman herself. I was puzzling, planning one way after another to solve the mystery, and throwing away each plan when it was made. My partner too was thinking; and so also, perhaps, was she, though neither

her face nor her acts gave any sign of what passed in her mind.

The sun beat down fiercely, and the day grew sweltering hot. There under the big trees we should have been fairly cool; but no breeze moved, and the hot air from the sluggish river crept over the hill and around us like unseen steam. I wished we were out of the place and on our way down the Tecuahy. The wish brought me to a decision.

"We thank you for your hospitality," I told her. "We should much like to know more of you and be your friends. But since you will not talk to us, we are only wasting time. So as soon as it grows cooler we shall go."

Her eyes opened at that. She shook her head.

"Let us go now instead of waiting," said Pedro. "It can not be hotter on the river. What is the good of delaying here?"

The woman gave him a look of sullen anger. As we arose she also stood up. Again she shook her head. Then she smiled at both of us and moved her hands as if swimming.

Now neither of us was a powerful swimmer, for, as I have said, we seldom swam because of the hidden dangers of the streams; but we could keep ourselves afloat well enough, and the thought of a cool swim in safe water struck us as pleasant. We agreed at once. She turned and led the way toward her enclosed bathing pool.

"Do you really intend to go?" Pedro asked softly.

"I intend now to swim," I returned. "Perhaps when we have soaked our heads we can think of something. If not, we had best go."

And we followed the wordless woman on through the forest and down her zigzag path to the little *moutá*.

There she coiled up her hair, loosed her belt, dropped the trousers which probably had belonged to some *seringueiro* now dead, and stood in only that close *tanga*. As we were wearing nothing but tattered shirts and breeches, we had only to lay our weapons in the path, pull off our shirts, and jump to the moutá. As I landed on that little platform she left it in a graceful dive.

Her spring made the thing sway under me, and I tottered and nearly fell off it. And before it grew steady I did fall.

"Have care!" came Pedro's cry as he leaped from the bank.

I had just caught my balance when his weight struck the moutá. It wobbled violently, we grabbed each other, and then we tumbled sousing into the water.

When we came up, snorting and coughing, the woman was floating nearby and laughing at us. We caught the posts and clung there, regaining our breath and grinning. She swam smoothly away, then went under and disappeared. While I was looking for her to come up beyond the spot where she had gone down, her head bobbed up almost in my face, startling me so that I nearly fell backward again. She had turned and come to me under the surface, and now she and Pedro both laughed at my sudden jump.

Feeling rather foolish, I let go my hold and struck out into the pool, enjoying its coolness and proving that I could swim. My strokes, I felt, were awkward compared to her easy movements, but I did not flounder. Behind me sounded a splash as Pedro also took to the water. I swam on until he caught up and passed me, when I turned back.

"Keep on!" he called. "I will race you to the other side."

But I was breathing a little hard, and as I now was nearer to the platform than he I panted:

"I will race you — to the *moutá*!"

Glancing back, I saw him swerve and knew he had accepted the challenge. So I began swimming my hardest. I beat him to the posts, but by only about two strokes; and the effort winded me. For that matter, it winded him too.

The woman had climbed up the ladder-pole to watch us from the top of the little stage. Looking up, I found a queer expression on her face. For the first time since we had come, she looked crafty. But as she caught my eye the expression disappeared and she smiled that slow smile. Pointing to the opposite shore, she vaulted out and began swimming the instant she struck the surface.

In less time than it had taken us two clumsy men to swim halfway across and back, she reached the other side and returned to the posts where we rested. And in spite of her speed she was not gasping when she ended her trip — only breathing a little faster. She looked at me as if expecting praise; so I spoke the simple truth.

"You are a wonderful swimmer," I said. "I have never seen a woman swim so well."

"Nor any man either," added Pedro. "You are a fish — a real *bouto*."

She smiled at my compliment; but when he called her "*bouto*" she lost the smile. For a second I thought her eyes gleamed with the same wild light which had shone there when she heard the word "Branco." But it quickly died. She glanced up, then motioned for us to climb the ladder. We were quite willing to sit and breathe a while, so up we went. She followed.

While we sat and rested Pedro and I argued jokingly as to which of us was the faster in the water. He declared he could have won if I had not kicked so much water into his face. I replied that excuses did not win races. The woman leaned forward quickly — almost as if she had expected some such argument — and began to talk in her sign language.

She pointed to the pole barrier at the farther end; then to me and to a point some twenty yards away; then to Pedro and to a place ten yards nearer; last to herself and the *moutá*. After that she moved her hands as if swimming, then swept one hand past us and again pointed to the poles.

"You will race both of us to that wall?" asked Pedro. "You will give my comrade a start of twenty yards, and me ten yards, and then beat us both?"

She nodded, teeth flashing and eyes alight.

"It is a long swim," he laughed, measuring the distance, "and I do not doubt that you can win. But you must swim to prove it. Lourenço, when she and I reach the poles I will come back to help you."

"Indeed?" I scoffed. "You will be much more than ten yards behind when I touch that wall. She may beat me, but you will not."

"You must swim to prove it," he repeated.

Without reply, I jumped off and headed for the wall.

Knowing that he would not start until I had gained my lead, I took my time. When I reached the ten-yard point I heard him splash in. I swam on, still slowly, until a second splash sounded. Then behind me came Pedro's shout:

"Swim! I am going to crawl right up your back!"

I grinned and struck out hard and fast.

The wall seemed very far away, but I knew Pedro was not much better at swimming than I, and I hoped to cover a good distance before being overtaken even by the dolphin woman. Once I looked back, finding that she already had gained on him, but that he was no nearer to me than before. Then I fixed my eyes on the wall and stroked onward without thought of anything except finishing the race as fast as possible.

Soon I was breathing hard. My legs began to feel a little tired. I wished I had done more walking lately, for many days of canoe travel had weakened me somewhat from the waist down. But the wall was growing larger, and still neither my comrade nor the woman had caught me. I began to think I might win over both of them. The thought gave me more power, and I struggled on faster than before.

Somewhere behind me sounded a gurgling gasp and a splash. I grinned again. Pedro had caught a mouthful of water, I thought, and would have to slow up. My arms were tiring now, but I still held the lead and I was determined to keep it if I could. I listened for other splashes which would show he too was tired, but none came.

Suddenly I felt that it was strangely still.

The thought drew my head around. I found myself alone. Both Pedro and the woman had gone down.

Instantly I swirled around and started back. The woman might be swimming under water, but Pedro would not; he could not hold his breath well enough. That gasp I had heard came back to me. Had Pedro drowned? Had they both drowned? Or was some monster here which had dragged them under to a death more frightful than drowning?

Madly I scooped water in my effort to reach the spot where my partner might be. I dropped my face and stared down, seeing only blackness. I lifted it again, gasped — and saw something ahead.

Something shapeless, something gone as soon as seen — a

heel, an elbow, a clenched hand, perhaps — showed for an instant on the surface. I fought toward it. It disappeared before I reached the place, but I knew where it had been. Lowering my head again, I peered down as I swam. Just as my straining lungs made me raise my mouth for air I caught a glimpse of something below.

Snatching a deep breath, I put my face under the surface once more. Beneath me floated a pale shape, moving very feebly. Something else seemed to be with it. I did not waste time in watching it. With all my power I threw myself down to the dying thing.

I looked into the swollen face of Pedro, staring upward with eyes that saw nothing. And as I grabbed at a limp arm I saw another face just below his. It, too, seemed swollen, but its eyes were alive. In them was a chill glare that was horrible to see. For a second it struck me cold, that awful face under him. Then I yanked at the arm I held and started clawing my way upward.

The terrible face moved away from him. An arm fell away from around his throat. A light body darted away and swiftly rose. Pedro too rose, and, strangling from pent breath, I broke out into the sun and air.

Another head was near me on the surface, its mouth open and gasping like mine. It was that of the woman. As I got my wind and turned to support Pedro's face above water she came at us both. I looked again into the glaring eyes I had seen under water — eyes agleam with murder. A hoarse, horrid sound came from her — a sound like a killing animal of the jungle. She was Death.

Pedro's arm moved a little in my clutch. I pulled him to one side, away from the woman, and stroked hard with my free hand. She came on, reaching for him and for me. Turning again, I stabbed my open hand at her, intending to shove her away. I did not quite reach her. But my hand, striking along the surface, spurted water into her face just as she drew breath. She choked, coughed and stopped.

At once I was off again, striking for the nearest bank and towing Pedro, who was still trying to swim. Thrashing along through the ripples, nearly exhausted, I had gone several yards when something under me clutched at one ankle.

The clutch missed, but it threw me into blind panic. Pulling up my legs, I kicked backward and down with all my force. One heel struck violently against something. I kicked again, but felt nothing. And then somehow I got myself and Pedro to the land.

Just above the water's edge was a small hollow in the bank, and I managed to climb into it and haul Pedro out. Then I fell, totally exhausted. For a few minutes I lay recovering some strength, Pedro lying across me, quivering and moaning and weakly belching water. When I was able to sit up his eyes showed that consciousness was coming back to him. I got to my knees and worked on him until he could breathe without choking.

While I helped him I looked around repeatedly for the woman, but saw her nowhere. If she had swum ashore she had done it quickly and quietly. I remembered our weapons, lying back there in the path by the *moutá*, and wished they were nearer. If that deadly woman got our guns she could come along the top of the bank and shoot us like cornered rats.

So, seeing that Pedro was in no further danger of suffocation, I scrambled up the bank to the top and ran to the *moutá*. Our guns, machetes, and shirts lay in the path as we had left them. The footprints in the path, too, all pointed toward the platform. Nobody had come up there since we three had gone down it together. And nowhere along the *enseada* could I see any person.

Back along the path I went with our belongings until I was above Pedro. There, as I stood looking down at the pool where we had just fought for life, I thought of the clutch at my ankle, remembered the thing I had kicked so hard — and I saw something. Down there in the darkness something light showed; something which seemed only a paler shadow than the rest, but which might be —

I slid down to my comrade. He was sitting up against the clay, looking weak and wan, but alive and awake.

"Where is she?" he whispered.

"I am afraid," I answered soberly, "that she is out there. I am going to see."

You can not guess, *senhores*, how I dreaded to enter that water again. But I did enter it, swam out to where I had seen that pale shadow, and went down. And when I came up I brought the Bouto woman with me.

Yes, she was there — very still now, and so far down that I had hard work to reach the top again. She made no movement when I towed her to shore, nor after that. I toiled long to bring back her life, but she never breathed again.

"God help me, I have killed her!" I told Pedro, who now was able to help me.

And I spoke of my kick at the thing which grasped my leg, and of what had gone before.

"You did not kill her," he said. "She drowned. She is full of water. Your kick stunned her, perhaps, or knocked out her breath; but the kick itself did not kill. And even if it had killed, she was trying to murder us. I was almost dead — I was blind and had lost my senses. Do not reproach yourself."

Then he told me what had taken place out there. She had caught up with him, as he had expected. But then, instead of passing, she had made a swooping dive, seized an arm, turned him on his back and dragged him down headfirst. She was under him, clutching him around the throat, and he could neither free himself nor even reach her. She had only to keep her grip and hold her breath while he drowned himself with his fierce struggles.

"But why?" I wondered.

"Do not ask me why any woman does anything. She did not like me, we know. Perhaps she thought that if she killed me you would stay and be her man. You were ahead, racing for the poles, and she probably thought you would not look back until you reached them. By that time she could stifle me, rise and swim after you as if nothing had happened. You would think I had exhausted myself and drowned alone after she passed me in the race."

I thought this over and disagreed.

"That may have been her plan," I said, "but I do not think

that was her reason. There is something else. We must look further for the cause of this thing. Let us see what is in her house."

So up the bank we worked, bearing with us the strangely silent woman who now was silent for all time. Back to the base of the *massaranduba* we carried her, and there we laid her down in her hammock and carefully looked over everything in the house. But we found nothing to show who she was or why she should wander under the midnight moon to our camp and try to destroy us when we in turn came to her.

As Pedro had said, the house had been made by fire and ax. We found the ax — an old rusty tool which had not been used for a long time, and which bore no mark to show whence it had come. We closely examined the guns, machetes and clothing, and became fully convinced that they were those of rubber-workers. We counted the money again, peered into cooking pots and gourds and everything that could possibly hold a clue. And when we ceased searching the place we were none the wiser.

"Why would you kill us?" Pedro mused, looking down at her. "We have no money — we are ragged rovers of the bush; and you did not care enough about money even to hide twelve thousand *milreis*. We offered you no harm, gave you no insult. And those other men — what did you do with them? Are their bones out there below that black water where you dragged me under?"

After a moment of thought I said:

"Let us go outside and look around. We have not yet been down behind this tree. Perhaps something is there."

Something was there. A little way back towered a big *moratinga* tree beneath which stood no bush. And in this natural clearing the ground was studded with five crosses.

"Five of them!" my partner exclaimed. "So there have been more than three men."

"Perhaps not. Perhaps there were three men and three women, and all died but she."

"The same hand made all those crosses," he pointed out. "Each leans a little to the left. Each cross-arm droops a little

downward at the left. And" — he bent and examined the bush-
cord holding the crosspieces — "each cord is knotted in the
same way."

It was true. We studied them, pondered, wondered, and
searched farther. And we found nothing.

AS WE returned to the house the sun smote into our eyes. We
squinted at each other and nodded. The day was going, and we
had no mind to spend the night there. Taking the rusty ax and
our machetes, we returned to the *moratinga* tree. After working there a while we made another trip to the house and back
to the little cemetery. And when we left the tree for the last
time a sixth cross stood beneath it — a cross which neither
leaned nor drooped, but stood straight.

Back at the empty *massaranduba* we looked at each other.

"Twelve thousand *milreis* do nobody any good here," Pedro
suggested.

"And there may be someone on the Branco who needs it," I
added.

"If we pass the Branco we can go up and see. Or better still,
we can go straight to Remate de Males as we intended, and
question some of the Branco men waiting there for the time to
go back to work. Old Jorge Faria might know."

In the glare of the dying day we tramped along the bank of
the *enseada*, down the zigzag path, past the *moutá* on which
still lay a dead man's breeches and machete, and over the pole-
wall beyond which our canoe floated. Out through the twisting,
bushy inlet we wormed our way to the sullen river, whose dirty
waters now looked like a golden path in the long sun-rays.
Then, with a long breath of relief, we shoved our paddles in
deep and jumped the dugout away toward the next bend,
bound for Remate de Males. With us went the twelve thousand
milreis.

DAYS LATER, gaunt and tattered, out of food and cartridges,
we reached the town. When we had left it the street was several feet under water; now it was bare ground. When we had

gone men had shaken their heads and said we went to death; now they stared as if we were ghosts. But at the store of our old friend Joaquim the trader we soon proved that we were not too dead to attack a jug of *cachassa*, and as the news spread that we had returned our fellow *seringueiros* came in from all around the town to help us drink and hear the tale of our wanderings.

Among them came Jorge Faria, a veteran rubber-worker of the Branco, always smoking and seldom speaking. We were watching for him, and as soon as he had had a drink we got him into a small room behind the store, where we could talk undisturbed. And to him we told the whole tale of the wordless woman who swam like a dolphin and was deadly as a *jacaré*.

His eyes widened as we talked, but he said no word. When we told of the leaning crosses he spat excitedly and put his pipe back in his mouth upside down. And when from under our waistbands we produced the money, which we had divided into two packets and fastened to our belts with strips torn from our shirts, he dropped the pipe.

"The Bouto!" he croaked.

"Oh, no," Pedro said wearily. "She swam like a *bouto*, but she was no fish turned woman. She was —"

"The Bouto," Jorge insisted. "Not the Bouto, of the Amazon story, but the mad daughter of Lino Cardozo — she who was called the Bouto because she had a madness for drowning. Have you not heard of her?"

We had not.

"She was mad from birth. Three months before she was born her father, Lino, a rubber-worker on the Branco *seringal* of Senhor Fontoura da Gama, stumbled and fell off the riverbank. Before he could get out of the water a *jacaré* rose and seized him. Lino grabbed a root in the bank and hung to it, screaming for help while the beast dragged at him. But before aid could reach him his hold broke and he was pulled down.

"Lino's wife saw it all, and the shock nearly turned her mind. And when the girl-child was born she had a twist in her brain. Yes, and a twist in her eye, for she never saw a thing exactly straight: anything which stood straight seemed to her to lean to the right, and if she stuck a stick in the ground she always slanted it a little to the left. This oddity soon became known, but of the kink in her mind nobody knew for years.

"It is true, she was not quite the same as the other children on the *seringal*, even when small. There was her habit of slanting things to the left, and besides that she was slow of speech —"

"She could talk, then?" I cut in.

"Yes, if she would. But once when she was about ten years old she said something that angered her mother, who beat her soundly. And from that day she held her tongue. Not one word did she ever speak after that. Queer, yes; but she was a queer girl. As I said, she was slow of speech before that day, and often she would stare in a vacant way as if her mind had flown for a moment. But she was a strong, plump child, and nobody suspected she was mad. 'Only a little odd,' was what the da Gama people thought of her.

"Perhaps her new habit of remaining dumb made her madness worse — I do not know. But before that time she had learned to swim, in a little *ygarapé* where the men built a wall of poles to keep out dangerous creatures, and had become a much better swimmer than any of the other children; and now the kink in her brain began to work. You might think her father's death and her mother's horror would make her fear the water, but it was not so. Instead, her twisted mind told her to drag things under the water, as the *jacaré* had dragged her father to death.

"At first she pulled down only sticks and pieces of log which she threw into the *ygarapé*. Then she began swimming below the other children and catching them by the feet or around the body, scaring them and often making them choke. And one day she pulled down a boy and almost drowned him before he could fight free.

"That made the rest fear her. They named her 'Bouto,' and they would not swim with her more. They drove her from the *ygarapé* when they swam there, and she had to do her swimming when they were not at the place. But every day she was there, seizing her logs and fighting to keep them under the surface. And I have heard — for I was not on the Branco in those days — that when a log escaped her she would pursue it with a glare in her eyes that chilled those who watched.

"Yet it was only in the water that she was dangerous. On land she was only a harmless, slow-smiling girl who slanted sticks to the left."

Jorge stopped, found his pipe, filled and lit it. When he went on his eyes were on Pedro.

"She was fifteen when I first went to the Branco. And in that year a tall, slim young fellow who had newly come to work on the da Gama estate made love to her. She had become quite handsome, and he — well, he did not intend to marry her. But she thought he did, and she liked him well until a *batelão* arrived from down the Javary, bringing a police officer who arrested the man for murdering his wife at Fonte Boa.

"The killer had a revolver, and so did the policeman. After the smoke cleared away the da Gama men had to bury them both.

"From that time on she hated men who were tall and slender — like you, Pedro. But men like Lourenço, shorter and more broad — she still liked them well enough."

I nodded, feeling that now her preference for me and her dislike for Pedro were explained.

"It was two years more," Jorge continued, "before another man really interested her. He was Bento Batalha, a heavy-muscled, cold-eyed man who was almost as silent and nearly as good a swimmer as she. Where he came from, and why, he never told, and we never asked. One does not ask too many questions on the Branco.

"Whether Bento and the Bouto ever talked to each other I do not know; nobody ever heard them. But whenever Bento went to headquarters he and she swam together in the walled *ygarapé*. There her madness broke out as before, and several times she tried to drown him. But he was too strong for her and always broke away. And instead of fearing these life-and-death struggles in the water he seemed to enjoy them, for he always had a grim smile when he came out. A queer man. A queer couple.

"Now the girl, being well-grown, helped her mother work around the house of Senhor da Gama, who, after the death of Lino, had taken the mother as his cook. She knew the house as well as Senhor da Gama himself — perhaps better. And when she and Bento disappeared together, as they did before long, something else disappeared also. Ten thousand *milreis*."

"Aha!" we cried, glancing at the money.

"Ten thousand *milreis*," Jorge repeated. "That and a canoe, Bento Batalha, the Bouto of the Branco — all gone between dark and dawn. And none has ever been found." We rolled cigarettes. Then I said:

"There were five crosses under the tree. There are twelve thousand *milreis* here — two thousand more than da Gama lost."

"Yes. And it is six years since the Bouto vanished. In that time quite a number of men have left the Branco and have not returned. Most of them have gone out to the Solimoes, but some were not seen after leaving the Branco. One of the crosses under that *mandiroba* may be that of Bento. The other four — who knows?"

"Four men could easily have had two thousand *milreis* among them," Pedro agreed. "Batalha, the thief, probably had more than one reason not to hurry out to the big river. He made that house, built those pole-walls, and perhaps lured a few *seringueiros* in there to visit him — and to go swimming with his woman. Then he himself swam with her once too often."

"Who knows?" Jorge said again.

We smoked on, looking at the money. We knew Jorge was honest and would soon return to the Branco. And I said —

"The mother of the Bouto — does she still live?"

"She lives," Jorge answered, reading my thought. "And the two thousand *milreis* which do not belong to Senhor da Gama would be a fortune to her. She grows old, and she has nothing."

We passed the packets to him.

"See that she gets it," I said. "Nobody knows of this but us three, and nobody shall know of it until you have returned to the Branco. And now I am thirsty again."

And when Jorge had tied the money under his waistband

we went back to the outer room, where the crowd waited to buy us more *cachassa* and hear more about us.

So ends the tale, *senhores*, of the Bouto — the killer who was born in madness, mated in turn with a murderer and a robber, and died at last under the heel of a man fighting to save his comrade. Tonight this big moon, which showed us that dolphin back yonder in the river, shines down also on the ruins of the *tambo* where she first came to me, the huge *massaranduba* in whose butt yawns a black and empty home, and the tall *mandiroba* beneath which stand six crosses — five leaning and one straight.

Under that straight cross lies a tale that is told. But under the slanting sticks rest five more stories which none of us shall ever hear. They are locked for all time in the jungle — which is forever dumb.

THE ANT-EATER

DID YOU know, *senhores*, that the ant-eater can kill the jaguar? It is true. Those long knife-claws with which he tears open rotten stumps in his search for food can also stab the king of the jungle.

I myself have seen it. I have cut my way through the bush to a place where I heard sounds of fighting, and there I found a dead ant-bear with his great claws hooked into the body of a dying jaguar. The big gray destroyer of ants had taken his slayer with him to death in a terrible grapple that could not be broken.

Yet the ant-bear never seeks trouble. He goes shambling along attending to his business in life, licking up ants with that long sticky tongue of his, and bothering no other animal if he is let alone.

He is a queer-looking thing, not at all handsome, but he is very useful. If you two Americans have ever been bitten by the accursed fire-ant while you were exploring the Javary jungles, or have seen a house fall to pieces because it had been eaten to a shell by termites, you will agree with me when I say that there is use for millions of ant-eaters here in Brazil.

I never kill one, for I feel that he is a friend. But if I should kill one I should do it from a distance, and not allow myself to be deceived by his clumsy appearance and his peaceful nature. For it is with animals as it is with men, *senhores* — often those that are usually harmless become dangerous when attacked.

There are other ways, too, in which animals and men sometimes resemble one another. Perhaps in your own United States you have met men who had the appearance and the nature of some beast or bird or reptile. But you would never suppose, would you, that any man could be like the ant-bear — even to his habit of eating ants?

Laugh if you will — it is droll, I admit. But perhaps you do not know that among the many kinds of ants crawling in our jungle there is one which is eatable by men — the *tanajura*, which is an inch long and can be fried in lard and eaten.

And once I met a man who ate these ants, and who was like a great gray ant-bear in more ways than that. So now, to pass the time while the steamer carries us on down the Amazon, I will tell you the tale of this man.

I came upon him while I was on an adventuring cruise in the flood season, when the low-lying rubber forests of old Coronel Nunes, my employer, were drowned by the rising waters and we *seringueiros* could work there no more. With a mate of mine, a tall young fellow named Pedro, I had paddled southward through the watery bush until we came into hill country higher than the flood level.

There we had followed a rain-swollen creek which now was a river, and we went on up the river, seeking anything that might be new and strange. To left and right of us rose the hills. Those to the left were low, but from the other bank they went up and up and up until, miles away, they became mountains — the mountains of Peru.

So far we had found easy paddling, for the flooded creek was smooth and deep. But as we went onward the hills grew more steep and the stream more narrow and swift, with white water now and then that gave us stiff work.

And at length the banks swung toward each other, holding between them a roaring rapid up which no canoe could go. So there we stopped.

Hanging to a drooping branch, we held the dugout steady and studied that leaping, lashing water and the steep banks beside it. And Pedro said:

"This far we go, and no farther. That *cachoeira* is more than we or any other men could mount, and no doubt it is even worse higher up.

"So, Lourenço, either we go ashore and tramp a while or go back downstream. Which shall it be?"

"Both," I answered. "I am going to land and stretch my legs, for I have the canoe-cramp. And after I have tramped along beside the cachoeira and tired of looking down into it, we may as well drift back down the current."

We swung the canoe over to the right bank, drew it well up on the shore and stretched ourselves. Then, taking our rifles, we worked up along the rapid, finding the bush not very thick, so that we could travel without much trouble over the rough ground and stop now and then to gaze at the tumbling waters below us. After a time we sat down and smoked.

"I have hunger," said Pedro, "and I want fresh meat. I am tired of *came secca* and *farinha* and dried fish. If a monkey comes along, shoot him."

Before our cigarettes were burned down a monkey did come along. I spied him peering at us from a tall *matamata* tree.

He was only a little fellow, not large enough to make a meal for two men; but still he was fresh meat, and I swung up my rifle. But he sprang behind the trunk where I could not see him.

We waited for him to leap for the branches of other trees, hoping to get a shot as he moved. He stayed where he was, however, and so we got up to work around the tree, Pedro on one side and I on the other. But before we found our prey something happened.

Somewhere off in the bush rose a long-drawn yell:

"Chico-o-o! Chico-o-o-o!"

We stood astonished, for we had thought no man but ourselves was in this place. The shout came again, a little nearer now. Up in the tree the little monkey made a chattering sound, and as we did not move he hopped up on to a branch, looking toward that call. We could easily have killed him, but we did not. The three of us, monkey and men, waited for that approaching man to come to us.

"Chico-o-o-o! Where are you, rascal?" called the voice, and we heard someone rustling through the bush.

The monkey fussed again, but did not jump. Then out from the trees came the man, who stopped short as he saw us.

He looked queer. That was my first thought as I looked at him — "queer."

At first, though, I did not see just why he seemed so. He wore almost nothing — only a tattered pair of breeches with belt and machete; but there was nothing strange about that, for we ourselves were not much better off except that our breeches were whole and we wore boots.

He was very hairy, and the hair was gray, though his face was not old; but that was not very odd either, for age is not a matter of hair. And though he was gray he looked stronger than either of us, for he was a big fellow and heavily muscled.

But then as I studied him I saw what was odd about him.

Above that powerful body were a long neck and a narrow head with small eyes and ears — a head that looked as if it had not much room for brains. And as he stood staring at us he ran out a long tongue and licked his lips in a way that made him look foolish.

And I thought, this is a big good-natured fellow who is not a fool but is not very wise either — a simple-minded man whose heart is bigger than his head. And soon I found that this was so.

Up overhead the monkey made another fussing sound. And though we were strangers, with rifles in our hands, the man looked up eagerly and then turned his back on us, walking up to the *matamata* tree.

"Chico, rascal!" he said in a half-scolding way. "Come here to me! You are a bad child, and if you do not stop running away I shall set you down on an anthill and hold you there until they eat all the hair off your tail! Come here!"

The monkey came down slowly while Pedro and I stood snickering at the thought of him hopping around with a tail full of ants. We knew very well that the threat was only a joke, and were very glad that we had not killed the little pet.

Chico came swinging down a long drooping vine, stopping near the ground as if he wanted his master to chase him up again. But the big gray man stood still, talking in a coaxing tone, and so Chico swung to other vines and came across until he was over his master. Then the man reached a hand to him and put him on his left shoulder where he perched and wrinkled his funny little face at us.

"Your bad child seems to make much trouble for you, friend," said Pedro.

"It is the truth," the man answered. "He is a mischievous fellow and a great care. If you have sons of your own perhaps you understand how it is."

He said it so seriously that we roared with laughter. The idea of this powerful man talking of that shriveled little monkey as his son was too much for us.

But he did not grow angry. He grinned slowly, scratched the monkey's neck with one big finger and let us laugh.

When we stopped he said:

"I have two sons besides this little Chico — real sons, who some day will be big men. Now they are not old enough to come out here with me, but must stay at home with their mother.

"So I have taken this little fellow as my son too, to keep me company while I stay here alone. He likes me, even if he is a bad boy at times — is it not so, Chico? I wonder if he would like you too."

Carefully he lifted the monkey from his shoulder and lowered him to the ground. Then he pointed toward us.

Smiling, Pedro squatted and spoke coaxingly to the little pet, and after watching him a minute Chico came over to us and let Pedro stroke him. Then he caught hold of one of my bootlaces and played with it.

He climbed up my leg, too, and slipped a paw into one of my pockets; but I lifted him away before he got anything and held him in my hands and scratched his neck and then set him down on the earth. He went to playing with my bootlace again. Then his master came up to us and lifted him again to his shoulder.

"You are honest men," he said simply, "If you were not, Chico would not make friends with you. Now if you wish to come to my *tambo* I shall be glad.

"I am Thomaz Nobrega, and I am here because I have been hunting gold. I have found it, too, and if you do not believe it you can come and see it."

We glanced at each other thinking he must be very simple indeed to tell two armed strangers that he had gold. He trusted us, of course, because Chico did.

And it is true, *senhores*, for I have noticed it myself, that sometimes animals can sense evil in a man when grown men and women can not. They seem to feel it as they feel an approaching storm and other dangerous things. Yet I would not trust the judgment of any monkey, or of most men either, where gold was concerned.

As if there could be no question of our good hearts, now that Chico had found us friends, the man Thomaz turned away and started back the way he had come. We followed.

Soon the pair ahead of us stopped, and Thomaz pointed up a small creek which probably held no water in the dry season, for now it was neither wide nor deep. Then he went on along the bank of this stream, and the four of us stopped again at a small *tambo*. And there on the ground near his hammock was a rough heap of ordinary dirt.

"This is my treasure," he said, pointing at the dirt-pile.

We frowned at it and then at him, wondering if he was crazed. He chuckled and added:

"It does not look as if it were worth much, does it? But now see what I shall show you."

Stooping, he clawed away a few handfuls of earth from the side of the pile. Then he stood up and pointed at the hole he had made.

Out from that hole shone a yellow gleam. And we saw that the dirt-pile was really a heap of gold concealed under a few inches of earth.

"You see, it is as I said," he told us. "I have found gold. Thomaz Nobrega, whom men laugh at and call Tamandua, has found fortune in this lonely forest where those who laughed were too lazy to go.

"Feel it, friends. Lift it. It is real gold."

We did not need to lift it, for one look showed us that it was true gold. And I was staring at the man himself. He had said that men called him Tamandua, and I thought how well the name fitted him.

For *tamandua bandeira*, as you probably know, is the great ant-bear; and Thomaz, with his thick gray hair and narrow head and that long tongue with which he licked his lips, did look much like that animal.

He lacked the broad black stripe over his chest and sides, and of course he had not the ant-bear's great bushy tail; but if ever there was a human ant-bear, it was he. And we soon found that he really ate ants.

"Sit down, friends, and be comfortable," he said, "and I will make you such a meal as I can."

So we leaned our rifles against a corner-post and sat in the hammock and rolled cigarettes. When these were lit we told him who we were and how we had come there, and watched him while he made a fire.

When this was going well he got out a pan, greased it with a piece of fat which he took from a small clay jar, and held it over the blaze until it was smoking hot. Then he picked up another jar plugged with a ball of leaves, took out the plug and shook the dish into the hot pan. At once came the sound and smell of something frying.

"What have you there, friend Thomaz?" I asked, for I could not see what he had shaken into the smoke. He grinned slowly and answered:

"Something very good, which I think you will like. Something that will probably be new to your tongue, although you must have seen them many times. *Tanajuras.*"

"*Por Deus!*" exclaimed Pedro. "Do you eat ants?"

Thomaz chuckled, and said:

"Yes, I do eat ants. I have eaten them since I was a child, for they are very good if you like them. But now I eat them because there is not much other food that I can get. I have been out for a long time, and my cartridges are all gone."

Looking around, we saw a rusty rifle lying across the poles overhead. We saw too that, excepting the useless weapon, his hammock, a few small tools and some things for cooking, there was nothing at all in the place — except that heap of gold. There was no food, and his only clothing was that ragged pair of breeches which were almost falling off him. And, he said, he had been out for a long time.

"I can kill a sloth with my machete whenever I find one, and eat that," he added. "But that is not often, and so I have to live on these ants, which are easy to get. I hope you will like them, Pedro and Lourenço."

"Why do you not take your gold, Thomaz, and go back to your home and get more cartridges and dried food and other things you need, and then come back?" asked Pedro. "Come back when the rains have gone and this place is dry, and it will be much easier to work."

But the gray man shook his head.

"I have lost this place once," he said, "and it took me a long time to find it again. If I should leave it now perhaps I should never see it more. I shall stay here until I have all the gold I can find, and then I will go out for good.

"You know how it is in the jungle — if you go away for only a little while from a place and then come back it does not look the same, because vines and bushes and creepers have grown and made it look strange; and so perhaps you will lose it."

I nodded, and he went on:

"I found this place first when I was out as a rubber scout, trying to find new trees so that I could ask Duarte Gomes for some money. Do you know Duarte Gomes? No? He is a hard man. He will do anything for money, and he will give money only when he expects to make much more money by doing so.

"And so, needing money, I tried to find a new rubber district, intending then to make him pay me well to tell him where it was. And while I was hunting I found this place of gold. But my mind was so full of rubber that I went away and left it, thinking I would come back here when I found rubber too."

I nodded again, for I could see that a simple mind like his might be so full of one thought that it would not change quickly to a bigger idea.

"But I did not find rubber, and when I tried to come back here I could not find this place either," he continued. "So I went home and told Gomes about the gold, offering to hunt for it if he would pay me.

"He laughed at me and told me to find the gold first and then he would help me to get it out if I would give him half. He would not give me even a cartridge. But I got some cartridges in other ways, and a few tools, and started out again.

"My wife said —

"'If you find gold keep it all yourself, and do not be so simple as to let him have any of it, for he has no right to it at all.'

"And she is right — it is my gold and he shall not have any of it. He gave me no help, and now I want no help. I had to hunt a long time, and the rains came, and my cartridges went, and it was only by luck that I finally reached this place again.

"And now when I go out Gomes will be sorry he did not help me. I shall be as rich as he, and my wife and boys will have everything grand.

"Am I not right, friends? Is not this gold all mine?"

We told him that it surely was, and that he must not let that Gomes or any other man take any of it from him. And we asked him whether he had told Gomes where this creek of gold was.

He said yes, he had, but Gomes did not believe it, so he would not be likely to look for it; and besides how could Gomes find it when Thomaz himself had had so hard a hunt? We said nothing, but we thought of the same thing — that Gomes might get an Indian to search the jungle and see if he could find either Thomaz or his gold.

We thought, too, that something might happen to Thomaz before he could reach home with his fortune. And we asked him how he planned to take it out when he had gotten it all from the creek.

"I do not know," he said. "First I must get all the gold. Perhaps then I will make a basket to hang on my back, and carry as much as I can to the water below the *cachoeira*, and then come back for more, until it is all there by the stream. And then with my machete and with fire perhaps I can make a canoe.

"But I do one thing at a time, and the thing to do now is to pile up all the gold.

"Chico, rascal, be still! You shall have some ants, yes."

He flipped out a hot ant from the pan, and Chico grabbed it. Then he dropped it. His master laughed.

"Perhaps that will teach you not to be so greedy," he said. "Wait until it is cool."

Chico poked at the insect with a finger, and finally seized it again and ate it.

"Now, friends, the meal is ready," Thomaz told us, bringing the pan to us. "Eat as much as you like, for I can easily catch more *tanajuras*."

But somehow we were not hungry now. We had never eaten ants, and these did not look very inviting. And so I said:

"I am sorry, friend, but we do not like the taste of ants. We have not eaten enough of them to become used to them. So eat them all, you and Chico, and we will go out and see if we can shoot something that we all will like."

He looked hurt and answered slowly:

"You do not like them? But you have not tried them. Eat a few and you will find them good."

But we shook our heads and arose.

"I know they are good if a man likes them," I said. "But, you see, we do not care for them. You know how it is — one man's taste is not the same as that of another man."

He nodded and said that was so, and he was sorry he had nothing else to offer us. Perhaps, he said, he could find a sloth somewhere and cook that for us if we wanted meat.

But we told him again that we would shoot something and then we would come back and share it with him. And we went away and left him sitting on his gold-pile, feeding himself and his monkey on those fried ants.

In the bush we stopped and looked back at him.

"Poor fellow!" said Pedro softly. "He is so trustful, just because that monkey made friends with us. Look at him — he is not even watching us.

"We could stand here and kill him and take all his gold. And so could any other men who found him.

"That man Gomes, now, who is a hard man and would do anything for gold — Lourenço, this big gray fellow needs protection. Let us give it to him."

"We will give him more than that," I added. "Let us give him food and cartridges. We are only on a rambling trip and can go back whenever we desire, while he is fighting for a life's ease for himself and his family. And though he likes ants he must be tired of them."

"That is just what I was thinking," nodded Pedro. "Perhaps our cartridges will not fit his gun, but if they do we will give him all we can spare. And whatever else we can do for him we will do."

We slipped away into the bush and headed toward our canoe, stepping softly in hope of seeing some fine fat *mutum* bird or other creature good to eat. But we met nothing of the kind, and we were nearing the river when Pedro halted.

He held up a hand for silence. We listened.

It seemed to me that I heard a murmur and a rustle off to our left, but I was not sure. No more sounds came to us, except the steady snarl of the rapids. We went on.

At the canoe we took out all the food and cartridges we could safely spare. And when this was done Pedro said —

"I thought I heard low voices back there in the bush, and the sound of men passing by."

"I thought I heard something of the sort too," I told him. "But probably it was only the noise of the *cachoeira*, and perhaps a little breeze up overhead."

He stared thoughtfully downstream, and asked —

"It was at the left?"

"At the left," I agreed.

"And that would be downstream," he said. "Lourenço, it may mean nothing, but let us paddle down a little way and look along the bank. It will not take much time."

So we pushed the canoe out from the tangle and dropped down the river close to the bank. Suddenly Pedro held his paddle and grunted. I looked. And there in a small cove, half-hidden by overhanging leaves, lay another canoe.

"Aha!" said Pedro. "I was right. Men passed us, going away from this stream. They were going toward the *tambo* of Thomaz, too."

He started, struck by a sudden thought.

"Lourenço! It may be that man Gomes! Gomes and others, seeking Thomaz and his treasure! What do you think?"

"It may be so," I answered. "This canoe has just come — the paddles are wet. Whoever these men are, if they find

Thomaz they will see his gold, for he did not cover up that hole he made for us in his pile. I think we had better waste no time in getting back to him."

We whirled and went swiftly back to our landing-place.

There we hid our canoe again, loaded ourselves with the food and cartridges for Thomaz and started toward his little *tambo*. It had seemed only a short distance on our first trip, but now that we were in haste we found it quite a tramp to that small creek.

Yet we took care not to rush but to go quietly, so that we could come up behind the strangers without their knowing it. When we stopped near the hut of the Ant-Eater we knew they had not heard us.

Four men stood now where we had left only one man and a monkey. One was long and lean with a yellow face and a cruel mouth half-hidden by a big blue-black mustache curving down toward his chin. Two were snake-eyed Indians.

The fourth was Thomaz. And Thomaz was the only one without a gun. The others held rifles, and the yellow man wore also a revolver.

"But the gold is not yours, Gomes," the gray man was saying in his slow way. "It is all mine. You would not give me even a cartridge or a mouthful of *farinha* to help me to live while I found this place again. You only laughed at me, and now you have no right to what I have found."

"I told you to come and find the gold and then I would help you take it out, and I should have half," Gomes growled. "Now I am here to take it out for you. Do not try to get out of your agreement."

Thomaz stared at him.

"But there was not any agreement," he said, "You did nothing to help me, and I did not make any agreement. I came back by myself and found it myself, and I will take it away myself. It is all mine."

"Did I not tell you to go and find it?" demanded Gomes.

"Yes, you did say so, but you were laughing at me."

"No; it is an agreement," Gomes insisted. "I am here, and half of that gold is mine. I will take it all out for you and give half of it to your family.

"You can stay here and dig more, and I will come back again until we have it all. Then I will take you home, and you will be very rich."

Pedro, beside me, growled something and would have stepped out. But I held him back.

"Not yet," I whispered. "We may be more useful to Thomaz if those others do not know we are here."

And he stayed where he was.

"I did not tell you to come after me," said the gray man patiently. "I did not want you to come. I do not want any help now. And you know it is not your gold. My wife told me it would all be mine if I found it, and it is so."

"Your wife?" Gomes sneered. "What does that old woman know? You can not cheat me, and you had better not try it."

"But the strangers also said it was all mine," persisted Thomaz. "Two fine honest men told me —"

"Strangers?"

Gomes turned quickly and looked all about. But we stood quiet, hidden in the bush.

"What strangers? Where are they?"

"I do not know where they are. They went away. Two fine men named Pedro and Lourenço who came and made me a visit. And they said the gold was all mine, and I must not let any man take it away from me. So I know I am right."

"Oh, they have gone," said the black-mustached man, looking relieved. "So they came and saw your gold and went away? You fool, they will come back and rob you. I will take the gold out at once before they return."

"No, they will not rob me," Thomaz answered. "They are honest men. Chico found them honest, and he knows. And Chico will not have anything to do with you, Gomes."

"That fool monkey?" the yellow man sneered. "You mean that I am not honest because that dirty little beast does not like me? Have care, Ant-Eater! I have had enough of your foolishness. Now get out of my way and give me that gold!"

His voice was a snarl. The two Indians leaned forward a little, their rifles ready. But Thomas stood unmoved.

"Whether you are honest or not is something you know better than I," he said. "But you shall not have one grain of my gold — unless Chico says so. Chico, rascal, come here!"

He looked upward, and so did the others. We knew the monkey must be up on one of the roof-poles, where we could not see him.

"Come down, rascal!" coaxed the gray man, "If this be an honest man who can be trusted, come down and show us that you trust him."

And he pointed at Gomes, holding his finger steady as he talked. For minutes the men stood there in that way. Then Thomaz said:

"You see, he will not come near you or have anything to do with you. He has gone back into the farthest corner. He knows! So go away, and do not bother us more."

The yellow man ripped out a string of curses.

"I will send your monkey to hell, and you too if you interfere!" he yelled.

His right hand dropped and rose. Flame spat from it. The crash of the revolver-shot made us jump. And down from the roof tumbled poor little Chico.

He struck the ground near a corner-post and struggled in the dirt. Then he got to his haunches and sat there facing Gomes.

With one little hand he pushed toward his slayer as if to drive him away. With the other he plucked feebly at his body.

After a moment he lifted that hand too and held it up for all to see. It was red with blood. And he held it there, *senhores*, until he crumpled over into a pitiful little heap and lay still.

I am not a soft-hearted man, but something came up in my throat as I saw that thing. And Pedro growled again and snapped up his rifle.

"I have got that yellow devil," he rasped in an undertone. "Cover one of the *caboclos!*"

I did so. But, though I too was hot with rage, I whispered:

"Do not shoot — yet. Wait until they attack Thomaz."

I heard him grit his teeth, but he did as I said. And there we stood, each covering a man and waiting. But those shots were not fired. For Thomaz Nobrega, good-humored eater of ants, suddenly became another man.

He stared down at his dead pet. Then he lifted a face that was black as the wrath of God.

Gomes, looking into that face, stepped back from him. His revolver swung up again and once more he fired — this time at Thomaz. And then things happened so fast that we forgot to shoot.

With a roaring yell the big gray man jumped at the yellow one. As he jumped his machete flashed out.

One of the Indians fired his rifle from the hip. A man swayed and fell — but that man was not Thomaz. So swiftly had he sprung past the *caboclo* that the bullet missed him and struck the other Indian in the heart.

For an instant the Indian who had fired stood dazed, staring at the mate he had killed. In that instant death came to him. Without even looking aside, the Ant-Eater swung his machete sidewise and backward. It caught the *caboclo* in the neck. He dropped sprawling, his head chopped nearly from his body.

Before the dead man struck the ground Thomaz had seized Gomes. He seemed to forget his machete, and to want to crush Gomes to death in his great arms.

Clinching, they went off their feet, the yellow man's revolver exploding again as they fell. Then on the ground they rolled and fought in a death-grapple.

Gomes got his gun-hand loose and shot again, but the bullet went wild. We heard him cry out with pain as that frightful grip tightened around him. He dropped his revolver and tore with his free hand at the gray man's eyes. But Thomaz turned his head away and ground his skull into his enemy's face, and Gomes quit that attempt.

Over they rolled, and somehow Gomes got his revolver back and clubbed Thomaz over the head. The Ant-Eater's grip seemed to loosen. Gomes fought him down under, on his back.

But Thomaz was not yet senseless. Though he was underneath he still held his enemy fast. As Gomes struggled to get the gun against the head of Thomaz and blow out his brains we

saw that Ant-Eater's big right hand, still clutching his machete, rise from the yellow man's back.

The machete turned downward. It slid between the ribs of
Gomes. The yellow man screamed once. Then he grew limp.
Both men lay still.

"Por Deus!" said Pedro, lowering his rifle. "And we thought
Thomaz needed protection!"

We ran to the *tambo* to see whether the Ant-Eater still
lived. We shouted to him, but got no answer. He lay as quiet as
the dead men around him.

And when we tried to lift Gomes from him we could not do
so. The terrible grip of Thomaz still held, and our tugs at
Gomes only forced the machete farther into his body.

"This is a true ant-eater, Pedro," I said. "Just as the ant-
bear of the jungle locks his great claws in the body of his enemy
and takes him to death with him, so Thomaz has done with
Gomes."

Pedro nodded, but said he thought Thomaz still lived. And
after each of us took one of those powerful arms and forced it
away from the body of the yellow man we found that this was
so.

Thomaz had lost his senses, and he had been shot through
the left side; but the wound was not bad, and when he became
conscious he would be in no danger. So we lifted him and carried him into the little creek, where the water washed off the
dirt and blood of his fight and revived him at the same time.

He woke up fighting. He knocked us both down in the
creek, and when we reached the shore and stopped coughing
up water he stood there staring at us in a puzzled way Then he
looked around him, saw what lay in his *tambo* and remembered.

Straight to Chico's little body he went. He lifted it tenderly
and sat down in his hammock, stroking the soft fur and
looking sadly down at the tiny companion whose judgment he
had trusted so.

Big tears rolled down his face, and though he made no
sound we saw that he could not have grieved more if Chico had
been truly his own flesh and blood. Not knowing what to say,

we stood silent.

After a time he got up, lifted his red machete from the ground and, limping a little from his wound, went out by himself into the bush. When he came back his hands were empty, and on the hilt of his bush knife was fresh dirt. And we knew Chico had been given burial.

Not until then did he give any attention to the bullet-hole in his side. As I have said, it was not bad, though the muscles were torn so that they would be very painful for a time. We patched him up as well as we could, and then we took out the bodies of the three intruders and put them where they would do no further harm.

When we returned he still sat in his hammock, looking soberly down at his pile of gold.

"Did you see what happened?" he asked. We nodded. Slowly he went on:

"I did not want trouble with Gomes and his men. If Chico had said so I might have given them some gold.

"But they killed my little baby comrade. And so they had to die."

And again we were glad we had not shot that monkey ourselves when first we met him, for now we knew we should have had to kill this big simple fellow too.

"I did not tell Gomes so, but I am almost ready to go out," he said after a while. "I am not finding much gold now."

"Then you had better go out at once," we told him.

But he shook his head and said that first he wanted to be sure. And so, having nothing else to do, we offered to work his creek for him and see what the prospect was.

We stayed there several days, searching that little stream while he sat on the bank nursing his sore side and talking to us. And we found he was right, there was no gold left worth staying for.

So then we packed his gold through the bush to the *cachoeira*, and there we loaded it into the canoe of the men who had come to rob him With the canoe, he said, it would be easy for him to reach his home, as it would take him within a day's march of the place where he lived, and he could hide canoe and gold in the bush while he went and got his wife and boys to help carry his treasure.

We gave him food and cartridges, too, and pushed his boat out into the stream. But he caught a vine and held it.

"Come and stay with me for a time — I should like to have you live with me forever," he urged us. "You have done everything for me, and I have done nothing for you except to offer you *tanajuras*, which you do not like."

But we laughed and refused.

"We have the wandering foot, Thomaz," we told him, "and we have stayed over-long in one place. Now we have decided to ramble on above this *cachoeira* and see whatever we may see there.

"So go home, and good luck go with you. And do not offer us any of that gold of yours or you will have a worse fight on your hands than you had with Gomes and his *caboclos*."

He grinned and rubbed his thick gray hair as if he did not know just what to say. Then he said only, "*Adeos*, comrades," and went away. But before the canoe had gone two lengths he turned and threw two little nuggets of gold at our feet.

"From me, Thomaz Nobrega, in memory of Chico!" he called.

And at once he began paddling in a way that must have hurt his side sorely, and quickly he and his treasure were gone around a bend.

We picked up the nuggets and kept them, as he had said, in memory. See, here is mine. I have smoothed it into the shape of an ant-eater's head, and whenever my fingers touch it I remember the man who was so queer and simple, and yet killed two men to avenge the murder of a monkey.

Yes, *senhores*, as I said at the beginning, the ant-bear is a harmless fellow when let alone, and he seeks no trouble with anyone. But if ever you meet with a man who looks and acts like that ant-bear, do not crowd him too far. If you should do so you might not live long enough to be sorry.

THE JARARACA

DEEP IN the Javary jungle stands a tree of death. Malevolent, repulsive, bristling with venomous thorns, it towers alone on the slimy clay bank of a nameless *ygarapé*. Near it grows no other tree; in its branches no monkeys play; nor do parrot nor toucan ever settle on it to rest their wings. It is shunned by all creatures save those hideous things which crawl and coil to strike death into the blood of the cleaner animals which walk on legs above them. Under it lurk only the dread *surucucu* — poisonous master of the bush — and the deadly *jararaca*.

Yet on the grisly trunk of this infernal growth gleams a symbol of hope. In the blazing sun of noonday, in the cool radiance of the midnight moon, this token shines on undimmed by the evil shade of the monstrous branches above. Its golden light strikes into the beady eyes of the serpents below, which rear their heads to hiss and dart forked tongues at it — in vain. Year by year it hangs there, flashing its message to the jungle creatures which see but do not understand; and year by year it shall hang there, until at last the malignant thing to which it clings shall fall in rot. For it is fastened deep and firm: fixed by sharp steel and the strength of a man's good right arm.

The keen steel still is there, driven far into the wood — the *machadinha* of a rubber-worker. But the man is there no more. He has gone out among other men, and with him he has taken the tale of the tree and the golden symbol.

The tree is the *assacu* — the poison-tree of the Amazon jungle.

The symbol is a cross of gold, its chain knotted hard around the head and handle of the hatchet. The man is Lourenço Moraes, a broad-chested, steady-eyed *seringueiro* of the Amazon headwaters. And this is the tale of Lourenço:

*   *   *

In the season of the *verao*, when the great floods had ebbed and we rubber-workers could return to our labors on the vast *seringal* of Coronel Nunes, I was called into the office of the *coronel* himself. He was making up his gangs, which would go out into those parts of the swampy jungle where were rubber areas and toil there through the few months before the next rise of the waters. As I had been in charge of a gang the previous season, I expected another assignment of the same sort. But Coronel Nunes had other ideas.

"Lourenço," he said briskly, "you have spent the time of the floods at Remate de Males, growing fat and lazy. Now I shall give you some work which will shrink your belt."

I blinked. I certainly was not fat, nor had I idled the time away at the Javary town he named. While the floods swept the land I had made two long roving canoe journeys with a comrade of mine, and the pair of us had undergone much hardship and faced death more than once. So now I was puzzled until I saw the twinkle in the black eyes of my employer.

"It is true, *coronel*," I grinned then. "I have done nothing but paddle hundreds of miles, fight head-hunting *barbaros* and demons with tails, starve on *farinha* and *pirarucu*, and suffer from wounds. So of course I am fat."

He laughed.

"So I have heard," he told me. "That is why I have picked you for the work I have in mind. I have plenty of men who can boss gangs in fixed camps, but few who are such jungle-tramps as you. Now you are to take eight men whose names are here —" he tapped a list on his desk " — and scout for new rubber. You know what I want, and you may use your own judgment as to where to go. Your men will pack the supplies tomorrow. That is all."

But I did not go yet.

"Who are my men?" I asked.

He read the list. I shook my head.

"If you will pardon me, *coronel*," I objected, "I do not want all of those men. I do not want half of them. No, I do not want any of them!"

"Why?" he demanded, frowning. "They are good men."

"Good workmen, yes. They are of the best — as workmen.

But a very good workman may be a very poor bushman. On a long scout into unknown jungle I should be so busy looking after those men that I should have no eyes left to see rubber."

He still frowned, but it was a frown of thought, not of anger. He had a very friendly feeling toward me because of some dangerous things I had done for him in the past, as well as much faith in my judgment. So now, instead of snapping out that I must obey orders, as he might have done with another man, he sat thinking. After a pause I added:

"Give me only one man, and let me pick the man. Two men travel more easily than nine, and —"

"And you will pick that rascal Pedro Andrada, your vagabond companion," he cut in.

"The same rascal who, though himself wounded, once saved the life of your son-in-law and afterward tracked down the man who had shot them both," I reminded him.

"Ah, yes," he admitted, his face softening.

"A stout-hearted, two-handed, merry comrade, and a better bushman than I," I went on.

He stared a moment at the list. Then he swiftly tore it in two and crumpled the pieces.

"As you will," he said. "That will give me seven more men for the gangs. You two reprobates may go as far as you like. But bring me back samples and reports of something big!"

"We shall try, *coronel*," I promised.

And out I went, hardly able to keep from singing and shouting. No dull labor in a fixed camp — weeks of prowling the bush with my comrade — permission to go as far as we liked! *Senhores*, while I hunted for Pedro I nearly burst with my news.

I found him at the big supply storehouse. With him were three of the men who had been listed to go with me. None of the four was working. Squatting in the shade, the three whom I had already rejected were listening to Pedro, who, with a cigarette between his fingers, leaned against the wall and talked lazily, as if only to pass the time. His back was toward me, and the squatting men were staring at him so fixedly that they neither saw nor heard me approach.

"At first I thought it must be a great *surucucu*, that giant snake which all men fear," Pedro was saying. "But it crept through the air, not along the ground. And then, as the glow of our little fire showed it more clearly, I saw that it had no head. Where a head should have been, comrades, was a great hand! And the thing which had seemed the body of a huge snake was a great dark arm, reaching stealthily toward that man who now slept.

"I could not move. I could not cry out. My tongue clung to my teeth and my blood turned to water. And while I lay there frozen, the awful hand closed over the head of that man and lifted him as easily as you or I would lift a frog. It drew him swiftly back into the blackness of the jungle — and we never saw him more.

"One scream he gave — one horrible groaning scream like that of a man crushed by the *surucucu*. That was the last sound he made. And though we seized torches and plunged into the bush seeking him after the arm disappeared, we found no sign of him. No, nor even the next day, when we searched every foot of ground — we never found a trace.

"And I can tell you, friends, I am glad I do not have to go where you are going. I do not want to be within reach of that demon again. The very memory of what I saw makes me cold even now."

I stood where I had stopped, staring hard at him. We two had roved the bush many times together and seen some terrifying things, but I never had seen this of which he spoke, nor even heard of it. The three who squatted there glanced at one another uneasily, and one of them dropped his cigarette as if it had lost its taste. He let it lie.

"Does the *coronel* know of this?" he asked.

"No," said Pedro, blowing a cloud of smoke. "We felt that it was as well to keep silent about the matter. I would not tell you of it now, but that I feel you should be on your guard against this thing when you go into that region. Say nothing of it to the others in your gang, Luis, until you are well on your way. If they knew of it sooner some of them might refuse to go."

"I refuse now," growled Luis. "I will take my chance

against snakes or savages or beasts, but not against such an infernal thing as that —"

He stopped suddenly as he saw me standing there. Then he stood up in a dogged way.

"Lourenço, you have heard," he said. "I shall not go in your band of scouts. I have a wife and children to think of —"

"Then stay here and think of them," I interrupted. "I want no man who fears the bush. You, Antonio — and you, Meldo — what say you? Do you too fear to go?"

"I fear nothing which belongs in the bush," answered Antonio. "But a fiend is another matter. I am in doubt —"

"That is enough," I told him. "No man who fears even the horned devil himself can come on this journey. All three of you can report to the *coronel* for new assignments. Pedro, come with me."

I scowled at him as if displeased, though I secretly rejoiced that those men had quit before learning from the *coronel* that I did not want them. When we had left them behind us I asked in a scolding tone:

"Why tell such a wild tale and scare away my gang?"

"Most illustrious *capitao*," he explained with a mocking bow, "I was only trying to attach myself to your honored company. I have been put into the gang of Arnado Pestana, which means nothing more exciting than tapping and smoking. Luis is no man of the bush, and I thought he might like to trade places with me — if I scared him enough. Now that he and the other two have quit, perhaps you can persuade the *coronel* to shift me."

"You are shifted already," I said. "The *coronel* has changed the orders. He decided that Luis and the rest were too valuable to be sent out on a long trip, while you and I were such worthless rascals that we should never be missed if we were lost. He also said that we could go as far as we liked and he did not care if we never came back. I hope you feel as highly flattered as I do."

"We go alone?" he asked, his brown eyes glowing. "We two and no others?"

I nodded.

"Of course we are expected to find several million *milreis* worth of new rubber," I added. "Except for that, we have nothing to do."

"Nothing to do but risk our lives," he laughed. "And the whole Javary jungle to risk them in. *Por Deus!* What a holiday! Perhaps we may find something more interesting than rubber before we return, Lourenço. Who knows?"

"Perhaps we may," I echoed. And we did.

II

SCOUTING FOR new rubber, *senhores*, is not so simple as it may seem to those who have not done it. You may think, perhaps, that since the only roads in our jungle are the streams, the best plan is to paddle along those streams until a rich rubber area is found, then explore that region and return to headquarters. And so it is a good plan — until all such places have been found. After that, men seeking new grounds must search the unknown bush. And of the scouts who go into the heart of the jungle on such hunts, those who come out usually are fewer than those who went in.

That is why, on a *seringal* so wide as that of our *coronel*, the search for new lands may be a grim venture. That is why the scouts are sent, not singly, but in bodies of six or more men: the more men, the more chances that some of them will live to bring back the report of the expedition. Yet to my mind there is another side to this practice: the more men, the greater the chance of sickness or accident coming to one and thus slowing up the whole journey — for of course you can not abandon a sick or wounded comrade.

The weakness of one man has hampered many a band of jungle-rangers so seriously that the expedition failed and the men returned in desperate condition — those who did return. And that is why I opposed the *coronel's* plan to send a squad of ordinary tappers and smokers, and chose instead the one man whom I knew and trusted above all others: my brother bush-rover, Pedro.

We outfitted ourselves with four weeks' supplies of salt *pirarucu* fish, dried beef, rice, coffee and sugar; new repeating rifles and plenty of .44 bullets; and, of course, our *machetes* and *machadinhas*. Also we made sure that we had a three-foot roll of tobacco, some packets of *tauari* bark for cigarette papers, and rubber-wrapped matches. We calculated that when we should leave our canoe and make up our bark-strip packs for travel through the dense *sertao* they would weigh about seventy pounds each. And that weight, *senhores*, is quite enough for a man forcing his way through sticky mud and thick bush, swinging his machete at every step and carrying his rifle ready in the other hand.

Yet, when we had stowed all in the canoe, Pedro stood frowning down at the load as if dissatisfied.

"What is the matter?" I asked. "We have all we need, and it is packed so that it balances well."

He nodded doubtfully. Then he swung on his heel and went away. Soon he returned with a small jug.

"Rum and ginger," he said in answer to my look. "I do not know why, but I feel that we should carry it. More than once we have seen the time when a drink would have been worth more than gold."

He spoke truth. There are times when a little strong liquor is priceless. So, though I had been about to grumble that a jug was too clumsy to pack through the bush, I held my tongue. The jug went into the bow of the boat; and before we saw the headquarters again I was to be thankful that we had taken it.

We had started our packing while the early morning mist still hung heavy along the river, and even now the bright sun was not high. A cool little breeze played along the water, brilliant butterflies floated flashing along the banks, and from the jungle on both sides of the stream sounded the morning racket of monkeys and macaws and other bush life. A perfect day for paddling awaited us; and as we took our places in the dugout and faced the start of our long journey we breathed deep with the joy of being alive and looking ahead to weeks of action.

"Adeos, amigos," Pedro called to the men standing on the edge of the bank above us. "Luis, if we meet that demon again

we will cut off his hand and bring it back to you."

And he laughed.

Luis made no answer in words. He looked straight at Pedro for a moment, his face somber. Then he raised an arm, pointing up the river. Following the motion, we saw, swinging slowly in the air, high above the stream, a vulture.

A grunt ran among the other men as they too saw the evil bird.

"Death waits," one muttered.

"Death waits everywhere," Pedro scoffed. "So long as it does nothing but wait, I am satisfied."

But the faces of Luis and his mates remained sober. And suddenly one pointed, not at the death-bird in the sky, but at the water before us.

"Death crosses your bow before you have taken one stroke!" he cried. "See!"

From my place in the stern I saw nothing alarming. But Pedro, in the bow, muttered something, swung up his paddle, and struck hard. The edge of the paddle bit into the water with a vicious chunking splash. Then, stretching my neck, I glimpsed something writhing in a reddening welter of ripples.

A flat, triangular head — a whip-like neck — a squirming tail — the thing came contorting itself down past me. It was in two pieces, cut apart by the force of Pedro's blow; and the two pieces together had formed that deadliest of snakes — the *jararaca*.

Under the surface something made a rush. Glistening heads, snapping teeth, glaring eyed — the snake was gone, chopped into fragments by blood-maddened *piranhas*. A few small ripples licked against the side of the canoe; the red stain disappeared; and Pedro laughed again.

"*Si*, Death crosses our bow," he jeered. "And you saw what happened to Death, did you not? Death or demons — let them come! Lourenço, are you ready? Let us leave these old women here to shake their heads and mutter. A long trail waits for our feet."

He surged at his paddle, and I at mine. Out into the river we swung, and up against the slow current we pushed our way.

And as we rounded a turn and the headquarters clearing disappeared I glanced up again at the spot where the vulture had circled. It was not wheeling there now.

Instead, a black blot was moving away from us across the blue bowl of sky; flapping straight up the river ahead of us as if speeding away for some dread purpose. And in spite of Pedro's jeers and my own common sense, the croaking voice of the man behind us echoed in my ears —

"Death waits!"

III

SIX DAYS we swung our paddles. Six nights we camped on hilltops or in little natural ports and slept without harm or alarm. No snake, no jaguar, no vampire bat, no other evil thing disturbed us by day or by dark, and the worst sound we heard was the hideous but harmless howling of *guariba* monkeys, to which we gave no attention. On the seventh day we paddled until noon. Then, entering the mouth of a slow, narrow creek, we unloaded all our supplies on the shore, slid the canoe under the deep shadow of some giant ferns, and, after eating, began to make our packs. We had reached the point where we must take to our legs. East of us lay the unknown section through which we had decided to travel first.

"Our little holiday has ended," my comrade sighed, scanning the dense growth around us. "No more free and easy swinging of the paddle. From now on we work for every foot of ground."

"You have it right," I agreed. "And now how do you intend to carry that awkward jug of yours?"

"On your back," he grinned. "You surely did not think I intended to burden myself with it?"

"If you do not it will not go far," I retorted. "I might carry what is in it, but not the jug itself."

"No? Pardon me, illustrious *capitao* — I forgot you were the commander of this two-man gang. I forgot, too, that you are too old and feeble to carry much weight. Since you refuse I will pack it myself. But of course if I carry it myself I will drink it myself. That is only fair."

"I will carry it today," I decided, changing my mind. "Perhaps if I lighten it a little first I can endure its weight. You can pack it tomorrow."

"What a sudden change!" he mocked. "But I agree that it might be well to lighten it by a couple of mouthfuls."

And he drew the plug.

"Here is to ourselves and the *coronel*," I said, lifting the jug. "May we return to this spot safe and successful."

I took one mouthful, and no more. The fiery liquid stung my throat so that I coughed and wept. Gasping, I passed the jug to him.

"A good thought," he laughed. "And here is another which I once heard from a North American *senhor* at my old home in Santare:

> *"Here's to those who love us well!*
> *Those who don't can go to hell!"*

"A beautiful sentiment," I agreed as he too lowered the jug and began to hiccough. "There are few who love us, but if the affection of those few is half as strong as this liquor we need no more friends."

He nodded, wiped his eyes, blew his nose, and looked reproachfully at the jug. Then he drove in the plug with a thump of his fist, set the vessel among his slabs of *pirarucu*, and began building his pack around it. When the pack was made and slung from his shoulders it balanced as well as if no jug at all were in it.

"That is the safest way to carry it — strapped in tight," he joked. "If it hung loose it might wriggle off and kick me from behind. Are we ready?"

Slinging my own pack and drawing my machete, I answered —

"Ready."

And we began cutting our way eastward.

For the rest of the day we worked on through the bush,

keeping near the little creek. Near night we halted at a good spot near the water, cleared away the usual space for a *tambo*, built a pole shed, roofed it with the great leaves of the *muru-muru* palm, slung our hammocks, made a fire, and ate heartily. Then we sprawled in the hammocks, smoked, and listened awhile to the cracking noise of the tree-toads and the rest of the early night uproar.

Presently Pedro began to laugh.

"I suppose Luis and Antonio and the rest have destroyed us a dozen times before now," he said. "The great demon with the clutching hand has pulled us apart and scattered our bones all around the forest. 'Death waits!' they moaned. And here we lie comfortable and well fed, without having seen danger of any sort."

"Except that we nearly strangled over your pet jug."

"Ah, yes. But we have killed many a jug before now, old bushman, and — Hark!"

For minutes we hung silent, listening. The racket of the frogs and the howling of some far-off monkeys went on, but I heard nothing else. My comrade settled back.

"I heard a scream, or thought I did. Some beast has made a kill, perhaps."

Without reply, I kept on smoking and listening. He too kept quiet. Then suddenly we both sat up.

Faint and far away to the southward, a long thin cry sounded across the animal din — a cry which seemed the shrill yell of a man in torment and despair. As it died the forest uproar hushed, as if the wild creatures were listening and wondering like ourselves. For the time of three long breaths there was no sound. Then the night chorus began again. The voice which had made that cry was still.

We looked at each other and at the black night shadows beyond the fire-glow. Travel through the pathless bush had been hard by day; it would be almost impossible now.

"A man?" Pedro muttered doubtfully.

"I do not know. It is silent now."

More time dragged past, and no further sound came from the south. Pedro arose and laid a small stick on the ground under his hammock, pointing toward the direction from which the cry had come. Then he lay down again.

"Probably some animal in distress," he said. "But tomorrow we might go southward and see whatever we may see. That cry could not carry far through bush as thick as this, and the place must be near."

"It may be farther off than you think," I disagreed. "The wind is from the south. But in the morning we shall see. There is nothing we can do now."

We said no more, and we heard no more. Soon we slept.

IN THE morning we shouldered our packs again, looked at Pedro's stick and at the jungle to which it pointed, and started to the south. And before long we found that my random guess had been near the truth: the sound had traveled farther than Pedro thought.

After cutting our way through matted undergrowth for some distance, we came out at water. Before us a long, weedy, winding *ygarapé* stretched away southward. How long it might be we could not tell; nor could we guess how far along it that cry had been borne on the night wind. We noticed, though, that it seemed to veer eastward. So, to avoid being turned away from our course, we took the right bank. And along this, chopping through thickets and jumping tiny streams and plowing heavily through sucking mud, we labored on for what seemed a long, long time.

Though we held a straight course, we never lost the *ygarapé*. It wound along like the *mai d'agoa* herself — that great serpent, the Mother of Water. Time and again we came out at the edge of the water, where we stopped to scan the other side and mop our streaming faces with our arms; then, seeing nothing strange, we went on through another belt of bush, watching all around us.

At length, pausing once more beside the water, we stood and stared. Over on the other low-lying bank a clay knoll swelled up and dropped again. On the crest of that hill a huge tree stood. And it stood alone. No other tree grew beside it, and under it was no bush. Grim, dingy, yellow-green, unwhole-some, it rose like a tremendous poison-plant avoided by all other trees. And a poison-plant it was.

"*Assacu,*" said Pedro. "The poison tree. Can you make out its evil spikes on the trunk?"

I could. And I made out something else — two rings of darker color around the bark; one about two feet from the ground, the other higher up.

"I never before saw an *assacu* with two stripes on its butt," I said.

"Nor I."

We stared thoughtfully at it. Then we looked up and down the *ygarapé.* We saw no way of crossing it. We knew it might wind on southward for miles before it ended, and even then its end might be an impassable lake or a vast swamp.

"I am going to look more closely at that tree," my partner said. "And there is only one sure way to reach it."

So we turned back. All the way to the spot where we had first found that *ygarapé* we worked, and then down the eastern shore. Noon passed, and still we toiled onward. The sun had swung well over to the west before we felt the soft ground beginning to grow firm and rise under our feet. And when we broke through the bush into the open at the base of that knoll we were so tired and hungry that it seemed we could go no far-ther that day.

Half blind with sweat, we gave only one glance at the tree before we dropped our heavy packs and sat down wearily on them. We had not yet grown hardened to pack travel, and my shoulders now ached cruelly and my breath came hard. Pedro too sat with head bowed and body slouching forward. For a little time we gave no attention to the strangely striped tree which we had worked so hard to see.

Then I caught a gasp from my partner. Lifting my head, I found him tense, staring at the tree. And as I peered at its butt and saw what he saw, my breath stopped.

Bolt upright against that venomous trunk, lashed tight to the cruel spikes by two bands of bark, stood the naked body of a man.

IV

FOR A dozen breaths we sat there as if frozen to our packs, watching that body whose yellowish skin blended with the yellow-green bark behind it. The drooping head, the dreadful stillness of the figure, showed beyond doubt that the man was dead. The bark bands showed that human fiends had bound him there. That much was plain. But the questions which jumped first to our minds found no answer — who he was, why he was there, and, more important still, who had put him there. And as we rose to go to him a thing happened which added to our perplexity.

The sun, rolling westward, struck down through an opening in the branches and lit up the body. At once a golden gleam flashed out from its naked breast. And as we mounted the hill that yellow radiance shone steadily into our eyes — the blaze of a gold cross dangling from the dead neck.

If Pedro had not looked down, that cross would have meant death to one or both of us. With our gaze fixed on it we should not have seen what lay before our feet. But something made my comrade drop his eyes an instant, and in that instant he swept an arm hard against my chest, stopping me with one foot in air. He leaped back, crowding me back with him; and in the same movement he dropped his gun hard.

"*Jararaca!*" he warned.

Held down by his rifle, a hideous shape lashed and squirmed. Pedro's machete flashed, and the deadly head flew off the creature. Picking up his gun, he crushed that head into the dirt with the butt. I slipped my own gun-muzzle under the body of the thing and snapped it writhing into the bush down below.

"Coiled before us in plain sight, and we almost walked on it," said Pedro. "Two steps more, and one of us would have talked with *Deus Padre* this night."

We stood searching every foot of ground. No other snake was in sight. But as our eyes roved along the earth we looked again on death. At the edge of the bush, down at our left, lay a jumble of bones.

Wordless, Pedro pointed his *machete* at them. I nodded. Then our eyes went back to the man who waited above, and on up the hill we went until we were within two spaces of him.

He was not tall, and his face was hidden from us by the droop of his head and the shaggy black hair hanging down over it — hair slightly streaked with gray, but not that of an old man. His body was lean but not gaunt, his shoulders were well muscled, and his skin to the waistline was darker than below. Yet his legs were not white. They too were dark, but with a different shade of darkness than that of the upper body. They seemed to have a bluish tinge. And they were swollen.

From head to foot, from foot to head and down again, we studied him. And our eyes rested longest on those puffed legs with their unwholesome color. Presently Pedro stooped, peered sharply at the feet and ankles, and grunted as if he saw what he expected. Still stooping, he looked up into the down-turned face. His own face tightened.

I slipped my gun-butt flatwise under the dead chin and lifted it. Somehow I did not feel like touching it with my hand. And when I looked squarely into the face I was glad I had not put my own flesh on it. Not only was it drawn into lines of horror and agony, but it was blotched with terrible sores.

Great livid patches were eaten into the hollow cheeks as if by some poison. One eye was raw and blind. And the nose —

"Ugh!" I grunted.

And I dropped my rifle-butt and stepped back. The head flopped stiffly forward and hung as before.

Pedro arose, and he too stepped back. After glancing around us he laid down his gun, got out his rubber smoking-pouch, made two cigarettes, and passed one to me. We stood and smoked a while before saying anything.

"Killed by snakes," he said at length, moving a thumb toward the distended and discolored legs. "Forced back against those poisonous *assacu* spikes, tied tight, and then struck again and again by snakes — probably *jararacas*. Before that — no one can say how long before — someone threw *assacu* poison in his face. I have seen such sores before."

I nodded, for I too had seen such things. The poison of the *assacu* not only is fatal if drunk, but if it is merely sprinkled on the skin it causes sores which can not be cured.

"He was a bush-traveler of some sort — perhaps like ourselves," he went on. "He is tanned to the waist, as we are, from going without a shirt. His muscles are those of a man who has paddled much. He is not more than forty-five years old, and he was strong and healthy not long ago. He died last night."

Again I nodded. That long despairing scream in the dark seemed to ring once more in my ears.

"But the big gold crucifix," I said. "What do you make of that?"

He made no answer until we finished our cigarettes. Then he said:

"Nothing. I do not believe he was a priest. He has not the face of a priest, nor even of a man who would wear such a thing. I doubt if it was his at all."

"Whose, then? It must be worth much money, and it is not a thing to be left hanging on a naked murdered man."

He only shrugged his shoulders. Then he strode down the hill to the bones at the edge of the bush. I followed.

The bones were those of men. Among them were seven skulls.

I bent to scan them more closely, but at once I sprang back. Just beyond them, in thick grass, sounded a hiss.

For a few seconds we saw nothing of the snake hidden there. Then among the stalks I spied a flat head and a darting tongue. I lifted my rifle, but let it sink again and pulled my machete, which would make no noise to tell other men we were here. Balancing it carefully, I threw it, point downward.

Up flew a thrashing tail. A louder hiss sounded. The grass heaved and bent. We glimpsed the body of a six-foot *surucucu*, into whose coil my blade had plunged. Pedro slipped forward, swung his bush-knife in a half-circle, and clipped off its head. I stepped in and got back my own weapon.

Leaving the twitching, headless coil where it lay, we turned away from the bones and walked cautiously around the rest of the knoll. We found no more bones, no more snakes. But at the edge of the water, south of the tree, we found the marks of men. In the clay were the prints of three canoe bows and the trampled tracks of human feet.

That was all. Looking southward along the *ygarapé* we saw only that the water wound another turn and disappeared. So we turned back to the tree.

"This is not only a poison tree — it is a murder tree," I said, "Those bones down there never fell naturally into that place. Seven men have met a frightful death strapped to these spikes, and one by one they have been kicked away when the murderers came with another victim. This man here is the eighth. Perhaps if we were found here we might be the ninth and tenth."

"Not without sending a few men howling to hell ahead of us," he answered grimly.

"And what is more, I have a great mind to send a few there anyway."

Looking at that mute body, I growled assent.

"Rubber-hunting will have to wait until we have settled this matter," I said. "Now let us give this poor fellow a decent bed to lie in if we can. After that we shall see.

So we went back on our trail a little way, found the best spot we could, and labored there at a grave. When it was done we returned with a pole bed to the spike-studded tree of death and, working carefully, cut the murdered man free without scratching ourselves against the bark behind him. And a little later he lay straight and still in the hole we had made for him.

We stood looking down at his poor tortured face for a time before packing the earth upon him. And then Pedro knelt, lifted the head, and drew off over it the heavy gold cross and chain.

"Friend," he said soberly, "this will do you no good now. It may be that the cross will lead us to those who gave you so foul a fate. And if it does and the good God fights with us, I promise you that those who did this thing shall pay!"

V

BACK IN the bush, well away from the *ygarapé* and that cursed tree, we made a poor camp. The ground was soggy and slimy, the only moving water we found was a stream less than a foot wide, and huge mosquitoes came by hundreds to attack us; but the day was so far gone that we must make some place to sling our hammocks, and we were faint from hunger. So we did the best we could, knowing we could endure the place for one night and glad we were not near that snaky *assacu*.

Between our hammocks we hung the cross of gold. And when we had eaten and lain down we stared at it and puzzled about it.

"Only savages could have given that poor fellow such a death," Pedro declared. "Yet where would savages get such a cross? And why would they leave it on him? There are *barbaros* who do not know what the cross means; there are some who do not know the value of gold; but even such brutes would keep this fine cross as an ornament, if for nothing more."

"If it is not his own cross, and if it was not put on him by those who murdered him, I can see only one way for him to get it," I said. "And that way is almost impossible."

"And what is that?"

"That some man of the church reached him before us and left it there."

"No. That is not at all possible. No priest travels this lonely bush, and no priest hangs gold crosses on dead men. I never saw a priest who even owned so good a cross as this. How it came here we can not know — at least not yet. But we can be sure that the men who did this thing are brutes as cruel as the *jararaca*. And tomorrow, before we go on, I am going to prepare for them some of their own medicine."

"How?"

"Wait and see."

And no more would he tell me.

In the morning, while the coffee was boiling, he said:

"There are two ugly things I want: a small *jacaré*, about

five or six feet long, and some snakes. I will hunt the snakes if you will find the alligator. Remember, no shooting! You must get him with the knife."

"Why waste time hunting such things?" I demanded.

"It is not a waste of time. When we have them I will show you."

So, knowing his habit of keeping his plans to himself until it pleased him to reveal them, and remembering more than one time when those plans had seemed foolish but had proved good, I went out that morning to kill an alligator.

On our way along the banks yesterday we had seen several of the brutes, and though it is not easy to kill a *jacaré* by the knife — for he is a tough, cunning, and wary beast — still it can be done. Out to the *ygarapé* I went, and there I crept stealthily along near the water, watching for a log-like form lurking in the weeds on shore.

It was a long hunt. Twice I found *jacarés* hidden in the rank growth, waiting for some animal to come from the jungle to drink; but both saw me too soon and clawed their way into the water. Two or three others were floating in the water itself, but these were beyond my reach. At length, when I had gone a long way from camp without success, I gave it up and started back. And I had nearly reached the place whence I started, when luck favored me.

Perhaps the creature was asleep. Perhaps he saw me but thought I did not see him — for, having nearly given up the search, I was walking along carelessly instead of sneaking on as before. At any rate, he lay motionless on the bank, and I was almost upon him before I spied him. Then, without an instant's pause, I attacked.

My machete was in my hand, and I dropped on the other hand and one knee and stabbed low and hard at his side. The blade sank into him nearly to the hilt. Instantly I jumped forward, straddled his back, grabbed his forelegs, and wrenched them up off the ground.

His struggle was short. He heaved, rolled, struck with his tail, tried to shove himself into the water. But the tail did not reach me, my weight and my grip on his forelegs kept him on land, and the long knife in his heart killed him.

When I was sure he was dead I released his legs, got up, and wiped my machete. He was a little longer than Pedro had asked, and heavy. But I rolled him over a few times until he was well away from the water's edge, and then returned to camp.

Pedro was in his hammock, chewing some beef. The sight made me hungry, and I took another strip of meat from our supplies and joined him. His mouth was so full and the meat so tough that at first he could not speak.

"Where is your *jacaré*?" he demanded after he got the chunk down his throat.

"In my hip pocket. Where are your snakes?"

"In my hat."

I laughed, thinking he had failed. But when we were through eating I found that he spoke truth. His hat lay in a corner of the little *tambo*, and, lifting it carefully, he brought it over and showed it to me. The crown was partly filled with earth, and on the earth lay the heads of eight *jararacas* and one *surucucu*.

"*Por Deus!*" I muttered. "This place must be alive with snakes."

"These were all I could find, but they will be enough," he said. "One *jararaca* head for each of the men who has died at that tree, and the *surucucu* for luck. Did you find a *jacaré*?"

"He awaits your pleasure back yonder."

"Good! Now we can get to work."

With his rifle in one hand and the hat dangling from the other, he followed me through the bush to the spot where the alligator lay.

"Good!" he repeated as he looked at the reptile. "Only one cut, and that one so small that we can easily hide it. Wait here until I come back. I must put this hat in a safe place."

So I squatted and smoked until he returned. Then he told me his plan. And after I thought it over I agreed that it was good, though I believed we could have done without the alligator.

We took the alligator to the tree. It was hard work, but the labor at the tree was harder. There, after mending the bark bands which we had cut yesterday in freeing the dead man, we hoisted the clumsy brute upright against the *assacu* thorns and managed to lash him firmly where the last victim had stood. And when this was done Pedro made a crude wooden cross with sticks and bush-cord and slung it over the reptile's neck.

Then he stepped to the bush and picked up his hat. Down the little hill he went to the spot where the canoes had left their marks. And from that point to the tree he laid a grim trail.

One by one, in little pockets scooped out with his machete, he buried those deadly snake-heads: buried them upside down, with the lower jaws cut away and the fangs pointing upward: covered them thinly with earth, so that they lurked just under the surface, a doom to the man whose bare feet trod on them. The largest and last head — that of the *surucucu* — he planted in front of the alligator.

Then he went to the water on the safe side of the hill, washed his hands, pounded his hat thoroughly on one knee, came back and made a cigarette. We stood as we had stood yesterday, smoking and looking up at the poison-tree. But different thoughts were in our minds.

"A dose of their own medicine," my partner said again. "Such fiends deserve nothing better. And no honest man ever will walk on that trap, for all men except these murderers avoid an *assacu* wherever found. Now let us look further and see what we can find."

Making sure that we had covered all signs of our visit here, we walked down to the edge of the bush. There we paused and looked back. All seemed the same, yet was not the same.

The monstrous *assacu* towered overhead, the ghastly bunch of bones lay at the edge of the bush, the bare dirt of the hill showed no new marks. But in place of a dead man and a gold cross now stood a dead alligator and a cross of wood. And from the water to the tree of poison led a trail of death.

VI

WITH THE packs once more slung from our shoulders and machetes swinging at the bush-tangles, we left our camp behind us and worked to the shore below the hill of death. There we again started southward, determined to follow the *ygarapé* until we found its end or something to turn us from it.

For some time we slugged on through mud and thickets, finding no path, no footprints but those of birds or beasts. Beside us the water wound along in the same aimless way, now veering westward, now swinging back to the east. Except for the creeping rustle of unseen life, the constant buzz of mosquitoes, and the noises of our own progress, there was no sound. The stillness of the hot hours of afternoon was on the forest.

Our advance was slow — far slower than if we had been in our canoe — and the *ygarapé* seemed to have no end. Another night of camping in swamp land with nothing new to think about seemed to be approaching. But the sun was still a couple of hours above the western land-line when the wandering water suddenly quit looping and began to go somewhere.

And at the same time the air brought to us a strange noise.

It swung to the east, that water, and broadened out into a good-sized *lagoa*. On a little point at the turn we stood amid shoulder-high grass and looked down its length. More than two miles of water lay open before us, and nowhere on it was any sign of men. But on the breeze, which blew straight from the east and stirred the surface into tiny waves, came the notes of an odd music.

Mellow, resonant, far away, those sounds rose and fell in a regular beat of four different tones: the notes of beaten wooden bars. Over and over they hammered in the same order — as if the music were trying to say something. Then they stopped as if waiting.

After a pause they started again in just the same way as before. But this time they ended differently: the last note was beaten repeatedly and rapidly. It sounded like a demand for an answer.

And the answer came. Nearer to us, louder and deeper, out boomed a reply from the same kind of wooden bars. Only two notes were in this message — if it was a message — one high and one low, following each other slowly and regularly until each had been struck half a dozen times.

At once the far-off sounds started anew. This time they came in a regular order, and the series was not repeated as before. And in spite of their mellowness they did not make music. They thumped through the air like words of something talking, telling some news to the other thing nearer to the place where we stood.

When they grew silent, that other thing again replied: a few deep, curt notes like an order. That was all.

Though we listened hard for further talk between those wooden tongues, none came. And though we watched the lagoon for canoes, we saw none. As before, the water was empty and the air still. Yet we knew that somewhere east of us men had talked across miles of distance, and that the deep-toned messages had started at a place not more than two or three long gunshots from the place where we stood.

We unslung our packs and squatted beside them in the tall grass, hidden from any eye which might watch from the east.

"Cannibals?" Pedro suggested, rubbing a shoulder worn tender by a pack-thong.

"Perhaps. You are thinking of that light-skinned tribe of Javary *barbaros* who send messages by beating wood?"

He nodded.

"I have heard sounds go through the air which were much like what we have just heard," he said. "That was when I was working on the western edge of the *coronel*'s *seringal*, two years ago, in the gang of Alves Feijo. The noises were very faint, and we never saw any Indians while we worked there, so I believed the sounds were made by birds. But old Nabuco Magalhaes, who worked in our gang, vowed they were messages beaten out on wood by those eaters of men."

"Nabuco was right," I told him. "Those cannibals do send messages in that way. I have been among them and heard the messages sent, but they never allowed me to see how it was done. But that was very far from here, and I do not believe any of those people live in this place."

"Perhaps they have moved here."

"No. Their country is far better than this — a land of hills, above the floods; and they never would leave it for this swamp-hole. What is more, I doubt if these men here are cannibals. If they were they would not lash a man to the *assacu* tree — they could find a better use for him."

"True."

After a few minutes of listening and thinking I added:

"We shall learn nothing by squatting here. I doubt if we shall learn much more today anywhere, for night is not far off. Our wisest plan is to make a secret camp and then scout without these infernal packs to hinder us."

"For once you have spoken sense, *capitao*," he smiled. "Let us find a sleeping-place."

So we lifted the packs once more and, stooping to keep below the grass-tops, left the little point. Back into the bush we went until we found a spot that would do for the night. Quickly we made camp. Then, leaving everything behind except our weapons, we struck off to the southeast, working on a slant toward the long *lagoa*.

Once more on the northern shore of that water, we stood behind trees and again looked along its rippling length. Pedro grunted.

"Aha! Now this dead water shows life!"

Far down the lagoon, almost at the end, four dark spots slowly grew larger. From them flashed little glints of light — the gleam of wet paddle-blades. Straight into the eye of the sun they came, heading directly for us. Behind our protecting trees we waited and watched.

The spots became bows topped by swaying shoulders and heads. On they came, and on, until we made out the naked copper bodies of the head paddlers. Then suddenly they swerved toward the northern bank and lengthened out into low-riding dugouts, each carrying six or more men. Bunched so closely that they seemed to blend into one boat, they surged straight at the shore; and, without slowing their speed, they slid into it and were gone.

"This *lagoa* must have an *enseada* on this side," Pedro muttered.

We left our trees and, working stealthily, passed along through the undergrowth until we reached water again. As my partner had guessed, an *enseada*, or bay, opened there in the bank. But it was empty. The canoes had disappeared.

The water curved eastward, and we knew the paddlers had gone around a turn. We knew, too, that the end of the bay was not far off; for beyond the turn the line of treetops rose high at one place, showing that under it must be a hill perhaps a hundred feet tall. There, we judged, should be an Indian settlement. A moment later we were sure of it. Out broke a sudden thunder of drums.

"A war party!" said Pedro, his mouth close to my ear. "Those canoes have been on a raid. And did you notice that one of the men in the first boat was hunched over as if wounded or a prisoner?"

I nodded. We moved on.

Keeping within the cover of the bush but near the edge, where we could see without being seen, we slipped on around the turn. Then beyond us we viewed the hill, rising steep-faced from the water, and at one side of it a number of canoes. But no men were in sight. All were up on the hill where the log drums boomed in triumph. And as fast as we could go without betraying ourselves we hastened to reach and climb that hill. We knew that up there something important was taking place, and that now, while it was going on, was the best time for us to spy without being caught.

Unexpectedly we found ourselves in a path. It came from the forest, turned sharply, and led on toward the hill. It showed signs of much use, but it was empty now. Along it we stole swiftly until we reached the base of the hill.

The hill was steep of side as well as of front, and almost bare of the undergrowth which had concealed us thus far. The many small stubs in the ground showed that the bush had been cleared away by the inhabitants of the place, perhaps to lessen the chances of any attack. But the big trees still stood, and by crawling upward from one to another of these we reached the upper edge unseen. And there, lying close to the ground and peering out from behind the same butt, we saw and heard.

Before the small doorway of a long, low house, which stretched back I know not how far among the trees, stood two closely packed crowds of Indians. Hard-faced, muscular, naked except for small loin-mats, all painted with wavy stripes of red, and some armed with clubs, bows, or spears, they were fighting-men every one.

Half of them stood with backs to the house, the rest facing toward it. In the space between these gangs, watched by all, were two things on which our gaze also fixed: a motionless, confused heap on the ground, and a man standing with hands tied behind him.

The prisoner was white.

VII

A LEAN bronzed man of medium height, with bushy blond hair and beard, and face hard-set; shirt ripped and mud-stained; breeches tight below the knee and also smeared with clay; boots laced to the knee — these were the things I noticed first. Then, looking him over once more, I saw that his light hair was stained with blood; that an empty cartridge-belt was around his hips; that from it hung a long holster, also empty; and that though he showed all the signs of a fierce fight, and though he now was a lone prisoner among scores of savages, he seemed to be not afraid but nearly bursting with rage.

My eye dropped to the heap on the earth near him. I saw a pair of copper-colored legs and a bare arm sticking out of the pile, which was still with the stillness of death.

Several dead savages, I thought. For an instant I wondered that even such hard-looking men as these should dump their dead in a pile like so much dirt. But then I thought no more of it, for a new thing took my attention.

The drums, somewhere but of sight beyond the crowd, stopped. The men before the door drew aside, leaving the way clear. And out from the house, moving with a smooth glide that reminded me of a snake, came a man who evidently was the chief.

Taller than the bound prisoner by half a head, he seemed higher still because of the lofty crown of brilliant long feathers which rose from his brow. He was painted like his men, as naked as they, and beardless like the rest; but otherwise he was no more like them than the lightning is like the thunder-clouds. Among their solid bodies he looked slender as a boy. Where their faces were broad and low his was long and thin. And that was not all. Every man of his warriors was copper-brown — but his sleek skin was white.

A white man with a black soul: that was my thought as I looked on him. Yes, a white man with the heart of a snake — and almost the body of a snake, too. That creeping glide of his — that slender, supple figure — and his eyes! As he stopped before the other white man and the sunlight fell on his face I saw that those eyes were as beady and venomous as if he were in truth a snake on legs. And the sneering smile he gave the prisoner was as deadly as the swift baring of a serpent's fangs.

The prisoner himself seemed to lose his tongue as he stared back at that white-skinned chief. For several breaths the two faced each other eye to eye, the men around them still as the trees. Then the blond man spoke.

"You the chief of these gory wolves?"

"*Sí, señor.*"

The snake-man's voice was a hiss.

"Spaniard, eh?" growled the other. "Might have known it, you dirty renegade! If there's anything lower, viler, or meaner than a Spaniard that's been kicked out by his own people and gone native I never yet saw it."

I looked to see the snake-faced chief strike him down for that. But he made no move. The cruel smile widened a little. In sneering Spanish his hissing voice sounded again.

"The *señor* is displeased about something?"

The blond man gulped.

"Speak English?" he snapped.

"Sí, señor, hablo inglés."

"Then speak it, damn you! And hear me speak it, damn you! You lousy, stinking, yellow-bellied son of two dogs, you sent these brutes of yours to wipe out my men, didn't you? And not only to kill them but to chop them up and bring them here to you, you filthy cannibal! Look at them!"

Still smiling that deadly smile, the feather-crowned man looked coolly down at the still heap on the dirt.

"The *señor* has it right. The men are cut even as he says. Perhaps the *señor* would like to say farewell to one of his friends?"

Swiftly he bent and lifted something from the pile. My breath stopped. The thing he had raised, *senhores*, was the bloody arm of a man, chopped off at the shoulder.

And before the prisoner could dodge or even guess his intention, that snaky fiend slapped him on the face with the dead hand on the end of that arm.

A choking yell broke from the blond man. Straining at the cords binding his wrists, he sprang at the grinning chief. He butted at him with his head, kicked at him, even tried to reach him with his teeth. But the snaky one moved about with the same smooth speed, avoiding all his attack and laughing in his face. Finally the red-eyed captive, unable to reach him, stood still and cursed him.

He cursed that chief with bitter, burning words until his voice failed. Then he stood panting, his face still working. And the chief grinned on.

"*Sí*, the *señor* is displeased," he mocked. "It is very sad. But the *señor* does me wrong when he calls me cannibal. I do not eat the flesh of men, for I do not like its taste. But my brothers here are fond of feasting on their enemies, and I am too soft of heart to deny them."

"Enemies!" the other rasped. "Those men of mine were not enemies to anyone. They were quiet, good-hearted fellows who came with me by the government's order. And I tell you you will pay for this! I am on government work, and when the government knows of this it will hunt you to your death — you and every brute in your gang!"

The chief laughed again in his hissing way.

"The *señor* forgets that the government may not hear. It is a true saying, is it not, that dead men carry no tales? My *capitán* reports that all your party were made unable to carry tales — all but you, who were kept alive by my order. And it may be, *señor*, that you also will lose the power to speak of this matter. *Quien sabe?*"

The blond man glared but said nothing. The chief went on:

"I have not heard what the *señor* does for the government. Perhaps the *señor* does not speak truth. What work of the government could be done so far from the home of the government?"

"Work that your ignorant brain would never comprehend, you son of a snake. Work of knowledge. I am commissioned by the government of Brazil to explore this region with especial reference to its resources, topography, and ethnology. By the government, understand? Behind me is the government's army. And if I don't come out the government will send in a force to learn why. And as sure as there's a God in the skies you will pay! Yes, you'll pay!"

"*Sí?* The government of Brazil is nothing to me, nor is any other. I am my own government. But it seems that I am something to the Brazilian government, or you would not know me by name."

His head lifted and his chest swelled as he continued:

"As the *señor* says, I am the Son of the Snake. Among my own men I am known as the Jararaca."

The captive stared. Then he laughed scornfully.

"Don't flatter yourself that you're anybody. I never heard of you, you bit of scum. When I called you 'son of a snake' I called you what you are, that's all — a dirty crawling thing too vile to live among men. 'Jararaca' is right!"

For the first time the chief scowled. Yet he spoke as softly as ever.

"It is unlucky that the *señor*, who is so wise and important, has not heard of the Son of the Snake. It is still more unfortunate that he speaks so harshly. And the *señor* spoke of God. He believes in the cross?"

"I'm no Catholic, if that's what you mean."

"Ah. But a Protestant, then? The *señor* believes in his 'God in the skies?'"

"Certainly. And in a hell for you, you yellow murderer. You — you —"

Again, with his eyes on the heap of butchered arms and legs before him, he burst into savage cursing of the Jararaca chief and all his men. And again the Jararaca listened as if amused. When the explorer stopped he said:

"The *señor* has the gift of tongues, is it not so? Perhaps this 'God in the skies' speaks through his mouth, yes? And perhaps the *señor* would like to leave this place and think about his God — even see him, it is possible. There is a quiet place not far from here where a fine gold cross hangs for those who believe in it, and where you may think all night undisturbed — except perhaps by a snake or two. I will send the *señor* there, and then he will not be offended by a little feast which my men will enjoy tonight.

"But while you are alone, *señor*, think about this word which I give you:

"Who lives by the cross dies by the snake."

For a moment longer the two fronted each other, the chief grinning, the prisoner scowling and trying to read his words. Then with a sudden wild screech the Jararaca leaped at the bound man.

Clawing, biting, attacking like a mad jungle beast, he knocked the prisoner down and fell on him. The blond man fought back in fury. Though his hands were useless, he did such damage with feet and teeth that soon the Son of the Snake squirmed away and stood up again.

I cocked my gun.

But Pedro, hearing the click, whispered fiercely:

"Wait! No shooting yet!"

I hesitated, burning to kill that chief where he stood. If he had attacked the captive again I probably would have shot — and I probably would not be here now. But I saved that bullet for another day. The Jararaca did not touch the man again.

His black eyes glittering, he laughed, the hiss in his voice louder than before. Then, turning toward the long house, he spoke two words to his men: two words in the Tupi *lengoa geral* which started us to creeping swiftly away down the hillside —

"*Boi euirah*. Snake tree."

VIII

IF THE gang of the Jararaca had not been intent on what was going on before them we might not have escaped unseen; for we went downhill too fast for good concealment. The little stubs jutting from the ground caught our clothes when we crawled, and stubbed our toes when we arose and flitted from tree to tree; and the trees themselves were not close enough together to hide us well from anyone at the top. But no yell of discovery sounded behind us, and soon we were hidden once more in the bush.

There we started back as we had come, hugging the shore. Neither of us spoke, but the same purpose was in our minds — to reach the *assacu* tree before the savages arrived there with their captive.

Half-way around the curve of the *enseada* we paused and peered across the water at the hill. Savages now were at the spot where the canoes lay, and among their ugly faces we made out the lighter skin and blond hair of the prisoner. Men shoved him roughly into a canoe, but no one entered the boat with him. Instead there seemed to be some argument among the warriors, and for the time all hung back.

"None of them wants to go now to the snake tree," Pedro guessed. "All want to stay here and prepare for the feast of man-flesh. So much the better for us — probably only a few will come with the white man. Let us hasten."

On we went until a thought struck me. I halted so suddenly that Pedro nearly knocked me down.

"Let us cut through to the *ygarapé* instead of following the shore," I urged. "It is shorter."

"No! By going the long way we make better speed — we follow the trail we have cut. And I want my *machadinha*."

I had not thought of the hatchet as a weapon, but now I agreed quickly. Those light, keen, silent *machadinhas* of ours might easily put two savages out of the fight. During the recent months of the great flood we had whiled away more than one idle hour by throwing them at marks, and had become so skilful at it that either of us could hit a man's head if we tried. Now was the time to try.

So we pressed on toward our camp, where the *machadinhas* lay with our packs. Now that we were far enough from the hill we ceased caring whether we shook the bushes, and dropped all attempts to move slyly. At top speed we raced over our back track until we stumbled panting into our *tambo*.

A swift search of our packs, and we were off again, the hatchets in our belts. And from that time on it was a steady, hard run along that never-ending *ygarapé*, fearing every minute that we should hear the drive of paddles and the swash of canoes overtaking and passing us. We wanted to save that man without shooting, for gunshots would bring the whole tribe of murderers out to hunt us down. But if the canoes caught up with us we must shoot.

At last, however, we burst gasping out upon the bare ground of the knoll of the *assacu*. Halting, we held our breath and listened until our straining lungs got the better of us. No sound came from the water behind. And you may be sure we did not creep to the edge to look back. Our feet were bare, and we were not sure we knew just where each of those nine buried snake-heads waited with upturned fangs.

"The American wears boots," said Pedro, his eyes roving up that bare ground.

"Yes. The fangs of snakes — alive or dead — are nothing to him."

"We had best go around to the other side. It is safe there, except that one spot before the *jacaré*."

Passing close to the bush, yet far enough from it to dodge any lurking snake, we strode around past the bones and on until we looked up at the alligator strapped against the poison-thorns. Then, after poking our guns into the undergrowth and making sure that nothing was coiled at that place, we stepped in and crouched out of sight.

"The day ends," said Pedro.

It was so. The sun was fast rolling down. Against its glare the great tree loomed black as a nightmare growth, towering over us like an awful giant about to step on us and crush us into nothing. Back in the jungle the dismal roar of a *guariba* broke out, and from thousands of throats the hammering of frogs swelled into the beginning of the night chorus. Less than a quarter-hour of daylight remained. I began to fear that night would find us still waiting.

Then, so near that I started, grunting voices sounded and water swashed. The *barbaros* had come.

We heard no bump of canoes against the bank, but we did hear snarling voices and the smack of a blow on flesh. The blow was answered by an angry curse in English. Then up over the crest of the knoll rose a blond head, followed close by other heads greasy-haired and brutal-faced.

The low sun struck across the face of the white man, and we saw that he recognized the *assacu* as a poison-tree and suspected that it meant death to him. He came straight on without a falter in his step, but his mouth was set grimly and his eyes darted this way and that as if he sought some line of escape. But then the two foremost savages closed in and gripped his arms, one on each side, to prevent any sudden break.

As they did this, one of them started slightly and jerked a foot upward as if something had stung it. He looked over his shoulder at the ground, but saw nothing. So he came on.

Another *barbaro* did the same thing. A third, though he did not jump like the other two, stopped a moment, leaned on a spear, lifted a foot, glanced at it, rubbed it with one finger as if something had hurt him, then resumed his stride.

By that time the first pair, clutching the captive, rounded the butt of the tree and saw what was bound there. They stopped short and stared. The others, following, pressed around them and also halted. Swiftly I counted them. Seven

Indians and one white. And no more were coming.

A sudden grunting started among them. The sight of that beast of the mud with its crude cross, where they had expected the corpse of a man weighted down with a crucifix of gold, had astounded them so that they could not think. Even the white man stood motionless, staring like the rest, and perhaps wondering what it all meant. And we stayed where we were, making no move; for we knew that death already was creeping upward along the veins of three of them, and we wanted it to creep as far as it could before we made our presence known.

Then a fourth, moving closer to the *jacaré* grunted sharply and drew up a foot. The buried head of the *surucucu* also had gotten its man.

But the man did not know it. He peered down at the ground, moved over a little, and turned toward the prisoner. The others remembered what they had come for. They too looked toward the white man and spoke growlingly among themselves. At the same moment the white made a desperate break for life.

With a heaving, twisting plunge he wrenched himself away from one of the men holding him and knocked the other staggering. In the same movement he whirled, bent low, and threw himself head-first at the two *barbaros* behind him. So swift and hard was his charge that he broke through between them and was clear of them before they could grasp him. And when he had passed them no man was in his way.

Straight for the bush he dashed — straight toward the spot where we crouched. Snarling, the nearest savages jumped after him. But in the next instant two of them died. We hurled our *machadinhas*.

In the last rays of the sun those hatchets whirled from our hands like streaks of lightning. And as if stricken down by thunderbolts, those two Indians plunged forward and down on their faces, our steel buried in their brains. Instantly we were out of the bush, charging with our machetes.

As we left the tangle the prisoner crashed headlong into it. Two more cannibals, leaping downhill after him, tried to stop themselves at sight of us, but could not. Slipping on the clay, they slid into our down-chopping blades.

I struck my man so fiercely that I too went down. The keen weapon, cutting into him at the base of the neck, sank into the chest-bones and stuck there as firmly as if driven into wood. As he fell, the downward yank of the fixed machete threw me off balance, and I tumbled on his body.

I was up in a second, straining to free the knife and watching the three remaining *barbaros*. If they had attacked me then they surely would have killed me. But they did not attack.

They had not come far from the tree, and they stood staring as if dazed. Not until I had put a foot on the dead man under me and worked the blade loose did one of them move. And his movement was clumsy — a sluggish sort of step like that of a man numb or sick. The other two did not move at all.

Then Pedro, standing beside me with red machete ready to meet any rush, spoke in Tupi.

"You are dead men. Even though we touch you not, death crawls through you. You are struck by the snake which is under the earth. Its bite is in your feet."

Silent they stood. In their faces grew fear. And every one of them looked suddenly back at the way they had come from the water, then down at his feet.

The sun dropped and was gone. Swift night deepened under the great *assacu*. The dead Indians on the ground, the three above still living but dying, blurred into dim shadows. The growing noise of the jungle swelled into a hammering, cracking, screaming roar of life.

"Senhor! Norte Americano!" shouted Pedro.

"Here!" came the answer from the bush behind us. And the white man strode out beside me.

Quickly I felt down his arms, found the thick bush-rope binding them, and cut it.

"Get to the canoes!" I ordered. "Shove them out. Work down the shore and wait for us. Hurry!"

Without a word he strode away through the dark.

"Get the rifles!" I told Pedro.

With the words I followed the American, watching for any

sign of a rush by those three above us. I went only as far as I thought the ground safe, and there I stood on guard. But no rush came. Straining my eyes, I made out that two of the three Indians had sunk down on the ground, where they sat hunched over with heads hanging. The third still stood bolt upright staring down at his legs.

"All right, you men!" came the blond man's call from the *ygarapé*.

Down the hill I stole to the bones, whose white glimmer showed faint at the bushline. There Pedro stood with the guns. Silently we worked along until we felt we were at the right point, when we began groping our way southward. And no man followed.

IX

FOR SOME distance we labored along the shore, advancing more by instinct and touch than by the use of our eyes. Then we halted and listened.

Only the night din came to our ears, and if any of the doomed three was trying to follow us we could not hear him. But we were sure they had not left the knoll. Not only were their hopeless attitudes those of men convinced they were about to die, but the loss of their boats would go far toward keeping them there. With their canoes they might have reached the Jararaca with their tale before they died, but to traverse the black, pathless jungle was another matter.

So we called to the blond man. From the gloomy water came an answering hail. A blurred shape glided into sight, and after one or two more calls to show where we were it floated within reach. We entered the canoe, found paddles, and shoved out and away from the shore tangle.

"Was there only one canoe?" I asked.

"That's all," the American answered. "Nobody wanted to come on this trip. Only one boatload did come, and they were ugly about it. Growled all the way over."

I said no more. Pedro and I began paddling quietly along

the *ygarapé*. The American took a few strokes, but soon stopped.

"Guess I'll let you boys do the paddling," he said. "My hands are bad. That rope damaged my wrists some."

Not another word was spoken until we reached the point where that afternoon we had heard the talking wood. There we landed and argued briefly about hiding the canoe. But it was a long craft — made for eight men — and too big to be easily concealed. So we decided merely to lift its bow on shore and leave it there for the time.

"We shall need it again at dawn," Pedro said. "I am going back to the *assacu* then and get our *machadinhas*. They are too good to be left to rust in the brains of *barbaros*. And we need them in our work."

The American still said nothing, standing quiet while we talked. And when we entered the bush and started for our camp he trailed us closely but silently. Not until we were in our *tambo* did he speak, and then it was in answer to a question.

"*Senhor,*" I said, "you have been through a bad experience. Will you have a little drink of rum?"

"I sure will!" was his instant response. "Now that things have quieted down I feel a little off color. Got a nasty rap on the head before I was captured."

I felt about until I found the jug, and when its plug was out I put it into his hands. A gurgle followed, and then a cough.

"Woof!" he sputtered. "Boy, oh boy! This is pure essence of hellfire! Got a recoil like a six-inch gun, I'll bet."

"In about two minutes you will know you have had a drink, *senhor*," Pedro laughed. "Could you eat something too?"

"Nope. Not just yet. Later, maybe, when my nerves loosen up. But I could smoke, if I had anything that would burn."

"You shall have it," I promised, taking back the jug and swallowing a mouthful from it, then passing it to Pedro.

When I stopped coughing I made two cigarettes, one for the stranger and one for myself, and held the match. He gave me a swift, straight look in the eyes as the light held, and when Pedro lit a smoke of his own he studied my partner, in the same rapid way. Then we sat down in the hammocks.

"We sleep with no fire tonight," I said, "but a cigarette or two will do no harm. It is time we became acquainted. I am Lourenço Moraes and this is my comrade Pedro Andrada — *seringueiros* of Coronel Nunes of the Javary, now scouting for new rubber. We are in this spot because two nights ago we heard a scream from the south and came this way to learn what made it. And then, having learned that, we kept on to find who was responsible. Now we know."

"That yellow snake who calls himself Jararaca?"

"The Jararaca. The man who told you that 'who lives by the cross dies by the snake.'"

His cigarette hung motionless a moment. Then he asked —

"How do you know he said that?"

"Because we were there, hidden behind a tree and spying. If we had not been there —"

"I would not be here," he finished. "I get you. And I hope I don't have to tell you chaps how eternally grateful I am for —"

"Say no more of that," Pedro cut in.

"All right. Just as you say. But I want to add that though I've seen some beautiful sights now and then, I never saw anything half as glorious as you two fellows rising up out of the bush and heaving tomahawks into those scuts behind me. Believe me, that's something that will stay with me until I reach the end of the long trail.

"It takes out a little of the rankle of seeing my men butchered for a cannibal holiday, too — a little, though not much. I'm going to do some slaughtering on my own hook before the score is even. And unless something bad happens to me right soon, that Jararaca is going to squirm around and bite himself for bucking up against Tom Mack.

"That's me. Thomas Gordon Mack of the U. S. A. Sort of a foot-loose cuss with some scientific knowledge and a constant urge to ramble into unknown places. I'm known to the Brazilian government, and while I was hanging around Rio a while ago and wondering what to do next they offered me a job nosing around this end of the country and looking things over, after which I'm supposed to write a weighty report of everything seen and done. So here I am.

"They'd have given me a young army, and maybe a brass band and a uniform, but that isn't my way of doing things. A few good men — the fewer the better — are what you want for bush work. And the boys I picked out were just built for the job. All caboclos except Joao, my *tenente*, who was a *mameluco*. Born *bushmen*. Good boys. Not a drop of yellow in the whole outfit. And now they're roasting on the hill over yonder to feed that nest of snakes."

He slammed his cigarette savagely down on the dirt.

"I was off in a canoe with one of the boys when it happened," he went on. "Heard shots and yells. Beat it back as fast as we could paddle. By the time I got there it was about over. The boys never had a chance. Surrounded, jumped, butchered.

"I got some of the raiders before my gun was empty. Then they got me. Must have thrown a club. The light went out, and I woke up disarmed and tied.

"By that time they had set up some sort of arrangement of slats, and one of them who looked more brainy than the rest was pounding out some message on it. Sounded like a big xylophone. After a while an answer came back, and when another message had gone and a reply came they took the thing down and threw me into a canoe. Guess they must have been telling their boss they had a live white man and wanted to know whether to chop me up or bring me in all in one piece.

"The rest of the boys they cut up — took their arms and legs — Ugh! But they'll pay, by Judas! They'll pay!"

"What will you do now, Senhor Mack?" asked Pedro. "Have the government send in an army, as you threatened?"

"Government? Hell, no! Governments are too slow, all of them. This is my own war. I'm going to get that Jararaca and get him good. Don't know just how; but I'm camping on his trail until one of us cashes in. You fellows haven't a gun to spare, have you?"

We hesitated. Then I said:

"We have no extra gun, *senhor*, and we do not like to part with our own."

"Of course. I wouldn't do it myself. Well, I'll dope out some way to get that bird or I'm not Tom Mack. And I'll clean up as many more as I can. Say, that rum of yours sure has a punch. Awhile ago my tongue was stuck at both ends, and now I can't stop it. Can you spare another smoke?"

With a new cigarette between his lips he was quiet a moment. Then he said:

"I hope you cleaned up those other three Indians after I boarded the canoe."

"They are dead by now," I judged.

"Huh? You left them alive?"

"Alive but not alive. There are some things you have not heard."

And I told him of the man whose body we had found and of the trap we had made.

"Ha! Good stuff!" he approved. "Turn about is fair play. And that alligator idea of yours helped me a lot in breaking loose, Pedro. But are you sure those three you left there all had stepped on snakes?"

"Quite, sure, *senhor*. Every one of them looked back when I told them they were snake-bitten, and I saw they thought of the stings they had felt as they came up."

"Uh-huh. We'll make sure in the morning. But now listen here; while we have a canoe I want to use it to get back to my camp tonight. Those mutts wrecked things pretty well, but I'm quite sure I can salvage some of my stuff, and I want all there is left. There'll be a moon tonight, probably in about an hour — enough light to get around with. If you chaps care to go with me —"

"Certainly, *senhor*," we said.

"Good! Let's start now. We can work down the lake all right in the dark and be so much nearer camp by moonrise. Say, do you mind if I waste a little rum on my wrists? They're cut up pretty bad, and the bush-rope they used on me may have been poisonous. If you'll just sop a little into the cuts I'll be much obliged."

While Pedro held matches I did as he asked. His jaws clicked together as the fiery liquor bit into the raw flesh, but he gave no other sound. When I corked the jug he spoke one word through his teeth.

"Thanks!"

Then we struck out through the bush to the point. The canoe lay as we had left it. I crawled into the stern, Mack took a place in the middle, and Pedro shoved the long boat out and jumped in over the bow. A moment later we were sliding quietly eastward on a lake of ink.

X

AN EIGHT-MAN *ubá*, or war-canoe, is a clumsy craft for three men to handle, and in darkness, on unknown waters where snags may lurk and noise may mean death, no speed can be made in such a boat. We three did not try to hasten on our way. We only crept along, our eyes and ears wide open and our paddles dipping silently, with rifles beside us ready for instant use. At any moment we might meet other canoes bound for the poison-tree to learn why this one did not return.

But we met none. Time after time we halted our paddles and reached swiftly for our guns as some splash or swashing sound came suddenly to us; but each time, after listening and peering around, we decided that the noise was made by alligator or fish, and began our quiet strokes again. And so, working, pausing, drifting, we journeyed on past the entrance of the bay at whose end lay the cannibal camp.

There we saw the glow of firelight shining in the black mass of jungle, though the fires which made it were out of our sight. Through the night noise also came the throb of drums beating at that place, and once we heard the voices of men yelling in savage celebration. At the thought of what was going on beside those fires I shut my teeth, and up ahead the blond man growled fierce curses. We put more power into our paddling than was wise, and slowed again only when the shouts and the light had died out behind us. Then we felt out way onward as before.

Moonrise found us rounding the turn at the far end of the lagoon. The first light dropping from the sky was very faint, but by it we could see the water ahead more clearly, and for the time that was enough. Here the broad water narrowed again into another winding *ygarapé*, along which we journeyed with fair speed but the same silence. The jungle noise had quieted somewhat, and the loudest sound we heard was the roar of some bad-tempered jaguar prowling the bush not far off. Nowhere was any sound of human life.

After a time the looping water widened once more, and now the light of the rising moon fell fair on it from our left.

Seeing nothing on the glittering surface, we put our shoulders into our strokes and surged along at far better speed. Before long Senhor Mack told us to swing in toward the right-hand shore. And after coasting along the edge of the jungle for a little way we turned into a small cove and found several small canoes floating at a landing.

On the sloping shore above was a clearing. In the clearing a big *tambo* stood out in the moonlight. As we stepped ashore and climbed into the open space beside that *tambo* we found only death and that life which preys on death.

Two big alligators crawled toward the water, opening their fearful jaws at us in menace and disappointment as they went. They had come too late, for the black birds of the sky had dropped on that spot long before they arrived. Now there remained only raw bones and skulls.

Senhor Mack made a choking sound as he looked down on those things which a few hours ago had been his men, And I too, though I had seen fleshless bodies more than once during my years in the Javary jungle, felt hot hate of the Jararaca and his crew boil up in my brain as I saw that no arm or leg bones were among those scattered remnants. Pedro, gazing about him, growled in his throat.

"Good-by, boys," the blond man said hoarsely. "You went out like men. And you went out quick — thank God for that! A damn right quicker than that yellow devil will go if I get him as I want him!"

He choked again and turned into the *tambo*. We stood silent and waited.

We saw him go slowly about inside the place, stooping now and then to pick up something, then dropping it. By and by he came out, bringing only a rolled-up hammock.

"Cleaned!" he said. "They carried away or ruined everything. Not a gun, knife, or cartridge left. Not a bite of grub. Even this hammock is cut, but it can be mended. Not another thing here worth taking. But I'm betting they missed my cache."

Tossing the hammock toward the landing, he walked to a tree at the edge of the open space. It looked as solid and firm as any other tree. But he stopped in the shadow beside it, put both hands on it, and pulled a large piece of bark away. Then his head and shoulders disappeared into the trunk.

Crossing to where he stood, we saw that in the tree yawned a large black hole. In this he was groping downward. Soon he straightened up and drew out a package wrapped in rubber-cloth.

"Hollow," he explained, nodding at the trunk. "I cut a chunk of the same kind of bark off another tree and trimmed it to fit this hole. When it's on you'd hardly know there was any hole here. Kept my notebooks and stuff like that in here — dry as a bone and out of harm's way. Sort of a bush safety-deposit vault."

He set the bundle on the ground, groped again in the tree, and brought up a smaller package.

"That's all," he said. "Wish I'd cached a gun in there, but wishing doesn't get me anything. I've got the records of the expedition intact, anyway. That and one bum hammock. Nothing else."

With the bundle in his arms he went down to the landing. I picked up the other, and we followed.

"Here are smaller canoes than ours," I said, looking over the boats whose paddlers never again would sit in them. "Let us take one of them and leave the big one."

"Right. We'll take my own. It's light and fast, and it will just about carry us three. But before I go I want to do one thing for my boys up yonder."

"What?"

"Put up a good big cross among them. We can't bury them, but — "

"If you will pardon me, *senhor*, I would not do that now," Pedro objected. "Later, perhaps, but not tonight."

"Why not?"

"Because the *barbaros* may come back tomorrow to see if they have missed any loot. To find a cross here would set them searching the bush for miles around for the men who put it up. Now they do not know of us, and it is not well to let them know until we are ready. And I think we had better not leave that big canoe of theirs here. Let us take it farther on and hide it in some place not easily found. I have been thinking, and I believe I have a plan to clean out that snakes' den."

"Good boy! What is it?"

"Later on, *senhor*, I will tell you," my partner smiled. "But now let us act, not talk."

"All right."

Mack dropped his bundle into a narrow, swift-looking canoe. We stowed the larger package where it would ride well. Then he climbed the bank once more and stood silent, his hand at his forehead in salute. When he came back his face was working and his eyes wet. Without a word we pushed out, towing the long *ubá* behind us.

Some distance farther on we found a bush-grown inlet where the boat of the *barbaros* could be entirely concealed. We drove it in, bent bushes far down to cover its stern, and left it there. With the moon rolling high above us we struck off toward our distant camp.

XI

AFTER OUR slow, blind trip to this place in the clumsy *ubá*, the return through the moon-glare in Senhor Mack's speedy little boat was like play. Swiftly we swept on, with the water purring pleasantly under our bow, until we had passed through the twisting channel and entered again the *lagoa* on whose banks stood the Jararaca's camp and our own. There we slowed and became cautious.

The moonlight flooded the whole sheet of water, and on it

we saw no boats. But that was no sign that it was not watched; and out of the many pairs of eyes in the Jararaca's gang it would take only one to spy us, and only one tongue to start an alarm. So we began to work along close to the southern bank, where we could blend with the jungle shadows. And as we neared the point opposite which the *enseada* opened, we paddled without lifting our blades, turning them under water at each slow stroke, so that the moon would not betray us by flashing off the wet wood.

On the northern jungle-line the firelight did not show now. Either the fires had sunk low or their glimmer was swallowed up by the brighter light of the moon. But the throb of the drums went on as before, floating to us across the water like the beating of some awful black heart. The cannibals still were awake.

No other sound of men came to us, and as we crawled on past the *enseada* we saw no blot on its surface. Down to the end of the wide water we traveled without any sign that we were seen. But we still stuck to the shoreline until that grassy point of land near our camp had slid out between us and the lagoon and we knew no watcher could possibly see us cut across the *ygarapé* to our own bank. Then I swung the stern. But Pedro swerved the bow back. In a low tone he said:

"Now is as good a time as any to get our *machadinhas*. Tomorrow may be too late. Perhaps it is too late now — the *barbaros* may have been there, may even be there at this moment. But let us go and see."

I grunted assent, and we moved on without crossing. Now we lifted our paddles and took a freer swing, but we made no attempt at speed. Loop after loop of the *ygarapé* crept behind us until we saw the awful head of the *assacu* towering from its knoll. At the last turn we barely moved, floating on as lightly as a fallen leaf, ready for anything. Then Pedro grunted and stroked boldly. Except for ourselves, the water was empty.

Across to the clay hill we slid, taking good care to pass the place where the snakehead trail began. As we drew up beyond the tree, where the ground was safe, Pedro rose to leap ashore. But he did not make that jump. For a second he stood poised. Then he gave the bank a sudden jolt with his paddle, swerving the canoe outward. In one swoop he had caught up his rifle.

I threw my own gun to my shoulder. Somewhere in the shadows under that poison-tree something was creeping toward us.

Down to the edge came a black, horrible shape. Over my rifle-barrel I stared at it, ready to shoot but not sure whether it was man, beast, or fiend. Then I saw. It was man and beast both — perhaps fiend too. A big alligator, clutching in his jaws the body of one of the Indians we had left there, was sliding into the water.

"*Por Deus!*" Pedro muttered. "Perhaps our *machadinhas* are gone even though no more *barbaros* have come."

When the reptile had sunk from sight we lowered our guns and sent the canoe back to the shore.

"Beware of snakes!" I warned.

Both Pedro and Senhor Mack grunted. We got out on shore very carefully.

"I'll go ahead," said the blond man. "You lads ought to wear boots. Hand me a machete, somebody."

I passed him mine, and he tramped on before us. Step by step we followed him up the slope.

"Back up!" he suddenly warned.

With the words he swung the knife. A hiss sounded. The machete thudded down. The hiss died.

"Good thing I came first," said our American partner. "He nailed my foot. Didn't get through, though. These boots are tough."

"*Jararaca?*" Pedro questioned.

"Don't know. Most likely. Something wicked anyhow. Say, you lads better stay back. You might step on his head or another live one. What do you want? Just your tomahawks?"

"I thought, senhor, it would be well to throw the *barbaros* into the water," Pedro answered. "There the *jacarés* will quickly take care of them, and if other cannibals came there will be no sign of a fight — except blood."

"Good idea. You stay there and I'll haul them over to you. Guess your hatchets are still here. Here's one cuss now, all curled up."

We saw him stoop and look.

"Ugh! He's swollen like a poisoned pup. One of the guys that stepped on your trap. If you fellows hadn't been here this afternoon I'd look like this thing now — or worse."

After a minute he came toward us, dragging a body by the hair. And he went straight past. We saw a bloated corpse slide by and go tumbling into the *ygarapé*, where it sank from sight.

"There goes one of the scuts that butchered my boys," he said grimly, coming back. "I wanted to heave him to the 'gators myself. You can have the others."

One by one he brought them to us, and we threw them out into the water. The first was swollen like the one he had dragged past. Then came one with a *machadinha* driven deep into his skull, and as we worked the blade out he pulled the other up and dropped it. Pedro drew the hatchet from that one's head. The two we had killed with machetes came last and ended the count.

"Two dead by tomahawks, two by machetes, two by snake-bite — and the one the 'gator got," Senhor Mack summed up. "That cleans up the pot, and we can call it a day. Maybe I'd better find that snake and chuck him into the bush, though. Then there'll be nothing left here but tracks. Phew! That 'gator tied to the tree is getting to smell out loud."

Lighting matches, he went about until he found the snake he had killed in the dark.

"Yep, a *jararaca*," he said. "Good sign, that. We'll clean up that yellow *jararaca* over on the hill — Judas! Here's another!"

Again the machete whistled in the air. Then we heard something soft go flying into the bush, and another thing of the same kind follow it.

"Suppose both of those squirmy cusses would have had a lot of fun slinging poison into my bare legs tonight if you lads hadn't stopped the cannibals from stripping me and trussing me up," said Mack as he returned to us. "But the boot's on the other foot. Anything more to do here?"

"Nothing, *senhor*," we told him.

And we went down to the canoe and shoved out and away from that accursed spot.

Back along the water we traveled swiftly until we neared the grassy point. There we slowed and sought a hiding-place for our canoe. After a little time we found it: a snug little spot under thick overhanging bush. We unloaded Senhor Mack's two bundles, got ashore, and started for our *tambo*. But somehow I got a desire to look again up the lagoon before we slept.

"All right," Mack agreed. "Never does any harm to look around. We'll squat here until you come back."

So I stepped toward the point. But I had gone less than a dozen steps when I halted. Into the air had come a sound which I felt rather than heard: a beat of paddles.

Back to the others I ran. Three words from me, and we were creeping to the edge of the water. There we crouched and watched.

The beat became plain. Water swashed. Before our eyes an eight-man *ubá* of savages surged past, bound for the *assacu*. Another followed, and another. They passed and were gone.

Wordless, motionless, we waited. The moon slid on westward. Life splashed in the water, howled in the forest, buzzed in the air. But no sound came from down the *ygarapé*.

Then came a confused murmur. Again sounded a rush of water. Paddles splashed as if driven in fear. The murmur became voices grunting excitedly. An *ubá* shot past, crowded hard by the other two. They swirled around the point and disappeared at top speed toward the camp of the Jararaca.

We arose and ran to the point, where we watched those ugly war-boats rush into their *enseada* and vanish. We waited long for them to come out again, but nothing came. So finally we turned back toward our camp. And as we went I thought of what I had heard.

Those cannibals, hurrying away from the place, had been mouthing one word —

"*Anyi!*"

And the Tupi word "*anyi*" means —

"Devil!"

XII

BACK AT our *tambo*, around which splotches of white light crawled along the ground as the moon crept westward, we helped our North American friend patch his hammock so that it would hold him up for the night. When the task was done and the bed hung beside ours, he asked:

"Now, friend Pedro, what's your big idea? How are we to smash the Son of the Snake?"

"My biggest idea just now, *senhor*," Pedro smiled, "is to sleep until morning."

"Oh, rats! We can sleep when there's nothing else to do. Come on, loosen up."

"In the morning, *senhor*. As you say, the time to sleep is when there is nothing else to do. We can do no more tonight. So now I sleep."

"You're an exasperating cuss," Mack grumbled. "But you're talking sense at that. I'm dog tired, and we can think better after we rest."

"Just so, *senhor*. Good night."

And we curled up in our nets and relaxed.

MORNING BROKE faint and gray, but after the sun sucked up the usual swamp mists the air grew clear and hot. We found a dead tree and cut from it wood which gave a swift fire with little smoke, and over this we boiled our coffee. As soon as the black liquid was hot we killed the blaze with mud. And after a spying trip to the point, where we saw only the bare water, we smoked and talked.

"Now, *senhor*," said Pedro, "you want most of all to kill the Jararaca. We are with you in that. But also you want to stamp out the gang of the Jararaca, leaving not one alive. We are with you in that also. Not only are such beasts unfit to live, but they make this place unsafe for any man.

"We seek rubber, and if we find it our fellow *seringueiros* must come in here to work it. But they can not work any region where lives so deadly a band of man-eaters as that of the *Jara-*

raca. And even if we find no rubber here, this is the *seringal* of our *coronel*, and as men of the *coronel* it is our duty as well as our desire to destroy these snakes before they strike at the *coronel*'s interests."

"Quite so," Mack nodded.

"But the job of destroying them is too great for three men armed as poorly as we are, You have no weapons at all; and though we two are well equipped to fight and run, we do not want to run. When we open our war we must stay with it to the end. I do not know how many men are against us, but they must number at least half a hundred. Lourenço and I have out-fought odds as great as that before now, but those were low creatures who were hardly more than beasts and who feared us as demons, so that they were defeated by their own terror. These fighters of the Son of the Snake are not such fools. What is more, their place on that hill is too strong for us to attack. Its front is a steep, bare slope of slippery clay rising out of the water of the *enseada*. The side where we crawled up yesterday and saw you face the Jararaca is almost as steep as the front, and its underbrush has been cleared away so that the cover would be very poor for anyone trying to storm the top. The other side, toward the *lagoa*, undoubtedly is the same."

"It is," the blond man agreed. "That's the side where I went up and down. Path leads from the canoe-landing to the top."

"So I thought. That leaves only the fourth side, back in the bush, of which we know nothing; but it is a safe guess that the rear is well protected. The place is almost a *forte*.

"The first thing for us to do, then, is to find enough men, with enough weapons, to give us a fighting chance against the *barbaros*. To go against them without a fighting chance would be to die like fools. Am I right?"

"Couldn't be any righter," Mack admitted. "But where are your men and guns?"

"On other parts of this *seringal*. And to get them we must first return to headquarters."

"Too slow! I want to clean up now."

"With what?" Pedro demanded. "Your bare hands? That is all you have now. I tell you frankly, *senhor*, I will not throw away my life for no good. I have no great objection to dying, but I do not intend to give my arms and legs to feed such brutes as those. If you will go against them alone, go. Perhaps the Jararaca and his men will stand in line and let you strangle them one by one. But I doubt it."

The other scowled and growled; but nodded grudgingly.

"You're right," he conceded. "How long does it take us to reach your *coronel?*"

"It took us nine days to reach this place, but we traveled slowly. This time we shall go fast. And have no fear that the *barbaros* will run away while we are gone. They will keep until we return."

"All right, let's go!" Mack snapped, rising swiftly. "And let's go light. Least weight, most speed."

"We take only our hammocks and what food we need," Pedro answered. "We shall have a good deal to pack when we return. There is another part to my plan, which I shall speak of later. Now our task is to make speed northward,"

Both Mack and I looked curiously at him, wondering what other thing he had in mind. But we asked no questions. We fell to making up light packs of food.

Then to me came a half-formed idea. I stopped my work.

"Pedro," I said, "I stay here until you return. There is no need of all three of us going to headquarters. You two are enough."

"Huh? Leave you here alone? Nothing doing!" Mack protested.

I smiled. Pedro laughed.

"Do not worry about Lourenço, *senhor*," he said. "He has gone alone more than once among the worst dangers of the jungle, and you see he is still alive. Even if the *barbaros* caught him they would find him hard to hold. If this Jararaca is a snake, Lourenço is an eel."

"I get you," the blond man said with a quick grin. "One of those electric eels that pack an awful wallop, eh? But what can you do here alone, Lourenço?"

"Perhaps I can learn a few things of value," I suggested. "And possibly some other victim may be brought to the *assacu* before you return. If I can not save him I can shoot him. That would be mercy."

"I'll say so," he agreed, his face darkening. "But listen here, old-timer — don't get too brash and kill the Jararaca on your own hook while I'm gone. He's my meat. Understand?"

"The time to kill a snake, *senhor*, is whenever you can," I told him coolly. "It does not matter who kills it, so long as it is killed. I make no promises."

For a moment I thought he would again refuse to go. But then he looked down at his empty cartridge-belt and holster, spread his hands in a hopeless way, shrugged his shoulders, and resumed his work on his pack. And a little later he and Pedro stood up with a scant week's rations on their shoulders, ready to go.

"I am leaving the gold cross with you," Pedro said. "It has led us to the demons who hung that poor fellow on the assacu, even as I thought it might. Now it may protect you while you are alone."

"You talk like a priest," I laughed. "Take it or leave it — I do not care. What interests me more is the fact that you are leaving the jug."

Senhor Mack snickered and Pedro grinned. We strode away to the *ygarapé*, leaving jug and cross behind us. While they settled themselves in the canoe I went again to the grassy point, saw nothing alarming, and returned to them. Then we struck off smartly down the winding water.

Reaching the *assacu*, Pedro and Mack again went ashore on the safe side of the tree, while I kept watch along the *ygarapé*. Quickly but thoroughly they removed the last traces of our fight and our moonlight visit — traces which the savages could not have seen last night in the deep shadows, but which they might perceive if they came again by daylight. They covered the bloodstains with fresh earth, which they patted down carefully and then smeared out smooth with hatfuls of water.

In the same way, working back toward the edge, they blotted out every track made by Senhor Mack's boot-soles and heels. And when they again entered the canoe we smoothed away the marks left in the bank last night by our bow and

Pedro's paddle.

"Now," said Pedro, "any *barbaros* coming here to investigate will get nothing for their pains — except, perhaps, more death from our snake-head trail. There is no sign that the *ubá* bringing you, Senhor Mack, ever reached here. You, and the seven cannibals with you, and the boat itself, have disappeared into nothing. Where a human corpse should stand against the tree is only a stinking *jacaré*. They will have something to think about."

"They had something to think about last night," I said. "They were panting '*Anyi*' as they fled. That means 'devil,' *senhor*."

"Yes? Thought the devil was after them, eh? Well, they'll be dead sure of it a few days from now, I'm thinking."

And Pedro, smiling at some thought of his own, echoed —

"I too am thinking so."

Down to the end of the *ygarapé* we pushed swiftly. Pedro and the blond man got out. I stayed in the boat.

"Dang it, I don't feel right to quit you like this!" Mack grumbled. "But it's the only thing to do if you won't come along. Take care of yourself, old chap."

"I am in the habit of taking care of myself," I smiled. "Go with God!"

Pedro waved a hand, turned, and plunged into the bush. Mack followed. They vanished, swallowed by the jungle. I was alone.

XIII

IF THE two who were gone expected me to spend my time lolling in my hammock and hugging the jug they were wrong. The first thing I did, after hiding the canoe and reaching camp, was to bury the jug at a rear corner of the *tambo*, where it would be safe and out from under foot. Then I cleared up the things left lying about in the hasty departure, oiled my gun, smoked a cigarette, and thought.

As the result of that thinking I went out that afternoon on

another spying trip. Halfway around the *enseada* I sneaked, almost to the place where that path of the *barbaros* turned so suddenly into the forest. I did not enter the path itself for two reasons: it was not necessary to my present purpose, and I felt a man in it.

Yes, *senhores*, I mean just that. I did not see him, hear him, or even smell him — I felt him. I knew he was there as surely as I knew I was there. And I took great care that he should not hear anything of me, for it was no part of my plan to kill any man there just then. I stole back a little distance, then wormed my way down to the water's edge and squatted there studying the hill of the cannibals and all I could see around it.

Pedro's estimate had been correct. The front of the place could not be scaled at any time, and the two sides were too steep and too well cleared to be rushed by anything less than a small army. Paths led to the top from both sides, I knew, but these probably were guarded at ordinary times, both above and below. The man in the path nearest to me undoubtedly was a sentry stationed at a fixed post, as he did not seem to go away — I still felt that he was there. And after watching awhile I became sure that the tongue of low land opposite me, running westward and forming a shore of both the *enseada* and the *lagoa*, also was guarded. Across the water I glimpsed an Indian passing slowly up and down through the undergrowth.

Not much chance of a few men reaching the hilltop from this direction, I decided. I began to speculate about the rear of the place, and half determined that I would take a look at it when the time was more favorable. That time must be at night, when I could pass unseen down the *lagoa* in the canoe and later prowl by moonlight.

While I thought of this, two *ubás* full of paddlers came swinging up the bay from the lake. Behind each of them trailed smaller canoes, empty. They passed in silence, and their men showed none of the fear I had observed among those who fled from the *ygarapé* last night. I had not seen nor heard any visitors to the *assacu* today, and was quite sure none had been there. These men evidently had done what Pedro predicted —

returned to the death-strewn camp of Senhor Mack to search for anything overlooked after the fight; and I silently blessed my partner for preventing the planting of any cross among the bones there.

The boats went to the usual place and the men got out in a calm, unhurried way. For a few minutes some of them stood talking. Then all faded away inland.

Having learned all I could at this spot, I crept away and returned to my *tambo*. The air now was stifling hot, and my head grew heavy. I decided to sleep for the rest of the afternoon, and then, after dark, to take out the canoe and go down the lagoon for further study of the Jararaca's place. Perhaps the paths along the *enseada* would be left unguarded after sundown — savages seldom keep sentries out at night, and these men did not know any enemy was near — and in that case I could safely prowl close to their camp. So I lay down, knowing the usual night clamor would wake me at dark.

But while I slept the weather changed. I awoke in blackness to hear rain pounding the jungle. It was not a thundersquall, but a hard steady rain that would last most of the night and blot the moon from the sky. After a smoke I went to sleep again and knew nothing more until day.

Now it is a habit of mine in the bush to glance around me as soon as I awake in the morning, before putting my feet to the ground. One never knows what sort of thing may have crawled into an open *tambo* during the night, and it is always well to look about before rising. Most of the time one sees nothing new, but now and then there may be something worth looking at. And this morning, after making my usual quick inspection of the ground, I kept my bare feet in the hammock.

Under me, coiled ready to strike, its wicked eyes watching me and its forked tongue quivering, was a *jararaca*.

It had crept in there, perhaps, to keep out of the rain, though a *jararaca* does not dislike water. At any rate, it was there, and it showed no intention of going away. And while it stayed under my hammock, I was in a bad position. I had no fear that it would strike straight up at me, though I have heard of snakes doing such things. But if I stepped out it surely would bury its fangs in my foot. And unless I did step out there was scant chance of my killing it.

As you *senhores* know, a hammock is a tipsy and tricksy bed at best. Many a time I have fallen out in my sleep while turning over or disturbed by a dream. When a hammock does dump you it does so very suddenly, giving you no chance whatever to save yourself. So you can see that it is no place from which to try to kill snakes.

This *jararaca* was not very large. My machete lay beside me, and my gun was within easy reach. But the deadliness of such a creature does not depend on its length, and any attempt to swing my bush-knife or rifle down on this snake would undoubtedly result in unbalancing myself so that I would sprawl beside him — and then I would no longer be a menace to that other Jararaca over on the hill. Even if I got my gun without tipping out it could be used only as a club, for of course any gunshot would reach the ears of the *barbaros*. And those two weapons were the only things within my reach. So I did the only thing possible — lay still and tried to plan some way to rid myself of the danger.

While I thought I looked all about the place, seeking something that would give me an idea. But I saw nothing useful. And the most useless thing of all seemed to be that big gold crucifix which still hung from the ridge-pole overhead. My eyes went from it to the snake, and from the snake to the cross, and all my looking at them did me no good. Each stayed where it was. And so did I.

After a time I tired of the sight of them and stared out at the bush, still puzzling over what to do. And suddenly I saw a thing so unexpected that it stopped my breath. There at the edge of the undergrowth, motionless as any bush, was the head and neck of another snake. And that snake was a *mussurana*.

XIV

NOW I am not at all religious, *senhores*, nor have I ever been. If I were, I probably should think that the cross hanging over me had brought that *mussurana* to aid me. But I do not believe in such things. I do not believe any cross, or any priest either, can save my life in this world or my soul in the next.

Yet I am not one of those who think there is no God. And I do believe that whenever *Deus Padre* allows an evil thing to come into the world he also creates a good thing to destroy it. And whether this be so or not, I know that as our jungle harbors the venomous *jararaca*, so also it protests the good *mussurana*, which slays the *jararaca*.

That is what the *mussurana* lives for. Though itself a serpent, it is a killer of serpents. And though the deadliest poison of another snake can not harm it, it has no poison of its own and does no harm to man. True, it is not at all handsome, and its flat head looks vicious and grim. But if ever I saw a snake which seemed beautiful and was as welcome as a friend in time of trouble, it was that morning when I spied that shining blue thing lying there with its fierce gaze fixed on the coil under me.

If I had lain still before, I now was motionless as a log. I hardly breathed, feeling that the slightest move might draw the attention of the *mussurana* to me and stop it from coming in. Yet I need not have feared. Its whole brain was centered on its enemy. And slowly, its head a little off the ground, its tongue darting, it crept smoothly out into the open.

Inch by inch, foot by foot, it came sliding forward until it was all in sight. In the watery morning sunlight its steely blue body shone like a four-foot gun-barrel slipping silently along the dirt. Into the shadow of the *tambo* it crept without a pause — on, on until it was within a yard of the *jararaca*.

Then under me sounded a startled hiss. The *jararaca*, which had been fixedly watching me, suddenly saw the danger almost upon it. At the sound the *mussurana* stopped an instant, and the two reptiles glared at each other. Then the *mussurana* resumed its glide.

It seemed to me that both snakes darted upon each other at the same instant. Such things happen so quickly that the eye can not follow them. But the *jararaca* flashed from its coil, and for a second the blue destroyer became a blur. Then I saw the *jararaca* jerk its fangs out of the side of the other snake;

and I saw also that the *mussurana* had whipped several folds of itself around the deadly reptile and sunk its own teeth into its enemy.

The fangs of the *mussurana* had struck several inches behind the neck, and this was not at all the hold it wanted. As the *jararaca* pulled away its head the other did the same; but it kept its twining body-grip. It reached for a hold nearer the head — and got it. As its fangs sank in for the second time, the *jararaca* also bit again. And then, locked together, they rolled about as I have seen two battling men roll when grappling on the ground.

Lashing, writhing, squirming, they struggled for minutes. But now I could see that the *jararaca* was trying, not to overpower its enemy, but to wriggle out of the gripping blue coils. And the *mussurana*, though it seemed trying to squeeze its prey to death, was not attempting that at all. It knew just how it wanted to kill that *jararaca*, and it was working very coolly toward carrying out its plan. While it gripped the venomous snake it was also creeping upward around it, working toward the deadly head. And at length it clamped its fangs into the head itself.

For a moment it lay quiet as if resting. Its body now was twined all down that of its enemy in a close, even spiral, and only the head and tail of the *jararaca* could be seen. Then the *mussurana*, moving its muscles upward, seemed to bunch itself around the throat of the other reptile.

The head of the *jararaca*, still held in the blue snake's teeth, came forward a little, then bent back. With sure, terrible power the destroyer was stretching the neck of its victim. When that neck was drawn taut the blue snake began twisting it from side to side.

How long that twisting kept on I do not know. But I do know it lasted until the bones of the *jararaca* were ground loose from one another and its neck was hopelessly shattered. At last the *mussurana* unclamped its jaws, loosened its coil, and let the weakly twitching body lie free. After another short rest it seized the head of the conquered snake and began to swallow it.

For some time longer I lay there, watching the blue-steel creature swell as it drew the quivering *jararaca* down its gullet. At last only the tip of the slender tail hung from its mouth. Then this too faded from sight. The deadly thing which had held me a prisoner in my hammock had vanished from the face of the earth.

I dropped my feet to the ground and stood up. The *mussurana*, which had given me no attention whatever, drew back in a startled way. But as I made no more sudden moves, it lay quietly watching me for a time, then calmly glided away toward the bush.

It was returning to the place from which it had come. I watched it, wishing I had some way of rewarding it for the good turn it had done for me. And as I thought this there came to me a curiosity to know where the creature had its lair. It was quite likely that before I left this part of the jungle I might kill another snake in my wanderings, and if I knew where my friend the *mussurana* lived I could take the dead thing there and give it a good meal without the work of slaying it first.

A foolish thought, yes. But just then I felt very grateful to that blue fighter; and so, having nothing better to do than to follow up my foolish thought, I stepped softly after the creature. It had vanished now into the undergrowth. But the wet ground was soft, and I have a pair of bush-trained eyes, so that it was not hard for me to trail the four-foot reptile, heavy with its swallowed prey. I felt that it would go straight to its den to sleep for the next few days, as is the habit of snakes after a good kill. And, traveling lightly to avoid alarming it, I followed its track until I neared a tree between whose buttress roots opened a hole.

At the bottom of this hole I spied the steely glint of the *mussurana*, creeping sluggishly in out of sight. Satisfied that this was its home, I went no farther. As I returned to the *tambo* I marked bushes lightly with my machete, so that I could come back at any time.

When I emerged in the clearing and set about getting breakfast I laughed at my foolishness. But before I finished my meal I stopped grinning.

Somehow the gold cross hanging in the *tambo* bothered me. Somehow there kept beating at my memory the sneering words of the Son of the Snake to Senhor Mack —

"Who lives by the cross dies by the snake!"

And suddenly, *senhores*, those words and the cross and the blue *mussurana* jumped together and struggled in my head as those two snakes had rolled about under my hammock. Then they straightened out into an idea — an idea that almost made me dizzy. And after staring at my coffee awhile I muttered:

"*Vive Deus!* I will do it!"

XV

DAYS PASSED before I put my idea to the test. It was not one of those ideas which can be tried as soon as thought of. Between the thought and the trial lay several steps which had to be taken slowly. The idea depended very largely on my newly found friend, the *mussurana*. And before doing anything else I had to make that blue snake acquainted with me. As you know, a snake which has gorged itself is sluggish for a while afterward. Not until it has digested its meal will it grow hungry and active again; and if it has fed well, this time of torpor lasts several days. If the *mussurana* was not alarmed it would stay in its retreat for a week or more before starting out on another hunt. So, since I knew just where to find it, I could visit it each day and let it become accustomed to me. And that is what I did.

The first day, going quietly to its hole, I squatted a yard away. The hole was not large, and in the blackness beyond the opening I could see nothing. But I was sure that the creature was there, and thought it might be sleepily watching me. So I remained quiet for some time. Then I began to whistle.

My whistling was not loud, you may be sure. I kept it low enough to be heard by no ear more than a few feet away, yet strong enough to reach the hidden snake. I did not try to make music, but whistled steadily on one note for a while, then shifted to another. And after a while, gazing fixedly at that hole, I saw within it a shadowy flat head. The *mussurana* was listening and watching.

For quite a long time I whistled away on that same note. I kept at it until my cheeks pained me, my eyes burned from the steady stare, and my legs cramped under me. During that time the dim head had slipped forward until I could see it plainly, as well as an inch or two of neck. But the snake was too sluggish or too uncertain of me to come any farther. So, rising as slowly as possible on my aching legs, I went away, knowing that my face and the sound of my whistle were planted firmly in the mussurana's brain.

The next day I did the same thing. Before I went away that time the shiny blue body had come out of its hole more than a foot; and as I arose to go, still softly whistling, it did not draw back. When, after a couple of slow steps, I paused and glanced down, it still lay there with eyes fixed on me. Probably it did not return to its doze until I had passed away through the bush to my camp.

So, day by day, I serenaded that *mussurana*. If the *coronel* and Pedro could have seen me squatting by the hour beside a hole and whistling to a snake they would have thought me stark mad. There were times when I too called myself a fool. What the snake thought about me I do not know, but I have no doubt it was puzzled.

Yet, as the swallowed *jararaca* digested and the blue fighter became more alert, it also grew friendly. By the sixth day it not only came out to meet me and listen to my noises, but it allowed me to pick it up. I handled it very gently and let it crawl along my arms, though I must confess that I did not like the feel of the thing. It made no effort to escape, and when I set it on the ground again it curled partly around itself and lay lazily in the sun, looking at me and listening as I talked to it in a crooning tone.

For a longer time than usual I stayed with it that day, mumbling to it. I told it what I intended to do, and it never winked an eye. I even gave it a name before I went away. I called it Matador Azul, meaning "Blue Killer." And in the days that followed I always thought of it by that name, though I dropped the "blue" part of it and called it only Matador.

This was not all I did during those days alone in the jungle. Twice I made the long trip by land to the poison-tree — by land, because it was wiser to keep hidden in the thick cover than to take chances of being caught in the canoe by *barbaros*. Nothing new had happened at the *assacu*, and at no time did I see or hear any savages going there. Those whom I did see were all on the lagoon or the bay or in the bush near the hill.

At night I made a couple of journeys, once by land and once by water, to the paths on each side of the bay. And I learned that both were watched after dark as well as during the day — at least while the moon shone. On the second journey I nearly got myself caught, for two guards were on the path at the time, and I nearly walked into them. As it happened, some sort of animal fight started in the bush near them just then, and while they looked and listened to the noise of it I slipped away unseen.

With these and other scouting trips, which gave me little new information but used up much time, I kept quite busy when I was not visiting my friend Matador. I also put in some hours at the work of weaving a small *atura* basket with a lid. This I took with me on the seventh day, when I went to see Matador. And when I came back to camp with the basket the *mussurana* was inside it.

Matador now was quite brisk and wide-awake, and I knew that unless he was confined he would soon seek another kill. If he found a good one he would be stupid for another week or more, and that was not what I wanted. At the same time I did not want him so hungry that he would slip away from me at the first chance. So, leaving the lid fastened down, I went hunting for a small *jararaca*.

I was lucky enough to find one less than a foot long. Using a forked stick and a cord, I took it alive, after which I carried it to camp and presented it to Matador as a light luncheon. He swallowed it promptly and then settled down in his new home, well content.

And now I was ready to test my idea.

It was as crazy and foolhardy an idea, no doubt, as a man ever had. Yet a bold, crazy plan sometimes succeeds where a more sane and cautious scheme would fail. And I now was so tired of hiding and sneaking and waiting for Pedro to return, and so curious about the Jararaca and his camp, that anything seemed better than more days and nights of skulking uselessly in the bush.

In my one view of the white-skinned cannibal chief I had seen that he was swollen with conceit; so vain that he twisted the name "son of a snake" into an indication that he was known to the world. I had learned that he had a murderous hatred for the cross and all it stood for. If he had any god at all it must be some foul serpent-god.

And whether or not he had such a god, I felt that he was crazed on the subject of snakes. His pride in his name, his snaky look and movements, his diabolical habit of sending white men to die in torment by snake-bites at the assacu, his boast that "who lives by the cross dies by the snake" — all these things indicated that his brain had a snaky twist.

So now, armed with a snake of my own and a jug of rum, I was going to pay a call on the Jararaca in his den.

XVI

VERY EARLY in the morning, while the waning moon still shone and the eastern sky gave no sign of dawn, I pushed the canoe out from its hiding-place and began paddling eastward. In the boat lay a small pack, consisting of my hammock and food arranged around the jug. With this, but not fastened to it, was the *atura* in which Matador dozed. My gun, my *machadinha*, and the gold cross I left behind. The only weapons likely to be useful to me in this venture were my machete and my wits.

Before daybreak I was safely out of sight beyond the other end of the lagoon. I had decided on what sort of story I was to tell, and my movements and appearance must bear out that tale. I had already attended to my looks. I was naked to the waist, my breeches were torn and mud-stained, my face was overgrown with a villainous black beard, and my hair was

matted and caked in places with dry clay. Besides this, I wore
on my head some long parrot feathers found days previously in
the bush, where some hawk or other prowler had made a kill. I
doubt if the men of the Jararaca themselves looked much more
wild and hard than I. And now, having reached the place from
which I was to appear, I dozed in the canoe until the sun was
well up.

Then I stroked slowly to the mouth of the *lagoa* and looked
down it, hoping to see some *barbaros*. Before long I spied a
canoe cruising along near shore, a tall savage in its bow,
spearing fish. At once I swung boldly out into the middle of the
lake and paddled westward.

Out swerved the canoe of the Jararaca's men. Straight for
me it drove. In its bow the tall Indian still stood, balancing
himself to the strokes, his spear held forward, I kept coolly on,
without either pause or haste, until their bow came within
twenty feet. Then I held my paddle and raised my empty right
hand.

They slowed, backed water, and stared. I said no word
while their eyes went over me, resting longest on those feathers in my hair. The boats slowly drifted toward each other. At
length, speaking in Tupi, I asked —

"Who are you?"

The spearman answered —

"Men of the Snake."

"What snake? The Jararaca?"

Surprise showed in their eyes. The spearman replied:

"The Son of the Snake. Jararaca."

I nodded as if well pleased.

"Take me to him. I have traveled far to find him."

Again they stared. An evil grin came into their faces. Here
was a fool asking for death! With a grunt the spearman moved
his head toward the *enseada*. The paddles stroked again, and
side by side we moved into the bay and on to the hill.

There I slung my pack on my shoulders, looped the line of
the *atura* around my forehead, and looked inquiringly at the
spearman as if I did not know which way to go. He pointed to
the path and up the hill. So up the hill I went, the canoe-men

following close on my heels.

On the flat hilltop more savages crowded around me, their faces ugly. But the spearman growled, and no hand was lifted against me. Onward we swung to that spot before the house where Senhor Mack had stood some days before. There the spearman motioned for me to halt. As I did so he turned into the house.

The other savages watched me with snaky eyes, saying nothing. I stood in a bold, careless manner, looking around at them. After a minute or two I unslung the *atura* and set it very gently on the ground before me. My care in handling it drew their attention to it. One fellow, curious, put out a foot and shoved it a little. I snarled and glared at him. He glowered back, but did not touch it again. The rest became all the more interested in it.

Thus we stood when through the doorway came the Jararaca.

My first straight stare into his face told me something. Before, when I had peered at him from behind a tree some distance away, I had thought him white. Now I saw that though his skin was white his blood was far from pure. His high cheekbones and slant eyes were those of the Peruvian Indian. His nose and mouth were those of a Negro. The blood of three races was in him. And of all mixtures of blood in our country, that of Spaniard, Indian and Negro is worst.

Black, glittering, evil, his eyes went over me as had those of his men. Like them, he looked longest at the feathers in my clayed hair. And, like them, he gazed narrow-lidded at the *atura* before me. While he still watched that basket I spoke, slow and deep.

"From the great chief Yacu, ruler of white Indians, and from the people of the Blue Snake, I bring greeting and a message to the famous Son of the Snake, Jararaca."

He lifted his head proudly.

"*Sí?* Speak on."

"The great name of the Jararaca has been borne across the rivers and the forest by the little snakes of the jungle and has come to the ears of Yacu. The little snakes have said that the mighty Son of the Snake has a white skin like that of Yacu himself; that the men of the Jararaca speak across the distances with tongues of talking wood, as do the white Indians of the west; that they also feast on their enemies, as do the men of the Blue Snake; and that the Jararaca hates, even as Yacu hates, the cross which the priests bring into this land."

At the name of the cross his face twisted savagely.

"If the little snakes have spoken truth," I went on, "then Yacu and the Jararaca are brothers at heart, and they may work together at that which may bring even greater power and glory to the Son of the Snake."

There I stopped. Silence hung around us while he thought about this amazing talk of mine, watching me without a flicker of the lids.

"I will hear the message of Yacu," he softly hissed.

"I, the messenger of Yacu, have come far and am worn by travel," I said as if displeased. "Is it fitting that the words of a chief be spoken to all the world, or that his messenger be kept standing among ordinary men?"

"Does Yacu send gifts?" he asked in return.

"Yacu, ruler of a thousand fighting men," I answered, glancing around to show him that I saw he had fewer than a hundred followers, "sends no gifts to a chief who has not yet shown himself friendly. When the Son of the Snake has spoken words of amity the gifts will come."

"Why does so powerful a chief send as his messenger only one man — and that man a white?"

There was a sneer in his tone.

"Because his own men know not this country. I, who have traveled the jungle far and wide, could find the Jararaca more quickly than a hundred of the Blue Snake men. I come alone because a lone man travels fastest. And I am sent because I speak more than one tongue, while no man of Yacu speaks any language other than this."

With that I made noises that meant nothing to him or to me either. They were only noises that sounded like words.

"I have said that Yacu sends no gifts," I continued. "By that I mean such gifts as he would send to a chief if he knew that chief to be one with him. Yet he sends, as a token of friend-ship, something which is on my back. And he sends, not as a gift but as a sign that my words are true, the Blue Snake of his people."

Squatting, I loosened the lid of the basket and whistled softly on the note which Matador liked best. Then, slipping my hands under him, I rose with the gleaming blue snake curled over my arms.

A sudden grunt came from the cannibals. Even the Jara-raca looked startled. Standing calmly, but hoping fervently that the *mussurana* would not start wriggling away from me, I held my arms still and let him do as he willed.

Matador behaved nobly. Looping himself easily over one arm, he crawled up along it, around my neck, and partly out on the other arm. There he paused, his head raised, his un-winking stare going from one to another of the faces around him.

Speaking in Tupi, so that all could understand me, I said —

"The Blue Snake of Yacu, leader of a thousand warriors, who devours his enemies as the snake swallows his prey, and who stretches the hand of brotherhood across the jungle to the Jararaca."

No man spoke. But they glanced sidewise at one another, and the Jararaca scowled but looked thoughtful too. Every man of them knew the *mussurana* was more powerful than the *jararaca*, and that against it all the *jararaca*'s venom was use-less. Whether my words and the sight of the blue snake made some of them think further and feel that, unless the Jararaca accepted the friendship of Yacu, the thousand warriors of the Blue Snake people would attack and devour them, I do not know. But the Jararaca himself, no doubt, thought of that instantly. He said nothing, but his eyes never lifted from Mat-ador.

Soon Matador tired of looking around him. Creeping on along my arm, he draped himself in curves again and looked down at his basket. I took his hint at once and lowered him into the *atura*, where he curled up lazily. Then I looked the Son of the Snake in the eye.

"The message of Yacu has not been spoken," I reminded him.

With a slow wave of the hand he pointed to the doorway. Turning, he glided into the house. With the snake-basket hanging from one hand, and the pack still on my back, I followed.

XVII

IN MANY ways the inside of the long house was much like the *malocas*, or tribal houses, of wild people I had seen in other parts of the jungle. But there were differences. In the *malocas* the hammocks generally are strung up with no idea of order, hanging wherever they may; while here they were arranged in two regular rows along the sides, divided by a wide aisle running from end to end of the house. Also, there was not one woman or child in the place. It was like a *caserna* — barracks.

The Jararaca, whose white man's brain no doubt had caused this orderly arrangement and the posting of guards on the paths by day and night, did not stop here. On down the aisle he went to another doorway at the end, and through this into a much smaller room. This, I could see, was his own private room — the quarters of the *commandante*.

Here were a rough but solid table, a chair, a gaudily decorated hammock, and other furnishings of sort. On one wall, beyond the hammock, were a number of rifles, each resting on two wooden pins. Machetes stood bunched in a corner. On the table lay a heavy revolver. It was just the right size to fit into the empty holster of Senhor Mack, and I had no doubt that it was his.

All these weapons probably had belonged to men captured by the savages.

The Jararaca, motioning toward the chair, went to the hammock and sat down. But when he sat, the revolver had disappeared from the table, and was in his hand. I did not see him seize it as he passed, but he had it. And as I glanced out into the big room I saw that it was now filled with *barbaros*, and that one very ugly brute who was holding a club stood just outside our door. No man entered the quarters of the chief, but all were ready to jump at me at a word.

I slipped the pack off my shoulders, laid it on the table, and leaned the basket against it. Folding my arms across my chest and paying no attention to the chair, I stood facing the Son of the Snake.

"The message of Yacu and his thousand men," I said, "is this:

"'The cross and the men of the cross have long been a threat to the power of the men of the jungle. There is no place where those skirted men of the cross will not go. They carry their false words to the men and women of the bush, and little by little the bush people grow tame, afraid, slaves of the cross and the gun of the white men.

"'The skirted men themselves carry no guns, but they are all the more dangerous for that. Preaching peace, they go safely where men with guns would die. Yet behind them always lurk the men with guns, and when the priests have conquered the people with smooth words, then come the guns to see that they stay conquered. So the power of the cross grows and the strength of the free people of the jungle wanes.

"'It is time that the jungle men band together and sweep the cross and all its followers from this land. It is time that the lying priests be destroyed and their settlements laid waste. What Yacu and the people of the Blue Snakes could do alone they have done, and in all their land no cross of priest can be found. Now he asks that his brother chiefs do their part, add their strength to his, and clean their own lands of this danger. So shall all this jungle be freed and the power of the chiefs increase.

"'Yacu has no wish to make himself chief or to swell his own power. His own lands are wide enough and his own people strong enough, and he wants no more. He grows old, and in time he will be buried in his clay jar under his house, like his fathers before him. Yet, though old, he is strong and long of arm, and he will reach far and strike hard against his enemies.

Any chief who opposes him in this cleaning of the land is not the friend of Yacu. He who is not the friend of Yacu is the enemy of Yacu. Yacu waits to know whether his brother chief, the Jararaca, is his friend.'"

I pause, staring steadily back into his unwavering eyes. Then I went on:

"Such is the message of Yacu. Now I speak to the Jararaca a thought which is not in the mind of Yacu, but which has come into my own mind since seeing the Jararaca, his men, and his camp. The soldierly arrangement here shows me that the Jararaca has the mind of a great leader. And Yacu, leader of a thousand warriors, grows old. He has no sons. The Jararaca could rule a thousand men as well as half a hundred."

Then I stopped. For minutes he sat motionless, wordless, his expression unchanged. But in his eyes grew a hot gleam that showed his mind was leaping along the trail I had opened to him.To become the ally of Yacu — to get control of Yacu's thousand men — to use this strength to crush other chiefs and add their warriors to his own — to make himself the terror of the whole land — it was a thought to fire a greater man than he.When at last he spoke he said only one word, but that word was a long, soft, pleased hiss.

"*Ssssi.*"

Calmly I turned to the table.With my back to the door I unwrapped my pack, removed the slabs of fish, and, shielding the jug with my body from the eyes of the *barbaros* outside, held it so that the Jararaca could see it.

"A slight token of friendship from Yacu," I said. "Is it well that the men of the Jararaca look upon it?"

Another kind of gleam shone in his face as he eyed the jug. Rising swiftly, he stepped to the door, shut it, and dropped a bar across it. Then he faced me, the revolver still in his hand.

"Let the messenger of Yacu taste first the gift of his master," he said with a snaky nod.

Knowing it was the last drink I was likely to get from that jug, and knowing also that he suspected poison, I took a hearty swallow. I tried to keep from coughing, but could not. So I said with a grin —

"The gift of Yacu, like Yacu himself, is strong."

With that I stepped around the table, where I again stood with arms folded. He slipped up to the board, tilted the jug with his left hand, poured liquor into a gourd cup, watched me keenly a minute, then lifted the cup and sipped at the fiery rum. For the first time something like a smile flitted across his face. With swift, thirsty gulps he drained the cup. And when he set it down he did not cough.

Without turning his back to me — though the table was between us and I had no gun — he returned to his hammock. Again he motioned toward the chair. This time I sat down. His eyes went to the jug, then back to me.

"Let the messenger tell me more of the people of the Blue Snake," he demanded.

So I told him. And now I told him truth — that is, almost truth. As you may know, it is true that along the Javary live Indians who are cannibals, who use that talking wood, and who are much lighter of skin than savages usually are. They have not the fairness of you North American *senhores*, but they are no darker than some of us Portuguese whites, especially when we are well tanned. They are the Mayorunas, who live in *malocas* holding from one hundred to two hundred people, each *maloca* governed by its own chief and usually miles from the next tribal house; fierce fighters, jealous of their women, and eaters of their enemies killed in battle. How many of them there may be I do not know, but if all were brought together they probably would make as deadly a body of warriors as could be found anywhere along our frontier.

I had been among these people more than once. Each time, through luck not likely to come my way again, I had managed to keep myself alive and get away again unharmed. So I knew a good deal about them, and what I knew I now told to the Jararaca, though I twisted some parts to fit into my tale of Yacu and his people. Indeed, I did not tell him I spoke of the Mayorunas, calling them always the men of the Blue Snake. It was quite possible that he knew something of the white cannibals and their ways. And the truth that I told would go far to support the other things I said which were not true.

While I talked he looked repeatedly from me to the jug. And long before I finished he had taken the jug into his hammock and poured two more gourds of the liquor into him.

His skin flushed, and the veins on his temples began to stand out. The hammock, which had been as still as my chair, rocked a little under him at times. He had laid the revolver beside him and seemed to have forgotten it. His eyes were not so steady as they had been. Yet he was far from drunk.

"Si," he said when I finished. "But how is it that though the men of Yacu live far west of here, the messenger of Yacu came from the east? And how is it that you, a Portuguese, are a man of Yacu, who hates believers in the cross?"

My real reason for coming from the east, of course, was so that I could appear ignorant of the *assacu* tree and everything else on that *ygarapé*. But I had an answer ready.

"I came from the east because I passed south of here, then found water which I could not cross, and followed the water north until I stumbled on a place of death where were bones and a hidden canoe. When I saw that no arms or legs were among those bones I felt sure that the men of the Jararaca had been there and that I was near the end of my long journey. So I took the canoe, came on down the water, and found the men of the Jararaca. And I am with Yacu because —"

I hesitated as if doubtful about telling him. Then I went on boldly:

"Because I have killed a priest. For that the slavish priest-worshipers hounded me into the jungle. A curse on them!"

I spat, looking as ugly as I could.

"*Si?*"

An evil grin flashed on his face, and he leaned forward.

"You killed a priest?"

"*Si.* I was drunk and sneered at him. He waved his cross and threatened me with damnation. So I sunk my machete in his fat belly and pulled upward."

I jerked my hand up as if doing that thing, and then made faces and clutching movements like a man disemboweled. And he laughed — a hideous hissing laugh that showed long yellow fang-teeth. The hammock swayed back and forth. The revolver slipped out and dropped. He did not notice its fall, or did not care.

"A killer of a priest!" he chuckled. "A ripper-up — so!"

And he jerked his hand as I had drawn mine.

"The messenger of Yacu and I are brothers! I too became a man of the jungle because I killed a priest. *Si*, a priest — and a woman. I slit both their throats — their throats wide open! Ha, ha, ha!

"Brother priest-killer, messenger of Yacu the cross-destroyer, you have done well to come to the Jararaca. I, the Son of the Snake, have destroyed all believers in the cross who have come into my hands. 'Who lives by the cross dies by the snake!' Such is the word of the men of the Jararaca.

"Our hunting has been to the east and south. Now it shall be to the west and north. Where the rubber gangs work, there shall the Jararaca strike. Where the rubber owners live, there shall the Son of the Snake leave only fire and death. I know their names, the numbers of their men, their locations. The nearest is one Nunes, two weeks' march from here. He dies first!"

XVIII

THE RUM had loosened his tongue. He drank another gourdful, and the tongue grew still more loose. He was fired as much by my talk as by the strong liquor. Either of these alone might not have overcome his snaky cunning, but the two together swept him off his balance. Besides playing my part as well as I could in word and manner, I had worked on his three passions — pride, ambition, cruel hate. He wanted to believe all I said. The powerful rum both inflamed that desire and dulled his suspicions. For the time, at least, he believed in me. And, believing, he talked.

He told me the things I most desired to know. Of his past — whence he had come, how long he had been a jungle outcast, and other things of that sort — he said nothing further, and I asked no questions on those points. But of his men and his handling of them he told more than I had dared hope for.

He now had sixty-eight men. They fought with bows, spears, clubs, blowguns, but not with rifles. Some rifles were here, but bullets were too few and hard to get to make the guns useful as regular equipment, and the wild men were not trained in their use.

Yet, though armed only with savage weapons, they were organized along military lines. Each eight-man canoe had its regular crew, and each crew was headed by a *cabo*, or squad-leader. On land marches there was a *sargento* in charge of each twenty-four men. When a raid was made the attack was led by a fighting captain, who was responsible only to the Jararaca himself.

"Look on them, man of Yacu, and see what fierce fighting men are mine!" he boasted, rising and stepping a little un-steadily to the door. "Not Yacu himself with his thousand has better fighters, man for man, than these!"

As he lifted the bar and opened the door I walked over to it, and together we looked out on that brutal gang of his. Loudly he bragged of their savagery, pointing at one after another, while the *barbaros* watched us wooden-faced. And while he talked he did a thing which later was to become most valuable to me: he curled an arm around my shoulders to steady him-self.

At the moment I had to fight down an impulse to pull away from his snaky clutch and fall on him with my machete. Once before — when he told me my old *coronel* would be first to die — I had almost dropped my hand to my bush-knife; and now his touch nearly made me show my hatred for him.

But I remained quiet, realizing that to his followers he would seem to be hugging me in brotherly fashion. I even praised those evil-faced eaters of human flesh, saying the things he wanted to hear. And he stood there hanging to me and grinning with pride, flattery — and rum.

"Anta! Here!" he called.

A solid, small-eyed man with an ugly scar across his nose and another down his chest strode forward.

"My *capitán*," the Jararaca explained, nodding toward him. "The best fighter of all my men — so good that I let him lead all attacks. He has not the brain to plan — only I, the Son of the Snake, can prepare the plans for an assault that can not fail — but when the order is issued he always carries it through without mistake. Would he not make an illustrious field general for Yacu — and for the Jararaca when Yacu is gone?"

To me the man Anta seemed hardly more than a merciless animal, but naturally I did not say so. Anta's stolid face did not change when I congratulated his master on having so mighty a warrior, and what thoughts passed in his bullet head I could not guess. But I could see that he noticed the slight lurching of the Jararaca and his hold on me. And this too was to help me later.

Suddenly tiring of looking at his men — or perhaps growing thirsty again — the chief stepped back, shut the door in Anta's face, barred it as before, and returned to his hammock. There, from boasting about his men, he went to telling of the strength of this hill of his.

The rear of his *forte*, I learned, was protected by wide swamps across which no man could pass — soft mud which would swallow anything stepping into it. The slippery front could not be climbed, the paths at the sides were guarded — there he broke off and took more liquor, after which he loudly declared that no men ever would dare attack this place, even if it had no guards at all. All the world feared the Jararaca. And he told why he was feared.

One tale after another of torture and butchery he related until I ached to kill him. But I made no move, for I was here to learn all I could, and I should be a fool to stop his talk now. Whatever thought came into his head came out of his mouth. And among those thoughts were the attack he planned on Coronel Nunes, the man whom we had found dead at the *assacu*, and the gold cross which had hung on that man's neck.

His intention of destroying the rubber-workers and rubber-owners to the north and west of him had not sprung into his brain as the result of my tale of Yacu. He had been planning it ever since capturing a stray bush-tramp who now had been sent to find out whether crosses were of any use on the other side of death.

From this man, who had been kept as a slave for a time — and, no doubt, treated with all the cruelty this white devil could think of — had been gained information concerning all the rubber estates of the Javary region. And now, since it was unlucky to start an important expedition on a waning moon, he awaited only the coming of the next new moon before marching out against the *coronel* and others like him.

When I asked how he had put that slave to death, he boasted of his infernal idea of lashing men to the *assacu*, where they would hang in torment until killed by snakes which always were near that spot. He told of throwing *assacu* poison into the face of that man when angered by his refusal to tell something he knew. And he pointed to a covered gourd in a corner, which, he said, held more of that poison, ready for the next man who dared try to thwart his wishes.

The hanging of the cross on that man's neck, and on others before him, was a grisly joke. Whence the cross itself had come he did not say, but as he had told me he was a priest-killer it was not hard to guess that he had robbed some church. He laughed in a blood-chilling way as he told of the screams and curses of men on whose necks that cross had hung when the snakes crawled up and struck death into them; and I did not doubt that more than once he must have gone himself to that tree and, from the safety of a canoe tying out on the *ygarapé*, watched the deaths of such victims.

But while he gloated he suddenly scowled and cursed. He had thought of a thing that spoiled his pride in the tree of thorns.

Some demon, he said, had come to the *ygarapé* where the *assacu* stood. The demon had swallowed a whole *ubá* and its men, changed the last victim of the tree into a foul alligator, turned the gold cross into wood, and put around the place snakes which had no bodies and struck down his men. Out of three boatloads of men who had gone by night to see why the others did not return, eight had come back dying from snake-bite in the feet, although not one snake had been seen. And when other men had gone by day, they too had come back with the same tale and with four more victims of those unseen snakes.

This was the first I knew of a daylight visit to that tree by the *barbaros*. They must have gone there while I was away on a spying journey. I nearly grinned as I figured that by our fight to save Senhor Mack and by Pedro's trail of death we had killed nineteen of these cannibals. But I pretended to be much amazed and asked whether he himself had visited that spot to see what sort of demon might be there.

At that he suddenly grew silent. By his expression I knew he had not gone there, and that he was afraid to go. He scowled at me so hard that I wished I had left that question unasked.

Perhaps he suddenly realized that this was no tale for me to carry back to the mighty Yacu — that the Jararaca's power was being wrecked by a demon and his men destroyed by devil-snakes. Perhaps that is why he began glowering at my basket holding Matador, as if he realized also that the blue snake always is death to the *jararaca*. And perhaps those were the reasons why he did what he did.

At the time, of course, I did not follow his thoughts. I took things as they came. And soon they came fast.

His glance went to the barred door beyond which his men lurked. Then he looked at me, and from me to the rear wall of the room. His scowl faded, and a cunning look crossed his face. He poured another drink — a small one — swallowed it, and began talking fast, as if the rum had started his tongue again.

"But the Jararaca cares nothing for demons," he declared. "A few men more or less — what matters it? The Jararaca is still the Jararaca, whom neither men nor gods nor devils can overcome. *Si!* And the tree of the snakes has grown stale. The Son of the Snake has a better idea for the next cross-kissers who fall in his way. Messenger of Yacu, look upon a sight that shall delight the hearts of the Blue Snake people when you tell of it!"

Across the room he went to that rear wall. Looking at it more closely, I now noticed that in it was the shape of a door, across which a bar lay in place. Still talking, he lifted this bar.

"When the Jararaca and his men go out on the war-trail, with them shall go the thing which you now shall see. And all slaves of the cross who live through the fighting shall kiss the living sign of the Jararaca's power. *Si*, it shall be put against their lips! And the lips — how they will swell! Ha! Look!"

I was standing beside him now. Swiftly he swung the door open. Beyond was a small room, not more than six feet square, lighted by a small hole above. Expecting to see some infernal image, I looked across the place and found nothing. My glance dropped to the floor, and then I saw the thing.

Lying on the dirt, about to coil, was an immense *jararaca*.

"Say to your master, Yacu," hissed the Son of the Snake, "that the *jararaca* is more powerful than the accursed *mussurana!*"

With the words he moved like lightning. One hand darted at the machete in my belt. The other struck me hard in the back, shoving me straight at that deadly snake.

XIX

MY OWN quickness was what saved me. That, and my unconscious recoil from the snake. If I had been standing flat-footed, or leaning the least bit forward, that violent push would have knocked me beyond the doorway, and a swift barring of the door would then have left me weaponless in a death-pen.

But the instant my eyes fell on that snake I drew back, and the blow of the Jararaca failed to throw me off balance. And the second his hands touched me my own hands flew out. One shot back and seized his wrist, stopping his attempt to disarm me. The other clutched the edge of the doorway, giving me a rigid support by which I could heave myself back. With all the power in that arm I forced myself away from the snake's den, and in the same movement I whirled and swung that arm around his neck.

So, at the moment when he expected me to be a helpless prisoner at the mercy of a reptile that knows no mercy, he found me crushing him in a death-grapple.

With all my weight I forced his wrist down until the machete had sunk back into its sheath and his grasp on it was broken. Still holding that wrist, I loosed my arm-hold on his neck and got a throat-grip.

Those two holds I meant to keep, especially that on the throat; for by it I could choke off any outcry as well as his breath. Just beyond the farther wall his whole cannibal army waited, and if once they heard their master yell it would not take them long to batter down that barred door and make an end of me. And whatever might come to me, I wanted no help to come to the Jararaca until he was past help.

But getting that throat-hold and keeping it were two different matters. I was fully as heavy as he, and more muscular; but he was wiry and as quick and wriggly as the snake he seemed to be, and he showed the strength of sudden murderous fury and of a man crazed by rum.

I had looked before into the eyes of men trying to kill me, but never into such eyes as his. They glared like infernal fires. Whether or not he was wholly sane at ordinary times, he now was a maniac. And he fought like one.

Time and again he twisted out of my clutch. But each time I was on him again before he could reach a weapon or even cry out. And each time I got that grip on the throat and clamped my fingers deep into his flesh.

He got a hand to my own throat more than once, but I always managed to break his hold. He bit at me, and so snaky was his look that I felt if his teeth ever sank into me I should die of poison. But his yellow fangs never quite reached me. Neither did the long nails of his free hand ever reach my eyes, though he slashed viciously at them.

Writhing, wrestling, wrenching, we threw each other around the room, falling to the floor, heaving each other over, plunging up again to fight the harder on our feet. His face grew dark, his mouth gaped for air, but he fought on furiously. My breath came in gasps; I began to feel my hold on him weakening; and still I could not down him.

At length we stumbled and fell across the table. It upset,

throwing us headlong on the floor. The shock broke our holds. Perhaps it dazed us a little too, or perhaps we were fought out. At any rate, we lay there a few seconds, both exhausted, neither moving, watching each other's eyes. I knew I ought to attack again at once, but somehow I felt numb. With the tabletop at my back and the Jararaca in front of me I lay like a log, waiting for new strength.

Suddenly he started as if thorns had struck him. His slant eyes widened. Terror flashed across his face. A hoarse sound came from his mouth. Before it could grow into a howl I nipped his throat again and choked it off. I started to force him down, determined now to jam him to the floor and throttle him with both hands until he died.

But as my head rose I glimpsed something beyond him; a thing that disappeared into a blur for a second, then took shape again. At the same instant my enemy twitched once more. And the terror in his face became awful fear.

I dropped back, holding him now not as a foe but as a shield. Only his body was between me and death. And death already had struck him twice.

The big *jararaca* had crawled through the open doorway of its pen. It had coiled and struck. Its fangs had sunk into the back of that other Jararaca, its captor. It had coiled again and struck again. And it would keep on striking.

That venomous creature had in it poison enough to kill ten men. If its fangs should reach me as well as my enemy I too would be dead before sunset. The Son of the Snake was a dead man now — dead, though yet alive and dangerous. Before long he would be a corpse. And if he succeeded in breaking from me, or even in turning me over to take one stroke from that flat head —

If I had held him hard before, I crushed him now. He lunged, yanked, squirmed in frenzy, but I kept him between me and that awful thing beyond. He tried to scream, but I cut off all sound except a few low wheezes. And again and again he quivered suddenly, and I knew the snake had shot more poison into his back.

All at once he stopped struggling and went limp.

He was not dead, nor even in a faint. Yet he lay like a wet rag. He did not even jump to show that another death-stroke had come to him.

Slowly, very slowly, I lifted my head to see whether the snake had stopped and crawled away. Before my eyes had risen high enough to see I heard a confused sound — a noise of hisses and small struggle. I dodged back, lay listening a moment, then rose again. This time I saw what was beyond us.

Where the *jararaca* had been was now a squirming, struggling ball. It rocked, rolled slowly over. Out of it stuck the head and neck of the *jararaca*. The rest of it was a scaly, gleaming mass that shone like blue steel.

Matador, friend of man and foe of *jararacas*, was out of his basket. That basket had been knocked off the table when it fell. The *mussurana*, jarred awake and angry, had seen his enemy and attacked.

His enemy was big and fighting viciously; but its death was as sure as that of the man beside me. Even as I looked at them the blue head of Matador shot out and closed like steel nippers on the under-jaw of the other serpent. The poison-snake was caught in a grip that never would loosen until its neck had been ground to fragments.

Then I looked down at the limp, motionless form of the Son of the Snake. Back to me came his words spoken as he had shoved me toward death. And with them came other words said before that.

"Son of the Snake," I said grimly, "you have said that the *jararaca* is mightier than the good blue snake. Look now on your mighty snake, helpless and doomed in the jaws of the *mussurana*!"

And I turned him over, holding a hand clamped over his mouth, and let him look.

"You have said also that 'who lives by the cross dies by the snake,'" I added. "Hear now this word —

"Who lives by the snake dies by the snake — and the cross shines on!"

He stared up at me, a strange horrid light in his eyes. He made no move. I lifted my hand from his mouth, holding it ready to smother any attempt to yell. But all he did was to gasp for air, breathing in hissing gulps.

I arose and dragged him around to the other side of the table, away from the snakes. He seemed unable to walk. He moved his arms and legs in a weak way, but he stayed limp. He reminded me of a snake with a broken back — the same venomous stare, the same useless movements. Never before nor since have I seen a snake-bitten man act as he did.

It may be that so many fierce bites in his back, so close to the heart — I counted seven wounds later on — had nearly paralyzed him. Perhaps the fangs had even pricked into his spinal cord. Or perhaps the poison and the sudden fearful knowledge of what had come to him caused some sort of stroke in his brain. I do not know. But I do know that he never spoke again. Nor did he ever again stand up like a man.

Beyond the table I dropped him. Bending over him, ready to strike if he tried to scream, I went on:

"*Si*, the cross shines on. The cross you hung in mockery on a tortured man sent to the poison-tree has struck you down. It led me here. It caused the deaths of your nineteen fellow-snakes on that *ygarapé*. It will cause the deaths of all the rest of your foul eaters of man-flesh. Even now men march through the jungle to destroy them — men of Coronel Nunes, my comrades, on whose lips you were to put the fangs of that *jararaca* which struck you in the back.

"I am no man of Yacu, the hater of the cross. There is no Yacu. There are no Blue Snake cannibals. I am a man of Coronel Nunes. And when you and all your tribe are only bones, scattered and forgotten in the jungle slime, the men of Coronel Nunes will travel this land and laugh loud and long at the tale of the Son of the Snake, who dreamed he could destroy the cross."

As before, he made no answer. He stared straight up, breathing in that hissing way. His eyes seemed fixed and glassy. When I moved my head aside his gaze did not follow me. I stood up, stood back from him; and still his eyes did not turn.

How long I stood there watching him, waiting for any word

or movement, I do not know. No word came. But movements did. *Senhores,* he began to wriggle like a snake.

Queer slow serpentine movements started at his neck and went down his body to his feet. Gradually he turned on one side. Still wriggling, he worked himself over on his stomach. He seemed to have forgotten that he had arms and legs. He turned himself only by squirming and working his muscles. And when he lay flat on his breast he began to crawl.

No, not as a man would crawl, using elbows and knees and feet. He tried to crawl as a snake would — by moving its muscles and worming from side to side. His arms dragged uselessly beside him. How he did it I do not know, but he did move forward a little. And as he went he held his head lifted — and he darted out his tongue.

I looked down at his back, swollen with poison. I looked at his snaky crawl, his darting tongue — and I felt cold. Though his body remained human, the thing inside it no longer was human — no, nor demon either. It was a snake, creeping on its belly — nothing more.

I touched its side with my foot. It curled around as if trying to go into a coil. It lashed with its teeth at me. I sprang back as if it were a snake in body as well as in mind. It lay there a few seconds in that twisted position. Then it straightened out. Its head dropped. It was still.

When I touched it again — this time with the point of my machete — it did not stir. When I pushed the head over and looked into the face I saw no life. No life was left.

The Jararaca, Son of the Snake, priest-murderer, woman-killer, torturer of Christians, who boasted that neither man nor God nor devil could overcome him, had passed out with his face in the dirt.

XX

A FEW feet away, the other *jararaca* — the real jararaca of the bush — also had met its death.

Its head already had disappeared into the jaws of Matador, who lay straight on the floor, his mouth wide, his neck bulging as he drew into himself the writhing body of his foe.

I looked from the good blue snake to the evil thing at my feet. Matador's enemy was dead, and so was mine. Now we both must return to the bush. But between us and safety waited nearly seventy man-eating savages.

I listened. It seemed that those savages ought to be tearing at the wall to get at me. But no sound came from the other room.

I stepped to the door, put an ear to the crack, listened again, and heard only the voices of men grunting in casual talk.

The fight between me and the Son of the Snake, though fierce, had been quiet. I had fought silently, had let no sound escape from my enemy, and had kept him from striking the walls. The table, hitting on solid earth when it overturned, had made little noise. The men outside had no suspicion that all was not well with their chief. I might yet escape.

At once I began seeking a way out. I found none. No door, nor even a window, opened outward from this room or the den of the snake. Light came in from high wall-slits and roof-holes, but nowhere was any opening big enough for me to pass through. So I drew my machete and started to dig a hole under a wall of the snake-house, intending to tunnel under the palm-logs and creep out that way.

But I did not dig long. The plan was not good. There must be men around the house, and in broad daylight I should have scant chance of escape. To wait until night was out of the question, for before that time the cannibals would be uneasy about their master's long silence and suspicious because he did not eat. Something whispered to me that my best hope lay in boldness. A bold front had brought me into this place; it might get me out again.

So I put back the dirt I had dug. I barred the door of the pen. I stood the table where it had been before, placed the upset chair on its feet, laid the *atura* on it, and eyed Matador. He was coolly swallowing away, his bulge growing longer as the *jararaca* gradually shortened. I had half a mind to put the pair of them into the snake-house and leave them, but decided against it, for it seemed like abandoning a friend in the midst of enemies. If I succeeded in getting away he would go with me.

Turning from him, I lifted the dead man and laid him in his hammock. I turned his face toward the wall and arranged him so that he sprawled as if in drunken sleep. I picked up the revolver, shoved it into my right-hand pocket, and lifted the jug. Some rum still remained. I drank. Then I put the jug back on the ground beside the hammock, and near it I placed the gourd from which the Son of the Snake had drunk. After that I made up my pack again.

When that was done I walked all about the room, looking carefully at everything to make sure that no sign of a conflict remained. Finding a jar of water in one corner, I washed the dirt and sweat of fight from myself. Then I put back into my hair the feathers which had been knocked out during the struggle. Last of all, I lifted the two snakes together and put them into the atura. Matador did not like it, for his meal was only half down. But I had given him all the time I could. Now we must get away as fast as possible.

Unbarring the door, I swung it partly open and slouched carelessly against it. The talk stopped. The savages all turned toward me. The ugly club-man, standing near, slipped forward and confronted me.

I gave him a glance, then straightened and looked past him until I found the scarred face of Anta. To him I raised a hand and beckoned. At once he came forward, shoving aside the club-man as he reached the door, and faced me with a cold stare.

"Anta," I said, "the mighty Jararaca sleeps."

With that I hiccoughed, staggered slightly, and grinned in a foolish way. Anta's eyes narrowed. He sniffed. He had caught the reek of rum on my breath — which was just what I wanted him to do.

"He sleeps," I repeated, with a drunken wink. "See."

And I stepped back.

He peered around the edge of the door. He saw the sprawling figure, the jug, and the gourd. He looked long at the jug, then up at his chief. I hiccoughed again and went on.

"The great Jararaca and his men now are the brothers of Yacu and the Blue Snake fighters. I go back to Yacu with his message of brotherhood. Soon, Anta, there will be work for us to do together. Much fighting.

"Now the Jararaca is tired from much talk. He orders that no man disturb him. Any man who does awake him will be sorry."

He nodded slightly. Probably he had seen more than one man made sorry for angering the chief. He himself did not think it wise, I noticed, to approach that hammock. It was well for him that he did not; for if he had I would have sent him after his master, even though I died the next instant under the weapons of his men.

"The Jararaca and I are comrades," I added in a boasting tone. "Did Anta see his chief lay an arm about my shoulders when the Jararaca told of the power of his men?"

He nodded again. He looked once more at the jug, then at me, swaying as if I had taken drink for drink with the Son of the Snake. I thought a grim smile showed in his eyes. Without turning, he moved a thumb toward the outer room and muttered —

"Walk straight."

Savage though he was, he was a good enough captain to wish his men to be ignorant of the drunkenness of the *commandante*. I straightened as if offended, replying —

"A man of Yacu always walks straight."

Quickly, yet without too much haste, I slung pack and basket and followed him out of the door. He softly shut it. Down the aisle we went side by side. In the middle of the room he stopped and grunted three names. Three men stepped forward. To these he gave the command that all be kept quiet. The three turned away and went among the others. They were the *sargentos*.

Without orders, eight men followed behind me and Anta. They trailed us to the door and outside, down the hill, and to the canoes. Still without orders, they manned an *ubá* and pushed it out. I got into the small canoe in which I had come, stowed my pack and basket, and took up the paddle.

"Farewell, Anta," I said. "Soon we shall meet again."

He grunted something. I shoved out. The *ubá* stroked beside me. Down the bay we swung to the lagoon. There the war-boat stopped. With no further word I turned eastward and paddled off as if hastening away on my long back-trail to Yacu.

Not until I had reached the end of the lagoon and rounded the turn did I look back. I knew I was watched. As soon as the bush swung in between me and the *barbaros* I stopped paddling and got ashore, where I spied back to see whether I was followed. The *ubá* still floated at the mouth of the bay. Soon it drew back and was gone.

Back in my canoe, I paddled on for some distance. Then I turned into a bushy cove and again went ashore. There I would stay until dark, when I could sneak back to my camp. And there I decided to let the blue snake go.

"Matador *meo*," I said as I opened his basket and slid him and his partly swallowed prey out on the ground, "I give you the best thing in life — freedom. Good hunting to you, *amigo*! May you live a thousand years and kill a *jararaca* every day."

Matador made the only answer he could. He gave a gulp, and another inch of *jararaca* slid out of sight.

XXI

AN HOUR after dark I was in my *tambo*. No sound had come from the *enseada* as I passed it, and I believed the secret of the Jararaca's sound sleep still was undiscovered. But I knew that soon after the next sunrise it would become known, and the noon must not find me here. The cannibals would comb the bush for me; and though most of them would go eastward, trying to find where I had gone ashore and then trail me on land, others might work westward and find traces which would lead them to this camp.

So, toiling by the dim light of a carefully concealed fire, I got together everything left behind by Pedro and made a new pack of food for myself. Then, with the gold crucifix hung around my neck, I got into my hammock and slept.

At dawn I was up and loading the canoe. A hasty break-fast, a pulling up of the poles of the *tambo*, and the camp was a camp no more. The mists had not yet burned away when I shoved out from shore and paddled swiftly away down the *ygarapé*.

At the end of the winding waterway I hid the canoe in one place and the spare equipment in another. Then I took the course by which Pedro and I had come southward and by which he and the blond American had gone back. Traveling light and fast, I pushed on all day without a pause to eat. And as I tramped, bending a little forward and naked to the belt-line, the cross swung from side to side before my chest as if it too were glad to get away from the accursed place I left behind.

Late in the day I halted suddenly. Not far ahead sounded the rustling, sloshing noise of men marching through a watery piece of bush. Low voices muttered. The sound was coming straight toward me. At once I slipped away from the trace and behind a tree, whence I watched with rifle ready. The men were marching fast. I had hardly concealed myself when the first moving form came into sight. Half a dozen more strides, and his face became clear. I lowered my gun. The leader was Pedro.

"*Alto lá!*" I called softly.

He halted so suddenly that he slipped. His gun-muzzle jumped at me. Then, as I stepped out, he dropped it and grinned.

"God bless your ugly face, old cannibal-lover!" he cried.

And as I came within arm's length he slapped my shoulder hard.

"How come you here so soon?" I asked. "I expected to have to wait days longer for you."

"We have traveled hard. We got ashore today. Look at the *bandidos* behind."

I was already looking at the "bandits," as he called them. Grim-faced, belted with cartridges, armed with rifles and ma-chetes, all bearing solid packs, they surely looked ready for battle and sudden death. Yet all were *seringueiros* like ourselves; all friends of ours and men of the *coronel.*

Only the few nearest us could see me because of the thick-ness of the bush, but the word was being passed back. Grins and hearty low greetings came from the men close by, and far-ther back hands rose among the leaves and waved to me, I sud-denly realized that all had feared they might not find me alive.

"How many?" I asked.

"Twenty-two. All we could find quickly."

"Twenty-two against sixty-eight," I muttered. "We should have more, but —"

"But these twenty-two are better than twice sixty-eight *barbaros,*" he cut in. "And besides these men we have a trick in our bag. Indeed, I brought the men only to work the trick. Wait, old snake-eater, and see us blow those cannibals to hell!"

"Nothing would suit me better," I told him, "But where is the American *senhor*? I do not see him."

"He walks last."

He gave me a slight wink, and I understood. The American was guarding against any loafing at the rear. And Pedro had hardly spoken when a word came up the line. Grinning, the man behind Pedro reported —

"The North American asks if you are paralyzed, and if not, why are you spending the day here?"

We chuckled. And I said: "He is right: we are losing time. Talking can wait. Twenty minutes' march from here is a dry place where we can make camp. Let us go."

So I turned back, leading the way, with the gold cross swaying now at the head of a band of straight-shooting, hard-stabbing *seringueiros* marching to storm the stronghold of those who mocked it.

An hour later we were in camp for the night. Shelters had been thrown together, hammocks slung, food eaten, pipes and cigarettes lit. Around a good fire which we made no effort to hide — for there was little chance that the *barbaros* would find us there that night — my comrades squatted and listened while I stood and told of all that had passed since Pedro left. When I finished, the American sat scowling.

"Curse it!" he grumbled. "That slimy mutt was my meat.

Not that I mourn his death — not much! But I wanted the satisfaction of cleaning up on him myself. Say, are you sure you didn't dream all this, Lourenço? It's a pretty tall story."

"Senhor!" Pedro cried hotly.

And others of my friends growled and looked sourly at Mack. I held up a hand and made my own answer.

"Perhaps it is a tall story, *senhor*. But if I dreamed, I picked this up while dreaming."

And I threw his revolver on the dirt before him.

"My gun!"

He pounced on it, peered at it, shook it as if rejoicing in the feel of it. Then he stood up.

"Old chap, I beg your pardon. You see I haven't known you very long, and — But I shouldn't have said it anyway."

"It is forgotten, *senhor*," I told him. "And do not feel cheated because the Jararaca died before you returned. There are sixty-eight other snake-men, and I think they will give you some action."

"Righto! And they're the ones who butchered my boys. Well, Pedro, I don't see that the situation is much changed.

"That bunch will be just as ready for a scrap as before, if not more so. What Lourenço tells us about the layout of the place changes things a bit, but your big idea still is perfectly good with a few variations. We'll have to tackle them on the water instead of in their fort, that's all."

"I think," I said, "that it is about time I was told about this big idea."

"And so you shall be," Pedro promised. "Do you remember that before we came away the *coronel* had decided to clear off a larger area around headquarters? And that he wanted stumps and all removed from the land?"

I blinked. Then I saw what he meant.

"Por Deus!" I said. "But how can we use that on the water?"

"Leave it to me," answered Senhor Mack. "Now come here and let's work out the details."

So, while the night life rioted around us and our fellow fighters took their ease, we made our battle plan. And when I went to my hammock I grinned. Pedro's boast, back on the trail, had been no empty threat. I was soon to see the cannibals blown to the hell where they were long overdue.

XXII

SOME DELAY was caused by the fact that we had to go after that war-canoe which we had hidden beyond the old camp of Senhor Mack. It meant another night trip and very careful paddling, for the savages now were savage indeed. Their drums thundered angrily through the darkness, and once we caught the dip of paddles and lay quiet a long time before continuing our groping journey. But we had to have that big boat, and we got it.

In the *ygarapé*, near the poison tree, where we felt sure the cannibals would not come because of their fear of the demon, we built over the bow of the *ubá* a tough woven basket-hood: a tight, rounded, strongly braced *toldo*, or cabin, which would stop arrows and stand firm before an air-shock that might tear away anything with a flat surface. This came well back from the bow, but protected the bow only. The rest of the canoe remained as it was.

When this was complete I added the last touch. With the toughest bush-cord I lashed to the front of that hood the gold cross. Our attack was to be in broad day, and I wanted the cross to flash in the sunshine as a maddening insult to the fiends facing it. That was my only thought in putting it there, but it was a good stroke. Some of the men with more religion than I felt that *Deus Padre* surely would fight with us now. And even Senhor Mack spoke approval.

"Good hunch, Lourenço," he said. "In a way we're a bunch of crusaders. It won't hurt us any to fight under the sign of our faith, even if some of us aren't over-burdened with piety. For that matter, I reckon any of us is just as good as some of the old-time Crusaders were, if all the tales I've read are true."

At the first ight of the next dawn the *ubá* and the small canoe filled with armed men. Down the *ygarapé* they went to the grassy point where the *lagoa* began. There all but two men got ashore and slipped away into the bush, heading for the point midway down the long curve of the *enseada* where the guarded path swung into the forest. Their task was to kill the guard silently and then lie low, watching the water, until the battle opened. After that they knew what to do.

The two paddlers brought back the war-boat, with the canoe trailing behind. Again the boats filled, and all our little army was on its way.

Reaching the lagoon, we pushed stealthily through the heavy mist to the mouth of the bay, where we floated to the tongue of land dividing the inner and outer waters. With hardly a sound our mates got ashore and disappeared. Like the men on the other shore, they went hunting the guard who patrolled the path. Leaving the small canoe there, the three of us who were left floated away into the fog, which now was thinning out.

Half of our fighting force now was on each shore of the *enseada*. When they took their positions they could rake the water with a cross-fire of heavy bullets. On the bay itself remained only three men in one boat — Pedro, Mack, and I. We had rifles, cartridges, and machetes. But those were not all. In a basket just inside the *toldo*, where they could be reached instantly, rested sticks of dynamite.

In each stick was a short fuse. In each fuse was a match. On the under side of the cabin roof was fastened a piece of sanded paper on which the matches could be lit with one twitch of the wrist. On the end of each stick, covering both fuse and match from dampness, was fitted a thin rubber cap. And as we stroked back toward the lagoon Senhor Mack held one of the sticks in his hand, waiting impatiently for the time to strip off its hood. We had to give our men on each shore time to reach their places, and also to await the vanishing of the fog from the water.

"Remember, now, you've got to hold her steady as a rock when I swing," the blond man warned. "Heaving from a boat isn't the same as working on solid ground. I'll use the regular bomber's throw — don't have to move my feet, except to turn on my right toe. But I've got to have firm footing. Only let me drop one of these babies and we'll go to hell in a handbasket Steady's the word."

"Steady is the word, *senhor*," we echoed. And we paddled on, hugging the shore.

The mist disappeared. Bright sunlight blazed on the water. Anxiously we scanned the bush along the farther bank, but saw no sign of our mates. Then from that shore, well behind us, came a short sound; a noise like a man starting to yell but killed before his voice could gain power.

"There goes the guard," Mack muttered.

With the words he stripped the rubber hood from the stick he held. Then he knelt and drew other hoods from other sticks.

"All right, boys. Over the top. Let's go."

While he still worked at the basket, we swung out into the middle of the bay and started for the hill of the cannibals.

We made no haste, but we did not delay. With regular, powerful strokes we pushed along to the turn, beyond which we could get our first view of the hill. But when we reached that spot we wasted no time in looking at the stronghold of the *barbaros*. Something much nearer took our eyes — an *ubá* heading for the place where that yell had started.

The *ubá* was not full. Only five men were in it. Probably they had been near the boats and jumped into this one to go and see what the sound meant. I feared that our men hidden in the bush would shoot and spoil our plans. But they had level heads, and they held their fire, though their fingers must have itched on the triggers.

The savage canoe, already near the shore, halted as we swung into sight. It was not more than forty yards away. Its men hung on their paddles and stared at the cross blazing in the sun.

"Rifle work, lads," said Mack. "Get 'em."

We got them. Swerving easily, we stopped our boat, picked up our rifles, and let drive. With the first belch of our guns two Indians slumped down; with the second, two more. The last man, howling something, stood up and tried to loose an arrow toward us, but it never left the bow. Our rifles barked together, and he flopped over and was gone.

"Guess that'll wake 'em up," the American said. "Yea, verily, I'll say so! Look at 'em come!"

Down at the boat-landing a boiling mass of men formed, rushing down from the hill and fighting to get into their own boats. Howls of rage came to us. An *ubá* swung out and started for us. Two more shot after it. And swiftly others crowded in the wake of the first three.

"Nine canoes," I counted. "Good! They are all here."

"They have seen that we are only three men," said Pedro. "Now they race to see who can kill us first."

"The first crew to get us eats us," I agreed.

Mack, grinning like a blond jaguar, swore and jeered the advancing cannibals.

"That's it; come on, you butchers! We're easy marks — perhaps! Come on and find out how it feels to have *your* arms and legs ripped off! *Yow-eeee!*"

His scream echoed down the water as he stooped to the basket.

"Give that first canoe some bullets!" he added. "Slow 'em up. Get 'em bunched. Then I'll hand 'em something."

We shot again — three shots each, fast. The leading boat swerved suddenly, two men pitching overboard. The *ubás* just behind it backed water, but one struck it. In a moment the war-boats were confused, trying to pass one another, dodging around, their speed broken. From them rose a flight of arrows which thudded into our *toldo* and plunked into the water around us.

"Here goes!" Mack snapped. "Steady!"

We brought the bow toward the *barbaros*, held it firm. A match flared. The blond man, standing straight, sidewise to the Indians, held his arms out like a cross. The left dropped, the right darted up, his body twisted at the waist. Up over the cabin, out over the water, a long stick of death rose, curved, dropped.

While we were still stretching our necks to watch it he was up with another match blazing. Another heave like the first; then he snapped —

"Duck!"

With the word he crouched under the *toldo*. We yanked our arms and paddles inboard, bent ourselves far down. An instant later the whole world seemed to explode.

A blow like that of a great ax swung by a giant struck our boat and knocked it backward. A smashing roar cracked our ears. Another blow — another roar. Then silence.

Slowly we straightened up, blinking at each other in a dazed way. Somewhere far off I heard screaming. And from a great distance Mack's voice came faintly.

"Great guns! Some kick in that nitro! I underestimated it. Can you hear me?"

I nodded, reached over the side, scooped a handful of water, and put it on the back of my neck. My deafness grew less. The screeching came louder. Waves rocked our boat, which had swung broadside to the cannibals. Looking toward our enemies, I found that many of them had disappeared.

Over there the water had turned red. Among the waves bobbed shattered *ubás*, smashed weapons, and things that looked like chunks of meat — small chunks. No screams came from that place; nothing was left there to scream. The cries came from farther back, where unbroken *ubás* still floated and savages held their heads as if blinded. Only in the last two canoes were men who still moved. And they were moving away as fast as they could, yelping louder than all the rest, fleeing for their hill.

Mack reached for another stick, hesitated, shook his head. Standing up, he roared:

"Fire! No quarter!"

Rifle shots ripped out from both shores. The two fleeing canoes slowed. Their men toppled, fell forward or back, sprawled over the side. Little spurts of water shot suddenly upward, glittering in the sun. Bullets whined as they glanced off the surface, thumped solidly as they hit the war-boats. Very soon those boats were empty. The firing dwindled to a few pops.

But it swelled again to a crackling roar. The *barbaros* in the other boats had regained their senses, and some were plying their paddles while others sent arrows curving at the shores. None came at us. None wanted to face again the boat of the gold cross, from which had leaped crashing death. They fought only to get away. But none got far.

Our swift-shooting comrades in the bush swept them with a hail through which no man could pass. A steady rip of gunfire sounded. Then it slackened and died. No living thing, except us three, floated on the *enseada*.

XXIII

A LONG yell of triumph rang back and forth from shore to shore. We began paddling again, moving toward the hill. Through the wreckage and the red water, past bullet-torn canoes filled with dead, and on to the boat-landing we pushed. Our comrades filed from the bush and joined us. Up the hill we trooped, alert to shoot down any enemy lurking there. But the hilltop was bare of life.

"This concludes the morning's entertainment," Senhor Mack said grimly. "Unless we use the rest of the dynamite on this fort. What say, gents?"

"That was what we brought it for," Pedro replied.

"True enough. Might as well use it up. There's a bunch of it left in camp. Send some of the boys after it. And have them bring plenty of fuse."

So we picked men to go back to camp in our *ubá* and bring up the rest of the explosive. Much dynamite had been packed in from headquarters, for Pedro's plan at first had been to plant it around the long house at night and blow house and cannibals to pieces all at once. The *seringueiros* who brought it had expected to do the work of planting the charges and, if the scheme failed, to do the usual bush-fighting with machete and gun. But when it was learned that the savages were always on guard the plan was changed to the one which we used.

"That cabin of ours was a lifesaver," the American added. "Without it we'd have been knocked cold. But if you boys want to see a regular blowout wait until we touch off this shebang. And that reminds me. We'll go back to camp by water, and none of us wants to be on this hill when the fireworks blow. There are a couple of war-boats lying idle down at the landing. Be sure you have paddles and everything ready for a quick get-away. Now let's look over this dump."

We went through the empty house, looking at everything and taking whatever was useful. In the room where the Jara-raca and I had fought we found that the table had been shoved against the wall, and in the middle of the floor was a low mound of fresh earth.

"If you still doubt that the Son of the Snake is dead, *senhor*," I said, pointing to the mound, "you might dig here and see what you will find."

"Not me. What's buried can stay buried unless the dyna-mite spatters it around, which is more than likely. All the rest are accounted for anyway."

"Except Anta, the fighting captain," I remembered. "I did not see him today. And the *barbaros* attacked like a leaderless mob, each crew for itself."

"If your Anta was a stocky man with a scar on his chest and another across his nose," a man spoke up, "he is down in the bush with two spear-wounds in his back. He has been dead at least one day."

I stared. Then I understood. There was no doubt that the dead man was Anta — murdered by his own men after the death of the chief became known.

We turned away and left the place, each man carrying with him some cannibal weapon or ornament as a trophy. At the outer door Senhor Mack paused, eying some three-foot slabs of thin wood leaning against the wall.

"Hm! Guess I'll take that along as an unwilling contribu-tion to science from the Son of the Snake," he said, "That's their bush telegraph I told you about. See? Each slab has a cord in it, and they hang four slabs in a sort of framework and then hang up the frame too, so there's no absorption by any-thing touching it. Then the guy with the bass drumstick — there it is, down on the ground — whangs away on different slabs, getting a different tone from each. The sound will carry for miles. Wish I knew their code, but there's no chance of learning it now. Hullo, there comes the powder-boat."

Gathering up the sticks of talking wood, we went down the hill to meet the *ubá* returning with the dynamite. When we came up the hill again we bore sticks of a different kind — sticks of destruction.

Senhor Mack himself set the fuses, cutting them in different lengths, and directed the placing of the charges. When all were set he and Pedro went swiftly along with matches, while the rest of us took to the boats. Two *ubás* started off at once. Soon Pedro and Mack came loping down the hill and scrambled into the third boat where the rest of us waited.

"Shove off!" Mack barked.

We shoved, and we kept on shoving. Not until we reached the turning point did we pause. There we held the boats and watched.

Suddenly a black mass heaved up from the jungle. A thunder-clap smashed the stillness. Torn pieces of wood and shapeless blobs of clay filled the sky. Fragments rained down into the waters of the *enseada*. A wave came rolling toward us, tossing the war-craft of the dead savages like chips. The cannibal hill was blown apart.

On the top of the wave we went out of that bay for the last time. Out on the lagoon we swung toward the *ygarapé*. But all at once *Senhor* Mack pointed back.

Swept free from shore by the wave, his little canoe was floating after us; the canoe he had used when his men were alive and loyally working for him.

"Turn back and get that boat," he demanded. "I'm going back to my camp and put up that cross for my boys."

"Let the canoe drift," said Pedro. "We will all go down there and give your men burial, and put up a bigger and better cross than you alone could make."

And it was done. Before we returned to our own camp the bones of Mack's men were under earth, each skull topped by a wooden crucifix; and a big cross towered above the spot where they had lived and laughed and fought and died. And when we reached the *assacu* tree we buried also the bones of the men who had perished there in torment and been kicked down the hill by the *barbaros*. When that was done, all the victims whom we could find had been laid away like men.

Then I looked at Pedro and Mack. And I said:

"Tomorrow, *senhor*, our ways part. You, of course, go back to headquarters with the other men. Pedro and I were sent to find new rubber, and we have not yet found it. So we go on."

But they both grinned.

"Guess we forgot to tell you what your boss said," Mack laughed. "He said that if you cleaned up this gang you'd be doing a much bigger job than merely finding rubber. He also said that unless you came straight back to headquarters to tell him the whole yarn you could consider yourself fired; and that if you did come back he would open a bottle of something smoother than the rum and ginger you took away. Oh, yes, he knows you swiped that jug. So you'd better come in."

"There can be only one answer to that, *senhor*." I smiled. "An order is an order. And an order to drink from the private stock of the *coronel* is not to be denied."

We turned toward the *ubá*. The gleam of the gold cross struck my eye. I looked up at the great grim *assacu*, from which we had cut away the foul alligator before we buried the bones.

"On this tree," I said, "we found the gold cross, hung in mockery on a victim of fiends. And on this tree I shall leave the cross, as a sign that the fiends have gone to their hell; and that though snakes may come and snakes may go, this place is safe for honest men."

So I took the cross from the arrow-studded *toldo* and knotted its chain hard around the head and handle of my *machadinha*. I cut big leaves from a nearby bush and held them before me as a shield against any flying drops of the poisonous sap of the *assacu*. And then, with all the power of my arm, I swung the hatchet, driving its head far into the tree.

Then we entered the *ubá*, pushed out, paddled to our camp, and began making up our packs for the return to headquarters.

Our work here was done. The gang of the Jararaca was gone. The jungle was safe. Among the wicked thorns of the poison tree, high over the heads of any *jararaca* or *surucucu* or other deadly thing which might crawl over the knoll when we were gone, shone the sign of the white man's rule; a golden token that here all was well, and that if at any future time it should not be well, we *seringueiros* were ready to return with lead and steel and make it so.

And now, with our grim work completed, we turned our thoughts from death and crosses to life and enjoyment, as is the way of men. And as we talked of what had passed we voiced only one regret. That was that nobody had been thoughtful enough to bring along another jug.